Dudley Bernard Egerton ancient Cornish seafaring family. He joined the Merchant Navy at the age of sixteen and spent much of his early life at sea. He was torpedoed during the Second World War and his resulting spinal injuries plagued him for the rest of his life. Towards the end of the war he turned to journalism becoming the Naval and Defence Correspondent for the London *Evening News*. Encouraged by Hornblower creator C S Forester, he began writing fiction using his own experiences in the Navy and his extensive historical research as a basis.

In 1965 he wrote *Ramage,* the first of his highly successful series of novels following the exploits of the heroic Lord Nicholas Ramage during the Napoleonic Wars. He continued to live aboard boats whenever possible and this was where he wrote the majority of his novels. Dudley Pope died in 1997 aged seventy-one.

FICTION

ADMIRAL

BUCCANEER

CONVOY

CORSAIR

GALLEON

RAMAGE

RAMAGE AND THE DRUMBEAT

RAMAGE AND THE FREEBOOTERS

GOVERNOR RAMAGE RN

RAMAGE'S PRIZE

RAMAGE AND THE GUILLOTINE

RAMAGE'S DIAMOND

RAMAGE'S MUTINY

RAMAGE AND THE REBELS

THE RAMAGE TOUCH

RAMAGE'S SIGNAL

RAMAGE'S DEVIL

RAMAGE'S TRIAL

RAMAGE'S CHALLENGE

RAMAGE AT TRAFALGAR

RAMAGE AND THE DIDO

NON-FICTION

THE BIOGRAPHY OF SIR HENRY MORGAN 1635–1688

DECOY

DUDLEY POPE

HOUSE OF
STRATUS

This edition published in 2001 by House of Stratus, an imprint of Stratus Books Ltd, Lisandra House, Fore Street, Looe, Cornwall, PL13 1AD, UK.

www.houseofstratus.com

Typeset, printed and bound by House of Stratus.

A catalogue record for this book is available from the British Library and the Library of Congress.

ISBN 0-7551-0442-0

In memory of my shipmates killed or wounded when Convoy SL 125 was caught in the 'Great Blackout'.

AUTHOR'S NOTE

Size and performance of U-boats varied with the type. The one described in this narrative is similar to one version of the Mark IX. The 'Great Blackout' occurred exactly as described: a convoy in which the author was serving was caught in it and attacked by a pack of ten U-boats with disastrous results. The criticisms of the Ministry of War Transport, previously the Board of Trade, are made from first-hand experience of their lamentable lifejackets and lifeboats which were probably responsible for more British seamen's deaths than torpedo hits.

Dudley Pope
Yacht Ramage
French Antilles

CHAPTER ONE

Yorke pulled down his tired-looking leather bag from the luggage rack, said a polite farewell to the old lady who had sat beside him in the train for the whole tedious and gritty night journey from Glasgow to London, and joined the crowd shuffling their way to the door at the end of the corridor. It had been a bitterly cold trip: the heat had never come on despite repeated assurances from the guard, and that combined with the blackout blinds ensured that the freezing air stayed stale.

The old lady was intriguing: small (about the same size as Clare, which meant a fraction under five feet), with white hair cut short in a severe style which made it seem she was wearing a Greek helmet. The inevitable venerable but comfortable cashmere jersey worn above an old tweed skirt of a dark green and black tartan matched the silk scarf, which was a folded square knotted at the back in cowboy fashion, with the triangle of material in front. Her shoes were black brogues, the tongues of which showed that they were more familiar with saddle soap than patent polishes.

Blue eyes, fading now; a thin and aristocratic nose which might have been carved from ivory. The lips had lost their colour but the rest of her features had the slight tan of a person who spent much time outdoors and showed that as a young woman she must have been one of the most beautiful in Scotland.

At first glance it was hard to tell if she was very poor and keeping up appearances or very rich and completely unconcerned. They had spent the night spasmodically dozing and waking in the dull blue light to find that one or the other's head had leaned to rest on a shoulder, and slowly, as was the way with Britons, they had begun to talk when the rattling of the train and sheer discomfort finally drove out sleep in a miasma of grit and locomotive smoke as it plunged through long tunnels.

She had casually asked if he was just starting convalescent leave, and when he had said no she had nodded at his left hand, whose skin was purple and criss-crossed with scars which had just healed.

No, he had been to sea since that happened, he told her and she asked no more: not because of the CARELESS TALK COSTS LIVES poster above the seats opposite but because she was leaving him to explain or not, as he wished.

Instead he asked her if she was coming down to London to shop. She had shaken her head ruefully. 'No coupons left. And at my age fashion is comfort. This skirt – I remember I was wearing it when I took the younger boy off to boarding school. That must be twenty years ago!'

For a few moments, although the blue eyes were looking at him, they were seeing only memories. Of that younger boy? What was he doing now, a grown man?

'And now I'm wearing it again.' She might have been talking to herself: Ned was not sure.

'To meet him?'

'No, to collect his medals. And one for his bro.'

She said 'bro' as a schoolboy might refer to his brother: obviously it was a familiar phrase in their family, and as an only child he felt envious for a moment.

A *mother* collecting her sons' gongs? That was strange. Normally, if the sons were serving abroad the local commander-in-chief presented them; if in Britain, most probably the King. He looked round at her, and she nodded, but with pride rather than sadness. 'Posthumous,' she said quietly, 'both of them.'

What medals, what service, what did they do? He would probably be at the next Investiture – a DSO for the *Aztec* affair, a DSC (so they told him) for this latest business. Should he mention it in case he saw her there? Yet if they met again what could one say to a woman who had given two sons in exchange for at least three medals?

'Both were pilots. The elder was at Cranwell when the war started,' she said. 'The younger was Volunteer Reserve. The elder flew through the Battle of Britain untouched. Spitfires. He finally commanded his squadron. He was killed two months ago. Intruder operations. It is such a long war.'

Yorke nodded. 'Their father?'

'He died a couple of months after the second boy. Now this old wreck,' she tapped a knee with the index finger of her hand, 'is left to farm 15,000 acres in the Highlands. Sheep mostly.'

Again Yorke nodded: there was nothing to say. By now, at this stage of the war, it was a familiar story, whether the bereaved woman farmed 15,000 acres or took in neighbours' washing. Death was very egalitarian.

'That's the ribbon of the DSO you're wearing.' Not a question, just an observation. The preliminary, he realized, to a reference to her sons. 'The eldest boy was invested in that, and he was awarded a DFC, too. Twenty kills. An ace,' she said.

He decided against mentioning that his DSO was the result of destroyer operations: she might ask details – although he thought not – but railway carriages were no place to discuss the *Aztec* affair, and the last business was sufficiently secret for even those in the know to keep silent.

'You'll be married?'

He shook his head. 'Engaged, I think.' As he was realizing how foolish the 'I think' must sound she nodded. 'I know. My husband never proposed to me either: it was an unspoken thing.'

Then he noticed that dawn had crept up beyond the blinds, and soon the train had started rattling into the grubby suburbs of London. Grubby from centuries of soot: battered from months of the Luftwaffe. Bombs had bitten ugly jagged gaps in terraces of houses, and where incendiaries had arbitrarily gutted factories and churches there were only blackened boxes. After the Great Fire of London, Christopher Wren had designed and built fifty-one churches, apart from St Paul's. An appropriate time to remember an odd fact.

She was being met, so she did not need any help with her luggage, she said, thanking him, and adding gently that, until his left hand had healed more thoroughly, he should avoid carrying old ladies' baggage.

And then he was being jostled along the platform. The small jagged potholes, as though someone had run amok with a pickaxe, were mementoes of the latest bomb splinters, and the bigger holes had been roughly touched up with cement. Ovaltine for Night Starvation, Peter the Planter and Mazzawattee Tea, Stephen's Ink with its blue blot – the metal advertising signs were still high on the walls but rusty measles marks revealed where they had been peppered by bomb splinters.

'Thetrennowstendinginpletfondsevingisthe…' The ghostly announcement reverberated across the station like an incantation. Foreign troops and old ladies sipping tea in the buffet cocked their heads alike in a hopeless attempt to understand what was being said and looked puzzled, defeated by the electrically amplified Essex accent or a bureaucratic fool who had never learned about punctuation. Experienced British travellers looked warily at the arrival and departures boards, usually discovering their train was being treated with the anonymity it did not deserve, so that harassed porters had to brush aside the anxious inquiries with hurried gestures.

The locomotive at the head of their train gave a relieved sigh, as though it was going to sleep, and most of the passengers in front of Ned disappeared in a cloud of drifting steam. A small Polish officer, noticeable in his czapka and smartly tailored battledress, stood beside several suitcases and a kitbag, looking for a porter, as though off for a social weekend instead of joining a new unit after having fought his way across Europe, and only Ned noticed that he was wearing the Virtuti Militari, Pour le Mérite, the Polish equivalent of the VC.

A ticket collector waited at the platform gateway, although all tickets had been taken on the train, and behind him two military policemen, red cap covers making them stand out like dowagers at a garden party, eyed the passing passengers. On the watch for deserters, men absent without leave? As Ned approached, one nudged the other and stepped towards him, blocking his way and giving a wrist-vibrating salute.

'Commander Yorke, sah?'

He has seen the Brigade at work, Ned thought. 'Yes?'

'Message from the h'Admiralty, sah. Would you telephone Capting Watts h'at once, sah?'

'Very well,' Ned said, 'thank you.' And realized he had no pennies. 'Can you change sixpence?'

'H'indeed, sah,' the man said, diving into his pocket. Yorke realized that the military policeman had anticipated that Lieutenant Commander Yorke was bound to arrive bereft of pennies. As a sixpence was exchanged for copper coins each man eyed the other's single medal ribbon. The military policeman had the Palestine General Service ribbon, indicating long service. Ned guessed that dilatory or nervous soldiers could offer few excuses to this MP that he had not heard many times before.

Ned squeezed into a telephone kiosk (wondering why they always smelled of urine even though the men's enormous lavatory was nearby), pushed in two pennies, dialled WHI 9000, and then asked for the extension.

Captain Watts, head of the Royal Navy's Anti-Submarine Intelligence Unit, was cheerful. 'Thought I'd save you coming in. Today's Thursday, so take the weekend off and start in again on Monday. You hoped you were finished with graphs, diagrams and statistics? Want to get back to sea duty, you say? Dammit, you've just *been* to sea! Anyway, this is an open line, so we'll discuss that on Monday. Not that there'll be any *discussion*. Well,

Joan's just put a note in front of me. Wish I could read her writing. Hold on a moment.'

Ned could picture Watts at his battered desk deep down in the Citadel, the new and supposedly bombproof operational centre next to the Admiralty building, sitting beside the Mall and looking like a Foreign Legion fort which had lost its desert and was manned by Tuaregs wearing bowler hats and armed with umbrellas. Joan, the Wren officer who was Watts' secretary but who seemed to keep the Unit functioning, would be explaining to Watts with ill-concealed impatience.

'You there? Yes, well, what Joan had written down in her execrable Roedean writing – ' there was a pause, when obviously Watts had his hand over the mouthpiece, 'well then, correction: it was Battle Abbey, she says. It seems to me she's listed your social engagements for next week. She thought you'd like to make sure you had some clean collars and your shoes polished. Ready? Monday, here in the office; Tuesday, see the PM at teatime. That's 5 p.m., so it means brandy time. You come with me. What about? This is an open line. Wednesday you work here like a peon. Thursday, Investiture. You can take two guests. Yes, yes, I've passed the word and she's being given the day off. Friday, you're back here, and you'll be expected to stand us all a gin. Remind me to tell you about having a hook sewn on your uniform for Thursday. Why? Do you expect His Majesty to sew on the bloody medal? Only one hook, for the DSC. The DSO goes on a ribbon round your manly and well-scrubbed neck. That's all for now. See you on Monday. You'll be at Palace Street until then? Good.'

Ned put down the telephone. Any conversation with Captain Watts was exhausting because he had a quick enough mind to anticipate most questions and answer them before they were asked.

Mr Churchill on Tuesday, the Palace on Thursday. And he was home. Should he 'phone? No, he had a key, and if Captain Watts had made sure that Clare had a day's leave from St Stephen's

Hospital to attend the Investiture with him and his mother on Thursday, news of his arrival would have been passed on. His left hand throbbed, as though there was too much blood in it. He had used it to hold the telephone, out of sheer habit, leaving his right hand free to write notes. Now it was slightly swollen, the skin purplish. Well, he had been warned to expect it.

Ned joined the queue outside the station.

He deliberately took his time paying off the cab, savouring Palace Street. The brick houses on one side, the malt smell from the brewery nearby. The brass doorknocker was polished (his mother refused to have a bell fitted: too shrill and unexpected, she said) and so was the letterbox. The cab driver flicked up the flag and drove off towards Victoria Street.

He carried his bag to the door, felt for his key and as he reached towards the lock, the door slowly opened. He pushed his way into the house and Clare was in his arms.

'Your train came in *hours* ago,' she said breathlessly.

'It could have been late!'

'But it wasn't – I 'phoned the station.'

'Is Mother home?'

'No, she's out until this evening.'

He picked up his bag. 'I'd love a bath.'

She rubbed his cheek. 'And you should shave first,' she said, in a sentence which ended in a row of dots.

'Yes, ma'am.'

'Carry on, Commander. And congratulations on the halfstripe. Oh Ned,' she said and burst into tears, 'it really *is* you!'

When he left the house on Monday morning after a weekend of the worst night bombing he had ever experienced – and made worse because Clare had to return to St Stephen's on Saturday, beginning a week of night duty – it seemed that all of London must have been blown up or burned down. Daylight when it came seemed little more than faded night: black, grey and white smoke coiling up from burning buildings and drifting to join up in low clouds driven on by a west wind made him think of Pompeii, when three days had been black as night. The last days of London? No, it was so huge that it would take the Luftwaffe fifty years of night bombing to destroy it. What they were destroying were the buildings that made London unique: the Wren churches, the Queen Anne and Georgian houses, even the stone water troughs for horses, relics from Victorian charities. The House of Commons was gone; Members had to meet in the House of Lords now. Yet Westminster Abbey, St Margaret's, St Paul's, the Tower of London – all were still standing. And Big Ben. The light in the tower showing that the House was sitting was of course extinguished for the war. Curious how bombs missed the really ugly buildings...

He turned right, up Buckingham Palace Road. As in Palace Street, odd sandbags, the sacking burned so that the sand spread into low and blackened pyramids, showed where incendiary bombs had landed in the road and on the pavement, and been stifled by sandbags placed by brave men risking blazing magnesium. Brave and usually middle-aged and elderly men who by day went about their ordinary business, running a local tobacconist's working in an office, acting as caretaker of a building. And women, too. Last night as he hurriedly dumped one sandbag on an incendiary in the road (after making sure none was lodged in the roof), a figure in an air raid warden's tin hat had called out encouragement while tackling another bomb, and it had been a woman.

As he strode along it seemed only a few days ago that, fresh from hospital, he had first made his way through St James's Park to the Admiralty to be given the task of finding out how ships in the middle of convoys were being torpedoed, apparently by phantoms. That had stayed a mystery until he went to sea in a convoy. Now, he wondered, what had Captain Watts in store for him? Nothing very exciting, from the sound of his voice on the telephone. Graphs and statistics of how many million tons of merchant ships were torpedoed last month, and how many million remained, and how long they would last at the present rapid rate of sinking and slow rate of construction.

There was the same old gardener in St James's Park collecting scraps of paper, stabbing them with a spear made of a broom handle with a nail at the end and then putting them in the sack slung across his shoulders on a piece of rope.

'Been away, then, guv!'

'Yes. I see you're still busy.'

'Ah.' He dug into a pocket as though he had been waiting to see Ned again. 'You're a naval man so you'll be able to tell me what this is what I've just found.'

Yorke walked towards him and took the proffered brass-coloured cone.

'Nose cap of an anti-aircraft shell.'

'Can I sell it?'

Yorke laughed at the man's uncomplicated approach. 'Yes, I'm sure someone would like it as a souvenir.'

'Not you, though?'

'Afraid not.'

'Seen too many, eh guv?' The old man gestured at the medal ribbon and then, catching sight of Yorke's left hand, exclaimed, ' 'Ere, you just done that?'

'No, it's quite a while ago now.'

'Didn't notice it a'fore when I used ter see yer,' he said, almost suspiciously.

'I was wearing a glove.'

'Ah, 'counts for it, dunnit? 'Fraid it'll put off the girls, eh?'

'I suppose so. That's how I felt then. Now you see I'm carrying my gloves!'

' 'Ave to, doncher? All part of the uniform. But take my tip, guv, don't worry about the girls. Them as'd be put orf, they ain't worth bothering with anyway. Wounded, was you?'

When Yorke nodded, the old man said, a complaining note in his voice, 'You ain't wearing a wound stripe. I 'ad two in the last lot, the proper war that was. Mortar bomb in the trench cut my legs up the first time. Got treated fer that in Boolong. Could see England on a fine day. Second one was a bullet – and a Blighty one, too! They sent me 'ome fer that and give me a pension, too. Wouldn't fink I'm ticking over with one lung, wouldjer?'

Yorke looked at his watch as he shook his head. The casual mention of a lung made him shiver. 'I must be off!'

' 'Ow much should I ask fer this?' the old man asked, holding up the nose cap.

'I don't know the going price. The guns fire a few thousand shells every night... Still, you might get a fiver from an American soldier. Or you might have to sell it for scrap!'

The Citadel was easier to see now: the trees had finally surrendered all their leaves to the twin blasts of high explosive and the cold winds of early winter. Only the pigeons seemed unconcerned whether there was war or peace: lunchtime always brought people scattering welcome crumbs, and one old man in pince-nez, who seemed to have come straight out of the *Pickwick Papers*, was always sitting in the same seat at this time of the morning scattering corn to an eagerly pecking circle of birds. Plump sparrows which always seemed slightly grubby weaved among the pigeons like cocky corvettes working through a lumbering convoy. Who was the old man? Ned pictured him at home sitting in an armchair, a fez-shaped velvet smoking cap on his head, a blue velvet smoking jacket round his shoulders, and reading. It would be something by Sir Walter Scott, and he would be quietly puffing Digger Shag in a meerschaum and probably existing on an Indian Civil Service pension.

And now Ned was almost abreast the Captain Cook statue, placed low as though Nelson's column, beyond Admiralty Arch, had made the Board shy of honouring yet another of Britain's heroes. That was one of the major faults of the Navy: it took the credit for the men like Cook and Nelson and Scott when the credit in fact was due to the country that bred them, since the Navy was anxious to forget its failures, the Hyde Parkers,

Roddams, Manns, and so on, and was skilled at putting unearned gloss on its Ansons, St Vincents and Jellicoes.

The messenger just inside the entrance recognized him and welcomed him back – but still wanted to examine his pass. The building with its mosaic floors, long corridors and high ceilings smelled as dusty as ever, a vast trap for hayfever victims. Then Ned turned off the corridor and down the steps to the thick steel doors and concrete of the Citadel, changing in half a dozen paces from the atmosphere of the 'down funnel, up screw' of the Victorian Navy slowly moving from sail to steam (and hating it) to the modern Navy with turbines spun by superheated steam.

The thick piping along the walls: hot and cold water, sewage, air conditioning – it was all here, so that the low-ceilinged bowels of the Citadel resembled the inside of a ship. The only thing missing was the distant rumble and vibration of propellers and their shafts, and the garbled bellows coming over the loudspeakers which, in the modern Navy, replaced with electrical incoherence the garbled bellows of the sailing Navy's bosun's mates.

He had reached his desk before Jemmy, the only person yet in the room, spotted him and leapt to his feet with a welcoming bellow.

'My hero!' he exclaimed. 'Hollywood wants to film us with you in the leading role: the Swedes are planting rows of turnips from sheer remorse; and keep your hands off Joan.' With that his head jerked back with the nervous twitch that had inspired his nickname, derived from the Earl of Sandwich who was First Lord of the Admiralty in Samuel Pepys' time and better known as Jemmy Twitcher, who was also a villain in John Gay's *Beggar's Opera*.

'How's Clare?' he continued. 'Glad to see you back, no doubt, the poor misguided wench. Watch your Ma – Captain Watts has been taking her out to dinner!'

'My turn now,' Ned said. 'It's wonderful to be back. I can't tell you how I've missed all this paperwork and – ' he waved at the

11

piping along the walls and overhead – 'all this tubing hissing and clanking and belching. And no one assassinates tea leaves like Joan, and I haven't seen a good twitch in weeks.'

Jemmy, thin-faced and with deepset eyes, gaunt of visage according to Joan, the Wren officer who was his mistress, had the kind of neck-twisting, head-jerking twitch that was a common sight in wartime, especially among air crews, submariners and men who served in the smaller fighting vessels (the large fighting vessels usually meant cruisers and upwards). It was usually a sign of an intelligent and imaginative man who had lived under intense mental strain for months on end, with the responsibility for the lives of many other men as well. Occasionally it led men to crack up. When this happened to the pilots of fighters, or a member of a bomber's crew, the Air Ministry bundled the man out of sight and labelled his file 'LMF', lacking in moral fibre, a polite way of calling him a coward. The Navy in its lack of wisdom was accidentally more humane. Not understanding what was happening to the man but unable to admit that a naval officer could be a coward (not in the numbers who were being affected), it gave him a shore job. This often cured him by relieving the strain, so that bureaucratic stupidity achieved a cure beyond the abilities of the doctors at the great naval hospital at Haslar.

Still, Jemmy looked less gaunt; his eyes were less sunken. Ned thought he had less of the 'lean and hungry' look of Cassius and more of the lean cat who had swallowed the canary – due no doubt to Joan.

The door swung open and the Croupier walked in, a gangling young lieutenant whose every joint seemed too loose, as though nuts and bolts needed a quarter turn with a spanner. Had he been serving in a ship, his long curly hair would have had the First Lieutenant suggesting a haircut, not merely a trim. The Croupier pointed an accusing finger at Ned.

'You owe us double gins!'

'I'll buy you gins, but I don't know about "owing"!' Ned said mildly.

'One of the oldest rules of ASIU,' the Croupier said nonchalantly, 'is that if you prove you're right, then it's doubles all round.'

'I've never heard of *that* one,' Jemmy protested. 'I'd be paying every day because I'm so often right.'

'You haven't heard of it because I've just made it up. Proposed, seconded, passed *nem. con.*'

'*Nem. con?*' Jemmy asked suspiciously.

'Latin,' the Croupier said airily. 'Means unanimous. Do you want a free gin or not?'

'No such thing as a free gin,' Jemmy grumbled. 'Chap buys you a gin, he wants a favour, or you have to listen to his boring stories, or he's lining up to pinch your girl. "You don't get owt for nowt", as our Yorkshire brethren say.'

'You had a bad weekend?' the Croupier asked sympathetically. 'This is no way to greet Ned. Welcome back, by the way. You've just made the ASIU into one of their Lordships' star turns. Much good joss comes our way from Number Ten. In fact Uncle expects a bottle of brandy from the PM any moment.'

'He's got it already, so Joan says,' Jemmy commented.

'Ah well, not all of us get the between-the-sheets confidences of Uncle's secretary. Nothing for Ned, then?'

'Well, he's got another gong.'

'And I am due at Number Ten for tea tomorrow,' Ned said. 'I go with Uncle.'

'Tea!' Jemmy snorted. 'Well, knock off a handful of his cigars: I haven't had a good smoke since Uncle Hubert left me his stock of Havanas in his will. Two gross of 'em. Never been able to touch a Havana since. I was fourteen at the time.'

At that moment Joan came in, honey-coloured hair neatly tied back, her uniform well pressed, and with several tan-coloured dockets under her arm. 'Ned! Welcome back! I've just been phoning Palace Street. Uncle is waiting impatiently, and here you are, gossiping with these derelict barrow boys!'

Ned kissed the proffered cheek. 'Lead me to him!'

As he came into the room Ned thought that Captain Henry Watts looked as though he had just stepped out of a Noël Coward war film. Those slightly heavy features, black wavy hair (in which Ned noticed the first flecks of grey at the temples), rugby player's build and excellently tailored uniform belonged on the bridge of a destroyer steaming at full speed on a cinema screen.

'Ah, Ned…' The two men shook hands. Watts had commanded his own destroyer flotilla and sunk four U-boats. Yet he still looks rather raffish, which is ten years older than debonair, thought Ned. Another ten years and he'll be combing his hair across the crown of his head to disguise the pink skin showing through like a maiden's blush, and telling himself that the bright light over the shaving mirror, not Nature, is to blame.

'Coffee?'

Ned shook his head. It was too early for Camp coffee poured from a bottle… For a man brought up on French coffee made in the French way, the artificial substitutes made unpleasant alternatives.

'Don't be too sure. Tell him, Joan.'

'One of the merchant ships in your convoy was so delighted by the way you found that U-boat that the captain presented a case of Brazilian coffee beans to the convoy boys in Liverpool. They had the decency to send half of it down to us. Seems merchant ships stock up with the scarce items when they visit places like Brazil. Pity there was no ship in the convoy from New York: I could have done with a few more pairs of silk stockings.' She looked down at her legs and raised her skirt an inch or two.

'They're silk,' Watts said.

'Yes,' Joan said matter-of-factly, 'but they don't last for ever.'

'I bet Jemmy doesn't know where you got those.'

'You always say you only bet on certainties, sir,' Joan said demurely. 'Jemmy's glad to be allowed to inspect them.'

'Well, we can all do that,' Watts observed.

'Can you?'

Ned pictured Joan, wearing only black silk stockings and perhaps a matching brassière, a carefully hoarded pre-war French one (what did they call those special ones? Slings?).

'Very well, I'll have some coffee,' he said. 'Black.'

'And you, sir?'

'Black for me, too, but not shiny,' Watts said, and Ned knew he had not been alone in his fantasy. A glance at Joan showed she too knew the thoughts going through their minds.

'Two blacks,' she said and walked over to plug in the battered electric kettle. She flicked on the switch. 'And when you're near a shop that sells children's chemistry sets, we need some new filter papers for these.' She gestured at the small metal coffee filters.

'How about grinding the beans?' Watts asked anxiously, and explained to Ned: 'I happened to have an old coffee grinder in the flat, but the lid can fly off. Makes an awful mess.'

'He speaks as though he cleans it up,' Joan said sarcastically.

'More respect, Third Officer Barclay, or I'll report to the Boss Wren that one of her eggs is addled.'

'If she knew one of her precious chicks was – '

'Yes?' Watts inquired as Joan paused. 'You know a surprising amount about periscopes for a Wren who has never served at sea.'

A blushing Joan gathered up the mugs. 'I must go and wash up.'

As the door shut behind her, Ned took a deep breath and before Watts had time to say anything said: 'I want to apply for sea duty, sir.'

'Very well, all such applications have to be in writing, as you know. Address it to me and leave it with Joan.'

Captain Watts was far too affable: he was speaking in a mild 'Knock and it shall be opened unto you' tone. Or had Ned misjudged the whole situation and would Watts in fact be glad to get rid of him? Had the convoy business been a naval success but, because of the revelation about the duplicity of the 'neutral' Swedes, a diplomatic disaster?

'So I'll get back to sea, sir?'

'Oh no,' Watts said cheerfully. 'I shall reply that your application is dismissed – I'll probably use some polite phrase like "cannot be acceded to", which is the sort of bashi-bazouk babu jargon patented by the Civil Servants. Anyway, why the hurry to leave ASIU?'

Ned shrugged his shoulders. 'I just want to get back to sea, sir. After all, that's what I'm trained for.'

'Listen,' Watts said, suddenly impatient, 'the way you waded through the dockets and finally solved that convoy business has got you a DSC. It took less than a month. If you'd been at sea in one of the King's ships for that month, you'd have spent most of your time censoring the matelots' mail, adding up mess chits or filling in the returns your predecessor let pile up or getting the additions to the Confidential Books up to date. In other words, my lad, while with ASIU you were helping to beat Hitler, but the rest of the jobs merely keep the Admiralty penpushers satisfied. Right?'

'I suppose so, sir,' Ned said gloomily.

'*Suppose?*' Watts exploded. 'Listen, I was commanding a *flotilla* of destroyers when they hauled me in for this job. You were simply the number one of a destroyer, and when you finally took command as the senior surviving officer, you had it sunk under your feet by bombers. So now I command a desk and a bag of nuts, including you, Jemmy, the Croupier and the rest of them in that room. Yet their Lordships – and the Prime Minister, incidentally – reckon they're getting a bargain.'

He looked round at the kettle, which had begun to boil, and bawled: 'Joan!'

She walked in with three small aluminium filters. 'No need to shout, sir.' There was just enough emphasis on the 'sir' to make it a term of abuse. 'Kettle takes exactly four minutes to boil...'

Watts looked at Ned, his eyebrows raised: he was admitting that despite practising on his former wives, he could not win where women were concerned.

As Joan poured hot water into the filter, spreading a tantalizing smell of fresh coffee across the room, Watts said casually: 'I met your mother at a party at the Ancasters' the other evening.'

'Did you, sir?' Ned kept his reply equally casual.

'Yes. Remarkable company. She has a lively mind.'

'Gets it from her son, sir.'

'We went out to dinner afterwards,' Watts said, ignoring Ned's comment. 'Most enjoyable evening. Best I've had for many months.'

'Indeed, sir? She didn't mention it.'

Watts glowered at Ned and then saw the comment was humorous, not malicious. 'She looks so young.'

'Much too young to have a grown-up son, sir.'

Joan put the filters in front of the men. 'Now, you two, discuss Ned's mum out of office hours. This'll take two or three minutes to drip through.' With that she left the room again, carefully shutting the door as if to make it clear that Captain Watts would not be disturbed.

'My application for sea service, sir – '

'Forget it, Ned,' Watts said quietly. 'I can't say anything for the time being except that the Navy – indeed the whole bloody country – faces an unexpected crisis. No,' he held up a hand, 'can't tell you the details at the moment. You'll hear more about it from the PM tomorrow. Providing,' he added, 'the security people get your new clearance through in time.'

'Security clearance, sir?' What the devil was that all about? Hell fire, he had been at sea only a few days ago shooting at Germans. 'Has DNI discovered that I've been passing trade secrets to the Germans? Seems a bit odd giving me a gong one week and running a security check on me the next!'

'Easy, Ned, easy. T'aint like that at all. And Naval Intelligence, or the Director thereof, has nothing to do with it. This is a different sort of check. The security boys – for the country, not just the Navy – have a set of rules. If Buggins has to see secret documents or receive secret information up to a certain level – say B3 – then he has to have at least a B3 security clearance. If he moves on to other and more secret work, he might need an A2 clearance, and so on. Each needs an increasing depth of checking.'

'I should have thought ASIU rated fairly high.'

'It does – about D7 metaphorically, compared with what is likely to be your next job, which by comparison would be A1.'

Ned scratched his head. Presumably A1 was the highest security classification. Did it allow you to listen to the PM chatting to President Roosevelt?

'Why would I want an A1 security rating, sir?' he asked suspiciously.

'That's what you're seeing the PM about tomorrow. I can tell you only this much: you need the highest security clearance just to *hear* your orders. To carry 'em out,' he added enigmatically, 'a metaphorical D7 would be quite enough, and a bloody hell of a lot of luck.'

CHAPTER TWO

The policeman saluted gravely as the door closed quietly behind the two men, and as Watts stepped out on to the pavement he glanced up at the low clouds and noted that it would rain soon. He turned right towards the steps at the end of Downing Street and, after glancing round to make sure no passers-by could hear, said: 'Well, Ned, now you've met the great man, what do you think of him?'

'A temperamental volcano stuffed with ideas and erupting spasmodically! But I didn't follow half of what he said. He was assuming I knew more than I did.'

'Yes, sorry about that,' Watts said apologetically. 'My fault – I was being too cautious. Wait until we get back to the office and I'll tell you the tale.'

As night slipped down over Whitehall, the two men walked diagonally across Horse Guards Parade towards the Citadel, and Ned confided his fantasy of the building being a Foreign Legion fort in the desert with Foreign Legion patrols emerging to do battle with marauding Tuaregs.

'Beau Geste and all that sort of thing, eh?' Watts commented. 'Well, it was a good film. And come to think of it, the fort simile isn't far wrong, when you think about it. Down in the cellars the Operations Room are fighting the Battle of the Atlantic against the U-boats who are the marauding Tuaregs. Lose that battle and Britain and the Citadel will be crushed by the Tuaregs. For "Tuaregs" read "Teds", if I may borrow your old Mediterranean hands' favourite description. Funny that the Italian for "German" is *Tedeschi*. It doesn't sound German enough!'

'It does in Italian,' Ned said. 'More so than "Jerry", which sounds almost affectionate.'

Watts, as the senior officer, returned the salute of a platoon of soldiers being marched up towards the Mall, the small peak of their caps showing they were Guardsmen, quite apart from the regular pace which made it sound as though a single giant was walking.

Both men had just sat down in Watts' office when Joan came into the room with a heavily sealed buff envelope.

'This came from NID "By Hand of Officer",' she said, giving it to Watts. 'Probably what you were waiting for.'

Watts grunted and reached for a paperknife. Ned saw there was a letter on Admiralty stationery clipped to several typed pages which were stapled together. Someone had run amok with a red TOP SECRET rubber stamp.

Joan walked to Ned's side of the desk as Watts quickly scanned the pages. 'How was the great man?' she asked.

'I've never seen him before, so I can't compare. But from where I cringed, he seemed ten feet tall with a skull the size of St Paul's dome. No, an enormous bulldog, really.'

'Did he really make you cringe?'

'No, he was charming. Flattering about the convoy affair and well briefed on the next business.'

Joan was too well trained to enquire. 'Does he really lisp the way it sounds on the radio?'

'Yes. You notice it for the first few minutes, then it seems to disappear. It doesn't, of course, but it is a natural part of the man. Bulldogs don't lisp, in other words! He made a meal out of my name, though. No one has ever got so much from the "k" before. "Mistah Yaw*k*".' Ned tried to imitate the Prime Minister and then shook his head. 'I can't imitate him. I just get angry at the thought of that grubby little Welshman in the House trying to claw him down all the time.'

'Don't be nasty to Welshmen!'

'I'm not, but I hate to see a fly trying to get attention by landing on a giant. Why doesn't he join up, instead of hiding in the House?'

Joan shrugged her shoulders. 'As a "reserved occupation" it's better than the Ministry of Fuel. But politics – they'd all stand on their heads at the Windmill if they thought it'd get them votes after the War.'

'When you two have…' Captain Watts said.

'Ah yes, sir. I have plenty of work to do,' Joan said brightly. 'There's that report you finally dictated last week – I'll type that up. One lump or two? Oh I mean one carbon or two?'

'Go and comfort Jemmy,' Watts growled, and when she left the room said to Ned as he waved the letter, 'This is your clearance. I broke the rules because I hadn't received it when I took you to see the PM. I talked to the Security boys before we left and they assured me that you were "secure" and the clearance was on its way round. Still, I could see the PM was a little puzzled by your lack of excitement.'

'I'm still a bit puzzled, sir. We want a Mark III Enigma machine with all its rotors. I know what an enigma is, but the one the PM's interested in obviously has a capital letter and is a machine of some sort. A triton, too. Neptune's triton?'

'Ah yes,' Watts said. 'Enigma and Triton. You'll be heartily sick of both words before you're finished. And you'll be so enveloped in secrecy that long after the war has ended you'll hesitate before mentioning so much as Elgar's *Enigma Variations*. But first, what I'm going to tell you is so secret that few ministers know of it, and only the operational commanders-in-chief and a few of their chaps who need the information for daily use. Even to hear about it, you need an A1 clearance – ' he waved the papers, 'which you now have.'

'Do any of the others in ASIU know about it?'

'Good grief, no!' Watts exclaimed. 'I knew very little until last week: just the tiny part that concerned ASIU. Then suddenly they fetched me in and told me everything.'

Ned thought for a few moments. Whatever it was, this was both urgent and the priority for Britain's survival: the PM had made that very clear. Ned recalled the resounding words: 'If we had to sacrifice a third of our surface fleet and half our bombers to achieve it, I'd agree and think I had a bargain.' But the PM had gone on to emphasize that the job would probably best be done by 'perhaps a couple of dozen men possessed of incredible courage and diabolical cunning – and you, Yorke, are just the man to lead 'em,' he had added with a lopsided grin. 'Diabolical cunning, that's what they need, eh, Watts?' And Watts had agreed, as though Ned knew what the deuce the 'diabolical cunning' was intended to achieve. Capture Hitler's moustache, puncture Goering, steam up Himmler's spectacles, pour mock turtle soup over Ribbentrop's dinner jacket? The scope for upsetting the German war machine was enormous – given diabolical cunning, he thought wryly.

'I'm now going to tell you what you need to know, but,' Watts added grimly, 'if you are ever taken prisoner you'll bite the L tablet with which you and your diabolically cunning chums will be issued. You'll see why in a few moments.'

'L tablet?' Ned asked, puzzled.

'L for lethal,' Watts said impatiently. 'Swift suicide to avoid interrogation. Now, we'll start at the beginning. Ciphers. Station A wants to send a secret signal by wireless to station B a thousand miles away. Anyone listening on that frequency can hear the transmission and note down the signal. If it's in plain language he can understand it; if in ciphers – well, his cryptographers can probably break it.'

Ned stared at him, unbelievingly. 'Do you mean our top Fleet ciphers are not safe?'

'You can raise quizzical eyebrows, my lad, but when you've heard what I've got to say, you'll wonder if *anything* is safe. Anyway, enciphering a message, as you well know, means the sender at Station A changes each letter according to a system, or cipher, that he knows and transmits what seems to be a jumble of random letters which are gibberish to anyone except Station B, which knows the system and can change the jumble back into the original signal.'

'I understand that much, sir,' Ned said heavily, having enciphered several scores of signals while at sea and deciphered traffic from the Admiralty – signals which often turned out to be queries about someone, owing to a clerical error, being paid a few shillings a week too much.

'Good,' Watts said, equally heavily. 'Now for the cryptographers. Say the signal from Station A to Station B, which are both British, was also picked up by Station X, which is German. The string of gibberish is handed over to the German cryptographers, who are a collection of mathematical wizards and chess fiends, and they start to break it. They look for repetitions, so they can work out the substitute letters for, say, the commonest letters, which I think are E, I, S and H. Gradually they work out the signal because the same substitute letter is always used for the same letter throughout the signal. In particular cipher, say, E is always enciphered as W, I is always B and so on. If they know who sent the signal and to whom it was addressed, they're usually helped in deciphering the beginning and the end of the signal.'

'That's true of all enciphered signals, except one-time pads,' Ned commented.

'True, and one-time pads are not practical for ships because Station A and Station B are using a particular page in the pad and destroying it after using it once. Such a cipher is virtually unbreakable but if you issue five hundred different one-time pads, the Admiralty (assuming they'll be signalling to the ships or getting signals from them) would need to have a quarter of a million corresponding pads.'

'I can see the problem,' Ned said.

'Now what we really want is a mechanical ciphering machine. A special sort of typewriter with a warped personality so that as you type the signal on it in plain language it actually enciphers the message by changing each letter, except that every time the same letter is repeated in the message, the typewriter gives a different one. For example, say the word was "bibliophile", just the sort of word the Admiralty would be sending to a corvette. The first B might come out as R, but the second B would be different, say Z. The first I might be W, the second A, the third K, and so on.

'The person receiving the signal would have to have the same kind of special typewriter and he would have to be able to set it to the same cipher to unscramble and punch it out as originally typed on the first machine.'

'What about the enemy Station X in between, eavesdropping, picking up the signal?'

'Doesn't mean a damn thing because there's no *repetition*. Because a particular letter is never enciphered the same way twice, it means the letters are completely random.'

'So it would be impossible for the cryptographers to solve.'

'Almost impossible, unless they had a similar typewriter – ciphering machine, rather – and could get some clue how it achieved its random choice in avoiding repeating the same letter. For instance,' Watts said, picking up an eraser from his desk. 'In typing the word "rubber", the machine would, say, make the first R into E, and the final one into F, while the first B might be G and the second Q, so "rubber" could be transmitted as EDGQYF. There's no indication that the first letter is the same as the last, nor that the middle two are the same.'

'Our cryptographers are lucky the Teds don't have such machines!'

'But the Ted have thousands of 'em with scores of different setting; that's the problem.'

Ned felt cold. He had been in action often enough to know the truth of the expression about bowels turning to water. Now the perspiration breaking out on his brow and upper lip seemed as chilly as the condensation inside a refrigerator. 'Possessed of incredible courage and diabolical cunning...and you're just the man to lead them.' Mr Churchill's words echoed in his mind, and he saw that lopsided smile. And a few minutes ago, Captain Watts had talked of L tablets, lethal poison capsules. Poison? Suicide to avoid interrogation (presumably by the Gestapo)? That seemed a bit drastic, just because the Germans were using some sort of cockeyed mechanical typewriter-cum-cipher machine. The problem might make a few frustrated British cryptographers beat their wives and kick the dog, but poison? Or for that matter, what was Mr Churchill talking about when he said that for the new Enigma and Triton he would swap a third of the Navy's surface ships and half our bombers?

Watts picked up a pencil and inspected it, giving Ned time to think. Clare would be going on night duty and by now the rescue squads would have dug out everyone trapped in buildings blasted by last night's bombing. Diabolical cunning. His left hand throbbed painfully, and one of the big pipes along the wall behind him gurgled in a way that would embarrass maiden aunts.

Watts put the pencil back in the jam jar which, Ned noticed for the first time, contained a dozen more, all well sharpened. He took a deep breath.

'You haven't put two and two together?'

'No, sir: I can't even find any twos.'

'Enigma, my dear Ned, is the name of the German cipher machines.'

Ned groaned. Diabolical cunning, indeed! 'I can see why the PM wants us to get one – and an instruction manual, too!'

Watts shook his head. 'No, it's not that: we've had an Enigma machine since the war began. We've been listening into German traffic for many months and the cryptographers have been breaking most of the ciphers within hours of the signals coming off the machine.'

'What am I and my diabolical couple of dozen men supposed to do then, pinch a patent Enigma oil can?' Ned was startled, puzzled and, for reasons he could not quite identify, apprehensive.

'Keep that grin on your face for as long as you can, Ned, while I tell you something about our Enigma machine. "Machines", I imagine, since we've built more. From what I hear, the Poles pinched one from the Germans before the war and passed it to the French, and we managed to get it out of Paris just before France fell, so the Germans still don't know we have it. Hence the L tablets if any of you are captured.'

'Pity we didn't keep Asdic to ourselves,' Ned grumbled. 'Giving the French the finest submarine detection device in the world means that after the Toulon debacle the Germans found out all its weaknesses.'

To Ned's surprise, Watts shook his head. 'Yes, I agree it was unfortunate that as a matter of honour the French did not destroy the Asdics before surrendering their ships, but have you ever thought about the Germans trying out their U-boats against the captured Asdics and after discovering its limitations, designing new attack tactics? They found out they are quite safe if they get below a deep layer of cold water because the Asdic ping won't penetrate. They discovered Asdic can't operate if the hunting ship is going at any speed because of the dome, and so on?'

'Yes, I've thought about it, sir. But…?'

'Have you ever thought it strange that the Germans did these trials in 1940, a year after the war began, and yet their resulting tactics caught us by surprise – we who had invented the bloody thing back in 1937 or '38?

'In other words, Ned my lad, no one in the Admiralty faces up to the fact that we were so dam' pleased with ourselves for inventing a machine that went "ping" and listened for it to echo back from a submarine with a "ding" that we never did proper trials *against* it. *Why* didn't we know about thermal layers? *Why* didn't we design a proper dome? *And* design depth-charges that can be fired ahead like a shell and sink quickly, not drums that are dropped or lobbed over the side and sink so slowly they give the U-boat time to get away? I'll tell you, Ned, and to hell with the Board of Admiralty. We were so smug that we thought Asdic was the *complete* answer. Asdic meant no U-boat could survive against a ship fitted with it: never again would we have the terrible merchant ship losses of the First World War. The Admiralty thought it was to a destroyer what a telescopic sight is to a sniper or Spanish fly to a seducer.'

Ned had never considered that aspect, and he realized that Watts spoke with the bitterness not of a destroyer man jeering at submariners, but of someone who hated the stupidity of authority – which meant both the Admiralty and the Treasury – which cost lives when the fighting started.

'It's an old story, sir, and the Merchant Navy chaps have suffered most from it. Remember those lifejackets made of cork blocks to Board of Trade specifications, which broke the wearers' necks when they jumped from sinking ships? Then the Ministry replaced them with thick waistcoats of light cloth filled with kapok. The poor devils in the merchant ships have long since found out that diesel fuel – always plenty of that floating on the water when a motorship sinks – penetrates the kapok so that in twenty-four hours it sinks. Those lifejackets are still standard issue. Lifeboats – they're the same design as the one rowed by Grace Darling, and in average bad weather they're impossible to get away from a sinking ship using only oars. Even a small merchant ship has four lifeboats – why isn't it compulsory, in peacetime let alone war, that at least one boat has to have an engine? After my trip in a merchant ship in that convoy business

I saw enough to want to send the last half-dozen presidents of the Board of Trade to sea on a sinking raft, along with their criminally stupid permanent secretaries. Anything with "Board of Trade Approved", or "Approved by the Ministry of War Transport" is designed by moronic landlubbers, made by profiteers, useless and probably dangerous at sea.'

He stopped, red faced and embarrassed, but noticed that after this outburst the queasiness had gone from his stomach and he was no longer perspiring.

'Well spoken, Ned. Pity this isn't the House of Commons. Still, remember the civil servants' union kept Wrens out of the Admiralty for months and months by claiming it was a "civilian" establishment and therefore all the paperwork should be done by their bloody members, and don't get saddened. All through our history, if you read carefully enough, at least a fifth of the population is really working for the enemy, whether they realize it or not. Useless lifejackets, out-of-date lifeboats, torpedoes unchanged since the last war and leaving a trail of compressed air while the Teds have electric ones, the same rifle and bayonet, no decent tanks – and we had to learn tank warfare from the Germans, who learned it from the books of one of our chaps, Liddell Hart, and that Frenchman, de Gaulle...

'Quite apart from all that, the standard light machine gun issued to the British Army is called the Bren, after the Czech town of Brno, whence it came; the standard light anti-aircraft gun issued to the Artillery is the Swedish Bofors; the 20 mm cannon fitted to our fighters is the Oerlikon, which I believe is Swiss.

'We won't embarrass anyone by mentioning the disastrous British-designed anti-tank rifle, which is even too awful for the Home Guard with their pikes, nor mention that we don't have our own anti-tank gun. Our tanks are more suitable for storing water. In fact all we can be proud of are the Tribal class destroyers and one class of cruisers. For this happy state thank senior permanent civil servants of the Treasury, Foreign Office and the three services, and that pipe-smoking scoundrel Baldwin, who instead of being impeached was created Earl Baldwin of Bewdley. Baldwin of Lewdly, more likely. But…' Watts made an effort to concentrate on the subject, 'we were discussing Enigma.'

'Enigma,' said Ned, 'and the fact that the Germans don't know we have it.'

'Yes, that's its value. The Luftwaffe seems to hate landline telephones: probably because the Resistance keep cutting the wires. Anyway, it bungs most of its traffic on the wireless, using Enigma: the targets for tonight, the losses last night, how many airmen in a particular squadron have contracted clap, and so on. All this is sent in various comparatively low-grade ciphers, of course. The Wehrmacht is not so good – the soldiers use the telephone more. But the Navy – the only way of communicating with a ship at sea is by wireless…'

'But surely they can keep wireless silence most of the time?'

'The U-boats can't, obviously. The German Navy uses about a dozen ciphers. The main one is Hydra. It started off at the beginning of the war as the one for German ships in the North Sea and Baltic, but by the time the Germans occupied Europe it was being used for all their operational U-boats – '

'And we can read it?' Ned exclaimed.

'Yes. Don't interrupt: you'll see the effect in a moment. Medusa is the cipher used for U-boats in the Med. Commerce raiders – pocket battleships and the like – use Aegir. The big ships, the *Bismarck, Scharnhorst, Gneisenau* and so on, use Neptun when they're at sea. Sud caters for surface ships in the Med. And when the *Oberkommando der Marine* wants to send a signal to a distant shore command (just as the Admiralty might send something to Suez) it uses Freya. And so on.'

Ned asked: 'And we are picking up all this traffic and breaking the ciphers?' The enormity of it, which could only mean that the Admirality was listening to every signal passing between the German Navy and its ships, left Ned almost dizzy, and deeply puzzled too. *Why were we losing the war at sea?*

'Picking up the traffic, yes, but not always breaking the ciphers quickly enough for the information to be of any use. It might take the cryptographers as little as twelve hours or as long as a week to break a particular signal – particularly Freya and Aegir, which are not used very often. That might be too long to make operational use of the information.'

'What about Hydra, then?'

'Ah yes, Hydra. Well, every U-boat operating in the Atlantic and the Mediterranean is fitted with a Mark II Enigma machine – ' he nodded his head and repeated, 'a Mark II, not a Mark III, and issued with a manual. I should have explained that no matter which service is using Enigma, or what cipher is being used, the actual settings are changed at midnight. Thus in today's setting, A might be K, in tomorrow's setting it could be, say, W. The daily settings of the three rotors are printed in a manual for each cipher,' Watts explained.

Ned was still puzzled. 'As I understand it, Admiral Dönitz, known to his loved one as *Befehlshaber der U.boote*, or Flag Officer, U-boats, sits at his headquarters at Kernével, within cycling distance of Lorient. A U-boat on patrol in the middle of the Atlantic spots a convoy, her captain drafts a signal to *Befehlshaber der U.boote* giving position, course and speed, Heinrich gets out the manual and looks up the Enigma setting for the day, adjusts it and taps away, clickety-clack, and the signal whizzes off to *B der U*.'

'Not quite,' Watts interrupted. 'Think of Enigma as merely a cipher typewriter which translates or scrambles the plain message into an Enigma signal in the Hydra code. Someone in the U-boat then takes the Hydra/Enigma version of the ciphered signal and then taps it out on a Morse key.'

'Very well,' Ned asked, 'So *B der U* looks at his specially gridded North Atlantic chart, sees where the nearest other U-boats are, and drafts a signal for them to form a pack at a particular position, and sends it through his Enigma machine in Hydra code to those boats?'

'Yes, as simple as that. And we've been able to pick up and read many of those signals going both ways. We have up-to-date approximate positions plotted of almost every U-boat at sea, and often know the quirks of the individual captains and wireless operators. Most good operators have an individual style which another operator can recognize, even though it's all Morse!'

'But if we know when a convoy has been spotted,' Ned said, 'surely we can see if it is steering for a particular concentration of U-boats?'

'Oh yes, but if the escort of each convoy about to be attacked by a pack was suddenly reinforced, or made a major alteration of course (much more than the usual zigzag), it wouldn't take long for Dönitz's boys to realize we must be breaking their ciphers. Anyway, we don't have nearly enough escorts to do any good. The best we can do, most of the time, is route the convoys through the safest areas.

'Enigma and our ability to break Hydra does mean, though, that we can make the best use of every escort vessel, merchant ship and Coastal Command aircraft that we've got. When we can sink a U-boat we make sure Dönitz's chaps never guess it was because we read any of their signals.'

Ned crossed his legs and cursed the hardness of the Ministry of Works Grade VII straightbacked chair, which seemed to have been designed by a Parliamentary committee advised by the Ministry's Permanent Secretary and a distinguished orthopaedist specializing in the problems of incontinent turtles.

Where the devil was all this leading? It was fascinating that Enigma and Hydra told us so much about the German side of the Battle of the Atlantic, and how Dönitz was operating his U-boats, but how…?

'What's the problem then, sir?'

'Simple, really. You now see where the Enigma machine and reading all the traffic fits in?'

'Yes, perfectly.'

31

'And you can see how important it is that we've cracked Hydra sufficiently to be able to decipher most signals to and from U-boats and thus know what's going on out there in the Atlantic?'

Ned nodded. Watts must be getting tired because it was quite obvious that his explanation had been detailed and clear.

'It took the cryptographers months to break Hydra, but they did it in about February of last year. Since then Enigma has been providing us with information about the U-boats which is absolutely vital. Even so, we're slowly losing. Without it, we could lose the Battle of the Atlantic completely in the next three months.'

'I can see that,' Ned said. 'But where does Mr Churchill and a third of our fleet and half our bombers come into it, sir?'

The skin of Watts' face went taut and he suddenly looked old. 'We've just discovered that the Germans will stop using Hydra any day now, and start using a completely new cipher, Triton. It's also believed they are introducing a Mark III Enigma for U-boats which will have four rotors instead of three, and two spare rotors, giving a choice of four out of six. I'll spare you the mathematics, but this gives them billions of different settings. The cryptographers estimate it might take at least a year to break Triton, and they don't guarantee that they can do it at all.'

'A complete blackout on what Dönitz is up to in the Atlantic, and at least a year to break Triton?'

'Yes,' Watts said. 'That leaves us losing the Battle of the Atlantic, which means this island falls. Some stooge of Hitler's will be installed in Buckingham Palace, all because of an extra Enigma rotor and a changed cipher. And the irony is that very probably the Germans are only changing the cipher as a matter of routine because what was their North Sea cipher at the beginning of the war has become the Atlantic operational U-boat cipher. Their tidy little minds have probably led them to prepare Triton so that Hydra can go back to North Sea use, though adding an extra wheel to the Enigma machine is probably for security alone.'

Ned shook his head, completely confused. 'Sir, I understand the probable effect of a year's blackout in the Atlantic, but I still don't see where I fit in. Nor the chaps with diabolical cunning.'

'That's quite simple. Somehow – without the Germans knowing – you have to steal a Mark III Enigma with the extra wheels, and a Triton manual. As soon as possible. More coffee? Perhaps you'd give Joan a call.'

CHAPTER THREE

Standing in the line of men and women in front of the King, freshly starched collar biting into his neck, wondering if his tie was straight, cursing because the only shoes which took a good polish were too narrow, so that his feet hurt, and wishing he could raise his left hand, which was beginning to throb painfully, he saw her.

She was at the head of the Royal Air Force recipients. Her white hair still looked like a helmet on her head. She was wearing a severely cut pearl-grey dress and a hat whose designer had been inspired by a Glengarry. Elegant, assured – and alone. To be close to seventy and about to receive from your monarch the medals won by your only sons, who had been killed in battle, was to be alone. She might have two dozen nephews and nieces, but the inheritance – the land, the money, the invisible and indescribable something that passes from parents to children but which becomes stronger with each generation – could not now be passed on directly. Ned had realised when he sat beside her in the train that somehow she had come to terms with it. But he imagined her at first, alone at home and hearing the BBC news bulletins about fighter sweeps and bomber raids…then the first bleak telegram telling her that one son had been killed. She would have realized then that the whole future of her little world depended on the remaining son. All she had to pass on to future generations (she would not use words like 'posterity') was vested in this young man... And then the second telegram: a future destroyed by a few capital letters stamped out by a machine.

He shuffled along slowly as someone stepped forward, an equerry moved with a small purple cushion holding the medal, and the King picked it up, hooked it on the man or woman's breast, said a few words... The Queen was sitting there, and one of the Princesses. It must be the elder one, Elizabeth.

Being in Buckingham Palace, among a hundred or more at the Investiture, was quite unreal. It seemed such a short time since he was on the bridge of the *Marynal*, trying desperately to think of a way to save the ships in the convoy, or standing on the bridge of the *Aztec* wondering how long such a battered destroyer could dodge German bombs and stay afloat, how long he could go on giving helm orders to keep the *Aztec* jinking, to confuse the German pilots as they began their dive. He remembered the signalman who kept calling out the number of bombs fallen and bombers shot down as though announcing football scores. Football at first; then the number of bombs began to sound like a cricket score. Curious, but he could not remember the final score before the last bomb hit the *Aztec*. Was it a hundred and thirty-eight bombs for three hits? It was all so remote from this large and high-ceilinged room which so fitted its purpose – chandeliers, a small dais where the King stood and which meant the recipient stepped up to receive the award...was that ancient Admiral some sort of chamberlain or equerry? He read each name from a list.

The fellow with crutches went up the dais without help: obviously he had made a point of being left alone. The King gave the medal and said something and then smiled as the man departed. What was going through His Majesty's mind? He was, after all, the chief of the tribe: in front of him were a tiny few of his warriors, men and women, and he and his family stayed on at the Palace despite the bombing.

Douglas! That was the name the Admiral had just added to an RAF rank. Was it 'squadron leader'? Anyway, the white-haired old lady was now walking up to the dais and she curtsied. The King took a medal from the cushion but spoke to her for two or three minutes. Then the equerry spoke again and Ned heard it quite clearly: 'Squadron Leader Kevin Douglas'. The cushion was proffered and again the King took a medal.

Douglas? One of the Battle of Britain aces had been called Douglas. Was he nicknamed 'Black Douglas' after the Douglas famous (or infamous) in Scottish history? Squadron Leader 'Black' Douglas. Didn't he have a number of Polish pilots in his squadron? It was coming back to Ned now – the cartoonist David Low had designed an eagle emblem that was the Douglas crest and the Air Ministry made a fuss and the Press was furious, so that the Air Ministry had to back down. He could imagine some ingratiating and overpaid civil servant, secure in his reserved occupation, genuflecting and saying: 'Don't you feel, Minister that...' Ned only hoped that Sir Archibald Sinclair remembered which Civil Servant had given him such small-minded and spiteful advice.

Two to go. The white-haired lady had gone; three men had received their awards since then. One to go. And now step forward, avoid catching a foot on the steps of the dais without looking down.

The King looked tired, but his face was far stronger than it appeared in photographs. Naval uniform, Admiral of the Fleet. Smiling. One cushion. Incline the head, as instructed, so the King can place the ribbon of the Order round the neck.

'The Aztecs are an interesting people, and it seems they get warlike when serving in destroyers!'

'Yes, Your Majesty.' No sign of the stammer which the King was said to have to control.

'And your hand?'

He remembered not to move it. This was polite conversation; a metaphorical 'How do you do,' and not to be answered with a medical history.

'It aches just before it's going to rain, sir!'

'A useful weathercock, eh? Now – ' The King reached for the medal, 'you've been busy, even if you left our neutral friends with red faces.'

Ned found himself walking away from the dais and seeing his mother's upraised hand. She sat next to Clare, with a vacant chair beside them. Lt Cdr Edward Yorke, DSO, DSC, RN. It was official now, even though both the Order and the actual Cross would probably spend the rest of his life in their velvet lined boxes, except for the rare invitation or order which said, 'Decorations will be worn.'

Unreal...unreal... Because of the *Aztec*'s sinking and his wound, he had been taken to St Stephen's Hospital to save his arm from what was known in Nelson's day as gangrene but today was called septicaemia, and he had met Clare. Then to the ASIU and briefly to sea again. Now, with Clare and his mother, they were all at a Buckingham Palace Investiture and he had an Order slung round his neck and a Cross pinned to his chest.

Clare tapped his knee and leaned over so she could whisper in his ear. 'I saw an old friend collect medals for two airmen. Why would she be doing that?'

She? There had been several women receiving decorations which they had won, but only one received posthumous awards. 'Do you mean the white-haired woman in a grey dress?'

'Yes, Lady Kelso.'

'She was receiving medals for her two sons. Both have been killed.'

When he saw Clare's face go white he knew he had not been paying enough attention.

'Boldro and Kevin? Dead?'

Ned nodded miserably as he saw tears forming in Clare's eyes. 'Poor Jeannie,' she murmured, 'now she's all alone.'

It took twenty minutes to complete the Investiture and then recipients and relatives slowly filed out of the great room, and Ned realized that they were a cross-section of Britain at war. An aircraftman pink with shyness marched stiffly with either his

wife or fiancée; a jaunty leading seaman with the DCM led out
his mother and father. A Navy captain with a DSO was alone –
victim of distance and divorce? A turbaned Sikh with a medal
Ned did not recognize stopped and gazed round the room, as if
soaking up enough memories to last him a lifetime. An ATS girl
had a BEM and led proud parents, the mother wearing a flowered
dress more appropriate to a summer garden party than a winter
Investiture. RAF pilots, a Fleet Air Arm pilot, and the man on
crutches, who now had a very beautiful Asiatic woman with him.
Balinese, Javanese, Indochinese? Ned was far from sure, but both
were proud of each other.

As they walked towards the door and through into the long
corridor they began to lose their shyness and started talking. Ned
detected dozens of accents – a WAAF from Wales, another from
the Midlands and another, judging by her father's proud
booming voice, from Yorkshire. An RAFVR pilot officer with a
DFC tried to quieten his mother, whose penetrating tone bore a
close resemblance to a Hampshire vicar's overbearing wife.

Then he heard a briefly familiar soft voice behind them. 'It's
Clare isn't it? And looking bonnie.'

Boldro or Kevin? Did they know Clare's husband, the
homosexual pilot killed before finishing his training course? She
had not loved him, but after his death had she loved Boldro or
Kevin? Had his meeting with the white-haired old trout on the
train been a ghastly coincidence? Doubt, jealousy, anger, each
chased through him as Clare stopped and clasped the woman to
her with a stifled: 'Jeannie, oh Jeannie!' How the devil did she
come to know the woman, if not through a son?

Ned and his mother waited, and then Clare, holding the
woman's hand, turned to introduce her. 'Mrs Yorke… Commander
Yorke, my fiancé… I want you to meet the Countess of Kelso,
Jeannie Douglas.'

'I've already met your fiancé,' the woman said. 'In fact, young
man, I think we can shock them by admitting we spent the night
together only a few days ago!'

The plump mother of a soldier who was passing at that moment, and heard only the last dozen words, stopped with popping eyes and exclaimed, ' 'Ere, jew 'ear that?' as her husband pulled her away. 'Ayemeentersay, at *er* age, it's...' By now Ned and the three women were listening to her outraged comments and all of them were smiling at the determined husband's back.

'It's no compliment that you accept my announcement so calmly, Clare,' the woman said.

'If you were thirty years younger I'd know I was beaten,' a smiling Clare admitted, 'but now I can give you a run for your money. Come on, we are in the way,' and she led them along the corridor. Olive-green suits her, Ned thought. He had not seen that dress before.

There was a pause as medals were put away in velvet-lined boxes, and his mother insisted Clare carried both of his, while the Countess put her three into her worn, alligator skin handbag, saying simply: 'The newspapers,' by way of explanation.

As they left the Palace building and walked across the wide courtyard at the front to where the Guardsmen stood at the gates and here and there a policeman looked round at the small waiting crowd of sightseers, they saw occasional sudden spurts of white light from the flash bulbs of the newspaper photographers.

'I'm dreading this,' the Countess said, pulling down her hat more firmly. 'Let me be in the middle, and behind you, Commander Yorke, then perhaps they won't notice me.'

For a few moments Ned was irritated. The old woman seemed to be making a meal out of it: the loudest cries for anonymity usually came from those who resented having it thrust upon them. After all, she was not the only Countess in the land, or the first mother to collect posthumous awards.

As they passed through the gates a photographer swung round.

'The Countess of Kelso? Hold it, ma'am!' The flash blinded them and they involuntarily stopped, and the photographer feverishly turned the plate at the back of the camera and fitted another flash bulb, calling: 'Just one more, ma'am!'

By now four other photographers were crouching or squatting, cameras clicking and flash bulbs exploding, and Ned heard one say urgently to another: 'This is 'er, isn't it?'

The photographers were grouped in front of them and there was no chance of moving so Ned, with an apologetic: 'You're trapped,' moved to one side to give the photographers a clear view.

As soon as they had finished, half a dozen waiting reporters crowded round and began calling questions.

'Lady Kelso, did you ask for Spitfires because your sons – ?'

' – cost of them? We understand the bill will be – '

' – name them? After each son, perhaps?'

' – *Glasgow Herald*, ma'am, so perhaps you would care – '

She held up a hand firmly. 'Gentleman, you're all asking questions at once and I can't understand a word you're saying. We've got all day and if my friend Commander Yorke will be kind enough to act as a master of ceremonies – '

With his back to the newspapermen, Ned whispered urgently: 'What's happened? They're not interested in just the medals.'

'I've just paid for two Spitfires,' she said quietly. 'The Douglases haven't finished with Hitler yet. The wretched Air Ministry had to announce it to coincide with the Investiture.'

Ned turned to the newspapermen. 'Very well, gentlemen, ask your questions. You – ' he pointed to a stocky, grey-haired man on the left. 'Why don't you start?'

'Aye. *Aberdeen Free Press*, m'Lady. Will the Spitfires be named after your sons?'

Ned turned and she looked at him. 'I hadn't thought about it,' she murmured.

'I think it would be a very good idea. Will you tell the men yourself?' He stood to one side and the Countess stepped forward, a tiny but resolute figure. By now there were passers-by standing two or three deep behind the newspapermen, and a policeman was among them.

'Yes… I want to call the aeroplanes…' Ned guessed she was trying to think of a phrase, and leaned forward to whisper in her ear.

'I want to call the aeroplanes "The Kelso Reply". I hope the Royal Air Force men can paint that on each aeroplane…with the name "Boldro Douglas" under one, and "Kevin Douglas" under the other.'

'With the crest, ma'am?'

'That would mean a lot of work for the artist.'

'I doubt they'll mind,' said the reporter in his calm Aberdonian accent.

Ned pointed to the next man. 'The *Telegraph*. My Lady, are there any other Douglases to carry on the fight?'

'No, they were the only two I had.'

'What happens to the title?'

'There's a wee bairn, the son of my late husband's younger brother.'

'Was it your idea to buy the planes?'

'Yes. It seemed appropriate.'

Ned pointed to the next man, who said querulously: '*Daily Herald*. Why didn't you buy a few field ambulances instead?'

'They would hardly serve my purpose so well,' she said firmly. 'We Scots are like the rest of the Allies: we want to kill the enemy, not carry them away on stretchers!'

She had neatly turned the question, and Ned pointed to the next man. '*Evening Standard*, ma'am. Will you be handing over the planes yourself at the factory?'

'Goodness, I don't know. They've only just cashed my cheque!'

The newspapermen laughed, and she was thankful when one of them, with an apologetic 'Press Association, ma'am – I must 'phone this,' hurried off to the nearest telephone, which Ned knew, since he passed it every day, was round the corner in Buckingham Palace Road.

The reporters obviously considered the impromptu Press conference over, and as Ned turned back to the three women, the Countess said: 'Can we get a taxi?'

'Why not have a scratch-round-the-larder lunch with us?' his mother said. 'We live just round the corner. Then we can talk as long as we want.'

Lunch was a typical 'unexpected guest' meal which bit into hoarded food coupons but justified the 'points' system, where the few issued each week could be used to buy some tinned and other foods which came under the heading of 'luxury' rather than 'essential'.

Clare changed her dress for a tweed skirt and cashmere jersey and then disappeared into the kitchen to produce a cold buffet of scraps, a salad of sliced cabbage with an oil and vinegar dressing, and, as the main item, a tin of herrings in tomato sauce. Clare apologized for the fact that the cheese ration was gone, that there was only margarine left, and the meat ration was still at the butcher's, intended for dinner on Sunday.

Lady Kelso shook her head regretfully. 'Up in Scotland we're very lucky. Plenty of rabbits and our own fresh vegetables. And now and again we share our venison.'

The four of them sat in the drawing room close to the one-bar electric fire, which only emphasized the chill, and Ned listened as Clare and Lady Kelso brought themselves up to date with their news. Lady Kelso was running the entire estate with the help of the former agent, who had retired before the war but had now come back, despite severe attacks of sciatica. The Ministry of Agriculture inspectors called once a week to tell him how they thought he should run the farm, but things had been a lot easier since a particular inspector had given instructions for a particular hillside to be ploughed and planted.

'McPherson – he's my agent – told him the hillside was so steep that a tractor would overturn, and none of the horses could work it. This inspector, a man with soft hands and clean nails and an ingratiating manner – I think he said he came from Huyton, in Lancashire, which I always thought was industrial – argued with McPherson so rudely that McPherson fetched out the tractor, hitched on the plough, and drove it to the hillside. He went back to his office for something and when he returned he told the inspector to show him how it was done. The inspector looked up the hill and promptly said he could not drive a tractor.

'McPherson, who had gone back to get his shotgun – an ancient twelve-bore hammer gun – cocked it and told the inspector to climb up and drive.

'I arrived just as McPherson had fired both barrels into the ground a couple of feet in front of the inspector and was reloading. I took the poor man to the railway station after giving him a whisky, and I must say the Ministry have been much more understanding since then.'

Her description of her life running the estate was, Ned realized, an outline of the kind of life one or other (or indeed both) boys would have enjoyed had they lived and when peace came again. Each had roamed the sky as a hunter, a Spitfire replacing the basket-handled sword of the forebears, but each had lost the last fight.

'There are plenty of grouse: they seem to know there are no guns about, apart from a few poachers. The deer, och they breed so fast and do so much damage, but I hate to have them shot, though it is for their own good. Rabbits – we have so many we could feed all England if they sent up a few ferrets and nets. Pheasants – enough to keep the poachers busy. They knock them out of the trees at night.'

The conversation then turned naturally to the two sons. Clare recalled happy childhood stays with the Douglases before the war, when she was not considered by the Countess old enough to travel alone on the night train down to London. Boldro's first stag – Clare and Kevin had been there when he shot it and, horrified, both vowed they would never shoot such a magnificent animal.

'And Kevin never did,' commented the countess. 'He never went hunting, or shooting, or even fishing. I think the only thing he ever hunted after that was Germans.'

'He certainly made up for it then,' Clare commented. 'How many did he shoot down?'

'Seventeen. But he was different from Boldro: he went his own way. He'd be at home reading while Boldro would be camping in one of the glens with a couple of his friends, cooking over a camp fire.'

The Countess and Clare reminisced and Ned felt the jealousy ebb away. Clare had been fond of both boys (and young men as they grew up) but they could have been her brothers or favourite cousins. One thing was very clear, though, and it accounted for Clare's ignorance of recent happenings in the Douglas family: the Countess neither read nor answered letters. If they came in manila envelopes they were given to McPherson, and the rest ended up, for a reason unclear to Ned, in a large zinc bin in the pantry.

The Countess stayed to tea and then took them out to an early dinner, before catching the night train back to Scotland. Ned sent his mother home by taxi before he and Clare took the old lady to the station. After the train pulled out and just as the sirens started their wailing warning that the night's bombing was about to begin, and with no taxis in sight, they walked down the steps to the Underground.

'It's been an extraordinary day,' Clare said. 'I'm so glad I don't have to do night duty as well tonight.'

'As well as what?' he turned to look at her.

'As well as travel on the Underground with you,' she said, blushing. 'Officers aren't supposed to use public transport.'

'Find me a taxi, then: I'd sooner take it. Tell me,' he said, 'what would have happened if I hadn't been sent to St Stephen's to have this hand mended?'

'Oh,' she said airily, 'if you'd gone to Haslar the Navy doctors might have made a better job of it – avoided the septicaemia, for example – but you'd have been bullied by SBAs, not me.'

'An unshaven sick-berth attendant after a night's bombing wouldn't have been as fierce as you.'

'No, but SBAs don't wear black stockings.'

He laughed, recalling the episode when he had teased her that a stocking seam was crooked. 'That was when I knew I loved you,' he said, talking as thought they were in the privacy of a sitting room or bedroom, not walking round people coming up the stairs. 'When did you, er...'

'It's often different with women, darling. Usually there isn't a blinding flash as they fall in love. It is slow and insidious, like getting a cold. One feels slightly odd, and then it gets worse. Finally one has to admit to having a cold and it is far too late to do anything about it.'

They reached the bottom of the steps and walked over to the ticket machines.

'When did you decide it was too late?' he asked.

'About a week before you wrote me that letter.'

'But...' he thought a few moments. 'But you had hardly spoken to me up to then. A couple of blanket baths, a few bottles, half a dozen changes of dressing...'

'And half a dozen times when I pushed your arm down into a dish of nearly scalding water and you simply grunted when I knew it must be agony.'

'But you never said anything sympathetic; you never hinted...'

'To be snubbed by the handsome wounded young war hero who had a girl in every port?'

The ticket machine remained silent after the coins were inserted and Ned shook it. It whirred and reluctantly produced a ticket. Then, as if ashamed of its previous tardiness, it ejected the second ticket. At almost the same instant Ned felt through the floor the vibrations of a stick of bombs landing nearby.

Ned had just sat down at his desk next morning, the first to arrive in the room, when Joan came in carrying a cup of coffee and greeting him cheerfully. 'With Captain Watts' compliments,' she said and put the cup on his desk. 'As soon as you have drunk it – he was emphatic that you take your time because this is the good coffee – he requests the pleasure of your company.'

'Where's Jemmy?'

'I left him trying to sharpen a safety razor blade with a new glass sharpener he'd just bought.'

'Honing it on the inside of an ordinary tumbler is as good as anything.'

'That's what he was discovering as I left.'

'Why doesn't he use a cut-throat?'

'With that twitch of his? He'd cut his head off!'

She obviously wanted to say something serious and Ned gave her time, slowly stirring the coffee and folding an old newspaper whose crossword he had not finished.

'Ned, I'm a bit worried about Jemmy. Can I say something very personal?'

'Dunno, girl. Shut your eyes, take a deep breath…!'

'He thinks of very little but sex. It's almost an obsession with him. There, I've said it now and I've probably broken all the rules, like "Never discuss women in the mess, chaps".'

Ned shook his head. 'If you're worried, come to Uncle Ned. But answer some questions. Are his demands bothering you?'

'No, not *bothering* me; in fact – ' she broke off, embarrassed.

'You look well on it. You enjoy it?'

'Yes. Just like the next girl.'

'So what are you really worried about?'

'Well, I feel he ought to have other interest than just me – and bed.'

Ned raised his eyebrows and looked at her directly. 'If you love each other – and I don't want to hear about that,' he said hastily – 'then think of what else he could get obsessed by. As a submariner, and with this bombing, obviously he could get obsessed with death. As a lieutenant, considering what we get paid, he could be obsessed about money. The way things are going out in the Atlantic –' Ned waved at a wall chart showing the ocean from Europe to the coast of the United States ' – he could be obsessed by U-boats, the progress of the war… There's plenty to be obsessed about. To be obsessed about sex with the girl you love – well, compared with death, money, bombs, torpedoes or losing the war, it seems a good choice!'

Joan reached out impulsively to grip his shoulder. 'You're right. That's how it is with you and that nurse, isn't it?'

'Yes, we try to live just for each day – and each night.'

'She must have been terrified when you went off to sea with that convoy.'

'She didn't say. I was, though.'

'That's hard to believe,' Joan said, gesturing at the two medal ribbons.

'I've a very special reason for staying alive now,' Ned said quietly. 'It makes a difference…'

'I hope it will with Jemmy. But you know his problem?'

'The confidence business?'

'Yes. It *isn't* cowardice,' she said fiercely. 'It's just that the responsibility for *other* people's lives is more than he can take.'

'Now,' Ned amended.

'Yes, now. He was all right for months. Obviously he was, since he's regarded by the Press as one of our submarine aces. But…'

'It happens easily enough. But command is like riding a bicycle. You never quite forget how to do it, although after a bad crash you might be nervous for a while.'

'Ned, you'd better go in to see Uncle. But thanks for listening. You're right. I feel a lot better already.'

'I should leer and say you've been looking better for quite a while. Does wonders for a girl's complexion, they do say!'

He found Captain Watts smoking a cigar, the wreathing smoke making him seem a handsome Satan smiling a welcome at an outer door of hell. Ned's view of the head of ASIU as satanic was increased as the welcoming grin enquired if he had enjoyed his coffee. 'Would you care for a cigar?'

'Too early for me, sir,' Ned said warily, thinking that a cigar this early rated with a tot of whisky to get the world in focus.

'Yes,' Watts said amiably. 'I agree. However, they help me think, and we've a lot of thinking to do today before the sun goes down.'

For the second time in less than ten minutes, Ned raised his eyebrows.

Watts' grin had gone. 'You remember what we were talking about after we saw the PM?'

Ned looked round to make sure the door was closed. 'Of course, sir.'

'And you have a shoal of ideas.' It was a statement not a question.

'No, sir.' How did one explain that a morning spent at a Buckingham Palace Investiture was not exactly a good preliminary to thinking about Hydra and Triton? And that, he admitted, was an excuse for the fact that he had puzzled a good deal about it anyway and could think of nothing. At least, several ideas had surfaced and sunk back again, waterlogged with embarrassment.

Watts puffed at the cigar. 'The pressure is being applied. I spent an hour with the First Sea Lord and then an hour with the First Lord. Mr Alexander is a skilful Labour politician whose only concern is to square his own yards: I had to take along a signed report, and then add to it in my own handwriting in his presence the burden of what I had just told him.'

'What did Admiral Pound have to say, sir?'

'Just telling me that ASIU must get cracking. Wanted to know what ideas we had. Incidentally I forgot to mention to you that any intelligence derived from Enigma is called "Ultra". They don't want anyone to use the word Enigma: if the Teds heard, it'd give the game away. Seems Enigma machines were on sale commercially years ago but none of our intelligence people were interested.'

'*Mein Kampf,*' Ned said sarcastically.

'What's that got to do with it?'

'It was published in the 1920s. In it, Hitler said exactly what he'd do with Germany. No one in our Foreign Office took it seriously, of course, so we missed a ten or fifteen year warning.'

'But you've read it?' Watts said, teasingly, then looked startled at Ned's bitter reply.

'Yes, sir. I read and understood it when I was fourteen years old.'

'At Dartmouth, eh?'

'Yes, sir. Very heavy going, but it's all there. If you'd read that, then the Rhineland occupation in 1936, the invasion of Austria and Czechoslovakia in 1938 and Poland the next year all fits in.'

'What's he going to do next, then?'

'He's done it. Now he has to consolidate what he's started. Defeat Russia and defeat us, then he – Germany, rather – rules the world.'

'What about America?'

'He ignores the United States in this context. I think he'll be content if he rules the Old World. There's been no great objection from the New so far.'

'But supposing the New World develops different ideas?'

Ned shrugged his shoulders. 'We'll have to wait and see, sir, but from what I hear the American Chief of Naval Operations, Admiral King, would be quite happy to leave Hitler to it, so that the US Navy can concentrate on the Pacific.'

Watts puffed his cigar, blew out the smoke in a stream towards the low ceiling and sighed. 'Yes, but technically at least Admiral Ernest J King is on our side, though I gather those of our people who have to work with him have their doubts. Nevertheless, our concern is with the Triton cipher and that dam' machine.'

'I've no ideas, sir.'

'Just like that, eh? No ideas?'

'Ideas yes, but none I'd want to be ordered to carry out.'

'Ned,' Watts said suddenly, putting his cigar in the ashtray, 'we're more likely to come up with something if a few of us are sitting round batting ideas back and forth.'

Ned almost sighed with relief. 'That's what I've been thinking, sir, but the security clearance business seemed a problem.'

'It has been, but I've asked for clearance for Jemmy and the Croupier. The four of us should be able to come up with something.'

'We'll sink ASIU if we don't.'

'That,' Watts said dryly, 'was the burden of Admiral Pound's remarks.'

'When will you get the clearances?'

'They promised them by noon. So go back to your room and finish *The Times* crossword puzzle, and bring Jemmy and the Croupier here at three o'clock. A no-alcoholic-beverages lunch for the three of you, eh?'

Watts said: 'Joan, m'dear, remove the coffee cups. I think these peasants appreciated it but we have work to do and I don't want them to think there is any chance of a second cup. And shut the door after you: I shall be conducting the rest of the service in total secrecy.'

'Aye aye, sir,' Joan said with just the right amount of sarcasm. 'They've heard the one about the Bishop of Salisbury's wife on a bobsleigh. Try the one about the Archbishop of Canterbury planning to assault the whorehouse.'

As soon as she had left the room Watts scratched his head. 'Anyone know a joke about the Bishop of Salisbury? I believe he's called Meacham? No? Dam' funny name. Ought to be engaged to Polly Peachum, the gal in "The Beggar's Opera".'

He began humming as the other three men tried to get comfortable in their Ministry of Works chairs.

'Very well, let's hear the ideas.' Watts started to clip off the end of another cigar, then caught Ned's eye and said: 'No, not black market. Friend just returned from a United States dockyard.'

The three young naval officers watched him strike a match, make sure it was burning well, and then proceed to light the cigar as though preparing it for a very rich potential father-in-law. He exhaled a cloud of smoke, sighed with satisfaction and then said, with unexpected sharpness: 'Did I miss hearing something as I struck that match?'

Jemmy's head jerked back in a prodigious twitch. 'No, sir. I haven't had a chance to talk to Ned but the Croupier and I don't have anything.'

'Ned?' Watts looked questioningly. 'Any blinding light shine on you while you were having lunch and NID were delivering the clearance for these twisted layabouts?'

'No sir. Q-ships?' He offered the word so carefully he felt he was pronouncing the hyphen and, seeing Watts' expression, wished he could hide under it.

'Q-ships? Disguised fishing vessels and merchant ships with guns hidden that wait for a U-boat to surface and capture it?' Watts repeated unbelievingly. 'Have you been reading some old copies of the *Boy's Own Paper*?'

'I'd been thinking on those lines, too, sir,' admitted the Croupier, 'although I was too shy to say so.'

'Me too,' Jemmy said, again twitching. 'Shyness has almost ruined my career so far. I'm fighting it all the time.'

Watts removed the cigar from his mouth with a Churchillian flourish. 'Tell Uncle what led you to Q-ships,' he asked Ned. 'You can be the spokesman for these other peasants.'

Ned was not fooled by the bantering tone. 'Starting off with the basic problem, it seems the only answer,' he said.

'What pray, is the basic problem?'

Ned decided that Uncle had been listening to too many speeches by Mr Churchill and it had gone to his mouth.

'First, we've got to get on board a U-boat to collect one of these Enigma machines and the manual. Second, we can only do that either by enlisting in the German Navy or capturing a U-boat, sir.'

'Marvellous,' Watts said. 'that's what comes of universal education, which ensures that all the peasants achieve the same abysmal level of stupidity!'

Jemmy's twitch was punctuated by a sneeze, which provoked Watts to exclaim: 'Don't say you're going to give us all colds. God, what a way to start the winter.'

'It's that dime store cigar smoke, *sir*,' Jemmy said, fanning with the docket he had been holding in his lap. 'I hope you didn't pay customs on those cigars. They sell 'em at ten cents each in the cigar stores in the States.'

'Damn and blast my cigar: I'm waiting for some sensible ideas from you three. You are supposed to be the bright boys, specially selected for a special unit. The brains of the ASIU.'

'Fact is,' Ned said gloomily, I'm more cut out to be a Naafi manager. Mars Bars for the masses: say "Please" if you want fifty Players. No Sherbert Dabs left, sergeant, and the Licorice Allsorts have gone – the colonel's wife pre-empted the last of them. Or maybe Director of No-Coke-This-Week at the Ministry of Fuel.'

'I'll get you transferred to ENSA,' Watts growled. 'As a stand-up comic you'll have 'em rolling off their seats – in somewhere like Aden. Anyway, let's hear some more *Comic Cuts* stuff, Ned.'

The grin took the sting out of the remark.

'Well, sir, I'd assumed we can't get into some German base and steal one. Or, rather, that we might be able to organize the Resistance people into pinching one for us, but that'd defeat the exercise because then the Teds would know we've got our hands on one of their toys and would start winding them up differently, or something.

'So we are back to getting our hands on a German warship and leading the Teds to think it has been sunk. Presumably it has to be a U-boat…' He paused a moment as something seemed to be waving from the edge of his memory. He looked up at Watts.

'Somewhere, sir, I've heard that the Teds get their long-range weather data not only from planes but, because of the distance involved, they have small weather reporting ships nipping in and out of the ice cap and playing hide-and-seek along the Greenland fjords. Could we…?'

Watts shook his head. 'Good thinking Ned. Yes and no. Yes, the Teds did have a couple of weather ships hiding in the fog and ice floes, wirelessing millibars and wind directions to their Met people in *Tedeschi* land, but no we can't go after them because they've already been "got". One was scuttled but we got on board the other. This was some time ago and it yielded a Mark II Enigma without alarming the Germans that we had one. It's the Mark III we want…'

'Can we count that in our score?' Jemmy enquired.

Watts took a puff and agreed.

'Peasants one, Forces of Evil nil,' Jemmy said.

The Croupier uncrossed his legs – a movement that, because of his height, made it look as if he was unwinding – and said in a cringing voice: 'Speaking as the Archbishop of Canterbury's aunt, sir, I cannot but feel you are taking a very unChristian attitude towards Q-ships.'

'Forgive the pun, but Croupier, how full of Cantuar. What had you in mind as a Q-ship? The *Queen Elizabeth*, a Thames barge, the Gosport Ferry or a drifter?'

Ned leaned forward. 'The type of ship depends on where we'd operate, sir. A U-boat'd be suspicious if she came across a Grimsby drifter in mid-Atlantic but might well surface to sink an old coal-burning merchant ship by gunfire to save a torpedo.'

'A cautious skipper might use a torpedo,' Watts said.

'None of the Ted skippers are cautious these days, sir,' Jemmy said. 'They're sinking so many of our ships they don't have to be, and I'm sure Dönitz has a special sweepstake going at Kernével. The month's top scorer gets a box of Tunisian dates, a bar of Hamburg rock and two yards of *Leberwurst*.'

'So?'

'Zo every skipper wants to make sure that each of his fourteen torpedoes gets a coconut, sir. Anything sunk by gunfire is a bonus. Even the best skipper is unlikely to get more than seven ships with fourteen fish, but let's say he got fourteen. That's obviously reckoned to be the top possible score of ships, but it could be equalled by some other sharp-eyed Teuton. But fourteen ships with fourteen fish, plus a couple more by gunfire, would be sure to win all the month's coconuts – and an Iron Cross with swords, diamonds, and lettuce leaves from the Führer's salad.'

'Very well,' Watts said carefully, 'so what you want is something inconspicuous which is not worth a torpedo but *is* worth a few rounds from the gun, eh?'

'And is well armed and manned by some properly-trained gunners. These Merchant Navy chaps are all right, but their enthusiasm exceeds their skill, doesn't it, Ned?'

'Most of the ships have DEMS gunners,' Ned said. 'They're a mixture of volunteers in the Maritime Regiment of the Royal Artillery, and Naval ratings. The men in Defensively Equipped Merchant Ships tend to have very little training and no practice, but enormous courage.'

'I can't see it,' the Croupier said unexpectedly.

'Can't see what, blast you!' Watts said crossly.

'I can't see the sequence. Or, rather, I can't see it working.'

'Jemmy, whisper in his ear,' Watts said. 'Tell him we're all sitting close and love him: there's no need to use a scrambler telephone.'

The Croupier grinned and apologized. 'I was thinking aloud, sir. Let's assume we have just the right clapped-out old coal-burner merchant ship, built in 1911. Every hour or so the bell rings and the stokers hurl into the furnace a few more shovels full of Welsh nuts – coal, not Members of Parliament – and the ancient and tall funnel suddenly emits a splendid cloud of black smoke which is visible for miles.

'Our Teutonic Knight spots the smoke and spurs his steed into position and suddenly surfaces close to the smoker, and orders it to heave-to and not transmit. Our TK may or may not give the smoker's men enough time to get the lifeboats away – that probably depends whether or not they're within range of Coastal Command planes.

'Up come the Teuton gunners, and they open fire with their 88 mm gun, which has a flat trajectory and is the weapon used in the Western Desert as an anti-tank gun against the 8th Army, and goes off with a nasty crack rather than a boom. A few cracks, down goes the ancient coal-burner, and if the TK is a keen chap he goes over to the lifeboats or rafts, if any, and takes the captain prisoner. If he's feeling liverish his chaps will throw a few hand grenades among the survivors or use the U-boat herself to run down the boats and rafts. All done as part of the code of the Teutonic Knights – *Krieg ist Krieg*, chums.'

Watts put down his cigar and clapped his hands. 'Oh *very* good, and what will you do as an encore? A sentimental number with Vera Lynn? You were rattling on about *sequences*. In your monologue, where you forgot to quote Masefield's "salt-caked smokestack" (may real sailors forgive him for using the word), you seemed to get lost.'

'Oh no, sir,' the Croupier said, 'I was allowing my listeners to use their imaginations. The sequence stops with the U-boat surfacing and starts again with it diving and resuming its patrol. The question is, how can any worthy sons of Albion get on board in between times? They're rowing for their lives, catching the grenades lobbed by the Teutons, or swimming (if they've survived the crunch) from smashed-up boats or rafts.'

Watts took a puff from his cigar and put it down again, and said acidly: 'Recently I had to go to a conference with some American naval officers, and noticed they prefaced several of their remarks with the phrase "Be advised". So Croupier, be advised that I'm the boss of this Fred Karno outfit and you, Jemmy and Ned are supposed to be brilliant young officers who feed me with equally brilliant plans to which I give my approval and get all the credit. Also be advised that I don't need three flatulent no-men bleating: "It can't be done." We all *know* it can't be done. Not so long ago we all agreed that there was no way ships could be torpedoed regularly from inside a convoy. Ned went off and found out how it could be done, stopped it, collected a DSC and is now back with us and joining in the "can't be done" liturgy.'

He inspected the ash on the end of his cigar. 'Go away, the three of you, and sit under a beech tree in St James's Park and think up a way. Don't let anyone hear what you are discussing. You will report here at 8 a.m. tomorrow. Bring your own coffee, unless you want Camp.'

CHAPTER FOUR

Jemmy looked round the half-panelled sitting room and subsided into a comfortable old leather armchair with a contented sigh. 'Nice house, Ned – so convenient for the Palace!'

'And Victoria Station,' Ned said. 'Actually I think the family originally bought it because it's only walking distance to Parliament.'

'Family owned it long?' The Croupier asked. 'Mortgage paid off?'

'Paid cash when it was built in the 1670s. One of my ancestors bought it from a speculator called Sir George Downing.'

'Any relation to the Number Ten bloke?' Jemmy asked.

'You're getting a history lesson. Yes, George Downing built strictly on spec a row of houses which were named Downing Street after him and then several more round here.'

'How did Downing Street get into the hands of the Mafia?' the Croupier demanded.

'I'm not sure. I know George II gave Number Ten to Sir Robert Walpole, who is supposed to be the first Prime Minister as we know the job.'

'Old George Downing didn't realize how famous he'd become!' Jemmy commented.

'He must have been an interesting character. He graduated from Harvard in the 1640s, went into the slum property building business, and died a knight.'

'Harvard, 1640s?' the Croupier exclaimed.

Ned pulled an encyclopaedia from a bookshelf. 'Yes, founded in 1636, just ten years after that Dutchman, Peter Minuit, bought Manhattan from the Man-a-hat-a Indians for twenty-four dollars' worth of trinkets.'

'If we don't apply our splendid brains to ASIU's problems,' the Croupier said gloomily, 'Adolf the Austrian will be buying the United Kingdom for fifty dollars' worth of ciphers.'

The house was cold and, without Clare, seemed very empty. Her absence made Jemmy and the Croupier seem strangers for reasons he could not explain. He had gone through to the pantry and looked in the tea caddy, but there was not enough left out of the meagre ration to make a pot for the three of them. A cold, empty house and no tea. War was getting tough. In another six months, he thought grimly, some of Himmler's SS men will probably be billeted in this house – unless we discover some of that diabolical cunning.

A dull, grey day, and even the carefully tended plants in his mother's window boxes seemed on the verge of surrender.

Suddenly and without warning the sitting room warmed and seemed to be comfortably full of people he could not see: grandfathers, third, fourth and fifth great-grandfathers facing similar problems – and, because the family had continued and the country carried on, presumably solving them. Affairs of state – his ninth great-grandfather was the Earl of Ilex, forced by Cromwell's Roundheads to flee to France, and who died before the Restoration. Affairs of the heart – his eighth great-grandfather, the Earl's younger son, had led the buccaneers of Jamaica and then brought his French wife home to live in this house for a few years. Most of the grandfathers between the buccaneer and himself had been Members of Parliament, with cousins successively inheriting the Earldom of Ilex. Being a Member then had been very much a thing one did, like belonging to a good club. Today many of its Members, taking subsidies from trade unions, brewers and the like in exchange for favourable votes, found it necessary to boast that being an MP was to be a member of the most exclusive club in the world, though convicts in Dartmoor probably had a better claim.

Curious how the Yorkes descended from the buccaneering eighth great-grandpa had generally gone to sea. He thought enviously that they had lived in the days when having a large estate and a seat in the Commons were no bar to owning a shipping company or serving in the Navy until one was forty or fifty, and then returning to the estate and going up to Town half a dozen times a year to speak and vote on some pet subject.

All the elder (or only) sons had been given Edward as a first name: all, as far as he could trace, had been called Ned by their families.

How often had one or other Ned Yorke and his political cronies gathered in this room to decide tactics over some new Parliamentary bill just being introduced. How often had a Ned Yorke in naval uniform sat here with fellow naval officers to discuss a coming or present war, or perhaps some new type of ship – the huge three-decker *Ville de Paris*, captured by Rodney at the Saintes, or the first ironclad. Perhaps Nelson had sat in here. One of the Neds – probably his great-grandfather – must have discussed the Crimean War here before sailing to take part in it and winning one of the first Victoria Crosses ever awarded. His grandfather would have talked of the Boer War; his father the Kaiser's War. Each in turn had inherited the estate, this house and a reasonable fortune (thanks to the buccaneer who had died a rich man). Affairs of state, service gossip, affairs of the heart (with chaperones present!): this room had heard many such discussions, but after all of them the United Kingdom – indeed the British Empire – had continued.

Now, he realized, with the eleventh Ned Yorke and a couple of war-strained lieutenants, the discussion (once it ever started) really concerned whether the United Kingdom would continue to exist, because if the Battle of the Atlantic was lost, then Britain would become part of Hitler's loudly proclaimed Thousand Year

Reich, which already stretched from the North Cape of Norway to the Tropic of Cancer.

Jemmy emerged from a day dream with a twitch that brought him upright in his chair. 'Q-ships,' he said. 'I thought Uncle sounded a bit on the turn about them.'

'All very well for him,' the Croupier grumbled. 'The Prime Minister and the First Sea Lord prodded him, now he's prodding us. Pity we don't have people to prod in turn. Still, Q-ships won't work.'

'I agree,' Ned said, 'but you didn't make your point clear to him.'

'What point?' the Croupier asked.

'Well, the Q-ship idea won't work because for the Q-ship to survive, it has to sink the U-boat first. There's no way it can stun the Teds long enough to get a boat load of boarders over to capture it. The wily Teutons will either drive 'em off or scuttle the boat.'

'Which means no Enigma machine, no manual, and an Aden posting for all in the ASIU: temperature 120° in the shade on a cool day and lots of sand,' Jemmy said gloomily, and twitched.

'The Resistance people,' the Croupier said morosely, 'I know Uncle will rule 'em out, but surely they might be able to do something.'

Ned shook his head and said quietly: 'It's not that the Resistance couldn't or wouldn't do it: they could snatch a Mark III machine and have it on its way to England by Lysander within two or three days, along with the Triton manual. But the moment the Teds know we have a Mark III and manual, they'll change the rotors, the settings, and cipher, and we'll be back at square one. In fact they would probably change *all* the ciphers. The only practical way is to get one from a Ted ship – U-boat or surface – and let the Teds think it was sunk in action. That means the Teds happily write off that particular Mark III and manual as down with Davy Jones.'

Jemmy sneezed unexpectedly. 'We're back to U-boats. Hey, what about Ted weather reports? What are they using now?'

'Aircraft – those bloody great Focke-Wulf Kondors and Kuriers.'

'Surely they use Enigmas? Can't we – no, I suppose not,' he finished lamely as he realized that shooting down a lumbering four-engined aircraft over the sea hardly solved the problem.

'They probably don't use Enigma anyway,' Ned said. 'They could report on their return, or radio home using an ordinary Luftwaffe weather cipher – there's nothing very secret about a Met report, especially when that same weather has just crossed Allied territory like Nova Scotia and Greenland. The ships were concerned more with long-range forecasting.'

'All right, all right,' Jemmy said. 'Cross out Goering's bloody aeroplanes. What about the Ted pongos?'

'The Teutonic soldiery are still using Mark IIs. Jemmy, just concentrate a moment; we are not interested in Enigma machines *as such* because we've captured Mark IIs in the Western Desert. We know all about Mark IIs using three rotors, and we have broken most of the ciphers used on the Mark IIs.'

'I know all that,' Jemmy said crossly.

'Then why are you rattling on about planes, which mean Luftwaffe and Luftwaffe ciphers?'

'All right,' Jemmy admitted, 'I was getting carried away with the idea of getting any blasted Enigma. Are we sure that, as the Atlantic boats come back to rearm, refuel and perhaps change crews, wily Ted experts with pockets full of nuts and bolts, and clutching metric spanners and screwdrivers, are fitting new Mark IIIs, and that Dönitz has set *Der Tag* for Triton?'

Ned sighed with exaggerated patience. 'I'm not sure when, Uncle isn't sure when, and the Prime Minister isn't sure when, but the codes and ciphers boys at BP are sure it'll be soon, and that's good enough for us.'

'BP?'

'Bletchley Park, the Government Codes and Ciphers place in Buckinghamshire. They're the Enigma wizards. They know what

Adolf's doing with his army, Goering with his flying machines and (up to now) Dönitz with his U-boats simply by picking up the Enigma stuff, finding out the day's settings for the various rotors, and then deciphering.'

'If they decipher all the German stuff, which means they cracked Hydra, why are they so worried about Triton?' the Croupier demanded.

Ned shrugged his shoulders. 'I know only what Uncle tells me, but obviously some of these top ciphers are hard to crack. Like our Fleet code. It took months for BP actually to break Hydra – a year, I believe – and obviously Triton is going to be a lot tougher, plus the fact that the Mark III has the fourth rotor. BP reckon they're being optimistic in saying a year. *For us that means a year's blackout on what the Teds are doing in the Atlantic.'*

'Bloody hell!' Jemmy exclaimed. 'We're losing badly enough now, even though we know roughly where every U-boat is. And we know through Enigma,' he marvelled. 'I always thought we were doing it by DF!'

'A direction-finding fix on a brief transmission fifteen hundred miles away can have an error of fifty or a hundred miles,' the Croupier said, 'but certainly I never realized…'

Jemmy gave a convulsive twitch and then sighed. 'Just imagine what the fly-boys could have done if they had had Ultra during the Battle of Britain!'

'They did,' Ned said. 'How the devil do you think we were matching a couple of dozen Hurricanes and Spits against a hundred Ted day after day? Simply because we knew when the big formations were coming and their targets. Our fighters could wait until the very last moment before taking off to intercept. That way they saved fuel and had more flying time.'

'So it's no Q-ships,' Jemmy said despondently. 'Let's get the Resistance to put up big posters in Brest offering huge rewards to any U-boat crew that will sail into Plymouth flying a white flag.'

'Those Teds are so convinced they're winning that they're likely to come over and demand that we surrender. Anyway,' Ned added wryly, 'that wouldn't help because Dönitz would know at once he'd lost a Mark III!'

'You know,' Jemmy said bitterly, 'I've been a submariner for most of my time in the King's Navee, from the lowliest of the low, keeping the Confidential Books up to date and trying to stay level with the Notices to Mariners, right up to commanding my own boat and sinking enough Ted and Italian ships to found Seabottom Shipping Limited, the largest line in the Mediterranean, but I feel nothing in common with these Ted skippers.'

'Why? They face the same problems. A depth-charge can kill them just as easily as you,' Ned said, curious at the tone in Jemmy's voice.

'Yes, we all operate best at 98.4 degrees. But they toss grenades into lifeboats to kill survivors, or ram the boats. Not my cup of tea. That's murder, pure and simple.'

Ned recalled the time he had spent on board the *Marynal*, a medium-sized dry cargo ship, solving the convoy problem. Her captain, officers and men all had one grudge against the Germans – the killing of survivors. He could picture the tiny lifeboat, probably overcrowded because a merchant ship was rarely able to launch all its boats, and a U-boat surfacing and coming up close. The Teds would use a loud-hailer to order them to row the last few yards, so they could take off the captain, and the boat would be close below the conning tower. Then a couple of stick grenades would be flung down into the boat... Supposing the survivors could grab the grenades and toss them back before they exploded! But they'd have to catch them, otherwise valuable seconds would be lost scrabbling round under the thwarts trying to find something the size of a jam jar.

Close enough to lob a grenade...

'Listen,' he said suddenly to Jemmy and the Croupier, 'this is only a crazy passing thought but it's a change from Q-ships.'

Ten minutes later they were leaving the house like a trio of excited schoolboys, and as Ned locked the door Jemmy was insisting they took a cab back to the Admiralty.

'We don't want to keep Uncle waiting,' he said.

'Uncle doesn't expect to see us for a week, and we need the exercise,' the Croupier said. 'You're so used to being under the sea or underground or in bed that daylight and open spaces scare you. Don't worry, no eagle will swoop down and snatch you up as you pass Queen Victoria's statue.'

'No, but a harpy might, and my mum warned me against harpies.'

Captain Watts listened carefully as Ned outlined his proposal and puffed at what he declared was his last cigar.

'It all depends on luck,' he said finally. 'One good storm could do you in.'

'We haven't much alternative, sir.'

'That's the only reason I'm sitting here listening to you, although for crackpot ideas this one takes the prize.'

He flicked the ash from the cigar. 'Have you two buffoons anything to contribute?'

'No sir,' Jemmy said brightly. 'We think he's wonderful. We stand beside him – not too close, of course, and always windward.'

Watts said: 'This is very secret but it might help. As you know, we've already captured a U-boat intact. What you don't know is that we also got Enigma, Hydra manual, the lot. A Mark II, of course.'

Jemmy's eyes widened. 'Any chance of us being allowed to prowl over her? It'd be an enormous help for Ned and the Croupier. U-boats are laid out differently from British boats.'

'In what way?'

'In British boats the skipper stands at the periscope with the attack team grouped round him in the control room at the same level, feeding target bearings and so on into their gadgets. They're close enough to pass him a cigarette. In a U-boat the skipper and periscope are up in the conning tower in a sort of attic, separated by a hatchway from the control room below him. He passes down orders like shouting down a dumb waiter.'

'Which would you prefer?' Watts asked, curious.

'Well, I prefer our way. More cosy. And I like to give the boys a running commentary on what's going on, and that's easier when they're close round you.'

He sat back, giving an occasional twitch, and then said: 'Well, sir, can we get a look at it?'

'With your new security rating, I think so. But wouldn't it be better to wait until you've drummed up your group of ruffians so that you can all go?'

Ned said quickly: 'That would be best, sir. No good just the three of us knowing our way about a U-boat. And any chance of having a chat with some Royal Marine commandos?'

'They'll be chary of lending you any of their chaps,' Watts said.

'Well, we'll need some Marines eventually, and our team of sailors will need a brisk course in close combat. The Jollies may have some new toys that can help.'

'Yes, "black bangers",' Jemmy said suddenly. 'Just the trick. My father's platoon of Home Guard have some. Like an ordinary Mills 36 hand grenade, but it's made of Bakelite and when it lands in the middle of a happy little group it goes off with such a frightful bang that everyone is stunned for several minutes, just as though the Archbishop of Canterbury went off his head and started talking sense at a tea party.'

'I know the things,' Ned said. 'Psychological warfare: stun the beggars! If you toss an ordinary Mills grenade into a crowd you can't hope to kill 'em all, but one of Jemmy's "black bangers" deafens and shocks them so you can nip in and snip their braces so their trousers fall down; then at your leisure you tie their bootlaces together. You can capture and tether a whole battalion of the Wehrmacht with a case of ten grenades.'

Watts grinned and said: 'I'll order a case. They probably make them now in red, white and blue, as well and black.' He suddenly became serious again. 'I hope your German is not too rusty?'

Jemmy said diffidently: 'I had a Swiss nanny. I'm still fluent but I have a heavy Swiss accent.'

'Mine's good,' the Croupier said, 'but I hate the sound of it.'

'Rusty,' Ned answered. 'Used to be good. Austrian nanny and my mother is fluent. I suppose it will come back with a bit of practice.'

Watts asked Jemmy: 'Is your accent too heavy to give Ned a few lessons?'

'No, we'll probably end up sounding like a pair of Swiss Guards but unless we're rigged out in that Vatican uniform it won't matter.'

'Very well. But be discreet about it. Anyone seeing two naval officers in uniform babbling German will get suspicious.'

'An obvious prelude to bombarding Berlin with the *Rodney* by sending her steaming up the Spree,' Ned said.

'That's it!' Watts exclaimed. 'We need a cover name for this caper and that's it, Operation Spree. I'll have to go through channels and get an official name, but among ourselves – just the four of us – "Spree" is the word.'

'Can we just run though what's been agreed so far, sir?' Ned said tentatively. 'Now we're on the spree,' he added.

'Yes,' Watts said. 'Incidentally, have any of you ever been on the Spree?'

'I have, when I was about eight,' the Croupier said. 'My parents spent a month in Berlin. Pa had business there and we had to go off for the day steaming down the Spree in a large ferry with all these ancient and portly Teds drinking steins of beer and talking business and celebrating with Pa. I remember I was fascinated by Ted tourists wearing embroidered shirts and shorts made of leather, and funny little trilby hats with small coloured feathers stuck in the bands. This little boy, for one, thought going on the Spree was a monumental bore. I remember that German lemonade was too fizzy; when you belched, bubbles of gas went up your nose. Made you sneeze.'

'You sound like a Zeppelin!' Watts said.

'Ha, wish I'd met him too, Graf von Zeppelin, but he was long dead by then. Remember the airship Hindenburg and when she came up the Channel – when was that, 1938?'

'Must have been earlier because she burned out in Lakehurst, New Jersey, in 1937. Anyway, I saw her before that,' Ned said. 'A long, thin silver pencil. Lovely day, too, just as though the pencil was lying on a pale blue tablecloth.'

'The German Zeppelin people were very cross with the Americans, I remember,' the Croupier said reminiscently. 'Seems they wouldn't sell helium to anyone – it's an inert gas and America's the only source. So the Germans had to use hydrogen, just as we did with the R 101. One spark and boom, it's all over: millions of cubic feet exploding – just imagine it.'

'I'd rather deal with Ned's question,' Watts said. 'We've agreed so far that I arrange for you to inspect the captured U-boat but we decide later whether there'll be just the three of you or your whole party; that the three of you (it may have to be restricted to Ned) visit BP and have a good look at an actual Enigma machine and get a briefing from the code and cipher boys; that you do a bashing and clubbing course with the Jollies and see what new in-fighting weapons are currently in fashion… And finally, I get you a supply of Jemmy's black bangers. That's all, isn't it?' he asked, eyebrows raised.

Ned nodded, admiring the man's mind. No touching one finger after another to tick off five very diverse items; no, his mind seemed like a five-barred mousetrap, each bar coming over with a brisk crash.

'Now you have to select and collect your gang of "diabolical cunnings",' Watts said. 'Any idea where such cunnings are kept?'

After glancing at the Croupier and Jemmy, Ned said: 'We'll work out a list of the jobs we'll all need to do; then we'll think who best can do them.'

'Very well, but remember that whoever you choose have to be in Britain: I can't get men back from the Med or some other unlikely spot.'

'No, sir, but – '

'No "buts",' Watts said firmly. 'It's no bloody good you coming to me and saying you want ERA Bloggs, last seen on board a sub at Malta, and CPO Raspberry, last seen lurching away from the destroyer pens in Gib with a couple of tarts in tow.'

'Quite, sir,' Ned said. 'Our chaps are more likely to be doing jankers in some Service prison.'

CHAPTER FIVE

The two Army sentries checked the three passes of the passengers in the Navy Humber, then demanded one for the Wren driver. She did not have one and the sentry with a corporal's stripes on his sleeves shook his head apologetically at Ned. 'I'm sorry, Commander, no one is allowed past the gate without a pass. We can't even,' he said hurriedly, anticipating Ned's protest, 'let the gentlemen we know and who've worked here for years through if they've forgotten their pass.'

Ned said: 'You are quite right. Have you a telephone?'

'In the guardhouse. I'll take you there, sir.'

Within a couple of minutes he was explaining the problem to the civilian with whom they had an appointment.

'Can one of you drive?'

'Yes. But what about the Wren?'

'Leave her with the guards. She'll enjoy herself drinking cups of weak tea.'

Ten minutes later Ned had parked the car and was tugging the sleeve of a bemused Jemmy as he stood twitching in front of one of the ugliest Victorian mansions that any of them had seen.

'Look at it!' Jemmy spluttered. 'I can just see some vulgar Victorian nabob, pockets full of money from textile mills or coalfields, instructing his architect what he wants built. Gothic, Perpendicular, Byzantine – it's all jumbled up here and you can see it adds up to a Victorian terrace stretched out and inflated.

Oh yes, he forgot to order a tower, a minaret, rather, from which the crier can call the hours of prayer to the Faithful.'

'Come on,' Ned said, 'you're neither a prospective tenant nor buying it. Look.' He pointed at some low wooden huts of the type found at every Service establishment. 'Perhaps that's more to your taste.'

'Ah yes, Ministry of Works Georgian. George VI, that is. Built of green wood that swells so that no window opens and you have to charge every door with your shoulder. Rot starts within six months: fungus flourishes under floorboards in a year.'

He was still grumbling as they were ushered into a sparse, cold, high-ceilinged room where an unpainted deal trestle table carried a scrambler telephone, 'In' and 'Out' trays, an ashtray almost full of cigarette stubs, and a dirty cup resting in a moat of cold tea within a fraction of an inch of slopping over the side of the saucer. The rest of the furniture consisted of three chairs from which the single coat of varnish was being worn away, and another small table nearby holding a mahogany box about a foot square and eight or ten inches high. The box stood out amid the shoddy Ministry furniture because it looked as if the original owner of the house had left behind a canteen of cutlery.

The man now standing in front of the larger table was comfortably dressed in tweeds, round-faced and cheerful with sandy hair thinning across the crown, and he wore horn-rimmed spectacles with lenses so thick that they might have been made from the bottom of lemon pop bottles.

Blinking myopically he took a step forward. 'One of you is Lieutenant Commander Yorke? I'm Jenson.'

Ned shook his hand and introduced Jemmy and the Croupier to the man, who seemed to be every cartoonist's dream of an absent-minded academic but, Ned guessed, was a lot sharper than he looked.

'You have a letter from some fellow in the Admiralty?'

Ned handed him the letter of introduction from Captain Watts and noticed that he glanced first at the signature before reading it.

'Ah yes, it all seems straightforward. If you'll just excuse me a moment...?' He picked up the telephone and muttered into it: 'Admiralty in Whitehall, ASIU, Captain Watts, please.' He replaced the receiver and waited until it rang.

'Ah, hello Henry, this is Rex. Shall we scramble?' He leaned over to push across the lever marked 'scramble', and carried on talking. 'I have three of your fellows here with a letter signed by you. Wait a moment – ' he pulled over a notebook and scribbled a few words. 'Right, can't be too careful. Very well, Henry, cheerio.'

He put down the telephone, slid the 'scramble' lever back to its original position and pointed at Ned. 'What are you usually called in your office?'

The unexpected question startled him but Jemmy growled: 'He's Ned!'

'Ah,' Jenson said and ticked off a name. 'And you would be?'

'Jemmy.'

'After that famous Earl of Sandwich, no doubt.' He looked up quickly, his eyes huge through the thick lenses. 'No offence meant, of course; I have a crossword puzzle mind and you have a twitch.' He turned and said: 'And you, Lieutenant?'

'I'm the Croupier. I pay when they want drinks.'

Jenson chuckled and then said: 'Very well, that's the first step. I'm sorry about the security but we have a lot of secrets in this Victorian pile. Now I'm the chap who is going to show you an Enigma machine, and explain how it works. I have managed to get a newish model for you – '

'A Mark III?' Jemmy asked hopefully.

'Good grief, no. I understand *you* are going to provide us with one of those!' He walked over to the small table and gestured at the mahogany box. 'This is a Mark II, the type used up to now by all the German services.'

Was it pedantry, Ned wondered, that prevented Jenson from saying 'all three German services'? Out of curiosity, he asked him: 'Who actually sends signals by Enigma?'

'Oh, goodness me, who doesn't! The Navy, Wehrmacht and Luftwaffe, of course; the Gestapo, SS – just about everyone, it seems. Our intercept people are almost swamped.'

He polished his glasses with a piece of toilet paper, torn from the remains of a roll which Ned saw he kept in a corner of his 'In' tray.

'Captain Watts has just asked me to go over the German signals system to make sure you understand fully where Enigma fits in. Do you gentlemen know anything about codes and ciphers?' When they all shook their heads, he clasped his hands like an earnest clergyman trying to explain a point of canon law. 'Well, the words "code" and "cipher" are used very loosely by the layman, but there is a difference – hence the official name of this place, the Government Code and Cipher School.

'A code is where a letter or number (or group of them) are used to mean complete phrases. For example, the figure seven sent by Morse could mean "The Fleet is to put to sea at once".

'A cipher is when you scramble the actual sentence, using the same number of letters. If you wanted to send "The Fleet is to put to sea" in cipher you would scramble up the letters of all the words and transmit the jumble. Of course, the receiver of the signal has to know how to unscramble it and read the original meaning.

'With Enigma, we are concerned only with ciphers,' he said. 'In fact ciphers are the key to wars. Ciphers, if you can break them, in effect let you listen to a microphone placed in the enemy's headquarters.

'The old way of sending a message in cipher meant referring to a book, rather like a dictionary, to change each letter of the signal into something else – into what would be a meaningless jumble to the enemy. There are problems. For example, take the word "add". In a particular cipher, A may become H, and D is W, so "add", in cipher is "HWW". Any cryptologist worth his salt would spot that, so having worked out that H is in fact A, and W is D, he looks for more clues like that and finally breaks the cipher and reads the signal.'

'How the hell can anyone send signals that the enemy can't break?' Jemmy demanded.

'Telepathy,' Ned muttered. 'That's the answer. Or tom-toms at short range.'

'I agree about telepathy,' Jenson answered, his face serious. 'I think it has great possibilities, but I can't interest my colleagues.'

'Where does Enigma come into all this?' Jemmy asked. 'Just a superior crystal ball?'

Ned decided that Jenson was completely humourless: no joke or wry remark ever intruded into his life (or, rather, was ever recognized).

In the flat tone of a true academic, Jenson began: 'Enciphering a message which has to be transmitted by a means the enemy can overhear (by wireless, for instance) means that the words of the message have to be scrambled in a completely *random* way, and the chances of it being broken are lessened if each time the same letter is repeated in the message it becomes a different one in the scramble.

'For example, say A is Z the first time it is used, K the second, R the third and so on.

'But war today is fast moving, particularly where armies are concerned. There isn't time to decipher long signals by turning the pages of a cipher book, particularly while you are being bombed or shelled, and it will probably be raining, too.'

'Enigma?' Jemmy prompted hopefully.

'So the ideal way to encipher a message before transmitting it by wireless is a mechanical means: in other words something like a special typewriter. You type the actual letters of the message in plain language on to the keyboard, but what you read as you hit each key is *another* letter, so instead of the original plain message you now have an apparently meaningless scramble. And a special refinement would be that, as you type each, it not only produces the enciphered letter but then changes, so that the next time that particular letter comes up, it is enciphered differently.'

'And that's what Enigma does?' Ned asked.

'That was my bird,' Jemmy complained.

'Basically that's what the Germans did when they produced Enigma,' Jenson said pedantically. 'They added a battery, a nice mahogany box, a manual for each cipher – and here you have it.' He patted the box. 'Just like a portable typewriter – which is what is really is.'

'But what happens when someone picks up the signal after Enigma has scrambled it?' the Croupier asked.

'Ah, that's quite simple. That person would need to be listening on an assigned frequency, have a manual for the particular cipher, and an Enigma machine – which have been issued by the hundred.

'Let's suppose Hans Schmidt is the wireless operator of the 15th Panzer Division in the Western Desert and the *Ober Kommando der Wehrmacht* in Berlin has a signal for the general commanding.

'The OKW signals people get the message at headquarters in plain language and will insert the prefix for that particular panzer division, say COD, then type the message on the Enigma machine in the appropriate Wehrmachit cipher, take the scrambled (and thus enciphered) result, and transmit it on that panzer wireless frequency.

'Out in the Western Desert, wireless operator Schmidt listening on his frequency hears the letters COD in Morse, recognizes it as the call sign of the 15th Panzer division and copies down the Morse signal. It is, of course, the letters COD followed by what seems to be gibberish.

'That signal is then taken to the 15th Panzer division's Enigma. Right at the beginning of the message, following COD, is another three-letter group which tells what the machine should be set at, and, if it is very secret, an indication that it must be deciphered by an officer. I'll show you all that on the machine in a moment.'

'As easy as that, eh?' Jemmy grunted.

'If you have an Enigma, and *if* you have the appropriate manual for the cipher being used and can set the machine correctly. For the eavesdropper – us, in fact, – it's more complex. We can usually work out for whom the signal is intended. Our problem is to work out the three-letter setting for the Enigma. Of course, a message can be *coded* first, and then sent by *cipher* using the Enigma. It's rare, but it really provides a headache. A double headache,' he said and smiled to indicate he had made a joke.

Ned said: 'I thought there were dozens of different ciphers – Hydra, Medusa, Thetis, Neptun and so on for the Navy…'

'Oh yes, for all the German services. These are the three-letter settings. The more important the cipher, the more difficult the setting. Look at the machine and you'll realize that one three-letter setting is not necessarily as easy as another.'

The trio grouped round him at the little table. 'Just a simple wooden box, and when you open the lid you see – ' he swung it up and back on its hinge as though to reveal a white rabbit, 'what looks like a complicated portable typewriter. And in many ways that's what it is, electrically operated.

'In front, you have an ordinary typewriter keyboard – Q,W,E,R,T,Y and so on. Then behind it, where you'd expect to find the platen, is this board with all the letters reproduced again, each behind a tiny glass window and in the same order. And then behind that you see the three small slots with metal wheels showing, each with a sort of thin disc, with a cogwheel rim, next to it. Now look carefully – '

Ned leaned over as Jenson opened a small cover.

'What do you see, Commander?'

'Letters of the alphabet are engraved round the rim of each wheel.'

'Exactly, and let's call that the rotor. But you can see – ' he turned the rotors beside the engraved rims, 'that each rotor is fitted to it own disc. Actually, we call the rim and disc together a rotor. You see three are fitted together here in the middle, but there are two more over in this rack on the right: they are spares or, rather, alternatives: the machine has five rotors but only uses three at any given time.'

'How does wireless operator Schmidt know which three to use?' the Croupier asked.

'The sequence is changed every twenty-four hours, so his manual tells him that for, say, the fifth of November he uses rotors number one, four and five. So he fits those – it's a simple pull-out and drop-in affair – depending on the date. Schmidt then picks up the call sign COD which shows the signal is for his own Panzer Division, and he copies it down as it comes over the wireless in Morse.

'Then – I'm guessing now – he takes his handwritten signal to the Enigma operator, who will set his machine to the same setting as the OKW Enigma was when it scrambled – enciphered, rather – this particular signal. There's another step too, but I'll explain that later.'

'How do the Germans actually pass messages to U-boats on this thing?' Ned asked.

'Well, let's look at it from the point of view of the U-boat at sea and of Dönitz's headquarters. The U-boat has the regular U-boat wireless frequency assigned to it, a call sign for that boat, a Mark II Enigma machine and a Hydra manual.

'At the start of the day – technically at 00.01 – the person responsible for Enigma (let's call him the U-boat Enigma man) looks at his manual for that day. Now, he knows that any signals sent to him will be in the Hydra cipher, so all he needs to listen for is the call sign for his own boat.

'The manual tells him which three of the five rotors he is to use, and the order (left to right) they are to be fitted. It also gives him three numbers – say 425.

'These tell him what letter on the wheel is to be set against the zero setting on each disc. The three numbers correspond to the letters in the alphabet, thus 425 means DBE. So he twists each of the three engraved rims one after the other until D, B and E are set against the zeros on the discs to which they are attached.

'Plug and socket settings are also given, and he puts each one into the right socket, making a pair which links one letter with another. I'll explain them later.'

Jenson looked round at the three men, taking off his spectacles and polishing them with toilet paper. 'Any questions?'

They shook their heads, though Ned wanted to ask if the paper did a good job, and Jenson continued. 'Very well, the U-boat is on patrol, but Dönitz has just received a sighting report of a convoy from another U-boat and wants to assemble a pack, including our U-boat, so he drafts a suitable signal. This is passed to his Enigma man, who looks up the particular U-boat's own call sign, and puts that in the Enigma signal preamble along with a three-letter group indicating that the Hydra cipher is being used. He then decides (at random) on a rotor setting, say ARP, and taps it out. This lights up three more letters, say SWL.

'Now he puts down SWL as the last group in the preamble, none of which is enciphered. He then sets his rotors to ARP – which does not appear anywhere in the signal – and types out the message, with someone noting down each letter as it lights up on the light board. That – with the preamble including the U-boat's call sign – is the Enigma-enciphered signal given to the wireless operator.

'The operator now sends it off in Morse, and thousands of miles out in the Atlantic our U-boat picks it up. There is the usual preamble telling the U-boat that *B der U* has a signal for them. Then the last group of three letters in the unenciphered part is, of course, SWL.

'The Enigma operator now types out SWL with the Enigma on the day's setting of DBE and lights up the letters ARP. He resets his rotors to ARP, and since he now has the correct setting for the message, types out the enciphered signal and someone else copies down the letters – which are of course now the deciphered signal – as light after light comes on.

'You see that Dönitz's Enigma man choosing three letters at random – in this case ARP – allows him in fact to encipher the actual setting that he is going to use as SWL. But of course both sender and receiver must each have copies of the same manual, and each must set up his Enigma machine – the right three rotors and the correct rotor-disc settings – as the manual lays down.

'Each cipher has a different manual which gives the settings for one month. Thus an Atlantic U-boat with the up-to-date Hydra manual can read only Hydra traffic. He could copy down a Neptun signal intended for a major war vessel but because he didn't have the Neptun manual he could not set up his Enigma to decipher and thus read it.

'Remember, the Enigma is only the machine for mechanically enciphering and deciphering a signal. The manual is what gives the settings. It's like going round the world with a perfectly accurate watch. Unless you have something that tells you your longitude you still don't know the local time.

'And remember, gentlemen, the one vital thing about an Enigma machine: it also works in reverse. If you tap A on the keyboard and P comes up on the lampboard, when you tap P on the keyboard A will come up on the lampboard. And if you keep on tapping P on the keyboard you'll get a different letter each time on the lampboard because a rotor turns one position with each letter and changes the circuit.'

'Seems unnecessarily complex,' the Croupier grumbled.

'It isn't really. If one didn't have an Enigma machine to experiment with, it'd be almost unbreakable – *providing* the users choose letters at random. With each new message the sender must select a new setting and choose at random the three letters for enciphering that setting. If, for example, he uses his girlfriend's initials a few times, his enemy's cryptographers will eventually break the cipher.'

'Do some operators do that – repeat themselves, in effect?'

Jenson smiled and said evasively: 'That kind of thing is one of BP's most closely guarded secrets. All I've told you is how Enigma works. You don't know how we read Hydra; you don't know exactly why Triton could take us a year or more to break unless we get a Mark III machine *and* a manual.'

'Even an out-of-date one?' Jemmy asked.

'Everything helps. Bring us a Mark III and last month's edition of the manual and I'm sure we would invite you in for a cup of tea and a slice of sponge cake. You can use your imagination to see just how much we could learn from even an out-of-date manual since we read Hydra.'

Jenson looked round at the three of them, as if trying to assess their intelligence, and asked: 'Can you picture the circuit?'

'I think I can,' said the Croupier, pointing with his finger at the right-hand end of the rotor assembly. 'The current comes in here on one wire of the disc corresponding to a letter of the alphabet, say Y, crosses the rotor and comes out the other side – '

'Cross-wired, of course, so that it is changed.'

' – yes, so it then leaves as, say, B and enters one side of the next disc as J, goes across the rotor and comes out as R because of the cross-wiring. To the third rotor the same way, in perhaps as D and out as X and then out through the disc at the other end still as X.'

Jenson shook his head. 'You were more or less correct up to the last disc. It doesn't exactly come out there – that last disc really reverses it, turning it round again so the circuit goes *back* through the cross-wire discs and rotors, so that there is in effect a double zigzag in the circuit. Now let me round it off for you all.

'As you press a key the first disc and rotor turns, and they eventually rotate the second disc and rotor one position, which in sequence turns the third rotor one position. So if you multiply 26 by 26 by 26, you get the variations –17,576 in fact.

'There are also thirteen plugs in the circuit – I mentioned them earlier. They are here in front, with the cover over them, looking like a telephone switchboard in miniature but which I won't bother you with other than to say each represents a letter connected to another, adding to the scramble. For deciphering, remember that the machine has five rotors, and three are used at any one time. Remembering that the chosen three have to be turned so that a particular combination is showing, there are six possible ways the rotors can be installed. Let us say rotors 1, 2 and 3 are to be used, leaving 4 and 5 in the rack. You can put them in as 123, 132, 213, 231, 312 or 321, so in fact you have actually many possible rotor positions. You also have 17,576 different circuits through the rotors, multiplied by the rotor possibilities.'

Jemmy sighed, overwhelmed by the figures. 'But surely this is all beyond the average German wireless operator or Enigma machine juggler?'

Jenson raised an eyebrow. 'I doubt it, but anyway, don't forget the "switchboard" plugs. There are thirteen pairs – thirteen, half the total number of letters of the alphabet. Each pair of plugs allows one letter to be linked to another – A to P, for example. On a really important cipher, all thirteen pairs could be used, so that there are a few more permutations…'

Ned noted the slight emphasis on 'few'. 'How many?' he asked.

'Well, the thirteen plugs means you have to multiply 25 by 23 by 21 and so on, and the answer is about eight followed by a dozen noughts, but there are other ways of introducing more permutations, so the final answer is about two hundred followed by a dozen noughts.'

'I'm beginning to see why everyone this side is worried about Triton!' Ned exclaimed.

'Not so much just Triton,' Jenson corrected. 'We want to look at the cross-wiring on the fourth rotor they are going to put to work on the Mark III. A choice of eight rotors… I'll spare you the mathematics. Now, any questions?'

'Yes, 'fraid so,' said Jemmy. 'I don't see the need for the first three letters in the preamble after the unit's call sign, whether an Army, Air Force or Navy unit.'

'Ah, we assume that's so that no one German service (or even unit) can read a signal intended for someone else. Himmler's Gestapo wouldn't want Goering's Luftwaffe to read their signals. So each unit has its own monthly manual giving the rotor settings which change every midnight and the operator or Enigma clerk knows at once whether he has the manual for that particular group, or key. If he hasn't, I expect he goes off for a smoke or continues reading his magazine. If he has, then he consults the manual and sets up his rotors.'

'You seem to know a lot about the Triton business?' Ned commented cautiously.

'Yes, Triton and Mark III. In fact I'm probably to blame for the three of you getting your present orders. My report went to the Prime Minister, and my old friend Henry Watts was sent for, as I guessed would be the case.'

'I went with him,' Ned said. 'Now, with Hydra, you know more or less exactly what's going on in the Atlantic?'

'Yes. There are delays at times because of the random settings until we break the individual signals, but rarely longer than twenty-four hours.'

'So when the Germans bring in Mark III with its extra rotor, and new manual, and start using Triton…?'

Jenson took his glasses off and began polishing them again. 'It will be a disaster. You understand by now that Triton (or Hydra, or any other cipher for that matter) is a particular setting of the rotors and of the plugs. What we have to know about a new Enigma with four rotors is how the four rotors and four alternative rotors are each wired up to their discs, or cross-wired, rather. Four rotors can be arranged eight ways…'

'Yes,' Jemmy said, 'so eight way with four rotors, and four more to choose from is – ' he stopped, defeated by the mathematics.

'There are a lot of permutations of the cross-wiring,' Jenson agreed, replacing his spectacles. 'With three rotors it is more than two hundred followed by twelve noughts. Just think of a three-figure number and add a dozen or so noughts…'

'Without a Mark III Enigma, the eight rotors and manual, what are you going to do?' Ned asked out of curiosity.

Jenson's face suddenly went blank, like a hurt child refusing to cry out. 'I have a wife and three small children, and there are more than fifty million other people on this island quite apart from all those in Occupied Europe,' he said simply. 'To stay sane, I don't think about it. I can only wish you luck, gentlemen: whether all these millions live or die now depends on you.'

The Marine sergeant instructor held up a black object the size of a large orange. 'And this,' he said, 'is – '

'A black banger!' exclaimed Jemmy.

The sergeant was not intimidated by naval lieutenants, even if they wore medal ribbons and were – as in the case of this smart alec here – famous submarine commanders. Anyone fool enough to serve in submarines when it was hard enough to stay alive on the top of the water deserved what came to him.

And, struth, what a bloody twitch; wonder he didn't break his bloody neck. There he goes, nearly twitches himself off the bloody chair. Black bangers, indeed; all that farting around beneath the waves must have sent him round the twist. Come to think of it, all three of 'em are a bit off, like Aunt Alice's piano: all the bloody notes are flat, no matter what key you hit, white or black, though he was not quite sure what the black ones did.

Anyway, the sarn't major, for all his winks and nods and nose-tapping with his finger, had not given much away yesterday. 'Sergeant Gill,' he had said, 'we 'ave a special task assigned to us.' That comes of working with the Americans for a week or two; every job is a 'task' and they're always 'assigning' things. Anyway, the sarn't major had said three naval officers were coming for a week's special training in close quarters combat. 'You're to assume they have to fight themselves into or out of a large chicken house filled with Jerries, and that they've got to kill, wound or otherwise render useless said Jerries without riddling the chicken house with bullets, bits of Mills grenades or other debris.'

Bloody *debris*, that's what he said. But why should a couple of lieutenants and a to-and-a-half ringer be fooling round in a hen house with a crowd of Jerries? Well, it must be something special because the sarn't major swore him to secrecy.

'You could call it a "black banger", sir,' the sergeant said, with what he considered just the right emphasis on 'could' and 'sir' to put the bloody fool in his place. 'Certainly five seconds after the pin has been pulled out and the handle allowed to fly up to release the detonator, it will hexplode with a very loud bang. Sufficient,' he quoted parrot fashion, 'to hinduce complete deafness, stunned sensation and considerable disorientation to anyone within a radius of twelve feet and alarm and discomfort to fifteen.'

'What happens if a piece of that Bakelite actually hits someone?' the Croupier asked.

'Cut, bruises, abrasions,' the sergeant said airily. 'this grenade, however, is not intended to be lethal. It is purely a training weapon. It could also be used as a psychological one, too.'

Ned considered the sergeant's pronunciation of the 'p' in the word and decided it sounded more effective.

'Panic, gentlemen, that's what the grenade caters for. Panic in confined quarters. If you want to kill 'em, then you use the standard Mills 36 fragmentation grenades – '

'With which we are familiar,' Jemmy said. 'How far can you chuck a "black banger"?'

The sergeant was not used to dealing with pupils adopting a light-hearted manner. 'Both the Bakelite grenade and the Mills are delivered with a bowling movement, as with a cricket ball, gentlemen.'

'Unless there's not much room and a quick lob is all that you can manage,' Jemmy said, and realized he had fallen into a trap.

'Ah, sir,' the sergeant said triumphantly, 'there you have the problem with grenades. Hit his himportant,' he said, being generous with his aspirates to emphasize the point, 'to hinsure the hoptimum distance between the hexploding grenade and the hurler thereof.'

And that, the sergeant thought to himself, was put over word-perfect: page seventeen of the manual, paragraph four, the third and fourth lines, and with three smart alecs it was just as well to get it right. Not, he admitted, that he wanted to see a two-and-a-half ringer with two good gongs stunned stupid by his own grenade, and that twitchy bloke's name for it, 'black banger', was good; in fact, he decided, he would work it into his next course.

'So for close-range work you have the black Bakelite grenade designed to cause panic, and the Mills grenade which will cause death and destruction. Now we come to the Sten sub-machine gun.'

He picked up a Sten and held it up. 'Has any of you gentlemen ever used one? No? Well, I'll start with a bit of 'istory.

'The gun itself is made of bits of cast-off gas pipe delicately welded together by beautiful young ladies conscripted into the munitions factories. Made in Britain. But the hammunition his a different story. Nine millimetre.' His eyes opened wider and his eyebrows lifted as he said it, and his voice dropped. Thus, Ned thought, would the rector's wife refer to the village's fallen woman.

'Has you know,' the sergeant continued, 'this is not a standard British calibre. Jerries and Eyeties use nine millimetre. And it's thanks to the Eyeties we've got the Sten, which is a lovely gun. Drop it in thick mud, spray it with water, hold it with one hand hanging upside-down from a tree, and the Sten always works.

'You see, as the Eighth Army chased the Eyeties across the Western Desert (this was before that Jerry general, Rommel, arrived) we captured Eyeties by the scores of thousands and nine millimetre ammunition by the millions. All those millions of rounds and we didn't have a gun to fire even one of 'em, except some Eyetie pistols and things. So what did we do?' he asked.

'Welded up some gas pipe and made the Sten,' Jemmy said.

The sergeant stared at him in disbelief. This twitching bastard had just shot his story stone-dead. 'You've 'eard about it already, then?'

'No,' Jemmy said quite truthfully. 'I just deduced it. Sherlock Homes was my mother's father, you see.'

'Ah, a very smart man 'e was,' the sergeant said, somewhat mollified. 'I've read most of 'is cases. You must be very proud.'

Jemmy nodded shyly and admitted he was. With that, the sergeant produced three more Stens and settled down to explain the mechanism.

After an hour's break for lunch the sergeant took them out to the range and that evening they dined at the officers' mess, heads aching and eardrums numbed by chattering Stens and the heart-stopping crash of the 'black bangers'.

Ned was just leaving the mess for the hut that would be the quarters for himself, Jemmy and the Croupier for the week while they went through the Marine commando course, when a 'phone call arrived.

It was Captain Watts, who started by reminding him it was an open line and then asked: 'How is it going?'

'Noisy but instructive. Today they concentrated on our brains, with Stens and grenades. Tomorrow they start on our bodies.'

'Bodies?' Watts exclaimed. 'What on earth do you mean?'

'The Tarzan stuff, sir. Swinging across rivers on ropes, climbing trees, that sort of thing.'

'That reminds me,' Watts said. 'Clare wants to know how your hand is standing up to this.'

'All right so far – I'm wearing a glove. I'm not sure about this rope stuff – the skin is still very soft.'

'Listen, what the hell use is swinging across rivers on ropes going to be? You need to be able to lob the "black bangers" into tea cups at ten yards, and use a Sten with more accuracy than a garden hose. Why not concentrate on those for the next two days, and then come home to Uncle?'

Ned sighed with relief. 'Aye aye, sir. The Jollies are keen to help us, but because we can't tell 'em anything, they think we are going to storm Berchtesgaden and kidnap Hitler.'

'A couple of days be enough?'

'Plenty, sir. Both Jemmy and the Croupier are keen cricketers, and I seem to be lucky with the Sten.'

'Lucky? That's an odd word to use about a sub-machine gun!'

'Well, I've outshot the instructor five out of the six times we've been to the butts!'

'I bet he's as mad as hell,' Watts commented.

'Oh no, sir: he reckons it proves how well he instructed me.'

'See if he's ever been to Whale Island. He sounds like one of their gunnery instructors. I've never heard of a Whale Island GI get caught out or admit he's wrong! I'll tell Clare and your mother you're a bit deaf but okay.'

'I think Clare is on duty tonight.'

'In a way. I'm taking 'em both out to dinner.'

'I sometimes suspect your motives, sir.'

'I should hope so,' Watts said. 'Makes me feel quite young, to hear you say that! By the way, the chaps you and Jemmy listed are being rounded up. No problems, so far.'

CHAPTER SIX

As she opened the front door her stance made him hesitate a moment. Black shadows under her eyes – that was normal after a week of night duty. But she was leaning to the left, the right side of her body still partly hidden by the door, and she was curiously still and now the welcoming smile was falling apart as her lips trembled.

Ned slid inside the hall and as he turned to grasp her saw the right leg below the knee was swathed in bandages and before she had time to speak she was holding him, her body jerking gently with dry sobs.

'What happened?' he whispered.

'St Stephen's – hit by three bombs. The surgical ward – only three of us… The rest were killed… Twenty-seven.'

'When? You weren't on duty last night.'

'Three night ago, early in the evening.'

'But Captain Watts took you and mother – '

'No, that was just a story we made up in case you heard the hospital had been hit.'

'Your legs – what happened?'

'I was buried in the rubble for a while. A beam trapped me.'

Realizing that they were still standing at the open door, he led her into the sitting room then hurried back to bring in his bag, and shut the door.

She was lying back on the settee, white-faced but still trying to smile. 'Just a few cuts,' she said, gesturing at the bandages. 'They didn't even keep me in.'

'With half the hospital knocked down, that doesn't surprise me. 'Where's mother?'

'She's out shopping. She's been nursing me. Not the biter bit, but the nurse nursed.'

He held her hand and, realizing that he was being too heavy-footed when the situation needed a light touch, he said: 'I hope she's bullying you, as you used to bully me.'

'She is, and I'm beginning to feel sorry for the way I treated you.'

There was something about the way she was lying back on the settee, as though trying to hold her breath. Pain from the leg? Her brow was covered in tiny pearls of perspiration.

'You ought to be in bed.'

'No, no… I just caught my ribs as I leaned back on the cushion.'

'You can't "just catch" your ribs. Did you bruise them?'

She smiled ruefully. 'I broke two and there is some bruising, but not too much.'

'And I hugged you at the door.'

'It was worth it. Don't worry, darling, everything is strapped up. Remember, I'm a nurse!'

'And I love you. Bed, that's where you belong. I'm surprised mother let you stay up.'

'She didn't actually. I guessed what time you'd get here if your train wasn't late and got up!'

He leaned forward and helped her stand. 'Come on. I don't have to go to the Admiralty until tomorrow, so I can sit with you and tell you tales of daring on the Spanish Main by eighth great-grandfather Yorke.'

'I'd sooner we made love,' she said, but winced as she put her bandaged leg to the floor.

'So would I – there, put an arm round my shoulder. No, that won't do because of your ribs. Keep still, I'll carry you. No, it's catching your ribs, isn't it?'

'Darling,' she said, 'a lacerated leg and two broken ribs is nothing. I love you spoiling me, but I dressed myself and came down the stairs to meet you, so I can get back up again.'

'I'll undress you, though.'

'Yes, that would be therapeutic.'

'I wish…'

'We probably can if you're gentle and I'm careful,' she murmured as she reached the door.

An hour later, as they were lying side by side on the bed, she said suddenly: 'The man in your bed was killed.'

'You do pick the oddest times to pass on news. Post-coital tristesse?'

'Perhaps, though I never normally get it. I was really just thinking for the thousandth time that it might have been you. Do you remember that night when – ?'

'Yes, I was expecting a bomb to land on me and it was Nurse Exton in the darkness trying to protect me.'

'Were you thinking of me at that moment? You hardly knew me!'

'Yes I was: we had just been teasing you about your twisted stocking.'

'Yes,' she said dreamily, 'I *thought* you might have been thinking about me.'

'How did you know?'

'Darling, I felt certain physical manifestations as I tried to cover you up against the bombs.'

'Yes,' he said, 'I remember wondering if you had, but after the bombs went off you hurried around the ward tidying things up.'

'It was very flattering, darling.'

'And now a bomb *has* hit the ward.'

'It was awful,' she said. 'the ward was full of patients. I was sitting at the desk in the middle with the green-shaded lamp, writing up notes. The raid had been going on for a couple of hours but it seemed to be Highgate and Hampstead that were getting the worst of it. Then the gunfire started creeping nearer, but as that happens most nights I didn't pay any attention.'

'Then what happened?'

'Well, I was so busy writing – I had a dressing to change in fifteen minutes, a burn case – I didn't hear the plane: just five or six quick whistles, or hisses. I knew they'd be close because you'd explained that the long whistles are passing safely over you.

'I heard two explosions – they fell some yards short – and then; well, not an explosion, just an enormous thump right overhead. The lights went out, the walls caved in and the floor collapsed – I felt the desk slide away and my chair tilted over backwards. There was an awful sensation like falling down a dusty well. Oh, that dust; I could hardly breathe. Things kept hitting me – falling beams from the floors above, plaster, and so on. Then suddenly it stopped and I couldn't move. It was pitch dark, of course, and there was something crushing my right leg yet I could move my left. And there was a big beam or something across my chest and the end of it – I could see this when the rescue team came with torches – was pinned down by a big piece of stone from the walls.

'The shouting and groaning from the other trapped people was worst. One man had been in agony in the ward and was put under morphia. Then after the bomb its effects began to wear off but he didn't realize what had happened. He was only a few feet away from me but separated by bricks and plaster and beams. He coughed as much from the dust of the plaster.' She shivered.

'No,' she said in answer to his question. 'I didn't feel pain. Shock numbs that for quite a while. No, I thought of you and thanked God you had not been in the ward. I thought – you mustn't laugh, but you know how absurd one's thoughts are in such a situation – about my hair being full of plaster dust and I would not have time to get it washed and set before you came back. Then I realized the beam across my chest might have cut into me. I couldn't move an arm or hand to feel, but I was afraid my breasts were cut and if they were scarred you wouldn't love them so much – oh, I know it was absurd but I was all alone in the dark with (or so it seemed) most of St Stephen's Hospital on top of me. Then I could smell gas, which was escaping from some pipes, and I hoped someone would shut it off at the main before we were blown up or suffocated.'

'How long before you were rescued?'

'About twenty hours. I think I passed out from time to time. Then I remember seeing dawn coming, with the light creeping through the debris like seeping water. The Heavy Rescue people had to be very careful when they tunnelled, shoring up as they moved. The worst of it was that the few they rescued alive were already surgical cases and in splints or plaster, or something. Most of them had to be hoisted on to stretchers, or splinted up, before they could be moved. Those tunnels through the wreckage: often not much bigger than the height of a prone person.'

'Often – how many tunnels did you see?'

'The three surgical cases near me, and myself, were the last to be got out alive. I suppose about fifty yards. The tunnels twisted and turned – they cleared them and shored them up wherever they could find gaps. I thought they'd stopped searching, thinking everyone was either dead or rescued. The poor morphia man was just groaning now. Suddenly somewhere above I heard a man shout "Quiet!" I guessed it must be the rescue team listening. So I called to them. Shouted, actually, and they answered, and said they were on their way. They shouted from time to time, to locate me. The man had stopped groaning by now, and I'm afraid he was dead when they found him.'

'So you were out in time for breakfast, eh?'

'No, it was nearer tea time. They had to saw through the two beams; but it took time to shore up the big piece of stone: they were afraid it would slip and crush me once the beam was not holding it.'

'And then?'

'Well, they dragged me out and put me in an ambulance. Your mother had been waiting there for hours – from the time she first heard we'd been hit. The ambulance was full so she could not come with me, but apparently she 'phoned Captain Watts and both came to St George's – that's where I was taken – and Captain Watts talked them into releasing me as soon as I was strapped up and bandaged.'

'He telephoned me. Said he was taking you and Mother out to dinner.'

'Yes, we agreed on that story, in case you heard rumours, and he said you'd all finished your work and could come back.'

'Playing with "black bangers" and rattling off Sten guns, while you were lying trapped in all that rubble.'

' "Black Bangers"? What are they?'

He realized that he had said too much and when he did not answer her question she said as though to herself (he was reminded momentarily of Ophelia): 'Sten guns are like Tommy guns, for close range, they have nothing to do with the Navy hunting U-boats.' Her hand reached out to hold him. 'Oh darling, are you going away again?'

She knew enough about secret operations not to ask why: she simply asked if, and she deserved an honest answer.

'Yes, as soon as possible, but that'll be at least two weeks.'

'You'll be away long?'

'I doubt it. A month, perhaps.'

'Will it be dangerous?'

'Not as dangerous as night duty at St Stephen's.'

As the grey-painted bus pulled up alongside the flooded dry-dock, Ned saw the U-boat lying low in the water, a long sausage covered with a strangely flat casing running its full length, forming the deck. The whole vessel had leprous patches of rust, and a white ensign drooped from a staff at the after end of the conning tower.

Buses were the same as ships' boats – the senior officer present was the last on board and first out – and he swung down to the ground to find himself facing an angry Captain. A captain 'E', in fact; the coloured bands between the four gold bands indicated that he was an engineer.

'Yorke? What the hell have you got a busload of people for? I understood there would be two, perhaps three of you.'

So this was Commander (E) Percy Shoar, temporarily in charge of the prize U-boat.

'Good morning, sir,' Ned said carefully, walking a couple of paces towards him and leaving the doorway clear for the passengers in the bus to disembark. 'I think there must be a misunderstanding.'

'I should dam' well think so!'

Shoar was about five feet six inches tall; he was a couple of stone overweight, and from his complexion he combined a liking for gin with high blood pressure.

'Perhaps we could go to your office?'

'Get those beggars back in the bus first!'

Ned gave the order to Jemmy and as the door slammed shut turned to follow Shoar, who led the way to a small, single-storey brick building at the end of the dock. His office was almost entirely filled by a large drawing-board along one wall, and lead weights held down several drawings. Instead of sitting at the desk and offering Ned the other chair, Shoar stood with his hands pressed down on the drawing board and, half turning to Ned, said: 'What the devil is this, a travelling circus?'

'Captain Watts has spoken to you, hasn't he sir?'

'Yes.'

'And he explained?'

'He told me some of you fellows wanted to examine our prize and familiarize yourselves with the deck and accommodation, yes?'

'That's what we've come to do, sir.'

'But there are more than a couple of dozen of you and some of them are ratings. Damnation, man, this whole business is highly secret. Secret – and you bring an excursion busload. Why, do you expect us to be selling Licorice Allsorts and Sherbet Dabs?'

By now, Shoar was shouting, and Ned waited a few moments. 'The men I have brought with me are a special team intended for a very special operation, sir.'

'*What* operation?'

'I'm afraid I'm not free to discuss it, sir.'

'Then you can keep away from the bloody prize! Get yourself and your busload out of the dock. Out, Yorke, out!' he shouted, pointing to the door.

Had the man not been so ill-tempered, Ned realized he would probably have lost his own temper. As it was the more Shoar shouted, the calmer Ned felt. He glanced at the telephone. It had the special switch so that it could use a 'scrambler'.

'Would you call Captain Watts at the Admiralty, sir? ASIU? He will explain.'

'No, I dam' well won't! Spoke to him last week and agreed to you and a couple of chaps having a look. That's quite enough. Not going to have my own chaps' work interrupted by a bunch of sightseers. They're doing highly secret and *vital* work.'

'May *I* use the telphone, sir?'

'I suppose so. But I must stay here,' he said, and gesturing at the drawings on the drawing board he added: 'All these are highly secret.'

Ned had already recognized the subject and as he asked the operator for the Admiralty said: 'Drawings of the electric wiring of a German U-boat can hardly be very secret, sir, but anyway I have an A1 security rating.'

'A1? I don't believe you!'

A distant voice answered and Ned asked for Captain Watts, spoke to Joan and then heard the familiar voice.

'Hello Ned, arrived safely?'

'Can we scramble, sir?'

'Yes. Over we go.'

'Thank you, sir. Did you speak to a Commander Shoar up here?'

'Yes, he's the engineer in charge. You've a couple of days on board with technical chaps around to help you.'

'Did you say how many would be in my party?'

'Don't believe so, but you've all got the right passes so what the hell does it matter?'

'Commander Shoar has just ordered us all out of the dockyard.'

'No sir, he regards us simply as rustic sightseers.'

'Put him on!'

Ned turned to Shoar, whose face now wore a smug and self-righteous expression. 'You can listen to this,' he told Ned. 'I shall be telling Watts *exactly* what the situation is.'

He took the receiver and sat down squarely at his desk, straightening his tie and removing his hat to reveal a remarkable head of wavy grey hair.

'Shoar here… Yes… Yes… Yes, I did… Well, I can't have a busload of… The First Sea Lord – what, Sir Dudley Pound?… Well, this young fellow claimed he was A1… and the two lieutenants?… The ratings and Marines are all B1? Why, that's absurd! I'm only B3, so here you have ratings with… Well, look here, Watts, perhaps… Just a misunderstanding… Surely you can see how disturbing it is – I mean, a whole busload… What's this prying into the boat all about, anyway?… Damnation, it *is* my business!… What do you mean, explain to Sir Dudley?… Oh, all right; but only two days… Yes, my officers will cooperate…'

He put down the telephone as though it was made of particularly fragile Meissen china. Looking straight ahead he said in a flat voice: 'Captain Watts has asked me to apologize to you, which I do. But none of you sets foot on board that boat until I know what you are up to.'

Ned gestured at the telephone. 'I can assure you, sir, that not even Captain Watts is allowed to tell you. Nor the First Sea Lord. May I use the telephone, sir?'

'Oh well, if you and your men want to swarm over the boat like so many bees, get on with it. The less you delay us the better. Two days and I want you all out of here!'

CHAPTER SEVEN

Ned sat in the U-boat's tiny wardroom with Jemmy and a lieutenant (E) named Heath and was reminded of the stoker's cubby hole in the boiler room of St Stephen's Hospital. The wardroom was cleaner but overhead there were dozens of pipes of various diameters and a special metal ducting for electrical wiring. Varnished pine planking hid the welding and riveting of the inside of the hull and the lack of noise was eerie, making it difficult to realize that one was in a ship, albeit a submarine (which was anyway always called a 'boat'). No generators, no pumps, no voices passing orders over the Tannoy, ghosts with strong lungs.

'Go over the basic details you gave me, to put Commander Yorke in the picture,' Jemmy told Heath.

Heath was clearly very impressed by the German technical achievement represented by the prize, and while Ned noted more signs and dials in German, the lieutenant said: 'I understand you are not a submariner, sir, so I'll keep it non-technical. This boat has twin diesels which give her nineteen knots on the surface. Submerged and using her electric motor, her batteries give her nine knots for an hour, or she can stay down for three days chugging along at one or two knots. Normally, though, she'd surface every twenty-four hours and run on diesels to charge the batteries. The dynamos that charge the batteries are also the electric motors that drive her submerged, of course.'

Ned nodded and asked: 'What armament?'

'She carries fourteen torpedoes. Electric-driven, of course, not compressed air like ours, so they don't leave a trail of bubbles. Four tubes firing forward and one astern. For surface action she has an 8.8 cm – you probably know it as the 88 mm, which is a fantastic gun with a very flat trajectory and used against our tanks in the Western Desert. Can also be used against aircraft. This sub also has two 20 mm cannons in anti-aircraft mountings.'

'Bust and hip measurements?' Ned could not remember the figures Jemmy had given him several days ago.

Heath allowed himself a wintry smile. Obviously the dimensions of a submarine were not figures that he as an engineer could joke about, but he accepted that others did.

'At full war load – fuel, torpedoes, ammunition and so on – about 770 tons. She's seventy-five metres over all, and six metres diameter. She can safely dive to 100 metres – that's 328 feet. Say 300 feet... And the new boats they're planning will get to twice that, we understand. Takes a long time for one of our present drum type depth-charges to sink to 300 feet. Just imagine a depth-charge sinking 300 feet to a spot from which the U-boat is moving at nine knots...'

Jemmy twitched and jerked. 'You see, Ned why we don't sink too many.'

'I hope the Director of Underwater Weapons is working on more streamlined depth-charges,' Heath said. 'They ought to be self-propelled, like torpedoes, only going downwards.'

Jemmy snorted angrily. 'I put up an idea for homing torpedoes – an escort fires one in the general direction of a U-boat and a sound device like Asdic, or a magnetic device, takes over. You know what they told me?'

'That you were another genius ahead of your time by two centuries?'

'No, the bastards,' Jemmy exclaimed, twitching violently. 'They said they'd consider it, but reckoned that, if the Germans found one and adopted the idea, it would be a greater menace to us in their hands than vice versa. This despite the fact that Otto

Kretschmer is reckoned to have sunk 325,00 tons of our ships in a few months...'

Ned looked up at Heath. 'Were you on board when this boat was brought in?'

'Yes. I have fluent German.'

'Do you know how these things operate?'

'You're not going to take this boat, are you? We've still – '

'No, no!' Ned reassured him. 'We're here just to get an idea of the way a U-boat is built and – if you can help us – the way it's operated. We're not interested in your baby as such.'

'Mistress rather than baby,' Heath admitted. 'Well, sir, I expect you know the broad details. The Lion roars from – '

'The Lion?'

'That's what the Jerry submariners called Dönitz otherwise *B de U*, Commander, U-boats. His headquarters are at a small place just south of Lorient.'

'By the way,' Ned interrupted, 'how many officers in a boat?'

'The skipper, who could be a lieutenant commander, but because they are losing a few boats now, more likely a lieutenant. The first lieutenant is responsible for torpedoes and gunnery, the second lieutenant for wireless and their code machine, a sub-lieutenant who is the navigator, and an engineer lieutenant who would be the second in command and responsible for all manoeuvring.'

Ned asked: 'Which bases are most used?'

'Well, they're busy building bombproof shelters at Lorient, St Nazaire, Brest, La Pallice and Bordeaux. They use La Rochelle, though at the moment it isn't bomb proof. Of course, to get into La Pallice or La Rochelle, you pass between the Île de Ré and the Île d'Oleron.

'We haven't quite got the drift of the actual control over the boats. Strictly speaking, U-boats and surface vessels come under the Senior Officer, West, but Dönitz and the Kernével people handle U-boat operations. Still, whatever the system, it works!'

Ned phrased the next question carefully. 'How was the wireless traffic handled?'

'Each boat usually had two wireless operators. They listened while on the surface charging (usually at night) and that's when they'd pick up the Kernével traffic. They'd get any signals intended for them individually, but since they all use the same cipher, one boat could pick up another's traffic. They did, too, because it was important for a skipper to have a good idea of what else was going on round him – that Heinrich in U-100 had sunk three ships, Bruno in U-150 had seven and was going home with no torpedoes, Hauptman in U-200 was going home with depth-charge damage – you can guess. Battle gossip, I suppose you could call it.'

'You know what cipher they used?'

'It's all right, I'm B1, like your chaps: I checked before you came (there's no need to mention that to Commander Shoar, by the way) and we're all cleared for Enigma. You know all the U-boat traffic is Hydra. One of the wireless operators would take down the signal and report it to the second lieutenant. The Enigma machine was usually kept in the wireless room, because of course the lieutenants slept in these bunks we're sitting on. Well, the lieutenant would tap out the ciphered signal on the keyboard, noting down the deciphered message letter by letter – you know the drill, I'm sure – and probably the skipper would be breathing down his neck, reading it as the letters lit up.

'Come along, the wireless room is just here.' He led the way to a tiny cabin and pointed to a small table which was no more than a sheet of metal welded to a bulkhead. 'The Enigma sat there – you can see the holes for the holding bolts, just four of them. Here's the swivel chair – ' he spun it round. 'Here is the drawer with a special lock. A bit flimsy, the whole thing. The Hydra manual was kept there or in the captain's safe. This little shelf was probably made specially for a particular officer – it holds signal forms, pencils and a sharpener.'

'You're fairly sure the Enigma would be in this position in the boats in service?' Ned asked. 'With four nuts and bolts?'

Heath shrugged his shoulders. 'I can't guarantee it, but it's a fairly obvious place, in the wireless cabin, and looking at the construction drawings, I'd say they've evolved an effective accommodation plan that'd suit any new design. It's a damn good one, isn't it?' He looked at Jemmy who nodded. 'But don't forget the Enigma is portable, with its own battery. The second lieutenant could work it while sitting in the head with it balanced on his knees.'

'Yes' Jemmy admitted, 'except for the skipper being up there with his periscope, like the rear gunner in a bomber, it's well designed.'

'You had better take me on a conducted tour of the rest of this bucket,' Ned said.

He followed Heath, crouching as they went through the oval-shaped watertight hatches, the actual doors now clipped back but able in an emergency to be slammed shut and clamped tight, dividing the boat into watertight sections to isolate a flooded compartment.

Then he finally recognized why the inside of a German U-boat seemed so strange. He had been on board British submarines many times before – visiting friends, usually – and he could understand the comradeship that set submariners apart from the rest of the Royal Navy: a feeling of being different and living in a long and narrow cylinder compared with the comparatively spacious destroyer or cruiser. Cosiness – an odd word but yachtsmen would understand it. In a similar but wooden shell, the yachtsman (in peacetime) drives to windward in showers of spray and discomfort: a mug of tea put down for a moment leaps up and spills over; a plate left for a second slides off the table or hits the fiddles and bounces over; hot soup in basins pours into the laps of the unwary who do not anticipate the next lee lurch. Those yachtsmen in soaking wet clothes thrashing along for days rarely enjoyed it moment by moment; but arriving at some distant port, the satisfaction was in having achieved it, and there were the occasional splendid dawns and sunsets. And in the same perverse way the submariners enjoyed it. Perhaps both came nearer to understanding 'the wonders of the deep'.

But the differences on board *this* German boat from what he remembered of the British: well the obvious and first one would be common to both – no machinery running, lying afloat alongside with only a dozen or so men working on board during the day, she was cold and damp; hot diesels warmed the boat and drove out damp, and there was usually the almost indescribable smell from batteries being charged, damp smells of wet woollen clothing, diesel fuel, damp or wet leather gear, oil – oh, dozens of things. Even the damned dials and the electric switchboards gave off their own smell, and the galley would forever be boiling cabbage – and occasionally baking bread and treating the boat to a welcome change of odour.

But this German boat? There was a pervasive and strange, sweet yet hospital-operating-room-antiseptic smell everywhere. He commented to Jemmy who, twitching as he ducked through a doorway, said: '*Ersatz*. German for "substitute"'.

Heath overheard him and stopped. 'If anyone's been wondering what IG Farben and the other big German chemical firms have been doing, I can tell 'em.'

Ned said: 'Well tell me. I've heard plenty of gossip.'

'Well, our blockade cut them off from natural rubber, so they went ahead and made a chemical version which is as effective as natural. Buna rubber, I think they call it. Doesn't last so long – but if it lasts four years and the war is over in three...

'Oil and all its byproducts: well, their hydraulic fluids and the like are artificial. And why waste steel and aluminium in making boxes, lockers and so on, when you can use a sort of Bakelite... These are the odd things you can smell.'

He pointed to the thick gasket round the edge of the watertight door. 'Look at that and feel it. Shinier and more slippery than you expect rubber should be? The answer is that it's not rubber, it's *Ersatz*. Does the job. Where they can save weight or scarce raw materials, the Jerries have invented a substitute.'

'So our blockade may not be all that effective,' Jemmy commented.

'It doesn't seem to be slowing them building subs and planes, no, but having to invent substitutes must make problems.'

Ned commented on the number of different smells.

'Ah,' said Heath. 'I was on leave in Sussex last year and a German fighter crashed into a neighbour's field. Piled in from about ten thousand feet: just left a hole about the size made by a five hundred pound bomb and sprayed out hundreds of small bits of wreckage. I went over within a few minutes and the smell was extraordinary: not burned oil that you'd expect from the engine – that was buried a dozen feet in the ground. No, sickly sweet smells. I picked up a couple of feet of ribbed hose from the oxygen mask. *Ersatz* rubber. A small section of the instrument panel – made of some Bakelite material with an odd smell. A piece of flying jacket – *Ersatz* leather, again with a curious odour. And this collection of unusual odours was the first thing I noticed when I came on board this bucket. If I had not seen the way some of it is used and works, I'd say *Ersatz* is another word for fake, but now I know it isn't. After the war we may find shoes made of *Ersatz* leather last longer than real leather. The Jerry scientists are creating a new fake world over there, *Ersatzburg*.'

With that he walked through to the engine room. 'Presumably I'll be spending a while here with your engineer, but you'd better know what makes it all tick.'

Below gratings were the great banks of batteries, and right aft the single torpedo tube, what Heath called 'the sting in the tail'. Working their way forward again, they inspected the captain's tiny cabin, the length of a bunk and little more than its width, the control position with all the diving controls, past the tiers of bunks fitted in every available inch of space along each side of the gangway, like metal frame cots in a busy corridor which ran almost the length of the boat.

Finally, right forward, was the torpedo room: several torpedoes, glistening steel cigars, were still in their racks – Heath explained that four had been taken away to a research establishment, to be stripped of their secrets – and Ned stared at them. Electric torpedoes: the first the merchant ship know of an attack was usually the deep boom as the torpedo exploded after its invisible approach.

The Royal Navy – Britain in fact – was paying a high price for Asdic, Ned reflected. Their Lordships had apparently regarded submarines as obsolete: Asdic had made submarines, submariners, torpedoes and underwater warfare in general as outdated as an aquatic dodo. So submarine design had been neglected and torpedo design relegated to a pigeon-hole. And now the Germans were winning the war with the same weapons with which it had nearly won the First World War and on the same battleground: U-boats in the Atlantic. The Navy in peacetime had suffered under a succession of mediocre time-servers as First Lords at the political and First Sea Lords at the naval head of the Admiralty. With the other two service ministries they provided convenient jobs for the various Bugginses that the party had collected, and the official residences became social centres dominated by the various Mrs Bugginses, all vying for minor titles that would, theoretically, make each of them a lady. Buggins was 'just the man' for First Lord of the Admiralty, War Minister or Air Minister. Buggins, in his various guises, was worth a fleet, an army or an entire air force – to a potential enemy. Leslie Hore-Belisha was remembered for his orange-topped beacons, telling pedestrians where to cross the road. How much better if he had (as War Minister) given his name to a tank. He was an exception who had the energy, but the generals were against him and the politicians deaf.

When they walked back to the wardroom, Ned said to Jemmy: 'Time for you to get the lads to begin the games. Pass the word for the military police to close off the dock.'

Heath looked puzzled, and Ned said: 'What you are going to see now must never be discussed with anyone. It may seem childish games to you, but it's highly secret. If you are working on board, keep away from the hatch.'

'What on earth are you going to do?' asked an alarmed Heath. 'Nothing that will damage the boat, I hope?'

The Croupier bellowed with laughter as Jemmy began climbing the ladder. 'Not the boat, but you might get hit for a six if you get in the way!'

Ned followed Jemmy up the steep ladder, stepped out into the conning tower and then up again through the hatch on to the tiny bridge, and blinked in the daylight.

'You don't realize how dim it is down there,' he grumbled to Jemmy. 'Makes even a winter's day seem gaudy.'

'And the smell!' Jemmy said. 'That *Ersatz* stink gets into everything.' Jemmy waved at the sergeant in a Marine commando beret. 'Sarn't Keeler, get the men ready.'

Further along the dock, near the U-boat's bow, an engine-room artificer in Ned's party, Hooper, was slow-bowling a worn cricket ball to a leading seaman who was catching it with the ease of a born wicket-keeper, making a comment as he returned each ball. As Jemmy spoke to Keeler, Hooper put on his cap and as he tucked the ball in his pocket called: 'Ready for us too, sir?'

'Ready for everyone! Into the boat!'

Ned looked round carefully: the gaunt and grey brick boxes which hid the dry-dock were either warehouses or workshops, once lit by windows in the roof, but the glass had long since been shattered by bomb blast. The only men in sight of the boat – the only men who could see what was happening, in fact – were the group of seamen and Marines who had arrived in the grey bus, which had long since departed.

'Let's get started,' Ned said, and stood at the forward end of the conning tower. It was tiny, a semicircular affair the size of an apartment balcony, and crowded with the thick pedestals of the two periscopes and the azimuth compass. The after side opened on to a gun platform and Ned imagined a heavy following sea washing everyone out. But as a vantage point the visibility was perfect. No excuse for hitting the dock when coming alongside, yet deep enough to duck to avoid a rogue wave.

Yet it was all unreal: the grey whale – for that was how Ned saw the boat – bore no relationship to an enemy; no relationship to the elusive enemy he had hunted as it turned and weaved and dived under the sea beneath his ship. This rusting and inert object was a sister ship of the U-boat he had recently been responsible for sinking – but there was no link. Until a few minutes before this one was captured and taken prize, the German lieutenant commanding her had stood here on the grating shouting orders in German. An hour or so before that he had no doubt sent signals in the Hydra cipher and used the Enigma machine to encipher them. And they had been tapped out by a wireless operator so that the wireless waves went out to those aerials, with the enormous porcelain insulators and running forward to the bow, and then at something around the speed of light went to Kernével. Was there a powerful shore station at Lorient, or did Kernével have its own? He tried to remember what the countryside around Kernével looked like. Hilly, but not mountainous.

Jemmy was calling from the dock. 'Duck down, sir!' The 'sir' was a politeness because of the ratings and Marines. If he crouched along the port side of the conning tower he would be safe from anything that did not bounce. The hatch, the cover clipped back, looked like a well.

He was just going to lean over and tell Jemmy to carry on when he saw a red-capped military policeman taking a reluctant step backwards, as though remonstrating with someone, and it brought the soldier right into view. He had his left arm up, as though keeping someone at bay, and a moment later Ned saw the stocky figure of Commander Shoar dodge round the military policeman like someone learning a complicated Scottish sword dance, and bellow: 'Yorke! Yorke! Tell this blasted fellow it's all right! The 'phone, Yorke, the 'phone: it's urgent!'

'I'll meet you in your office, sir.' Ned beckoned to Jemmy. 'Take over up here and once I've got this joker out of sight carry on with the exercise.' With that he scrambled down the steps welded into the side of the conning tower, ran down the side of the casing and up on to the dock.

He found Commander Shoar sitting behind his desk, dignity restored but now replaced by outrage.

'Really, Yorke, that MP! Said he was acting under direct orders from – '

'He was, sir. The 'phone?' He gestured at the receiver, lying on the top of the desk.

'Yes. Admiralty. Now, about this insolent MP – '

Ned picked up the receiver and just stared at Shoar. It had no effect, so Ned spoke into the mouthpiece.

'Yorke here.'

'Watts. Are you on scramble?'

'No, sir, and I'm not alone.'

'Scramble and make yourself alone!'

'Aye aye, sir.' To Shoar he said: 'This is a confidential call, sir...'

Shoar did not move. 'Well, go ahead.'

'I have been ordered to take it alone, sir.'

'Good God!' Shoar exploded. 'First an MP threatens to shoot me, and now a wretched two and a half ringer wants to throw me out of my office while he talks to his girlfriend!'

Ned spoke into the telephone. 'Commander Shoar insists on listening in, sir.'

'Put him on,' Watts growled, 'and stand by to pick up the pieces!'

Ned held out the receiver. 'Captain Watts would like to speak to you, sir.'

Shoar stood up suddenly, grabbed his cap and made for the door. He slammed it shut, and Ned spoke into the 'phone to hear, before Watts recognized the voice, a cutting voice say: 'Shoar, you were a soft cock as a sub – you haven't changed!'

'He's gone, sir,' Ned said.

'Oh, pity. That'd be news to him. Very well, you're on scramble – that I can hear – and now you're alone now, right?'

'Yes, sir.'

'And you're concentrating?'

'Oh, furiously, sir.'

'Well, what I'm going to tell you will wipe that silly grin off your face.'

'I'm concentrating even more furiously, sir, with a stern expression on my face.'

'They start using Triton at one minute past midnight Greenwich tonight. At zero zero zero one.'

'Hmm, very thoughtless of them. We wanted another couple of weeks.'

'Finish what you're doing and then come down here.'

'Very well, sir,' Ned said, and thought a moment. 'Before you go, sir, there's a chap here we want in our happy band of pilgrims: a lieutenant (E) called Heath. Can you fix it?'

Watts laughed. 'I can hear Shoar's screams from here! Any more of his chaps you want?'

'No, just Heath. These U-boats are set up for the engineer to be the second-in-command, and although we're not playing that game we need an enginer office rather than just an ERA – even though our chap's very good.'

'Do you want to give Heath a hint?'

Ned thought for a moment. 'No, sir, I think not: I don't want to risk him refusing because he thinks his present job is more important, but I can't tell him yet why we want him!'

'What's his clearance, any idea?'

'B2, he said.'

'Easy. The rest of your chaps are B1 anyway, and upping him to A1 will be easy, for this job. Now listen, Ned: the intelligence people reckon they won't dry up entirely on Hydra for three or four weeks, until all the Ted boats on patrol at the moment are replaced. Meanwhile, the Great Blackout begins at midnight, Ned m'lad.'

CHAPTER EIGHT

The *City of Norwich* started going through the boom gate across the river Clyde just as, the Croupier complained, decent people were settling down for afternoon tea. At 17,000 tons, the *City of Norwich* was in peacetime one of the smaller twin-screw passenger liners engaged in taking passengers to and from the United Kingdom and India. She was a favourite among Army officers and their wives because, in the tedious part of the voyage up the Red Sea, her cabins were cool. Yet none of the other competing shipping lines had realized what really made the City Line ships so popular – that they went to a great deal of trouble to provide large daytime nurseries with trained staff to look after and amuse the passengers' bored and querulous children (spoiled in India by doting amahs).

This left the parents to enjoy the voyage, lying back in deckchairs reading or playing deck tennis, or being unfaithful to each other, as the mood or opportunity overtook them.

Now the *City of Norwich*'s hull and superstructure were painted a dull grey, along with her once-famous blue funnel, with the vertical white sword (symbolizing the city's civic dignity) on each side. Her topmasts (like all merchant ships) had been removed to lower her profile, and an ancient 4-inch gun now sat on the poop deck where once peacetime passengers gathered for the first whisky and soda of the evening.

A gun emplacement looking like a roofless chicken coop had been built on each wing of the bridge, overhanging the ship's side and fitted with twin Hotchkiss machine guns. The armour plating in front of the gunner reminded Ned of two sections of an altarpiece triptych. Up on the monkey island above the bridge a pair of 20 mm Oerlikon cannons nestled in a circular emplacement shaped like the small, wooden bull rings, miniature amphitheatres, so common in French towns near the Pyrenees. Various other Hotchkiss guns were mounted on the boat deck, where there was a clear field of fire.

Down in the cabins all the comfortable furniture of peacetime, mahogany tables, chintz-covered armchairs and settees, had been removed to avoid damage by the brutal and licentious soldiery and stored in a warehouse in Liverpool which had been burned to the ground during one of the first air raids. Now each cabin was crammed with bunks which were crude steel frames welded to the bulkheads and usually fitted in pairs one above the other, four to a cabin, giving it the egalitarian appearance of a prison cell.

Ned, Jemmy, the Croupier and the Lieutenant (E), Heath (who on joining the party, still slightly bewildered at the sudden transition, had immediately been nicknamed by Jemmy 'Yon blasted', abbreviated to 'Yon'), shared one cabin on the boat deck. Rectangular, with the door on one long side, two bunks one above the other on a short side and another two opposite the door, its furniture comprised a heavy mahogany table in the centre, bolted to the deck, a settee with rattling fans aimed at it from each end, four hanging lockers, a large chest of drawers with four drawers, and a gramophone with five records, four rusted needles and, presumably left by the previous inhabitants, a small piece of sandpaper to polish the points. In peacetime the cabin belonged to the wireless operators employed by the Marconi Company.

The cabin reeked of O-Cedar, the wood polish which was, Jemmy declared, the Merchant Navy's elixir. It was to the chief officers of merchant ships what Brasso was to the first lieutenants of warships, and reflected a curious difference between the two:

the Royal Navy worshipped polished brass and the Merchant Navy polished wood.

The *City of Norwich* had been launched from a Scottish builder's yard two years before the war: when the Labour Party and the Conservatives under Baldwin thought of 'rearming' in the same way as the Vatican regarded 'Satan', and in the Conservative Party the strongest voices (although a small minority) belonged to the Anglo-German Society. She was designed to make a 16-knot passage, which meant she could average sixteen knots in near gale conditions, although in peacetime she would not, because her captain had to consider the comfort of his passengers and account to the Line's marine superintendent for the cost of the extra fuel consumed. But the war bringing in the convoy system meant that the *City of Norwich* was a lucky ship.

Convoys were made up of between twenty and a hundred ships: the average was about forty. Sailing together in a box formation of several columns, with the escort round the outside, their speed was the speed of the slowest ship. This meant that most of the convoys bringing food and armaments to Britain, and carrying arms to distant war theatres, sailed at six knots, a mile an hour faster than a reasonably fit man walks down the road for his Sunday paper.

Thus a merchant ship carrying tanks and ammunition, cases of dried egg, fighters, or seven or eight thousand tons of food from the assembly port of Halifax, in Nova Scotia, to Liverpool or Glasgow, covered the two thousand five hundred miles across the Atlantic at a not very brisk walking pace; a speed which showed the advantages of the U-boats – nineteen knots on the surface, or nine knots submerged for an hour. It meant, in fact, that a U-boat on the surface could cross the Atlantic three times faster than its target.

There were several reasons why the 'slow' convoys were so slow (the 'fast' ones varied but ten to twelve knots was normal). In peacetime, shipowners wanted a ship of the lowest possible net tonnage, to keep down the cost of harbour and canal dues, and the highest possible gross tonnage, to carry as much cargo as possible. Neither tonnage bore any relation to a ton as a weight: net and gross tons were based on a ton comprising one hundred cubic feet. Into the largest practical cargo-carrying hull the shipowners put the smallest and most economical engine that would propel her at the lowest speed acceptable to the shipper and producing in peacetime the highest possible profit to the shareholders.

In wartime, of course, all such ships were, like militant prelates, complete disasters: prime examples of the compromise that kills. Crossing the Atlantic at walking pace meant that a U-boat could attack a convoy, use all her torpedoes, race back to Lorient on the surface (except for the last couple of hundred miles, when she would have to dive at daylight), refuel, rearm, and race back again to make another attack on the same convoy. Did they do that? Ned wondered. Dönitz did not seem very short of boats, although just as Nelson was always crying out for frigates, so too *B der U* no doubt always cried out for more U-boats.

Shipowners, excluding the respectable and well-known lines like Blue Funnel, Shaw Savill, New Zealand Shipping Company, Royal Mail and a few others, regarded the war as a good thing: they were carrying assured cargoes at high rates, which was the first consideration. But if their old ships, the depreciation long ago written down on the companies' books, were sunk by the enemy, the government replaced them with new ships and new crews drawn from the Pool of seamen organized by the Ministry of War Transport. And, Ned remembered bitterly, supplied them with those infamous life jackets and lifeboats.

Once the *City of Norwich* was out in the open Atlantic, her engines throbbing comfortably and the ship pitching slightly as she met swells which could be the distant outriders of yet another depression sweeping across the Atlantic to the north-east, a seaman knocked on the door of the cabin with a request for Ned to visit the *City of Norwich*'s captain.

Yorke was surprised to find that Captain Painter was a tall, thin-faced and ascetic man who looked as though he would be more at home in a pulpit than on the bridge of a ship. Then he remembered that Painter was the City Line's senior captain and that he had taken the *City of Norwich* through an out-of-season typhoon, reputedly breaking only half a dozen teacups.

'Commander Yorke,' he said after they had shaken hands, 'I do believe these orders, every spare inch of which is stamped "TOP SECRET", are the oddest I've yet received, and I'd be glad to go over them with you, so there's no chance of mistakes.'

Ned nodded as Painter went to his desk, sat down and unlocked a drawer, taking out several sheets of paper clipped together. He read through them, after putting on a pair of tortoiseshell glasses.

'We're not unused to picking up survivors from lifeboats – in fact we rarely make a crossing without sighting a boat, though now winter's here again I'm afraid we often arrive a few days too late: the poor beggars have died of exposure.'

Ned waited, nodding understandingly.

'It's bitter in an open boat out there in mid-Atlantic. We go up as close to the ice as we dare, you know.'

'Yes I know,' Ned said. 'I went over your routeing chart for this voyage.'

'But abandoning some twenty men in one of our own lifeboats – it's asking a lot. It goes against what I've been trained to do since I first went to sea.'

'Think of it as "delivering", not "abandoning",' Ned said. 'And I've no need to assure you that there's a very good reason for it.'

'I'm sure there is, and I'm certainly not questioning it, but I just want you to be sure you know what you're doing. In gale force winds, you'll need all you've got to survive in one of those dam' lifeboats. If it gets up to storm force...'

'We shall be very uncomfortable,' Ned agreed. 'But please don't worry.'

'But you don't realize what it's like in a lifeboat!' Painter exclaimed.

'Not a lifeboat, no; but in a lifejacket, yes.'

'Oh, then you've...'

'We are all picked men. Several of my chaps have things like DSCs.'

'It's impossible to tell since you're all wearing, ah – '

'Fake Merchant Navy uniforms,' Ned said, grinning. 'There's a reason why the officers have them, and anyway the seamen and Marines very sensibly prefer thick jerseys. When the time comes probably we'll all be wearing oilskins!'

Painter looked at him closely. 'I don't want to pry into whatever it is you are doing, but does it depend on people thinking you are a boatload of survivors?'

Ned thought for a moment or two and then nodded.

'Well,' said Painter, 'if we spotted you through glasses, I'll tell you straight, we'd alter course ninety degrees away and leave you to it!'

A puzzled Ned tried to think what would raise Painter's suspicions and finally shook his head. 'Tell me why!'

'Oilskins! Most survivors split into two types: the few chaps on watch or who had time to drag on some clothes – they'll be wearing uniform if officers, and anyway lifejackets. The rest will be in whatever they can scrounge – engineers, greasers and so on would have been down in the engine room in shorts, singlet and sweat rags round their necks. A few might be wearing those yellow survival suits, but they rarely do.'

'Why? Surely they help to keep spray and the wind out.'

'Yes, in theory anyway they should help, but the chaps can't be persuaded to carry those little packs around with them everywhere they go. So when the torpedo hits they're in one place and the packs in the other. Anyway, they're flimsy things, just what you'd expect from the Ministry of War Transport. Row a lifeboat in bad weather wearing one of those things and first you get soaked with perspiration because the material doesn't "breathe"; then it chafes across the shoulders and under the arms; then it splits; and one size fits all. They'd be all right if everyone wearing them crouched in the bottom of the boat without having to row... But it's not like that. Comes of having these Ministry chaps having war-winning ideas...'

Ned thought back to the convoy he had been sailing in only a few weeks earlier. 'Yes', he said, 'I know it's not going to be easy. But please don't worry about us. If we weren't sitting in a lifeboat we'd be doing something else equally uncomfortable.'

'Your hand,' Painter said. 'You need a glove for it. Hasn't had time to heal properly. Skin's too soft. What happened?'

'Destroyer in the Bay of Biscay...air attack. We zigged when we should have zagged.'

'The Bay's no place to be these days,' Painter commented. 'Still, I have my special charts and my zigzag diagrams, so I'm quite content: Halifax and back with another brigade or two of Canadians.'

He took a pipe from the rack on his desk and began stuffing it with Three Nuns Empire blend. As soon as he had puffed the pipe into life he said conversationally: 'Great things, those Admiralty routeing charts. The courses they give seem to keep us out of trouble. Do you know how they find out where the U-boats are concentrated?'

Ned shrugged his shoulders, and thought of all the signals being tapped out between the U-boats and *B der U* at Kernével in the new Triton cipher using the four-rotor Enigma. Signals that BP could not now read. In two or three weeks the effects of the Great Blackout would be felt. Routeing charts from there on would be merely inspired guesses, as much use as giving Red Riding Hood written instructions about how to avoid the Big Bad Wolf. There would be no more enciphered signals sending a ship like the *City of Norwich*, or even a convoy, on a sudden jink to avoid a concentration of U-boats. Captain Painter, like everyone else, would be playing blind man's buff. He could be steaming along in broad daylight, with the *City of Norwich* fitting accurately between the graticules of a U-boat periscope.

Fortunately, Captain Painter had no idea of the danger he and his ship (and his country, for that matter) were now in; nor did he, or could he, know how important it was for all of them that he abandon one of his lifeboats in mid-Atlantic with twenty-three men in it.

'I've no idea,' Ned said. 'There's a whole section in the Admiralty dealing with routeing ships: I expect it's them.'

'It's a great responsibility they have,' Painter said admiringly, relighting his pipe. 'After all, they could easily route a ship or whole convoy – ' he paused as there was a knock on his door. 'Excuse me a moment: time for blackout, and the lad's come to close the deadlights. Come in!' he called.

A steward came in and swiftly worked his way round the cabin, swinging the deadlights, solid metal covers hinging over the glass portholes, and screwing them down tight. They had originally been fitted as protection in case enormous seas broke the thick glass of the portholes; now they were used not to stop great seas coming in, but chinks of light getting out. The steward went into the other cabin to screw down the rest of the deadlights and Painter relit his pipe.

'A drink – whisky, gin or something?' he asked Ned, who replied that he had some paperwork to finish up, refusing the offer.

Once the steward had left the cabin, Painter said: 'Is there anything special I can provide for your chaps?'

At that moment Ned contemplated exactly what was meant by the fact that in a few days they would be living on lifeboat rations, and the success or failure of the whole operation might ultimately depend on how long they could last out physically. In the rush of planning, learning cipher data and commando tactics, getting to know the inside of a U-boat and how to lob black bangers and all this being cut short by Captain Watts' telephone call to say that Triton was now being used, the question of survival in an open boat had somehow been pushed to one side.

The more he thought about it, the more absurd the omission became. There were plenty of excuses – he or Jemmy or the Croupier would have worked on it had the training and planning part of the operation not been speeded up. But even when they were doing extra physical jerks and balancing exercises – running up and down the casing of the prize U-boat and scrambling up the welded steel ladder of the conning tower, everyone obsessed with stopwatch times and noting whether or not a Sten slung over the shoulder caught one of the rungs – they forgot to ask one question: are you sure you can survive, for a couple of weeks if necessary, in a lifeboat in the middle of the Atlantic in the depth of winter? Not just survive, but still function rapidly and efficiently at the end of it.

'Yes, perhaps,' Ned said 'First, your doctor – you do carry a doctor, don't you? – could provide a crash menu so that we can get as many proteins or carbohydrates, or whatever they are, tucked under our belts to help us through the long winter nights rowing that dam' boat. Perhaps he can also draw up a list of the special things – which I hope your Chief Steward can provide – which will help keep us in as good condition as possible? It's not a question of cheating and not wanting to live on just lifeboat rations, but – '

'I understand,' Painter interrupted. 'Whatever it is you're up to (and I know better than to enquire), obviously your health is the main concern. "Winter North Atlantic" is, as you know, one of the marks on Mr Samuel Plimsoll's load line, but it's not the time to go boating!'

'No, I'd prefer the one at the other end of the scale, "TF" – Tropical Fresh,' Ned admitted.

'The tropical sun can scorch you black: I found a boat full of bodies down close to Freetown and even though they'd cut up a sail for an awning, they were so dried up they reminded me of some biltong I saw in South Africa – sun-dried meat.'

'So we have the choice – sun-dried or refrigerated!' Ned laughed but, with the *City of Norwich*'s engines making the whole ship throb, and the chosen lifeboat hanging in the davits outside his cabin door, the diagonal gripes holding it in so that it did not swing sideways out and back with the ship's roll, the joke was hollow.

Not refrigerated, but more probably so sodden with bitterly cold sea, flung at them as spray hour after hour, day after day, that they might die of exposure; the body unable to stand more wet, cold, exhaustion. The sheer effort of rowing the lifeboat to keep its bow heading into the seas to avoid getting the boat sideways on, so that it broached by rolling down the side of a wave or was capsized by a crest, was the greatest danger they would face: greater than U-boats, starvation or exposure.

'Very well,' Painter said. 'You chaps go on a special diet. And doc will prepare some special lifeboat rations, in addition to the stuff already in the lockers. By the way, those galvanized food lockers under the thwarts – you know them?'

Ned shook his head. 'I've seen them, that's all. In the RN we have Carley Floats – balsa frames with nets across.'

'Well, these galvanized lockers are bolted on under the thwarts and you get at the food inside by unscrewing a circular plate on one side, about the size of a tea plate.

'I once found a lifeboat with ten survivors in it. They were only just surviving. They were starving – with both food lockers full, and the water breakers nearly empty.'

'What happened?'

'It was almost tragic. Instead of having the food locker lids unscrewed once a week, greased and put back on every trip, and the water breakers topped up – they're made of wood, of course, and in hot weather there's seepage – the chief officer on this ship had the lockers checked and the breakers topped whenever he thought of it, which was at the beginning of a trip: every three or four months, often longer.'

'He must have cursed himself,' Ned commented.

'He did. His carelessness killed him. When the ship was hit, twenty-nine got away in this one boat, including the chief officer. But they couldn't get at the food because the threads on the lids had rusted up. They broke all their knives trying to dent a locker and make a hole. Then they bashed with an oar, but the lockers were too tough. So after a week or so the weaker men began to die. As I said, only ten left when we sighted them, and one of them died after we got him on board. So watch the threads of those lids – anhydrous lanolin's what you need. I'll add a tin to the list.'

Dying of starvation while separated from concentrated food by a sheet of galvanized steel – Ned reflected on the thoughts of that chief officer: dying because of his own negligence, and knowing his shipmates were dying too. He was unlucky not to have died at once, in the blast of the torpedo.

Painter looked at his watch. 'Nearly dusk – we copy the Navy and go to action stations at dusk and dawn. We don't have many guns but there's no harm having everyone at action stations – more eyes watching for periscopes. They tell me the German torpedoes don't leave a track.'

'No, they're driven by electric motors, not compressed air,' Ned said, and there was an apologetic note in his voice.

Painter opened the door and all the lights went out automatically: Ned thought irrelevantly that the small metal hinge forming the on-off switch, and which was pushed back and forth as the door opened and closed, was like a kissing-gate. Lovers' gate, some called it.

Climbing the steps of the companionway up to the bridge with dusk closing in on the ship like a noose tightening and the sea cold and unfriendly and spattered with white horses, inviting more victims to drown in its grasp, it was almost impossible to imagine that hundreds of lovers' gates still punctuated hedgerows in Britain; lovers' gates now rarely used and sitting in a silence broken by the occasional hysterical squawking of a blackbird frightening itself, or the metallic warning of a jay, and perhaps occasionally the methodical tapping of a woodpecker.

'Evenin', Mr Harding,' Painter said as he came on to the port side of the bridge and greeting the Chief Officer. 'About ready, eh?'

Harding, a burly man of perhaps fifty, deliberate in his movements and slow of speech, who gave the impression of enormous reliability but no imagination, dug below the folds of his duffel coat and brought out what looked to Ned like an enormous hunter. He pressed the knob at the top of the winding stem and the solid front hinged down to reveal the watch face.

'Four minutes to go, sir,' he announced, and replaced his watch.

'We've none of your Navy loudspeaker system – what do you call it? Tannoy? – so we use the action station bells but starting with a "G" in Morse. The dash-dash-dot gets their attention and tells them it's not actually an air, surface or submarine attack, but the regular call to action stations.'

Painter pulled his cap more firmly on to his head as he walked to the forward side of the bridge. The *City of Norwich*'s speed of sixteen knots, straight into a westerly wind of fifteen or twenty knots, meant that looking over the fore side of the bridge was like standing up in an open sports car doing more than thirty miles an hour – at twilight, a month before Christmas.

'Glass is going down,' Harding commented. Yes, it was a Newcastle accent, Ned decided. Usually ships' engineers were Geordies; deck officers came from anywhere between the Orkneys and Westward Ho.

'Hmmm…the forecasters before we left said there was a low which'd go up over Iceland.'

'Must be passing south a bit.'

'Maybe,' Painter said, and turned to Ned. 'We'll probably run out of it by the time we reach your spot.'

Ned shrugged his shoulders and wished he was wearing his duffel coat. 'We'll see. As the poet said, you can break the glass, but it won't hold up the weather.'

'Aye, that's true,' Painter said, 'but what if it *is* blowing a gale when we reach your spot?'

'If you can heave-to and give us enough of a lee to launch the boat, we'll go.'

'But if we can't,' Painter persisted.

Ned grinned to soften his words. 'If this ship was torpedoed, you wouldn't have any choice.'

'Touch wood while you're saying something that that!' Painter exclaimed. 'But he's right, isn't he, Mr Harding.'

'Aye, he's right,' Harding said. 'Not that I trust those boats. Nothing approved and required by the Board of Trade – the Ministry of War Transport, rather, though a tatty leopard can't change its spots – is any good. Ha!' he snorted, 'd'you remember that last Ministry fellow we had on board?'

'Straight off the boards of a music hall, he was,' Painter told Ned. 'Anyway, he had to inspect the lifeboats. We got the covers off for him. He climbs into the first one – and he loses his bowler hat, which the wind blows over the side into the Queen's Dock, Liverpool. Bald as a badger, he was, so we find him a knitted balaclava. Then, getting out of that first boat, he rips the seat of his trousers – the seam split, so he's strutting round with a balaclava on his top and his bottom hanging out. Then he complained he couldn't find the bung, didn't he, Mr Harding?'

'Aye, he did that and I waited until he'd brushed himself down and someone found some safety pins for his split trousers, and then I led him back into the lifeboat and showed him the bung stowed just where the Ministry of War Transport regulations said.'

Painter returned to his original question. 'You'll embark in the boat more or less whatever the conditions, even if it's going to get worse?'

Ned considered carefully, because it was a good seamanlike question and (although Painter did not know it) really boiled down to how important it was that the lifeboat be launched at the exact latitude and longitude they had decided on back in the Citadel. That was after poring over the ASIU charts and looking at the Trade and Operations plots, seeing where the heaviest sinkings were and where the U-boats seemed to be most heavily concentrated. Or, rather, where they had been until the Blackout started.

Yet Ned remembered how they had grouped round the chart in ASIU, Captain Watts, Jemmy, the Croupier and himself. One of them had jabbed a finger down here, another favoured there… In the end they decided that there was a great square in the Atlantic, probably 800 miles from east to west, and 400 miles from north to south, which was agreed to be 'most favourable'. They picked on a latitude and longitude exactly in the middle.

The rest of the box stretched away to the west of them, so they had about 400 miles of westing in reserve: the *City of Norwich* could steam for a day and night after passing their chosen position before she passed the western end of the 'most favourable' area. If it was blowing a full gale at the chosen spot – they could wait twenty-four hours, particularly since the ship would probably have reduced speed considerably because of heavy seas heading her. In twenty-four hours the centre of the low should have moved nearly 700 miles or so, since ship and low would be approaching each other at a combined speed approaching thirty knots and the weather would be improving. Damn, it was cold standing out here on the open bridge, but Painter knew better than to discuss this sort of thing in the wheelhouse, where the quartermaster at the wheel, being human, would be listening.

'It's very hospitable of you not to want us to go, Captain! The position I've given you is the ideal one for our purpose, but if it is blowing too hard, we can move it four or five hundred miles westward. No more, though.'

'Ah, that should find a clearance in the weather. Or at least save you a couple of very uncomfortable days during which, whatever you're *supposed* to be doing, I'm dam' sure you *couldn't*!'

Harding nodded his head vigorously. 'In those kind of conditions, Commander, I can tell you that you're rowing for your lives like madmen just to keep the boat heading into the seas. Get beam-on and you broach. Only takes a few seconds, and then it's all over: you get washed out, the boat is gunwales under or upside-down, and away you drift in your useless Ministry of War Transport lifejackets, and you die of exposure or you drown because you don't have the strength to keep your head up out of the water.'

'The Mate should know,' Painter said. 'He was in one of our sister ships, the *City of Winchester*, when she was hit by two torpedoes last year.'

'Any tips?' Ned asked Harding.

'Watch the men rowing. A good man will keep rowing until he collapses exhausted – and then he lets go of the oar. Double-bank if necessary. The inboard man can be resting as he sits on the thwart, and all he has to do is keep a couple of hands on the loom of the oar, so when the outboard chap passes out, the oar isn't lost.

'Keep the chaps cheerful, obviously. If there's a lot of spray there's no point in bailing out the boat all the time: every quarter or half an hour. Better to sit with the water swilling around your feet a bit than have half a dozen men sloshing away with bailers like kids on the beach. If anyone is wearing boots – rubber Wellingtons, half-boots, mess boots, call 'em what you will – watch the feet: they swell and then it's damn difficult cutting boots free without drawing blood. Jacket sleeves wet at the cuffs: they chafe the skin and start salt water boils. Roll-neck wool jerseys do the same round the neck, so cut 'em into a V. That's about all. Watch for the moaner!'

'The moaner?'

'Yes, there's usually at least one man in a crowd – rabble-rouser, union shop steward, Bolshie, sea lawyer, Trotskyite, radical person, call him what you will – that starts making trouble. Argues about the water ration, length of the spells at the oars, any wretched thing he can turn into a grievance. Jump on him quick – not *too* quick though, because sometimes the other men shut him up, and save you the trouble.'

Ned thanked the Mate. There was good advice in what he had just said, information learned at first hand. Obviously just surviving in bad weather was a full-time occupation for survivors, he thought grimly, without the added task they had been given! And at least he did not think any of his picked men would turn out to be moaners.

Harding looked at his watch again, glanced round the horizon and walked to the forward side of the bridge, jabbing the heavy metal button that sounded action stations throughout the ship, shrill bells which, Ned knew only too well, scared the wits out of you even before the enemy put in an appearance.

Dash-dash-dot: the Morse letter 'G', indicating that what followed was routine, not emergency. Action stations, and the bells sounded through the ship, fast and urgent. Almost at once doors slammed, the switches automatically shutting off the lights before they swung open, and he could imagine cursing men pulling on duffel coats and grabbing lifejackets and steel helmets before running to their action stations.

Several were coming up the ladder to the bridge, dodging round Painter and Harding to get to the square box at the end of the bridge, overhanging the sea and containing the two Hotchkiss machine guns. With an ease obviously coming from long practice, they unlaced the canvas cover and pulled it off the guns. While one folded it and put it in a corner out of the way, another man pulled a heavy leather belt round himself, grasped the pistol grips of the two machine guns, and leaned back against the belt. At the same time the first man checked the belts of ammunition.

Both said something to the third man: Yorke guessed it meant that they were ready.

Hotchkiss…there must have been a great store of them somewhere, relics of the First World War, because most British merchant ships seemed to be armed with them. They were reliable guns and, like most (except the ubiquitous Lewis, which was without peer), worked well apart from one nasty trick. The Hotchkiss' trick was that the lever putting the action on Safe or Repeat (when the gun fired a single shot each time the trigger was squeezed), or Automatic, was at the end of the breech. The sequence was anticlockwise as you faced it, Safe, Automatic and then Repeat, which meant that in a rush, or in the dark, it was easy when slapping the lever across from Safe to Automatic to go one click too far so it stopped at Repeat. This meant in turn that as the gunner (nestling against the leather belt, a hand on each of the butts, an index finger round each trigger and tracking the target) squeezed the triggers, instead of a stream of fire, each gun fired one round; a defiant 'bang-bang' of Repeat instead of the tearing calico, racing belts and metallic clicking of ejected cartridges of the guns firing on Automatic. The gunner's curse as he wrenched the two levers back to Automatic usually indicated that he could no longer track the target, which was most likely to be a diving bomber. Ned reflected that strangers listening to merchant ship gunners might well wonder why they had never previously heard of an arms manufacturer called 'Soddinotchkiss', the name by which the guns came to be called. This became almost as much part of the nautical vocabulary as 'tramsmash', the usual description of tomato ketchup when asking someone farther along the table to pass it, or 'slide', the more usual word for butter or margarine.

Ned looked round the horizon. Astern it was already nearly dark; ahead, to the westward, the sky was still light. He then looked at his watch, comparing the time with sunset.

Captain Painter seemed to read his thoughts. 'We're a touch late, eh, Commander?'

'Ten or fifteen minutes later than we're accustomed to do it in the RN,' Ned said tactfully, 'particularly since you haven't zigzagged for twenty minutes or so.'

'That's a good point. Mr Harding, make a note that we go to action stations a quarter of an hour earlier, and are we following the zigzag diagram from the book?'

'Yes, sir: number seven. It's one with short legs to the south-west and longer legs to the north-west, so we increase our northing and westing.'

'Ah yes, of course.'

'But I agree with the Commander,' Harding said. 'I'm glad we'll be going to action stations earlier: I've often felt we left it a bit late.'

'But you didn't mention it because you were too shy,' Painter said sarcastically, although with no malice in his voice.

'See a grey goose at a mile,' Ned said suddenly, and was as startled as if someone else had spoken.

'What's that?' Painter asked.

An embarrassed Ned searched his memory. 'I read somewhere that in Nelson's day – perhaps even earlier – the lookouts at dawn were sent aloft, and brought down on deck again at night, when they reckoned they could see a grey goose at a mile.'

'Good enough yardstick,' Harding commented.

'Old naval family, yours?' Painter enquired, obviously interested.

'Seafaring, if not always Royal Navy.'

'Some pirates back there hanging from the family tree, eh?'

Ned laughed at the allusion, which was almost correct. 'A buccaneer or two in Jamaica before Henry Morgan's day.'

'Buccaneer, pirate – what's the difference?'

'Quite a lot, particularly if your eighth great-grandfather was a buccaneer,' Ned said lightly. 'I'd happily own up to a pirate, if we'd had one in the family, but the best we can do is a buccaneer – with the same name and nickname as myself.'

'What's that, then?'

'He was Edward Yorke but, like me, usually known as "Ned".'

'Ned Yorke…Ned York…' Painter repeated. 'Wait a minute, I've read about him.'

Harding chuckled happily. 'Raided Portobello, didn't he? Captured so many Spanish pieces of eight that when he got back to Jamaica, they made them the official currency. And he's an ancestor of yours, by gum!'

'With respect, Commander,' Painter said, 'what's the real difference – what *was* the real difference,' he corrected himself, 'between a buccaneer and a pirate?'

'In spirit I doubt if there was much,' Ned explained, 'but legally a great deal. Think of the buccaneer of my eighth great-grandfather's day as being the equivalent of the privateer of Nelson's day.'

'Oh, I get it: he had a sort of licence to capture enemy ships!' Painter exclaimed.

'Exactly. My forebear (and the rest of the buccaneers whom at one time he led) had a commission signed by the Governor of Jamaica allowing him to make war against the Spaniards, using his own ship.

'If he lost or damaged his ship, that was his affair. But if he took prizes, whether sacks of gold from some town on the Spanish Main or Spanish ships, he had to bring it back to Jamaica and in effect declare it, paying the King and his brother (Charles II and James) their share.'

'A private navy, in fact,' Painter said. 'I'm beginning to remember now. Weren't those buccaneers given a special name?'

'They called themselves "The Brethren of the Coast".'

'And their leader – he was called something special, too.'

'Yes. My eighth great-grandfather was given the title of "Admiral of the Brethren".'

'Good for him,' exclaimed Harding, obviously reaching back into boyhood memories of books he had read; florid Victorian histories condemning piracy competing with overblown Edwardian novels describing the buccaneers as heroes and the

Spanish as villains. Few books that he had ever read gave any hint of the story told in ancestor Ned's letters, written in the 1670s. Buccaneers, pirates... Standing on the bridge of the *City of Norwich* as she zigzagged her way towards Halifax, Nova Scotia, a lone and almost insignificant protagonist in the Battle of the Atlantic, he found that the Ned Yorke of three centuries earlier had suddenly become closer.

The *City of Norwich*, a tiny moving island of steel carrying a few men who were caught up in a great war now affecting most of the world, thanks to the Japs bringing in the Americans and Hitler's megalomania involving the Russians – yes, some of the phrases in the Restoration Ned's letters took on, well, not a new meaning but somehow a real life: Ned seemed to be looking over his forebear's shoulders as the quill pen scratched.

'We are so few,' he had written, 'about a thousand undisciplined men hailing from half a dozen countries, to dispute the might of Spain. We have the tiny island of Jamaica while Spain holds the Main, thousands of miles of coast from Trinidad in the east round to the Strait of Florida, and the great islands of Cuba and Hispaniola and Puerto Rico. Yet even as a tiny horse-fly can make a great plough horse bolt with pain, so can we sally out from Jamaica in our little ships (as sorry a collection as you could assemble for a debtor's sale at the Nore on a windy day in midwinter, vessels on which no mortgagor would bother to foreclose nor any insurer write cover: a score of men to each and perhaps a couple of small guns) and keep the Spaniards away. If only the King would send up a ship or two: we are defending his possessions with our own ships, lives and pennies, and yet he does not abate by one penny his and his brother's share in the prize money.

'Picture us, if you will.' (This phrase was always very clear in Ned's memory: a quiet voice echoing through centuries like a whisper in a cathedral.) 'Jamaica is situated about like Guernsey, in the Channel Islands, and all the land around (be it France or Britain, Spain to the south or the Netherlands and Denmark and

Sweden to the north) belongs to Spain, who is determined to possess this tiny speck in the ocean.

'Yet we who defend this speck are given no assistance from England. We have had to capture our cannon and our ships, our powder and our shot, and more recently the very gold coins we now use as currency with which to trade, to buy food and clothing, the very necessities of life. Yet we are called pirates by some, even though we do possess the only thing the King grants us for our defence – our commissions. With these flimsy parchments (for which we have to pay, of course) we defend his island and capture prizes which yield a goodly share for the King's purse.

'Yet all the time we wonder if the King has a secret agreement with Spain to hand back the island after a decent interval as his reward to the King of Spain for allowing him to live there in exile while Cromwell ruled Britain.'

Well, little has changed in three centuries, Ned thought: Britain had been completely unprepared for Hitler's attack, and judging from the dockers' recent strike and the Civil Service union's attitude over Wrens, the unions had taken over the role held in Restoration days by absentee landlords enjoying themselves at Court while others kept the country secure. What would the dockers have thought as they stopped unloading the merchant ships, which had reached British ports only because the convoys had been fought across the western ocean, if the anti-aircraft gunners defending the ports in which their homes were situated had gone on strike for more sugar in their tea, and the German bombers had flown in unopposed?

'Hope you still have some of the old boy's money left,' Painter said enviously. 'Should keep you in the best Havana cigars!'

'Very little. Gets a bit watered down in seven or eight generations, you know, and my direct line lost a fair sum of money as shipowners.'

'Yes, I can see that, and I suppose it needs only one eldest son to blow his inheritance at the backgammon table!'

'Yes, but luckily most of it was – and still is – heavily entailed: old Ned (then a young lad of course) saw the family lose everything to the Roundheads, although they got some of it back at the Restoration, and made sure his buccaneering and later landowning wealth was well tied up.'

'Inherited wealth,' Painter said vaguely, 'I've often wondered about it.'

'Have you any children?' Ned asked casually.

'Son and daughter, both at school.'

'Do you believe in saving money?'

'Of course! Don't want to leave my wife without a penny when I go, and I want the boy to have a decent education, with something left over to set him up in a little business when this bloody war is over.'

'That's inherited wealth,' Yorke said gently. 'What's the difference between your son inheriting it from you, and me inheriting it from my father? Who do most men struggle and save if not to give their children a better chance than they had themselves? That my eighth great-grandfather took enormous risks which let him provide for his descendants is really the same as you commanding this ship and dodging U-boats while your pay accumulates in your bank for the benefit of your family.'

'So, I'm a buccaneer, eh?' Painter asked humorously.

'No different from the Commander's ancestor,' Harding said unexpectedly, 'except you're paid regularly in English quids and he got his irregularly in pieces of eight!'

Painter looked round the horizon: night had fallen except for a lighter patch ahead, to the west.

'Different scale, surely, Commander?'

'Yes, up to now. I shan't have much to leave any children I might have (I'm a bachelor at the moment), but say you leave £5,000 to your son, who becomes a clever businessman and dies of old age leaving £500,000 to *his* son, who is a clever financier and leaves a couple of million…'

'Some hopes, with taxation the way it is!' Painter said.

'My buccaneer forebear complained bitterly that the King took ten per cent and the Lord High Admiral, the King's brother, fifteen of the gross, not net. So buccaneers were paying twenty-five per cent income tax in the 1660s, and no doubt they took the same view as you!'

Painter laughed heartily. 'Yes, I see what you mean. "Inherited wealth" is someone else doing it, but when you do it yourself it's looking after the wife and kids!'

Ned held up his hand. 'I didn't bring my glove, and this is beginning to feel a little frail.'

Painter shivered. 'That's a polite way of saying it's bloody cold! Very well, Mr Harding, stand 'em down.'

CHAPTER NINE

The depression was small and quickly slid up to the north-east to bring more gloom on Iceland, thickening the snowfalls and sending bitterly cold winds scouring the bare and striated hills forming anchorages like Seidisfjord, where merchant ships and escorts were assembling.

The convoys to Murmansk were sailing again now that the nights were long, with fourteen hours and more of darkness, increasing through the winter until at the latitude of northern Norway half an hour's twilight was the day's ration.

The *City of Norwich* steamed westwards – seemingly in increments, Ned thought, when she turned a couple of points to port as the buzzer attached to the special clock in the wheelhouse signalled the next leg of this particular zigzag. The wind waves superimposed on the broad swell gave the ship an awkward roll, and glancing astern at the wake he saw that the quartermaster was still settling down to the different conditions as he tried to keep the ship on the new course.

How the *City of Norwich*'s quartermaster must hate that zigzag clock and buzzer! It was usually the second officer's job, as the man responsible for navigation, to set the clock, which was like an ordinary ship's clock but had a rim round the outside of the face along which small sliding metal contacts could be adjusted. Using details for a particular zigzag diagram listed in the manual, the contacts were set at various times, so that a buzzer sounded when the minute hand touched them. At each buzz the ship zigged or zagged on to a new course, the theory being that a lurking U-boat sighting the ship would be manoeuvring into a firing position just as the ship turned away on the next leg of its zigzag, steaming out of range. Ned, like a number of naval officers, had grave doubts about zigzagging. By all means change course every few hours – especially at dawn and dusk – so that a U-boat sighting a ship could not make an accurate estimate of her future position and alert other U-boats farther ahead – but these shorter zigzags were just as likely to bring a ship into range of a U-boat as avoid it. With the U-boat able to move underwater only at nine knots, a 16-knot merchant ship steering a straight course was likely to pass out of range of a random U-boat faster than another which was zigzagging. Perhaps the mathematics showed zigzagging gave a slight advantage, but Ned reckoned the longer distance steamed over the zigzag course gave the ship many more chances of getting within the range of torpedoes than a straight course. Jemmy, with all the experience of having very successfully commanded a submarine, could not make up his mind for sure but tended to agree with Ned. He reckoned he had lost many chances of sinking enemy ships because they were passing too far off, and he had also sunk ships that started off too far away and then zigzagged into range. But he had also had a promising target zigzag out of range minutes before he was going to fire.

'Our torpedoes are too slow,' Jemmy had said. 'The dam' things go only a knot or two faster than a Tribal class destroyer with the wick turned up... Let's fit destroyers with explosive bowsprits and go back to battering rams!'

Both Jemmy and the Croupier were sitting back in their bunks, legs hanging over the bunkboard, as they reported the day's activities. Yon, the engineer, sat along the settee from Ned, working on a drawing and occasionally getting up to sharpen some crayons into the wastepaper basket.

'The men,' the Croupier reported, 'are living like fighting cocks. Enormous breakfasts, steak for lunch and steak for dinner:

seems the doctor once advised in preparing a Welsh boxer for a title fight. Two hours' PT in the morning, and two hours' scrambling round the ship, up and down vertical ladders. And the cricket balls are a success.'

Ned nodded, having thought of them before they left England. He had been watching the men sitting in the lifeboat and trying to lob the balls into a bucket perched on top of the radio operator's cabin just above the inboard of the boat. It was somehow typical of the British Civil Service, fighting the war behind the armour plate of reserved occupations, that they could not supply a couple of dozen cricket balls for the present enterprise. Ned had finally hired a cab, driven round central London finding sports shops which had some left in stock, and paid for them with his own money. The Triton cipher might well be broken by a couple of dozen cricket balls, paid for by Lt Cdr Edward Yorke, because (as the bureaucrats delighted in telling him) cricket balls could not be supplied "for the public service".'

'Yes,' the Croupier continued, 'one in a dozen lands in the bucket.'

'No coconut!' Jemmy said. 'They have to get at least half in the bucket to win a coconut.'

'Done!' the Croupier exclaimed. 'A couple of 'em, that hefty Marine corporal, Davis, and the skinny hooky, leading seaman Jarvis, can get nine out of a dozen in the bucket. I was giving you the figures allowing one man one throw. But if a man can throw a couple of dozen obviously he gets his eye in.'

'Whoa, there!' Ned said. 'We'll award the coconuts on the basis of one man, one throw. That's what it'll be on the day of the village fête. No one will be able to shy even half a dozen balls, let alone a couple of dozen.'

'So how does it work out with each man throwing one?' Jemmy asked.

'Well, only one or two actually land in the bucket, but I've had 'em paint a circle a yard in diameter with the bucket in the middle, and all the throws land inside the circle,' the Croupier replied.

'When thrown from a stationary lifeboat,' Jemmy pointed out.

'We can't avoid that,' the Croupier protested. 'Anyway, the ship and lifeboat are rolling or pitching. We can only train the horses and enter them in the race. We can't guarantee the bloody winner. Not every penny gets a coconut, mate. That's why bookies drive Rolls Royces and punter pedal bicycles.'

'So the bowling is good. What about the batting?' Ned asked. 'None of 'em have heard a shot fired for a fortnight.'

'Ah, well, that's been the subject of some delicate negotiation between the Chief Officer and me,' Jemmy said.

'*Negotiation?*' Ned repeated, as though unable to believe his ears. 'It's war that's broken out, not peace!'

'Don't get alarmed,' Jemmy said, 'I was trying to get a laugh, guv. Any time we want, we can roll an oil drum off the fo'c'sle and blaze away with the Stens as we hurtle past it, but Harding has never fired a sub-machine gun and he fancies himself at the butts shooting grouse.'

'Blasting away at the fairground at sixpence a time, using a .22 with a wonky sight,' growled the Croupier. 'That's more his mark!'

'Agreed, agreed,' said Jemmy, 'but since the Chief Officer's our only source of big oil drums, we need him on our side. Remember, one drum is one blast from the Stens, and if we're doing sixteen knots we pass it in, let me see, three and three-quarter seconds. So it'll be in effective range of those shuddering gas pipes for between a minute and a minute and a half.'

'I don't want everyone firing from the poop, though,' Ned said firmly. 'We'll never keep track of who's doing what, and in the excitement someone will empty a magazine into his next door neighbour's navel! So spread them out – between the two hatches forward, wing of the bridge, along the boat deck, and so on.'

Jemmy asked: 'What if the fellows forward sink the drum before it reaches the bridge?'

'Give them a box of chocolates and bring me my smelling salts,' Ned said. 'Don't forget the Sten is a short-range weapon. You're more likely to sink the drum with Captain Painter's 4-inch on the poop.'

'Oh yes, why don't we suggest to Painter that he gives his chaps some practice with the 4-inch?' the Croupier exclaimed.

Ned eyed him coldly. 'Are you mad? Do you want to be on the poop squirting away with a Sten while those DEMS gunners are right behind you with a loaded 4-inch? You'd get blown over the side with the muzzle blast!'

'True, true,' the Croupier agreed. 'It could also scorch my lovely locks.'

'Not only that,' Ned said, 'It can destroy the balance chambers in your ears. A friend of mine has just had the left one destroyed, so he progresses in circles to the right, walking into the arms of fat old ladies. He created a sensation as he ambled down Oxford Street. Or at least, he did until he called in at Swaine, Adeney and Brigg and bought himself a decent walking stick. Now he uses it to make his own straight line.'

'A right-winger, eh? Ought to go in for politics.'

'It's not so funny having balance problems. In fact this chap gets dizzy and he uses a shooting stick, not an ordinary walking stick. When he feels dizzy he opens up the stick and sits on it, just as though he's at the butts waiting to pot a passing pheasant.'

'Must alarm people, seeing a chap sitting on a shooting stick in Oxford Street.'

'No doubt. Doesn't bother him though – they'd be even more alarmed if he fell flat on his face in front of them.'

'Very well, Ned, point taken, beware of muzzle blast. Now, with a couple of men at each position, and perhaps ten spaced out along the boat deck, shooting clear of the boats, we should have sixteen blazing away. If I can squeeze in another seven it means we all get a shot or two at the barrel.'

'Yes, do what you can. The three of us had better be on the poop.'

'To watch the drum sink!' the Croupier said cheerfully.

'To watch it float past entirely unharmed,' Ned said.

'Oh, come *on*, Ned don't be so gloomy.'

'You should have seen us in the *Aztec* when the Teds dive-bombed us in the Bay. We fired thousands of rounds of 20 mm Oerlikon and .303 Vickers at 'em, but they trumped us.'

'You should have had your chum at the wheel – the one who keeps turning to the right!' Jemmy said.

'We were doing high-speed turns all the time: as far as those Ted bombers were concerned they were shooting at snipe.'

'Two snipe with two barrels,' Jammy said, 'that's the mark of a good shot.'

'I know,' Ned said, 'but those Ju 88s carried four bombs each, so for them it was one snipe with four barrels.' He remembered that last half an hour, with the *Aztec* leaking from damage caused by near-misses. 'One snipe flying on one wing.'

The Croupier nodded sympathetically. 'Still, I guarantee we'll sink that first drum before it gets abreast the bridge.'

Jemmy jerked his head in a twitch which thumped the bulkhead. 'Okay, I'll hold the stakes. Who's betting what?'

'Case of champagne that we sink it before it reaches the bridge!' the Croupier said.

'Very well, a case that you don't!' Ned said.

'Oh no you don't, Ned,' the Croupier said firmly. 'You said it would float past the poop unharmed.'

Ned sighed. 'This is taking champagne from babies. Very well, you say it'll sink before it's abreast the bridge and I say it'll reach the poop unharmed. Case of champagne and Jemmy's the witness and judge.'

'Agreed,' said the Croupier. 'But we'd better check with the ship's chief steward that he *has* a case of champagne.'

'I'll do that,' Jemmy said. 'If no champagne, its cost equivalent, but these ships are well provisioned – they stock up with whatever's going wherever they call. D'you know why we eat such glorious steaks? Last trip took the *City of Norwich* to New York, where the chief steward stocked up with choice steaks from Chicago.'

The next day was not very typical for the North Atlantic in winter. The wind was about Force 5 on the Beaufort Scale and from the south-west, and (on this leg of the zigzag) the *City of Norwich* was steaming south-west at revolutions for sixteen knots. Ned was standing on the bridge muffled in duffel coat, woollen balaclava helmet and two pairs of gloves: an inner pair of silk (Clare had cadged them from an RAF pilot patient) to keep his left hand warm, and an outer of thick wool. The wind seemed as sharp as a knife, whipping round the men on the bridge at better than thirty knots.

The *City of Norwich's* bow was rising and falling as she butted into swell waves, so that the seamen on the fo'c'sle had to hold on with one hand as they hauled the big, empty oil drum to the starboard side. Ned knew how difficult such a seemingly easy job could be: as the bow dropped one seemed to become weightless, and it was difficult to walk, as in a dream. Then, as the bow began rising, one's weight increased. He had seen men having to work on the foredeck of a destroyer in a seaway alternately forced to their knees and then spreading out their arms like wings to keep balanced.

Painter looked at the Sten guns. Yorke's was slung over his shoulder but the Chief Officer, Harding, could not get used to such a small weapon: it could not be held with the butt under the arm like a shotgun, and he was not used to handling a gun that was a cross between an automatic and a 12-bore shotgun in size.

'You look like somebody's grandma trying to make up her mind whether to rob the bank or nip into the White Swan for a glass of Guinness and an arrowroot biscuit.' Painter told Harding unsympathetically, adding hastily: 'And don't point the blasted thing at me!'

'It's such an odd shape,' Harding grumbled. 'This butt thing – it's just a piece of gas pipe welded on to the breech and with a flat plate to go against your shoulder. Butt, I suppose you'd call it.'

Ned nodded sympathetically. 'Just imagine you were a commando with a blackened face creeping through a blackberry hedge with it. Respirator, webbing belts all over the place, spare magazines, probably a water bottle as well – you'd be glad of a nice simple gun. A Purdey is best for rocketing pheasant, but give me a Sten for battling the Wehrmacht at close range on a dark night.'

'What about the Thompson sub-machine gun?' Harding asked nervously.

Ned remembered a brief course on the different types of small arms that were coming over from the United States and Canada, held in a quarry near Glasgow. The instructor, a raw-boned sergeant from the King's Own Scottish Borderers, was clearly bored stiff with having to explain the same weapons week after week to what he no doubt regarded as a supercilious and idle bunch of naval officers.

Browning automatic rifles, Ross bolt-action from the First World War, Springfield which was very much like it, Hotchkiss machine guns... Different ammunition, too: none of the British .303 with rim – now it was .300 rimless. And then came the famous Tommy gun with the round drum, reminding one of the film *Scarface*, with Paul Muni, and gangs fighting for control of Chicago. Well, God knows how they did it with Tommy guns, unless the chatter of them firing made the enemy drop dead from fear. All the gangster films where the villains poked Tommy guns through car windows, and, a cold smile on their faces, proceeded to riddle the targets in the next cars with magazines full of bullets, had turned out to be sheer rubbish.

The only way to fire a Thompson sub-machine gun accurately (at least those early models with the circular drum magazines) was to have an elephant sitting on the foresight to keep the barrel down. Ned had been the first to be chosen at the quarry to fire the damned gun, and the dour sergeant had made no mention of recoil: he gave the impression that the gun was the answer to the German Schmeisser, and a dozen men from his regiment equipped with it could liberate Holland and, with a few extra magazines and a packet of sandwiches, Belgium as well.

The gun had fitted the body snugly: butt tucked in under the right arm and the pistol grip and trigger nicely placed for the right hand, and the left hand on the grip forward of the magazine. As the sergeant explained, it was a piece of cake. Fire a few rounds from the hip, sir, the sergeant had said: sense where you're aiming, like a cowboy with a six-gun.

Squeeze the trigger...and the gun started climbing, hammering away like a run-amok pneumatic drill with the muzzle lifting and combining with the recoil, becoming too much for the left hand to hold down. So stop firing – but the bloody gun leaping up and forward like a seasoned warhorse meant he could not get his finger off the trigger: the gun pressed forward and up and up and up and – then it stopped firing.

'You'll find the magazine is empty now, sir,' the sergeant said laconically. 'The magazine release is – ah, that's it sir. Ran away with you, did it?'

'Runs away with everybody, I should think,' Ned had said sourly, ears ringing and so deafened he could hardly hear what the man was saying.

'Those American gangsters you see on the films seem to have the hang of them,' the sergeant said, fitting another magazine, 'and I'm told they're sending over straight magazines, instead of these things that look like what my mum baked flans in, but nothing'll ever make 'em any good for anything but scarin' birds in a cherry orchard.'

And that, Ned remembered, had been an accurate assessment. By comparison the Sten handled like a tame dove.

'The Thompson sub-machine gun?' he asked Harding. 'Well, if you can imagine trying to handle a well-greased hysterical pneumatic drill which has no "off" switch, then you'll know!'

'But in the films – '

'In the films,' Ned said, 'the heroine can kiss the hero a dozen times and his hair stays straight and so does hers, and her lipstick… You try it and you'll find you've got lipstick all over your collar – '

' – and she's cussing you for messing up her hair!' Painter interrupted. 'But Commander, I think they're ready on the fo'c'sle to let the first drum go.'

Ned saw the muffled figures standing beside one drum which was ready to be pitched over. 'Very well, I'll go aft and wait on the poop. When I wave with both arms, perhaps you'll pass the word. I'll wave each time we're ready for another barrel. I see we have six, thanks to Mr Harding and the Chief Engineer.'

Painter nodded. 'Since Mr Harding is going to be firing his share of the bullets that will defeat Hitler, I'll handle the telephone to the fo'c'sle. I'll make sure they drop it promptly when I give the order.'

As Ned clambered down the companionway on his way to the poop, Painter went into the wheelhouse and picked up one of the telephones, pressing the call button below it.

Through one of the horizontal slits in the armour plating blocks of special concrete on the forward side of the bridge, he saw the third officer, muffled in oilskins against the spray, move across the fo'c'sle to answer the 'phone, normally only used for passing orders and reports when the ship was anchoring or weighing. Painter gave him his orders and put down the telephone.

He turned to the quartermaster, a thin and lugubrious-looking man wearing a knitted red woollen hat, a thick jersey of unbleached wool, which Painter guessed was a gift from one of the Australian or New Zealand organizations which sent gifts for seamen, and a pair of Navy bell-bottom trousers, bought or exchanged from one of the DEMS gunners. For all his sad appearance, this man was one of the ship's wits and practical jokers, as well as being one of the two best quartermasters.

'Judkins – a nice straight course, eh?' He glanced up at the clock on the bulkhead behind Judkins where he stood at the wheel, and saw from the settings of the contacts that the next zigzag was not due for twenty minutes. 'We've got to give them a fair chance of hitting the drums.'

'Ho yes, sir,' Judkins said. 'After all, we're all on the same side.' With that he sucked his teeth and bent his head to peer at the compass in front of him. 'I can keep her within three degrees either side of the course.'

'Good enough.' With that Painter went out to the starboard side of the bridge, where he had a good view of the poop with its solitary 4-inch gun and three men wearing duffels and holding Sten guns. He then saw that the 4-inch gun's regular DEMS crew were over on the port side, out of the way.

He could just distinguish Ned by his distinctive stance and waved in acknowledgment as he saw him lift both arms in the air. He went back into the wheelhouse, picked up the fo'c'sle telephone and as soon as the third officer answered said: 'First barrel over the side, and make sure it lands well outboard.'

By the time he was outside again he heard the rapid stuttering of the Stens of the two men abreast the foremast and a few moments later froze for a moment, even though he was expecting it, as Harding opened fire, followed a moment later by the Marine sergeant, who was in the gun position with him. The Marine was cursing, but Harding was happily shooting short bursts. Then more Stens opened fire from the boatdeck as the drum passed down the ship's side and Painter saw the three men on the poop lift their guns and fire in what seemed a casual manner. He caught sight of the drum and saw it was much closer to the ship than he expected. If any of those bullets ricocheted against the ship's hull by way of the engine room, there would be complaints from the Chief Engineer that he had not been warned.

'Chiefie' was, as an exasperated Harding had once exclaimed, 'a long unshaven complaint wrapped up in a sweat rag'. But Harding had never been on board with Chiefie when the *City of Norwich* had been in convoy. In the early days, before independent sailing was either the policy or organized, she had at times been in 6-knot convoys. Station-keeping was a nightmare, with the helmsman's two-hour watch leaving the man worn out with the concentration of keeping the lubberline against the course on the compass card. Worse, because it took longer for the correction to come into effect, was the changes in speed. The officer on watch, seeing that the ship was creeping up on her next ahead, would telephone down to the engine room (engine room telegraphs being a thing of the past in wartime) to say 'Up two revs, please,' or 'Down three revs, please,' and if Chiefie had answered hastily putting down the receiver before the explosion, which was invariably preceded with a rumbling: 'You silly buggers up there don't...' Like all merchant ships there was a sharp division between 'deck' and 'engine room'. In most ships where it was a rule that all officers eating in the saloon had to be properly dressed in uniform (which meant leaving lifejacket and steel helmet in a pile outside the door), the engineers preferred to eat in their own mess where they need not scrub up and wear uniform, especially if they were in the middle of a massive overhaul of some piece of machinery which would coat them in oil and grease.

The only contact between the engineers and 'you silly buggers up there' was in port, when those engineers not on leave usually had their wives on board and all had their meals in the saloon.

Painter's thoughts were interrupted by the realization that Ned, at whom he had been staring for some seconds, was waving his arms. He went into the wheelhouse and spoke into the fo'c'sle telephone once again.

On the poop an angry Croupier was protesting: 'Yes, Ned, I *see* that the bloody drum hasn't sunk – '

'Or apparently been hit once.'

' – or apparently been hit once, but the bet's off if we have to shoot at a drum almost alongside. Christ, we're likely to shoot our toes off!'

Ned nodded and held up a hand, both to silence the Croupier and pick up the telephone to the bridge. He pressed the waterproofed call button.

'Bridge here,' Painter said.

'Captain Yorke here. We've a problem. The drum is too close alongside so we can't get any realistic target practice.'

'Thought not,' Painter said. 'I was expecting a call for the quack to come up and bandage some feet! What shall I do, drop a drum and circle it?'

Ned knew enough not to ask for such a favour, but Painter was a helpful man who could be relied on to do his best without risking his ship.

'That would be perfect. If your chaps could drop a drum every five hundred yards, then, as we turn, we'll have plenty of targets.'

'I don't think I'll reduce speed, but what sort of range?'

That, Ned thought, is just the trouble. The Sten is a fine close-range weapon, but don't expect it to pepper oil drums at two hundred yards... He visualized the angle for his party lining the *City of Norwich*'s deck.

'Can you keep the drums say forty yards from the hull? That's difficult, I know, but I'd like 'em just clear of our bow wave abreast the foremast.'

'I know what you mean,' Painter said. 'Luckily your 'phone buzzed just as I was going to tell the fo'c'sle party to drop another drum. Shall I announce the change of plan?'

'If you would. Tell them to open fire when within range.'

Ned put the telephone down. 'Is the bet on or off now?' he asked the Croupier sarcastically.

'On, I suppose.'

'You'd better change your magazine, then.'

'Blast you – sir.'

Jemmy coughed. 'As stakeholder, I must know if insubordination cancels the wager.'

'It does, but only from now on.'

'But sir,' the Croupier protested, 'this is like shooting down at rats in a sewer.'

'You didn't hit the drum,' Ned pointed out. 'What do you want, the drums circling the ship like unemployed albatrosses? Look, we're beginning to turn.'

They could see the men on the fo'c'sle heaving over an oil drum from time to time and soon they appeared in the *City of Norwich*'s curving wake, gradually forming up in a half moon, bobbing like playful porpoises as the liner continued a long and wide turn which, Ned could see, would soon bring her round to meet the first of the drums.

As she was half-way round the turn the swell waves caught the *City of Norwich* abeam and made her roll, and for a moment a metallic rattling startled Ned until he realized it was the spent Sten cartridges which had been ejected and now rolled the steel deck.

Jemmy looked down at them and grinned. 'Like a giant pinball machine.'

'Yes,' Ned agreed, 'only it's registered "Missed", not "Tilt".'

They could feel the vibration of the ship's engines slow down slightly, and the thrusting movement against the seas lessened, as though a restive and jostling crowd was quietening down.

'He's making it easier for us,' Ned said. 'We've dropped a couple of knots. Hope no U-boat is watching!'

'If the target suddenly changes speed,' Jemmy said professionally, 'it's much harder to hit her. If she *decreased* speed

– which isn't what a submarine commander would expect – torpedoes will pass well ahead.'

'As long as they don't bounce off one of the oil-drums and explode!'

'They've probably got magnetic pistols which explode the torpedo as soon as she gets within the powerful magnetic field caused by ferrous metals – a ship's hull, for instance,' Jemmy said with the reproving seriousness of an expert whose subject had been broached in too lighthearted a manner. 'An oil drum's magnetic field is *much* too weak.'

'You don't say!' the Croupier said sarcastically. 'And polarized all wrong too because it's twisting about and doesn't know its north end from the bung.'

'The first drum is coming up,' Ned warned. 'Stand by to fire broadsides and then board in the smoke.'

Captain Painter and the quartermaster brought the great bulk of the *City of Norwich* up to the first in the semi-lune of bobbing drums and then steered in a curve conforming to them as they had spread out under the influence of wind and the waves.

The Stens forward began barking, sounding faint like excited poodles playing in the park; then Harding and the Marine joined in from the wing of the bridge, followed by the men stationed at intervals along the boatdeck. Finally the three men on the poop could see the drum floating high in the water, slowly turning as wind waves butted it. The three Sten guns thudded in short bursts – just as the instructor ordered, Ned thought – and finally stopped as the drum passed astern out of range.

'My dad's got shares in Shell, and these are Shell drums.' Jemmy said conversationally. 'He'll be so pleased to hear we aren't damaging Company property!'

'I don't understand it,' the Croupier grumbled. 'We must have fired three or four hundred rounds at it. They can't *all* have missed.'

Ned turned round and called 'Corporal.' From behind the gun, where he had been standing with the DEMS gunners, a pair of binoculars hanging on their strap round his neck, came Corporal Davis.

'Well, how are we doing?' Ned asked.

'Shooting in a pattern about four times the size of the drum, and most going over it, sir. I saw about ten holes in the drum. No more.'

'All the holes being at the top means the drum won't sink for a few hours, until it turns enough times to let water in. Well, here's the next drum. You two shoot,' Ned said. 'I'm going to have a word with Captain Painter.'

He turned away, picked up the bridge telephone and a few moments later was saying to Painter: 'Can you tell 'em that everyone is shooting too high: the shots are landing in the sea beyond the drums.'

Ned had hardly replaced the receiver before Painter's voice boomed out. The moment he stopped speaking the forward Stens began firing.

'Stay close with those binoculars, Corporal, and sing out what you see,' Ned said as he picked up his Sten and swiftly fitted a new magazine.

The bridge guns fired and then, the noise creeping aft as though men were walking towards the poop firing as they came, the boat deck group.

'Bridge pair still too high,' said the Corporal. 'Ah, that's better – boat deck group (most Marines, sir) getting hits. Twenty, perhaps thirty. Oh, very nice!' he shouted above the hammering of Jemmy's Sten, and then sharp bursts from the guns of Ned and the Croupier drowned his voice.

As the drum drew astern, Ned took the Corporal's binoculars. The black-painted drum was pocked with rusty marks and as it turned slowly the light reflecting from its wet surface showed how the impact of the bullets had flattened the curve slightly.

As he returned the binoculars he said to the Croupier: 'You'd better get some ice from the Chief Steward. We'll share out the champagne among our prize crew.'

'I wonder if he has champagne buckets,' Jemmy said.

'Galvanized iron ones will do the job. Most of the chaps will be drinking out of mugs, so let's not be too fussy.'

He turned to Corporal Davis. 'When we've finished shooting, I want you to make sure these guns are properly cleaned and all the magazines filled. Next time we fire 'em, it won't be at oil drums.'

CHAPTER TEN

In the darkness the *City of Norwich* slowly came to a stop. The steady rumbling of her engines quietened until by comparison they were purring: the vibration through the hull, caused by the long shafts spinning on their bearings and finally going out through the hull to turn the propellers, came to a stop. What had been a gentle pitching while the ship drove on westward now became more violent, with the ship losing way and finally lying inert, like a log in the water.

On the bridge Ned shook hands with Harding as Captain Painter talked to the Chief Engineer on the telephone. He put it down and, walking carefully into the wheelhouse, lit by a single blue bulb which distorted the colours and made the men look like animated corpses, said: 'The Chief says the screws are stopped, so now's the time, I suppose… The barograph seems fairly steady…'

Ned shook Painter's hand. Neither man knew quite what to say. Painter still did not know what strange quirk of warfare dictated that men like Yorke had to be abandoned in a lifeboat in the middle of a North Atlantic winter; Ned knew the chances were that the *City of Norwich* would be torpedoed within a month or two because of the Great Blackout. The routeing charts given to Painter for later voyages would be as much use as directions given to a deaf aunt by a whispering nephew who did not know the way. Painter would follow them optimistically because in the past the routes given had kept him out of trouble.

On the boat deck the motley collection of men waited by the lifeboat with Jemmy, the Croupier and Yon. The *City of Norwich*'s second officer stood by with a handful of seamen ready to man the falls and lower the boat.

'All ready here, sir,' Jemmy reported out of the darkness.

'Everything stowed in the boat?'

'The Croupier's just checked over the list, sir.'

'Very well. You and three men in the boat when she's lowered: you've chosen the men?'

Jemmy said something to the group and three joined him to climb into the lifeboat as it hung in its davits, the only one in the row of six boats whose davits had been swung outboard so that when she was lowered she would not hit the ship's side.

Ned looked across at the second officer. 'Right, lower away!'

Ned reckoned this was the most dangerous part of the whole operation. At the bow and at the stern of the lifeboat was a large metal eye. From each davit hung the falls – which peacetime passengers called by the more familiar word 'pulleys' – each having a hook which fitted into the eyes on the boat.

The *City of Norwich*'s seamen had to be very careful that they paid out the rope of each fall at the same speed, so that the boat remained level (preferably, in fact, with the bow slightly higher than the stern) until it reached the water. In the excitement and darkness, all too frequently one fall was lowered faster than the other: if the seamen had not taken enough turns of the rope round a cleat, so that the friction slowed it down, they found it racing through their hands. Many a lifeboat ended up hanging vertically by one fall: then the crest of a wave gave it a nudge which unhooked the remaining fall and the lifeboat fell into the water, usually upside-down, and pitched the three or four men into the water, to drift away to leeward and a lonely death.

Ned saw that at the roller of the rope one seaman was crouched down making sure that as it turned the rope came off without kinks; the second officer at the ship's side was watching the lifeboat as it was lowered.

He turned forward and bellowed: 'You forward – are you ready with the painter?' As soon as he had a reassuring answer he turned aft. 'You, aft there: are you ready with the sternfast?'

There was enough surge of the sea, the crests and troughs rising and falling a good ten feet, for Ned to see that, as soon as the lifeboat was properly in the water, both falls must be unhooked quickly and cast off, otherwise, if the boat had landed on a crest, as she tried to drop into the trough the falls would hold her up. Once the falls were unhooked then the painter leading forward would hold in her bow and the sternfast would keep her close to the ship's side.

'Falls clear!' the second officer called, and the men began hauling the ropes in to lift the heavy blocks and hooks clear of the lifeboat and back up to the davits.

'Over with the ladder!' the second officer ordered, and as the rope ladder was pushed over the side, unrolling from where it was secured at the top, he said to Ned: 'Your men can board now.'

The men dressed in a variety of clothes, but unencumbered by Sten guns or bags of black bangers, which had long since been stowed, scrambled down the ladder. Ned counted them, and finally only the Croupier was left, the two gold rings on his arm conspicuous because now instead of the 'executive curl' worn by the Navy, his jacket had the diamond shape of the Merchant Navy, indicating that he was a second officer, known colloquially as a 'second mate'. The Merchant Navy, Ned thought irrelevantly are just like the Royal Navy in their quirkish ranks. The Merchant Navy's equivalent of the Royal Navy's 'number one' was the chief officer, who was rarely called the 'first mate', although in effect he was. The chief officer in fact had passed his examination for master mariner and was usually as well qualified as the captain (who might have taken his 'extra master's' certificate). But the chief officer had to have more sea time as a chief officer before getting a command. The next down the line was the second officer, who held a first officer's certificate, and in most ships was responsible for navigation. The junior was the third officer, who had passed his second mate's examination and held the certificate. Below him were the cadets – called midshipmen in some companies, apprentices in others – busy (or supposed to be) studying to take their second mate's examination. In the Merchant Navy, an officer usually served in one grade below the one for which he was qualified.

And now the Croupier was climbing down the rope ladder and the *City of Norwich*'s second officer was waiting at the head of it.

'Good luck, sir,' he muttered. 'Dunno what you're all doing, but I hope you succeed!'

Ned shook him by the hand and started off down the rope ladder. At each step down, the ladder swung in against the ship's side. Going down was always more difficult than climbing up, and the rough paint of the ship's side scraped his knuckles as the ladder kept banging against the hull.

Suddenly hands were grasping him and he was in the boat sitting on a thwart. It did not seem so dark down here, and he realized that the water sluicing between the lifeboat and the ship was slightly phosphorescent.

He scrambled aft and found that Jemmy had already shipped the rudder. 'Is the bung in?' he demanded.

'Put it in myself,' Jemmy said.

Ned shouted preliminary orders and men grasped oars, holding them vertically on the port side, ready to use them to shove the boat clear of the ship.

'Right, cast off the sternfast... Fend us off there...' Then, as the gap opened up between the lifeboat and the ship, enough for the oars to get to work, 'Cast off the painter...'

Five minutes later, the men rowing briskly yet appearing to make no progress in the darkness, among waves much larger than Ned had expected and passing under the boat with a hiss as though a giant was exhaling, the dark blob of the *City of Norwich* finally disappeared ahead, and for a few moments a whiff of her funnel smoke caught the back of his throat and made him cough.

He saw that the men were settling into the rhythm of rowing, thanks to the practice they had had back in England, but they were not used to the high waves: every now and then a man who had not dipped the blade deep enough cursed as the loom jerked back and hit him across the chest.

But Ned could not throw off the air of unreality that was wrapped round him, as though he was an inert chrysalis in a cocoon. A chrysalis, he thought, making a wry joke, waiting to turn into something.

It would be hard to tell someone on land that having just been left in a lifeboat in the middle of the night in the middle of winter in the middle of the Atlantic one felt cocooned, as though the wind and seas, the grey lifeboat, the cursing men, the oars more like twitching frogs' legs than the Boat Race, were disconnected memories. Yet this was the beginning of their weird gamble. It was quite impossible to connect this pitching and rolling boat and the men at the oars with the bespectacled boffins at Bletchley Park, to whom a cipher was simply a mathematical problem – one that might take months to solve. Nor was there any apparent link between this boat (water was already swilling around his feet) and the plump and pink yet bulldog face in Number Ten Downing Street, who had told him to collect men of diabolical cunning. Well, full of diabolical cunning they might be inside, but at the moment they were just dark lumps of misery, already sodden with spray and rapidly chilling with the wind which, as it evaporated the water from the clothes, acted as an efficient refrigerator.

Then the absurdity of it all hit him simultaneously as the wind sliced off a breaking crest and flung it in his face, the cold water soaking down round the neck of his duffel coat, cold tentacles gradually becoming clammy as they went lower. 'Keep your stomach warm and you'll survive…' How many times had he heard that in lectures on survival at sea: how many times had he told his own men the same thing? But like the lecturers and instructors, he had skated lightly over the 'how'. Keep your stomach warm and the rest of your body won't worry about the cold. But *how* to stop the stomach gradually chilling as all one's clothing became sodden and cold, the doeskin material of a uniform jacket turning into fine sandpaper to chafe skin, where every move exposed to another cold compress a tender part of the body that still retained a tiny, previously unrecognized area of warmth?

A standard ship's lifeboat containing twenty-three shivering, cursing and sodden men thought to be possessed of diabolical cunning (it must have been a sunny day) yet already wishing they had never heard of the sea, a few Sten guns greased and wrapped in oiled canvas, a few metal boxes with 'black bangers' sitting in them like emu eggs – this miserable bunch were Britain's champions in the contest against Germany. Hitler had pitted Commodore – no, Admiral, he had recently been promoted – Dönitz and all his U-boats, about five hundred by now, and all his Enigma makers and cipher experts, and electric torpedoes with magnetic pistols which exploded the torpedo when triggered off by a ship's magnetic field, against them. Laughable. Had history juggled the time so that, instead of the Armada, Spain sent Don Quixote astride his spavined Rosinante, to be met by the Black Prince on the playing fields of Eton, the whole affair to be reported by Beachcomber? What a one-sided tourney that would have been. Yet as the British crowd prefers supporting the underdog, they'd probably have cheered the Don and hooted so loud against the Black Prince that his charger would have bolted, although his wife Joan, the Fair Maid of Kent, would certainly have then gone on to the field and put the crowd to flight.

There was some comfort in thinking about jousting, because the heavy armour must have kept the wind out, and presumably one had armourers ready to clean the armour and polish it after the battle – and grease it, too: a squeaky visor or one which stuck open, exposing one's cowardly grin to swift dentistry from an opponent's sword, could be troublesome.

Knightly combat – now all that was left of it was proof of some of Newton's laws, and phrases used mostly in heraldry. A coat of arms – how many realized that it was originally a way of identifying yourself? A dozen knights in a dozen suits of shining armour sitting on a dozen heavy horses also clad in armour looked as alike as a dozen wine glasses. So each wore a sleeveless silk coat, like the colours a modern jockey wears to distinguish his horse's owner, and on the silk his lady embroidered the arms of his family. Some Yorke forebears five hundred years ago must have pulled on their silken coats of arms, been hoisted up on to their horses (a knight in full armour was done for if he fell: some wretched fellow could creep up, flip open the visor and cut his throat!), raised their lances to their wives or mistresses, and galloped off to find glory or a clangorous end. They certainly never thought that one of their descendants would be pulling down the hood of his duffel coat as he sat in a lifeboat, the tiller tucked under his arm as a vastly foreshortened lance. Gentlemen of England now abed shall think themselves accurs'd... Well, perhaps, but he was prepared to swear that the twenty-three gentlemen of England (and Scotland, Wales and Ireland) now in this boat wished they were abed at this moment – as no doubt was Hitler's champion, *B der U* himself. Ned visualized the hard-faced little man Dönitz, with his large ears and close-cropped hair (several photographs of him were pinned up on the wall of ASIU, on the 'Know Your Enemy' principle), tucked up in a warm bed near Kernével. No doubt a comfortable French chateau had been requisitioned, and German Navy cooks probably sliced leberwurst where previously a gourmet cook juggled truffles which pigs had rooted up in the chateau's own grounds...

Jemmy was shaking his arm insistently. 'Two hours, Ned: time to change the watch!'

So two hours had passed while he had been riding with Rosinante, picturing Joan, the Fair Maid of Kent – who was by chance one of his forebears – along with the Black Prince, whose tomb in Canterbury Catherdral was a reproach to all the

Cromwells, Harry Pollitts and James Maxtons of this world – and the Major Gateses, too, the pro-Germans now interned on the Isle of Man because of their opinions before the war.

Changing the watch involved only physical contortions: as soon as Ned passed the word, the man at the inboard end of each oar changed places with the man sitting outboard. The inboard man had been doing the work, from the position of most leverage. The man outboard had tried to doze, holding on to the oar as instructed, so that it should not be lost overboard if the inboard man let go.

Jemmy slid across the short aftermost thwart and took the tiller. 'Sweet dreams,' he said. 'Now you see why I'm a submariner.'

Dawn came with the dreary slowness of departing toothache. The Croupier commented sourly: 'You can now *see* what's making you miserable. I prefer the dark.'

Daylight revealed a desolate scene: wave heaping upon grey wave, white crest after white crest ripping off its top and scattering to leeward in cold spray which made eyes raw. But was it so cold? Ned felt warmer, until he considered it, pulling the hood of his duffel over his face to keep out the spray. No, it was no warmer because obviously it could not be; quite simply he was getting used to it. He knew from bitter experience when the *Aztec* sank that after a while one did not really feel the cold. One could see the effect of it – pinching flesh did not produce pain – but not feel it. One just grew weaker, and the onset of hunger produced that stage in the process of surviving where the strong came through and the weak gave up; where the real leaders still made the decisions and gave the rest the will to live, and the hearty blusterers who in less stringent times passed for leaders, kept quiet, only too glad to leave decisions to others.

Strange how if you covered your head and face it seemed less harsh. The man who invented duffel coats should die a millionaire. Yet it was somehow symptomatic of – well, the

British Isles – that the duffels issued to the Royal Navy were thin compared with the Royal Canadian Navy type. Yes, here in the tiny tent formed by the duffel's hood you did not hear the hiss of the wind. It did not whine because there was no wire rigging or anything else to cause a whine. What did wind sound like in a desert, with no buildings to buffet and no trees? Presumably just a hiss; a roar if it was very strong. The sea was not comparable to the desert because the wind tossed up the waves and there was always the sound and feel of waves and spray. Oh to be a Bedouin safely in his tent in a sandstorm. Yet no doubt the stifling Bedouin, breathing in sand, dreamed of being in a boat at sea, where there was no sand and no heat. No satisfying the customers, Ned thought, and dozed off.

He woke momentarily lost – the hospital after the operation on his hand, with Clare at the Palace Street house, on board the *Marynal* while chasing the U-boat in the convoy, in a desert somewhere… He pulled back the duffel hood and saw a grey and white desert of waves that moved eastwards with an awe-inspiring relentlessness. Perhaps not so high as when he had dozed off, though pushing back the hood brought back the drumming and buffeting in his ears.

'Want a spell?' he asked Jemmy.

'No, I'm all right. Wind is easing. Sea flattening a bit, too.'

'Still not gentlemen's yachting weather, though.'

'But we're not gentlemen,' Jemmy said.

Ned pulled back the sleeve of his duffel to see his watch. 'Seven o'clock. Time for breakfast.' He leaned forward. 'Sergeant Keeler, are you awake?'

A burly figure in kapok lifejacket and duffel swivelled round to face aft, thin strands of blond hair plastered over his brow, blue eyes red-rimmed from salt spray. He looked like the amiable village baker; in fact he was a Royal Marine commando and was more skilled in killing men than anyone else Ned had ever seen. A quick flip with a cheese wire from behind and a knee in the back killed a sentry silently; an edge-of-the-hand blow across the windpipe from the front was as effective. Dagger, cosh, rifle butt, length of gas pipe, Bunsen burner hose filled with lead shot, an old sock containing beach-worn pebbles, Sten gun, Bren, Lewis, revolvers, automatics… Sergeant Keeler handled them with such familiarity as if they were childhood toys.

Yet he was softly spoken, with a Midland country accent, perhaps Herefordshire, and his round face and ruddy complexion seemed to belong on a farm. Keeler was a kindly man; the sort of person that made a good father. The only thing was that at the earliest age possible he had entered the Royal Marines – this before Hitler's attack on Poland – and as soon as the special Marine commando units were formed, had volunteered. From what Ned could make out, being a Royal Marine commando made Keeler flourish like a well-manured and expertly pruned rose tree: corporal, sergeant instructor, and then a reputation for being the best man with a cheese wire, able to lob a grenade into a bucket at twenty paces, the best all-rounder with a Sten, the best with what Keeler always referred to as 'the small stuff', revolver and automatic… When Ned had called on the Marines with a letter from Captain Watts and said he wanted the loan of some Marines and their best sergeant for a month, the Marine colonel had nodded and said at once: 'Keeler's your man, from what Captain Watts says,' – what *had* Watts written? Ned wondered – 'I'd be inclined to let Keeler pick his own team. Sounds a bit "death or glory", so you want the best.'

Well, the colonel had been right: Keeler had kept his team on their toes and also trained the seamen in the finer points of close-range fighting. An innocent cheese wire, normally seen on a cheese board with a wooden toggle at the end, became a murderous garrotte; the place in the human body to insert a dagger for maximum effect… Keeler had turned a blasé Jemmy and a bored Croupier into keen students of silent killing and, with Ned, they had been fascinated by Keeler's descriptions of the three commando raids on the French coast in which he had taken part. None had ever been made public. None had involved more than thirty men, and each had a specific task. One had been to take a couple of scientists (put into uniform in case they were captured, and so that they would not be shot as spies) to attack a radar station on the cliffs close to a French village.

Jemmy had added a few words to the story: putting the two boffins into uniform would not help: since Hitler had announced his notorious 'Commando Order', all captured commandos were executed anyway. Keeler had laughed and admitted that the boffins had worn uniform for another reason: it was important, if they had been captured, that the Germans did not guess the real reason for the raid. Two men who obviously were not commandos might give the game away, so the boffins had to be beefy men who, like the rest of the party, were well equipped with vicious weapons.

But now crouched on the lifeboat thwarts, Sergeant Keeler and him team of professional killers looked just as weary and weather-beaten as the rest: unshaven, faces grey with cold and fatigue, hunched over oars like galley slaves in their tenth year of rowing Barbarossa. They would stand a close inspection through a U-boat periscope: they looked like genuine survivors. Still, Ned thought, after twelve hours in a lifeboat in this weather everyone *was* a survivor.

'Sergeant, will you deal with the rations?'

For two or three days they would eat well: the chief steward of the *City of Norwich* had put sliced hams and cuts of roast lamb, well cooked chops and steaks in one box: in another were sliced bread, a selection of boiled and roast potatoes, cucumber cut into thick discs, radishes, carrots and hard-boiled eggs, as well as jars of piccalilli and bottles of Lea and Perrins. A third box held a selection of fresh and dried fruit, bought on previous trips to other lands and now stored: dates and currants, apricots, oranges and apples, huge raisins…

As Jemmy watched Keeler begin to hand round the sliced meat and another man passed round bread from the other box, he commented: 'We're going to notice it when we're reduced to lifeboat rations!'

'Yes, but with this lifeboat gourmet food you all have to stay alert: the quickness of your hands must deceive the Teds' eyes.'

'Guaranteed,' Jemmy said, 'as long as the cold cutlets last.'

'The chief steward reckons three days, and the ham longer. The bread was specially baked.'

Jemmy shivered. 'I'd have thought it was cold enough to keep the meat longer. You didn't tell me that being in a lifeboat is like trying to get comfortable in a draughty refrigerator.'

'Ah, thanks Sarn't,' Ned took a thick slice of cold lamb and passed it to Jemmy, and then took another piece for himself.

Keeler apologized for the lack of piccalilli. 'Bloody onions keep rolling off, sir. Thought I'd keep it for calmer weather.'

'Yes, and when the meat's not so fresh,' Ned said.

Ned munched and Jemmy took bites as he moved the tiller with the other hand, frequently having to push with his body to overcome the oars on one side.

'I'm sure this bloody boat's warped,' he complained. 'It keeps turning to port.'

'The chaps on the starboard side are pulling harder,' Ned said, and called them. A couple of minutes later he asked Jemmy: 'That better?'

'Yes, Sorry Ned, I'm not thinking too well at the moment.'

'I'll give you a spell.'

'No, it's the Croupier's turn.' He shouted, and the Croupier, sitting in the forward part of the boat beside Yon, heaved himself upright and began to scramble aft, climbing over the thwarts and careful not to get jabbed in the ribs by the looms of the oars as they moved backwards and forwards in erratic rhythm.

'Not much hope of spotting anything – anything spotting us, rather,' Jemmy said. 'A U-boat would have to have its periscope raised twenty feet to keep the lens clear of this spray.'

'Wouldn't it surface?' Ned asked. 'Not much chance of being spotted by aircraft out here!'

'That'd depend on the skipper. What luck has he had so far, how many torpedoes he has left, what fuel, how many days to the end of his patrol. Yes, and crew morale. That's likely to be a problem for Dönitz these days. Okay, the Teds are winning the Battle of the Atlantic – the figures make that clear enough – but we are sinking quite a few boats. They're building so many it doesn't make much difference to the balance, but it does to the men.'

'In what way?' Ned asked. 'They know they're winning, they know new and better boats are being designed and launched, and according to the Resistance boys, the submariners are the heroes – even to the French girls in places like Brest.'

'Oh yes, the survivors have a fine time. But I wonder how many officers and men in U-boats on the day war broke out are still alive today? The engine-room artificers of September 1939 who have survived are probably lieutenants (E) by now; the nervous sub-lieutenant who was then general dogsbody is probably one of the ace commanders – if he's lived this long.'

Ned gave a dry laugh. 'You sound like a Ministry of Information hand-out to the Press!'

Jemmy slid a couple of feet across the thwart so that the Croupier could sit down and take the tiller. Jemmy, his head jutting out of the hood of his duffel like a hen staring from its nest, leaned across towards Ned.

'Plain statistics, old boy. Say they had fifty subs then and now have four hundred. What are the chances of those early subs surviving? But even if they do, the best men get moved on to the newer boats. The newer boats get the tougher jobs and (because they certainly have longer range) the most distant ones, with more chances of being intercepted and sunk.

'Do some sums, Ned. How many of those original fifty young sub-lieutenants have survived? How many commanding officers, and, probably more important, how many engineers? How many of those original crews? More than two years of war, so say half at the most, scattered among the other boats. Each has a memory of Old Heinrich, or Herman, or Ernst, who went out on patrol with U-so-and-so and never came back.'

'Hold on a moment,' Ned protested, 'you make it sound as though they're losing!'

'No, I'm not, I'm trying to make you see it through an ordinary submariner's eyes. Yes, he knows the Reich is winning; he hears of little else but numbers of Allied ships sunk and gross tonnages. He hears that one of the aces has just sunk his hundredth ship. He knows Kretschmer sank 325,000 tons, but also knows that one day Kretschmer didn't come back. Prien may have sunk the *Royal Oak* in Scapa, but Prien too is dead.

'So Heinrich, commanding *U-555* at the age of twenty-six, hero on shore, a sub-lieutenant only a year ago, an *Oberleutnant* six months ago, and now making his first trip as *Kapitänleutnant* and with an Iron Cross round his neck like a priest with his rosary, hoping it will ward off the devil in the shape of depth-charges, has his hopes – and his memories.

'Just as I dream of potting two snipe with two barrels, so *Kapitänleutnant* Heinrich dreams of potting the *Queen Mary* with one torpedo and a battleship with another, and returning triumphantly to Brest or Lorient or Sant-Nazaire, where *B der U* welcomes him with a brass band and the news that an admiring Führer has made an immediate award of the Knight's Cross with Diamonds, Oak Leaves and Tea Leaves.

'But – there's always a but – while Heinrich dreams of sink the *Queen Mary*, he has *nightmares* about a pattern of depth-charges going bang in the night followed by the sound of spurting water as the lights go out and the hull starts crumpling up. Ned, I know how *Kapitänleutnant* Heinrich feels as he tries to sleep in his cabin. I know because my cabin was probably about the same size.'

Ned finished chewing the last piece of lamb and looked round, half expecting to see a black-painted and rust-streaked tube like a drainpipe, with a large prism on the top, sticking up out of the sea and eyeing them, like a giraffe looking over a wall.

'Yes, I follow all that, but what's it got to do with Heinrich not thundering along on the surface?'

'Oh, don't misunderstand me. Heinrich might be a born killer whose vocation is sinking enemy ships and bumping off survivors, but he'll probably be the only such man on board. It's more likely that Heinrich has finally learned he can live without a Knight's Cross and the Führer's embrace: he comes up to periscope depth every hour or so in daylight, takes a look round, and goes back to a hundred feet where he doesn't feel the swell waves.

'He doesn't get any dirty looks from his lieutenants, either. The sub-lieutenant might still be inexperienced enough to be breathing fire and Nazi brimstone, but the first depth-charging will cool him off. I'm only saying, really, that I reckon most of the Heinrichs of this world are doing their duty but no more. They know that the Tommies have learned a few tricks about escorting convoys, so the days of easy killings are gone for good. They know they'll never be a new Schepke, or a Kretschmer.'

CHAPTER ELEVEN

The slice of bread passed along by Sergeant Keeler tasted delicious, taking away the greasiness left by the meat, but Ned's mouth felt dry and salty. Every dam' thing was salty – his eyelids, lips, hands: rubbing an itching eyelid resulted in a sharp sting as encrusted salt grains caught the eyeball.

Bobbing around this blustery and cold sea in a lifeboat, Ned thought to himself, seems far removed from the bold talk in the ASIU. He took a dipper of water held out to him by Keeler. A dipper a day keeps the doctor away. They had plenty of water, in addition to the two wooden breakers, but it was so cold they were not losing it by perspiration and did not need so much. Dipper – an odd word, but it certainly described the narrow cylinder of metal, closed at one end and with a line secured at the open end so that it could be dipped into the small barrel, quaintly called a breaker. A memory stirred…was not 'breaker' a corruption of the Spanish word for a cask, *barrica*? Why the blasted thing was not called a keg he did not know.

As he handed the dipper back to Keeler, slowing swilling the small ration round his mouth as a portly cardinal would savour a rare wine, spray hit him in the face and, as he swallowed the fresh water, the salt trickled inside his jacket and soaked down his spine. His neck was becoming sore from the chafing and his shirt collar did little more than lodge round his neck after he pulled out the stud. Ironically, the fact that he wore a shirt and tie might matter on a calm day, when wearing it was no inconvenience: but it certainly did not matter in this weather, when collar, tie, coat with the four gold stripes and diamond of the master of a merchant ship were hidden under a duffel.

The Croupier said unexpectedly: 'Thank God for duffel coats.'

'Wrong chap,' Jemmy growled. 'They're Spanish.'

'Rubbish!' the Croupier exclaimed. 'Did Ferdinand and Isabella give Columbus one to wear on his first voyage to the New World?'

'They might well have,' Jemmy retorted. 'It started life as a huntsman's coat in Brabant – which, I am sure you don't know, was a Spanish province in what is now Belgium – and gets its name from the town of Duffel.'

'Coo!' the Croupier said in mock amazement. 'And to what do you owe this erudition?'

'Reading guide books. I was taken to Belgium on holiday as a child. Pouring with rain, no toys in the bloody hotel, father in a temper – I retreated and read a guide book. Hence Duffel, in Brabant.'

'And wet duffels, as in lifeboats,' said the Croupier and in the few moments before he drifted into unsettled sleep Ned remembered his earlier thought that he hoped the inventor of the coat had become a millionaire.

Daybreak on the third day confirmed what they had felt and hoped during the dark hours of the night: the weather was improving. The heavy, grey nimbus cloud had lifted; patches of pale sky appeared fleetingly, like a teasing girl at a window. The sea was slowly easing, freed from the urgent thrusting of the previous week's strong winds.

The oars had been shipped; they were lashed down along the centre-line of the boat, which drifted like a large piece of flotsam, sometimes rolling heavily as it twisted beam-on to the waves, sometimes pitching.

As Ned watched the men eating what passed for breakfast (the last of the bread and meat from the *City of Norwich*, followed by sections of concentrated chocolate from the lifeboat rations, and washed down by a dipper of water), he took stock. All the men needed a good shave: the bristling chins made them look like a gang of cut-throats, or maybe a guerrilla band operating in the mountains, busily blowing up bridges and generally irking the enemy. For three days their only rest had been sleeping where they sat, in sodden clothes. But they were no longer numbed by the cold. It had not become warmer, but after the first day and night the cold no longer soaked into their bodies and occupied all their thoughts. They were still cold, but they accepted it as though it was normal, and few could really remember what it was like to be pleasantly warm. Ned found himself trying to recall life in the Tropics: wearing white shorts and shirt, white cap cover and epaulettes and cursing them all because they were too hot now seemed an absurd reaction. In fact the phrase 'too hot' was absurd: nothing could be too hot. In the past he had complained of a cup of tea or coffee being 'too hot'. Just let them try to serve it too hot now! Anyway, that was the first problem overcome, the cold.

The next was morale. The third and fourth, hunger and thirst, would come later, but morale was good. Not just good but almost absurdly good. Even though wet, cold and tired the men were cheerful, teasing each other as if they were in Chatham barracks, making private jokes, swapping their slices of meat because some preferred a fatty piece, others wanted lean.

Their morale was high because…? An interesting point. They were trained to kill effectively and usually silently – not skills that helped you keep cheerful in a lifeboat. None of them came from the Marines, a corps famous for its comradeship, and ten were RN petty officers and seamen, yet the strongest comradeship did not help you keep dry and warm, or stop you getting cold and wet. The officers – yes, Ned admitted he was lucky. Both Jemmy and the Croupier were as much 'at home' in the boat as Yon, who although a newcomer fitted in perfectly with the ASIU trio.

How would survivors from a torpedoed merchant ship be feeling three days after they had abandoned her in a near-gale? Well, it would take a couple of days to get over the shock – more for the nervous or imaginative. Not the incapacitating white-faced, pain-deadening shock from being wounded, but the dazed, almost numbing feeling after discovering that what cannot happen has just happened: that one's ship is not immune, but like other ships in the convoy she can be torpedoed, and indeed just has been.

Real survivors would be rowing, and several of them would be imagining the time before the hit: when that periscope was watching in the darkness, unseen by them, but seeing. The German captain at the periscope would have been calling ranges and bearings and speeds, and other men would have been calculating the speed of the target (their ship) and the number of degrees the torpedo would have to be 'aimed off' to intercept the ship at some point along her course. That thought alone, that an unseen hunter had been watching from the darkness, had aimed and fired and hit, could leave men lethargic from this particular form of battle shock.

Purpose – that was important, too. A genuine survivor getting into a lifeboat had only one hope, or purpose: to be picked up. Yet he knew the odds were against him. For a start there was the Admiralty order that no ship in the convoy was allowed to stop to pick up survivors. That order had been accepted by the Merchant Navy because it made good sense: with a pack of, say, a dozen U-boats attacking a convoy (and by today's standards that would be a small pack), an individual U-boat could, and often did, torpedo one ship and then wait for the next astern in the column to stop to pick up survivors. The second ship had to stop almost alongside the victim – providing the U-boat with a second target: a stopped sitting duck needing only a single torpedo to bring the score to two.

So the survivors now sat in their lifeboat and waited. Did they hope or did they despair? Probably half of them despaired and half hoped, when the weather was bad. The important point was that they did not know whether or not they would ever be picked up – and fear, Ned knew only too well, is *not knowing*. Once you know for certain one way or the other, fear usually disappears. Knowing for sure that you were going to die did not mean you danced and cheered, but it gave life some certainty, if only the certainty that circumstances had put a term on it, and helped most men to keep up a brave face. But a survivor in a lifeboat was never certain until he was either rescued or eventually lost consciousness from exposure, hunger, thirst or cold, or a combination of them all. Thus, from the time he found himself in a lifeboat, a survivor was really in a state of shocked apprehension. He might laugh and joke to keep up the spirits of his shipmates, but beneath it all he knew his chances of rescue were low.

What about his own men, now hunched on their thwarts, some taking off their duffels like bears shredding their furs, in the hope that their clothes beneath would start to dry out? First of all, they had not suffered the shock of a torpedo sinking their ship, so they still felt invulnerable. And they were in the lifeboat for a reason they knew all about and for which they had been trained, so knowing that, they had no reason for fear. No shock, no fear, just a few uncomfortable days to be endured, and which were probably preferable to conditions in their early commando training, which was designed to weed out the men who were tough from the men who thought they were.

Two weeks of this, and then if nothing had happened, they'd open the special suitcase that contained a wireless already tuned in to 500 metres, the distress frequency, and start calling every hour on the hour. A corvette at sea and specially detailed for the task would be listening and, all being well, would find them. All being well. If there was not another gale lasting a week, and if the corvette left Halifax, Nova Scotia, at the appointed time. And if her wireless was working properly and her operators were listening all the time and not looking through copies of *Men*

Only, or *Razzle*, or playing uckers. Why the Navy had taken to ludo, renaming it, he did not know. What was apparently a mild dice-and-counters game for children brought out the worst in adults on the Navy's messdecks.

'You know,' Jemmy said suddenly, in a conversational tone of voice, 'I went back to my old school just before we left.'

'Did you?' Ned responded, knowing that the series of violent twitches showed that whatever Jemmy had to say was important to him.

'Yes. The headmaster wanted me to give a talk to the boys, and the Admiralty loved it. Submarine ace stuff all makes good propaganda, and we'll eventually need these kids, the way this war is dragging out.'

'And they cheered the hero home from the wars, eh?'

'Yes, and it was all very embarrassing. But I told 'em a few tales about some of the Med operations. If I could have signed 'em on then and there the whole school would have volunteered for submarine service.'

'Bit young, though.'

'It's a young man's game. You're old at thirty. Twenty-five is middle-aged. Twenty is good.' He twitched again and added gloomily: 'I reckon about sixteen is ideal. Plenty of dash and fire and you think you're immortal.'

'What,' Ned enquired, 'brings on this bout of bullshit and misery?'

'Oh, yes, well, in the assembly hall, where the whole school starts off the day with prayers, a hymn, and the headmaster's announcements, there's a large wooden panel, with the school's crest carved at the top. In the middle of the panel are three columns of the names of all the school old boys who were killed in the Great War. I remember as a kid I used to read them, while the headmaster said the prayer, trying to picture what they looked like. I remember I visualized them as being as old as sixth formers.'

Jemmy stopped, having clearly slipped back in time, his eyes dull as he looked unseeingly across the toppling waves.

'Yes,' he said suddenly. 'the headmaster was the same chap that used to give me the whack – six whacks, rather; he always awarded them in half-dozens – every week. He'd retired, then come back when the new headmaster that replaced him went off into the Army for this war.

'What was I rattling on about? Oh yes, the war memorial. There were sixty-three names on it. Three were the same, brothers, all in the same battalion, all killed on the Somme. There were four pairs of brothers.' He paused a moment. 'My own family's surname was up there three times – my father, in the RN, one uncle in the Royal Flying Corps, and the other a soldier who won a posthumous DSO commanding his battalion at Gallipoli. He raised the battalion as a territorial unit, and took it into action. Must have been gratifying.'

Ned nodded, and noticed that the Croupier and Sergeant Keeler were listening.

'Sixty-three names,' Jemmy repeated. 'Lot for such a small school. Mostly Army of course: when you think we lost a million and a half in the trenches. That's why we're so short of leaders in their forties and fifties today: the chaps that should be leading are lying in all those great war cemeteries.

'Then the headmaster showed me a list of the chaps already killed in this war. Seventy-eight. Nine of them were from my class. Made me feel guilty to be still alive. The eerie thing was that in bed that night, and just before I went to sleep, I found I could remember the names of everyone in my class, and in alphabetical order…'

'Most of us can,' Ned said, 'and as you recite them to yourself you see them as the kids they were, and then you remember the ones that have been killed. That spotty little chap you never liked was a fighter pilot, killed in the Battle of Britain; the fellow who was captain of the cricket team and bowled faster than cannon balls died at Dunkirk, covering his men with a Bren gun as they waded out to a cabin cruiser brought to the beaches by a drunken yachtsman.'

'What you're saying is that I'm not telling an unusual story, eh?'

As Ned nodded, Sergeant Keeler coughed and said: 'Beggin' yer pardon, sir, it's the officers.'

A startled Ned raised his eyebrows. 'Not all the chaps from my school who were killed in the Great War were officers.'

'Oh no, sir, I didn't mean that. This war's what I'm talking about. More officers and more of them get killed. Take the RAF blokes. When the war began only the pilot and perhaps the navigator of a bomber was commissioned: the rest were sergeants.

'Then, as the Germans shot down more and more of our bombers and the aircrews were taken prisoner, so they started commissioning the sergeants so they'd get better treatment. So all those bombers and fighters shot down – it's officers what get the chop. Not that being commissioned means much if you're dead. But the Navy's the same. More small boats – take Coastal Forces. Blow one up and you've knocked off three officers, and a mid, and six or eight seamen. Twenty-five per cent officers. All mounts up. In the last war it was the Army slugging it out in the mud of the trenches. This time the Army, apart from Dunkirk, can only get at the Jerries in the Western Desert. S'pect they've heavy casualties to come, but not so far. Hope I 'aven't spoken out of turn.'

'You're quite right,' Jemmy said. 'Never thought of it like that.'

'Yes, well sir, I expect your school provided more officers than mine, too. You got to know sums to get into the Air Force – if you want to fly, that is.' He eyed the three officers who looked like three down-and-outs drinking meths. 'And to get through Dartmouth, too. And Keyham,' he added, nodding towards Yon in the bow.

'If we win the war – *when* we win the war,' the Croupier corrected himself, 'it means in about thirty years' time Britain is once again going to be short of leaders: all the good ones will have been killed in this war, just like the last. I suppose that frightful little Aneurin Bevan, who keeps attacking Churchill, and places like the Ministry of Fuel and Power are riddled with some pretty weird chaps. They'll come out after the war – T E Lawrence was right.'

'Wait!' Ned exclaimed. 'Seven Pillars of Wisdom, the Introduction where he says "we were wrought up with ideas inexpressible and vaporous, but to be fought for." He says something about living many lives in those campaigns but "when we achieved and the new world dawned, the old men came out again and took our victory to re-make in the likeness of the former world they knew..." Then that bitter phrase, "we stammered that we had worked for a new heaven and a new earth, and they thanked us kindly and made their peace."

'But if we win, it'll be very different this time. It won't be "old men" creeping out, it'll be the young men who have been hiding in reserved occupations in the ministries, reading Karl Marx or Fabian Society pamphlets. They'll make damned sure that no one who was away achieving anything in the war will get a look in.'

Ned stopped suddenly. A lifeboat in the middle of the Atlantic was not the place to express contempt for the dodgers, nor criticize the weird crowd who had a firm grip on such curious organizations as the Army Education Corps, most of whose members were either incapable of coherent speech or were mousy men wearing steel-rimmed spectacles and nervously clutching Fabian pamphlets as though they were lucky charms.

'Sergeant,' he said briskly, 'mark the day!'

Keeler slid a hand inside his duffel and brought out a heavy knife. He moved along the thwart and then twisted round to cut another notch alongside earlier ones.

Ned reflected that the earliest calendars were probably notches cut on twigs, recording the passing of the day and the seasons, and perhaps some were specially marked, indicating the time for sowing certain seeds and reaping harvests. Oddly rural thoughts in a giant meadow of a sea.

The next meal would be plain lifeboat rations. The three days' extra sustaining food from the *City of Norwich* had gone. Assuming she too found good weather, she should be approaching Halifax, Nova Scotia, by now. Apart from a fondness for her officers and men, Ned had other grounds for hoping that she arrived safely: Captain Painter was to report where he had finally launched the lifeboat, well to the west of the anticipated position, so if the operation failed, the corvette would know roughly where to search at the end of the two weeks. Where – in which five hundred square miles – to begin looking!

He looked round the horizon again. The whole operation when they talked it over in the Citadel had seemed extraordinarily simple: its great merit was that so little could go wrong. Most operations that foundered did so because they were too complicated, each successive part resting on its predecessor, so that one failure doomed everything else. Training in the captured German U-boat had been an unexpected bonus for everyone, particularly Jemmy, and finding Yon, who was still a bright and cheerful fellow, as though being in the infernal din of an engine room had left him unmoved, quite able to tease the men who did not share that life. The commando training had been tough, but it left the team (particularly those not commandos) with enormous confidence, certain that Stens, black bangers and the heavy commando knives would carry the day. Ned's own feeling of confidence had held until they had sailed in the *City of Norwich*. There once again he had realized how enormous was the ocean, both in area and weather.

Here he sat on the thwart of a lifeboat, wet (well, now simply damp because the heat of the body, which one could hardly credit, had helped dry at least the inner layers), tired, every muscle aching as the body moved erratically to compensate for the pitching and rolling.

The buttocks were long since numbed as they tried to stay four-square on the hard thwart; feet had long since stopped communicating with the body, and when inspected (as Ned had insisted daily) were sodden and white, like a woman's hands after a day's laundry... Yes, out here in the middle of the Atlantic it all seemed absurd: he felt a sudden and violent resentment against Captain Watts for letting them attempt such a piece of absurdity.

Supper tonight would be lifeboat rations. From now on, there would be a slow weakening of all the men. Suddenly, as though sitting high above the lifeboat and looking down at himself, he realized that his morale was probably the lowest of all the men. He was supposed to be the leader, the one who kept them cheerful, alert for instant reaction to whatever might happen. At the moment he seemed more like an old lag weeping into his beer.

He shook his head and sat up straight and looked round just in time to catch Jemmy's eye. Jemmy winked and murmured. 'Happens to all of us, like constipation. Better now?'

Ned nodded, then grinned as Jemmy confided: 'I had my attack yesterday. You lasted out the longest.'

CHAPTER TWELVE

Sergeant Keeler chopped the eighth notch in the thwart, and as he returned his knife to its sheath commented to no one in particular: 'What I miss most is Naafi tea.'

'So do my kidneys,' said a Marine called Taylor. 'They're convalescing. But now it's a bit warmer, I'd like to spend an evening in the pub, playing darts. A hundred and one up and the loser buys the beer.'

Another Marine, Andrews, said jeeringly: 'That'd mean you'd be paying. You have enough trouble hitting the board, let alone a double top.'

'Only when I'm playing with your darts. You've clipped the feathers so only you know the aim off.'

'My oath, are you saying I cheat?'

'Oh no,' Taylor said airily, 'just that the bird those feathers came from spent its life flying in ever decreasing circles, with the inevitable result.'

'Watch it' Andrews warned darkly, 'or else I'll let on about your set of shove-ha'pennies.'

'*What* about his ha'pennies?' demanded Keeler, who reckoned himself of champion class when he could get the ball of his thumb to work at a well-chalked board.

'He's jealous,' Taylor said quickly. 'Nothing wrong with my set. I can win with ha'pennies taken out of the pub till.'

'Let's see 'em,' said Keeler, holding out a hand.

'You don't think I've brought 'em with me, do you Sarge?'

'Why not, if they're just ordinary ha'pennies? Why didn't you bring them? Where are they?'

'My oppo's got 'em back in Chatham,' Taylor said. 'And just think a minute, Sarge. That twerp plays darts. If you weight a dart or trim one of the flight feathers, you – and only you – know it'll curve one way. You know how much and can allow for it. You give those darts to your opponent and he'll be throwing googlies all over the shop – '

'Hey,' Andrews interrupted, 'are you still saying my darts is nobbled?'

'No, your darts are as untouched as a virgin's top hat. But wiv ha'pennies,' he continued explaining to Keeler, 'you want them to go straight where you aim 'em. There's no advantage in curving to the left or right. Running smooth, yes: that's why we use worn coins. Use a new coin, with a side as rough as a quartermaster's tongue, and it'll stop dead on the board when it should still have some slide.'

'So what's so special about your set – the ones you've left in Chatham?'

'Nothing special: they're just my lucky ones. If you must know, my bird gave 'em to me. She works the cash register in a big shop in Canterbury, and she kept an eye open for smooth ones. Not just smooth: that's not enough. Smooth but still enough metal so there's weight enough to skyve another ha'penny over the line. And smooth enough to go a bit farther than expected when the other chap tries to skyve it.'

Ned found his respect for the humble shove-ha'penny board increasing. Obviously it was not just a question of thumping away and putting chalk marks to one side. The game probably had its own jargon. But he saw that, since a coin once played stayed on the board, using one's own coins had little or no advantage. He waited to hear if Taylor had any more gems of information to reveal about the two great pub sports, but Keeler seemed satisfied, and Andrews obviously reckoned he had wrung an apology from Taylor, though Ned found himself considering a dart as something more than the object thrown at a dartboard and landing with a thud that brought cheers, groans or curses. Yes, perhaps taking the scissors and trimming an eighth of an inch or so off one of the three flight feathers would affect the dart's accuracy. Yet a dart was thrown with such vigour that...oh well, it was time to shake up everyone's liver.

'Sergeant, time for PT.' He called forward to Yon, telling him to come aft to join them.

There were groans from most of the men in the boat. Jemmy turned to the Croupier and offered to take the tiller, an offer which was politely refused, since the Croupier hated any form of physical exercise, claiming that having to do PT at school was the reason why he was so thin.

As Keeler barked orders, the men in the boat dived into two parties by sliding along the thwarts, so that half of them were on the port side and the rest to starboard, leaving the centre-line clear except for the oars.

Ned took his stopwatch from an inside pocket, rolled off the contraceptive that kept it waterproof, and handed it to Keeler, who wound it and set it at zero.

'Right now,' he glanced at Ned. 'Start with you, sir?'

Ned took off his duffel and put it on one side of the thwart with his cap. He stood on the centre of the thwart, balancing himself against the roll of the boat. He spread his arms out to help his balance.

'Ready sir? Right, one, two three, off!'

Ned jumped from one thwart to the other, cheered on by the seated men, reached the bow and touched the stem, turned and made his way aft, thinking yet again that he must look like a startled hen making for the hedge. He reached Jemmy, reached over the Croupier and touched the top of the rudder before turning forward again. He had to make four circuits, knowing that the stopwatch was ticking away and that all the Marine commandos could beat his time hopping on one leg.

Finally he leapt on to his thwart amid cheers, and Keeler announced the time in a lugubrious voice. 'Eleven seconds faster than yesterday, sir – but the sea's calmer.'

'Wait till there's a gale blowing, I'll beat the lot of you,' Ned gasped. 'Come on, Jemmy, your turn.'

'I'll break my bloody ankle, then I'll be no use to anyone,' he grumbled, but stood up and shrugged and twitched himself out of his duffel coat. 'I should have brought my ballet shoes, but I didn't know you girls would ask me to dance.'

A grinning Keeler held up the stopwatch. 'Ready, sir?'

Jemmy was eight seconds slower than the previous day, and as Keeler announced it everyone groaned and several shouted: 'Shame, sir, shame!'

Jemmy bowed ironically, and held up his hand for silence. 'Commander, Lieutenants, Sergeant and you hairy lot swept out of the gutters by Marine sergeant majors and Whale Island GIs, you don't recognize a thoroughbred when you see one. I'm a heavy-weather boat-runner; this semi-calm stuff is too easy!'

Jemmy sat down amid ironic boos and took the tiller from the Croupier, whose erratic progress along the boat reminded Ned of a crippled grasshopper, but who nevertheless was cheered because he had beaten Ned by three seconds.

Ned moved forward to sit beside Keeler, leaving his usual seat clear as the starting place for the rest of the men in the boat. Yon beat the Croupier by four seconds, but the officers' times began to look absurd as the seamen started running. The nimbleness of three of the sailors made up for the generally heavier build of commandos. As the last of them finished his run, Ned held out his hand for the watch, Keeler reset it at zero and handed it over before climbing on to the thwart.

As Ned watched the burly sergeant leaping from thwart to thwart in what seemed to be a controlled forward dive, he was once more startled by the man's agility. By the time Keeler was sitting down again it was clear he had won today's round of what Jemmy dubbed the Western Atlantic Gold Cup.

Keeler then stood up in the boat and took everyone through the rest of the day's exercises: lying on their backs on the thwarts with their legs in the air and 'cycling'; press-ups on the thwarts; lifting each other by standing back to back and linking arms, each man alternately bending forward to raise the other.

At the end of it, Yon grumbled mournfully: 'Although I know we aren't eating any bulky food, I can't get used to not having a regular bowel movement. I feel my injectors will get sooted up!'

'My bowels are reconciled,' Jemmy said. 'It's not shaving that's killing me. My face itches as though it's resting on an anthill.'

'Submariners are supposed to be famous for their beards,' Ned commented. 'Especially submarine "aces".'

'This "ace" was trumped very early on in the beard stakes,' Jemmy said. 'I'm far too beautiful to hide my light under a beard. Anyway, it makes Joan giggle too much: she can't stand being tickled.'

'But you've only known her a few weeks,' Ned said, recalling Captain Watts' Wren secretary. 'From after you came back from the Med.'

'Oh no!' the Croupier exclaimed. 'You've got it the wrong way round. He's known her for years – '

'Two years,' Jemmy interjected.

' – for two years. For half of that time he was in the Med, and Joan was Wrenning up in Harwich, doing a fandango with the Coastal Forces chaps, I expect. Then when Captain Watts set up ASIU with Jemmy and me, and needed a Wren to help feather the nest, guess what?'

'Jemmy just happened to know...'

'Yes. That's why we get such rotten tea. She knows Jemmy likes it weak so the rest of us must have our kidneys waterlogged just to keep him company. That weak stuff saps your sex drive,' he warned Jemmy as an afterthought. 'The tannin dissolves your libido.'

'So now we can count ourselves lucky,' Jemmy said smugly. 'An overabundance of libido – '

He suddenly broke off, eyes staring over the port bow.

'Ned, periscope red two-oh.'

'Don't look round anyone,' Ned shouted. 'Move slowly and casually, hand out the Stens and black bangers.'

'See it?' Jemmy hissed. 'He'll lower it as soon as he's sure there are men in the boat. There! Five seconds from when I saw him. Don't know how long he'd been there.'

'Hundred yards?'

'Hard to say. Perhaps more.'

Most of the men in the lifeboat kept in the same positions they were in when Ned gave his orders, but every third or fourth man was now crouched down between the thwarts, slashing at the lashings of oiled canvas bags that held the Sten guns, black bangers and knives.

The guns were cocked out of sight and the safety catches slid on before they were put on to the thwarts, alongside each man. The black bangers followed, each man putting a total of four in various pockets.

'Bloody marvel we haven't got our duffels on,' the Croupier said. 'Must have been telepathy, Ned, that made you time the PT!'

'Yes, but that Ted at the periscope must have wondered what was going on if he saw us running up and down! Could he see that much detail, Jemmy?'

'Yes, if he flips the close-range lever. Narrows the field of vision but increases the magnification. If he saw the runners he'll be entering it in the log. No sense of humour, these Teds!'

Ned felt a hand offering him black bangers, and Sergeant Keeler's voice from below the thwart muttered: 'Hot cross bun day, sir. Four be enough? Right?' There was the slight grating of metal. 'Sten's beside you on the right. Ready for three spare magazines? One, two, three. Now the knife. That's the lot, sir.'

Keeping his eyes on the patch of sea to port, and cursing that he had not spotted any feather of spray which would have indicated the direction the submarine was travelling, Ned bent his knees sideways to let Keeler pass to give weapons to Jemmy and the Croupier.

He began to see dozens of periscopes and closed his eyes for a few moments. Was this really it? Finally the moment when Mr Churchill's 'diabolical cunning' was needed? Hydra, Triton, Watts, Clare, BP, black bangers, the pain in his left hand, Enigma...thoughts, pictures forming memories, raced through his mind as though a cine projector was running wild.

Jemmy said anxiously: 'You did see it, didn't you Ned?'

For a moment the unreality left Ned unsure. Sitting in a lifeboat was unreal. The thought of pockets full of black bangers was unreal. The Croupier had been rattling on about libido, which was an unreal sort of conversation to be going on in a lifeboat in the middle of the western Atlantic. The whole bloody thing was unreal – but so had been the dive-bombing attacks on the *Aztec* and the clatter of her guns hour after hour, until finally the *Aztec* had wallowed to a stop, and sunk.

'Yes, I saw it for a moment.'

'Good, I was afraid I'd imagined it.'

'I can see dozens now,' Ned admitted.

'That's normal. Shut your eyes tight. They'll be gone when you open 'em again.'

Then Ned saw it. 'Same place, couple of hundred yards,' he hissed.

'Got it. Ah, see the flash of the lens? He's having a look round for aircraft. Just like they teach 'em at the Baltic training schools.'

'I *didn't,*' the Croupier said emphatically. 'Are you sure it wasn't just a floating piece of dunnage?'

Dunnage in the form of pieces of timber used to prevent cargo shifting in merchant ships was often left floating after a torpedoing. The wood went grey and became waterlogged. More dunnage had been fired at or bombed, Ned thought ironically, than real U-boats. Rarely did a baulk of six by four float vertically, yet the more he thought about that fleeting glimpse, the less sure he was.

Yon had no doubts and Jemmy was certain: 'That was a periscope. I saw the reflection on the prism. Keep your eyes open; it'll be the only time you can look at a Ted periscope without the risk of being torpedoed.'

'No,' the Croupier said bitterly, 'the bastards will probably just ram us, like so many of them have already. Not us, but all the other lifeboats.'

CHAPTER THIRTEEN

The four men sat silently watching while pretending to be talking normally, gesticulating from time to time. The rest of the men in the boat resumed their conversations with phlegmatic acceptance.

'Five minutes exactly, I make it,' Jemmy said. 'He'll be – '

'Abeam to port, two hundred yards,' Ned said quickly, 'Not so high this time.'

Jemmy, counting the seconds, was just saying: '…nineteen… and twenty…' when the periscope disappeared again.

'Tell us,' Ned told Jemmy. 'What's he doing and what's he going to do?'

'Christ, Ned, have a heart. I'll nip down and ask him! But I'd guess the first time we saw him he'd just put up his periscope for a routine look round and spotted us. Very sensibly he lowered it and sent his lads to action stations. Then he pops up his looking glass for another precautionary look to make sure it's not a trap. He'll take one more look and then deal with us, one way or another.'

'That's what you'd do?' Ned asked.

'No bloody fear. We don't go in for ramming lifeboats or dropping grenades into 'em, and surfacing just out of curiosity would have been suicide in the Med because the Luftwaffe is so busy. Still, Coastal Command planes and the Americans aren't exactly deafening us out here.'

Ned raised his voice so all the men could hear. 'Well, lads, the chap we've been waiting for is having a look at us. The two men nearest the lashings on the oars should cast them off without making a meal of it. Keep the Stens out of sight. Up to now it's all happening as we expected. One last thing – put your earplugs in as late as you can: I want you to hear orders right up to the last moment. Oh yes, and take the plugs out when it's all over!'

The men laughed and then resumed their chatting, not looking very 'diabolical'. Yet on second thoughts, perhaps they did. He had become accustomed to them being unshaven with hair matted, and to their dress, which ranged from roll-neck jerseys to once-gaudy but now drab tartan lumberjack's coats.

'Any moment now,' Jemmy warned. 'He's moving aft, so he might turn up on our starboard side. Obviously he doesn't know we've spotted him: expects to take us by surprise.'

Ned eased himself round so that he could watch the starboard side and told Sergeant Keeler, who was facing aft: 'Keep a sharp lookout on the quarter.'

The grey paint on the lifeboat had obviously lasted well enough while the boat was slung in its davits on board the *City of Norwich*, but now, constantly soaked with salt water, it was beginning to peel and flake. Ned made a conscious effort to concentrate on the U-boat, and as he focused his eyes he saw the rust-streaked, grey tube poke up on the starboard beam, much closer.

'Green nine oh, fifty yards – hell, it's gone again!'

'Okay,' Jemmy said, 'this is it: he's just taking a last look, to position himself. He's turned, putting us to leeward of him.'

As if her captain heard Jemmy's words the U-boat began to surface. Ned watched fascinated as first the periscopes – there were two, one much shorter than the other – rose a few feet, and then the conning tower surfaced, surprisingly small and spilling water like an enormous overfilled saucepan. There was the 88 mm gun and its platform emerging like a small twisted sea monster with a long snout. Then under the water the waves were still for a moment as finally the great whale-like dark-grey hull of the submarine surfaced, lean and menacing, its plating mottled with streaks of rust like dried bloodstains, streams of water pouring from slots in the casing. Cabbage water, Ned thought; green and smelly, the side of restaurants the patrons never saw.

'She's a type IX,' Jemmy hissed. 'Two diesels, about twenty knots on the surface, nine or ten submerged for a short period – you can see the 88 mm, and there's a pair of 20 mm cannons on AA mountings.'

She was the first U-boat Ned had ever seen at sea, yet the visit to the prize boat had not prepared him for it: as usual, a vessel at sea seemed much larger than lying alongside in a dock.

Her bow seemed sharper and the flatness of the deck more pronounced as swell waves swept across in whorls of white and green water, and he could now hear the suck and gurgle as it swirled out of the long line of scuppers formed by the flat deck plating fitting on to the hull which, now higher out of the water, looked more like a pregnant monster.

'Here we go,' Ned said as he saw a figure in a peaked cap suddenly appear in the surprisingly narrow and pear-shaped conning tower. The man was followed by three more.

'The skipper is usually first out,' Jemmy muttered, 'so watch for him: he'll be the only one with a white cap cover – it's a German affectation.'

The lifeboat now lying parallel to the U-boat soon rolled less as the comparatively huge hull, most of it still below the water, began to make a lee, a giant grey breakwater appearing out of nowhere in the western Atlantic to block the swells. The Captain's face went black – he was obviously holding up binoculars.

'He's inspecting us,' Jemmy said, as though carrying on a cricket commentary through a pause in the game.

Ned called to his men. 'Turn and take a normal interest. Don't wave, though: think of him as having sunk your ship last week.'

'That's a lousy paint job,' Leading Seaman Jarvis said contemptuously. 'They didn't use a primer. Can't put undercoat on bare metal and expect it to hold.'

'Belt up Jarvis,' said Keeler amiably. 'If they hear you they'll rig a stage special and give you a pot o' paint and a brush.'

'They're not manning the Oerlikons,' Jemmy murmured. 'I'd been having nightmares about them using cannons to rouse us out.'

'We'd get 'em with Stens before they could fit the magazines and cock the guns,' Ned said. 'That's the main reason we've got the bloody things.'

'You're a marvel, guv'nor,' Jemmy said sarcastically.

The Croupier grunted. 'No good relying on you, Jemmy. You're supposed to be the sub expert. That great lump of rusty steel over there is probably Vichy French and has got lost trying to smuggle Gauloises from Dakar to Devil's Island. He's simply going to ask the way. Tell him to go west until he sees land, turn left and then keep the land on his right. Bound to get to French Guiana eventually.'

The U-boat captain's face reappeared as he let the binoculars drop to hang on their straps. He bent his head, obviously to speak to someone below, and then lifted something like a stubby and bulbous trumpet.

'Here we go,' said Jemmy. 'We now sing "The Ride of the Valkyries", royalties payable to *B der U*.'

The voice over the loud-hailer was curiously distorted and had an echo like a cry from a deep cave.

'Vot sheep?'

'Tell him we're Bo-Peep and we've *lost* our sheep,' growled Jemmy.

Ned stood up, careful to make sure that the four gold bands on his sleeve were visible, so the German Commander would know he was either the chief engineer (since at this distance he would be unable to distinguish the coloured stripes that engineers wore next to the gold) or the captain.

'The *Silver Star*,' Ned shouted through cupped hands, slurring the words and giving his men more time to size up the task. He could vaguely hear Sergeant Keeler giving last-minute instructions.

'Vot sheep? I no hear!'

'The *Silver Star*.'

'Ah, see *Zilver Zaar*. Ja?'

'Christ, he'll have me talking in rhyme soon,' Ned muttered, and then to add to any confusion, shouted back: 'No, the *Silver Star*!'

'Ja, I hear. *Zilver Zaar*.'

Ned waved an affirmative and sat down.

'Now for it,' he murmured. 'Have they given up collecting captains, or are they tossing grenades to the starving seamen...'

'I'd like to take off the top of his skull with a burst from my Sten,' the Croupier said. 'I've got Indian blood in me.'

'*Ja*, ver' gut,' the disembodied voice came across the water. 'The captain – stand up!'

Ned stood up, carefully miming reluctance and cursing as the two black bangers in his left-hand pocket jabbed his bottom rib and made him gasp.

'You look very stern and determined,' Jemmy said. 'As the Press photographers say: "Hold it, sir, just one more!" '

'Bringk you boat alongzide.'

Ah yes, Ned thought. 'Come into my parlour' said the spider, but don't let us make it seem easy. Nor too hard, he suddenly realized. Now the U-boat Commander had the sunken ship's name (or thought he had), a couple of grenades tossed in the boat would finish the job. Still, captains could be questioned about convoy routes...

He turned forward and gave orders to the men to ship the oars. 'Be lubberly about it, though: merchant seamen don't often row.'

'Lucky bleeders,' Able Seaman Coles said loudly, betraying his Cockney origin.

'And make sure you're sitting on your Stens,' Ned cautioned. 'Your grandmothers may have warned you it'd give you piles, but that fellow over there has a pair of Zeiss eight-fifties slung round his neck and can spot which of you hasn't washed behind your ears.'

By now the oars were in the rowlocks, but the men were taking a delight in being lubberly.

'Capitan – I do not haff all *die Nacht.*'

'We're coming!' Ned called, his voice quavery. 'Very weak...no food.'

'*Ja, ja.* Hurry!'

'Croupier, stay at the tiller,' Ned said. 'Jemmy, get these beggars rowing evenly. I want to sit here like a poacher waiting for a rabbit to pop out.'

'Bloody hell,' Jemmy complained, 'we'll be lucky if I don't pop the boat on top of that son of a bitch.'

'Leave it to my unerring eye,' the Croupier announced.

'Row you buggers!' Jemmy suddenly bellowed. 'In...out...in...out... Mortlake Bridge coming up, Oxford leads by a canvas...in...out...half of you sods are Cambridge... in...out... That's the time. My learned colleague will now bash us all against that horrible rusty monster. Abide with me...'

Ned, hand in each pocket, turned the black bangers so that the safety pins were uppermost. The Sten was uncomfortable to sit on. Looks as though bringing them was a waste of time. Jesus, only a few more yards to go.

Every man in the lifeboat had his orders about what to do next; every man had practised it on the prize U-boat. So here we go. Clumsily Ned stood up to make his way to the bow.

'No change in plan,' he said to Jemmy and the Croupier, and as he threaded his way past the rowers, careful not to be hit by a loom or upset the careful lack of rhythm, he repeated to all the men, 'no change...no change.'

Then he was standing at the bow, clear of the oarsmen, and he saw that the Croupier was steering the boat so that it would go alongside just beneath the gun platform, whose guard rails stuck outwards like the bottom set of buck teeth.

He felt in a pocket and then crouched down, as though he was being seasick, and pressed in the rubber earplugs. Suddenly he was in a curious almost silent world where the only noise was the pumping of his own blood.

He stood up again to find the lifeboat within ten yards of the U-boat and quickly noted a line of stanchions with a single wire running along the deck beside the conning tower, obviously intended to save anyone on deck from falling overboard or being washed away by a wave. The forward side of the conning tower with the bridge above was thin and parallel sided, jam jar shaped, but the after side tapered like a wedge of cheese to form the gun platform, wide enough to give the gunners plenty of room.

The sudden surge of a swell wave lifted the lifeboat and thrust it forward, and as the stem grazed the stanchions Ned leapt on board.

Even as he jumped he realized that the deck would be more slippery than he had expected: a skin of slimy green weed mottled the steel plating like an unshaven man with a skin disease, and there were speckles of the rough pyramids of barnacles. A red shield painted on the side of the conning tower had a black battleaxe in the middle.

Just as Ned was regaining his balance on the U-boat's deck and noting that the lifeboat was slewing round slightly, still pinned against the stanchions, an amplified voice bellowed from above: 'Captain commen op here! Stand from the rail!'

Ned stepped back and glanced up, looking for a steel ladder or footplates. A German sailor, blond-bearded and burly, was standing beside the German captain. Ned saw him cock an ugly-looking sub-machine gun, and rest its barrel on the fore side of the conning tower. A Schmeisser – he recognized the shape. Fired more than a thousand rounds a minute.

Now they had the *Silver Star*'s captain on board they were going to use the rest of the survivors in the boat for target practice.

Ned pressed himself against the conning tower, hidden by a welded plate jutting out for twelve inches like a hat brim and obviously intended to deflect spray.

One banger might stop that blond bastard starting to shoot; a second should give the lads in the boat time to get on board.

His right hand came out of his coat pocket with a black banger and his left index finger slid into the ring of the safety pin. A quick jerk pulled it free: now only the curved handle, shaped into the grenade, stopped it exploding. As he threw it the handle would fly free, and five seconds later...

Jemmy was watching from the boat but the commandos had not moved: Ned guessed Jemmy could clearly see the man with the Schmeisser and was waiting to see if Ned could do anything before letting the men try to cut the sailor down with the Stens.

Ned took a quick step back and lobbed the grenade up into the conning tower six feet above him, ducking back under the metal skirting. Five seconds. Obviously the Germans were not expecting anything; in fact once the English captain was hauled below, that Schmeisser would open up with its distinctive whiplash noise. Three...four...five. The explosion inside the narrow cupola formed by the conning tower was shocking, despite his earplugs.

He pulled the pin from a second black banger, took a step back and lobbed the grenade upwards into the centre of what he now saw looked like a smoking stubby funnel of a coaster.

Just as he began counting and realized he was within three feet of steps welded into the conning tower, he saw his commandos and seamen rising up in the boat like crouching animals beginning to leap, and in the second before the grenade burst he realized that Jemmy, the Croupier, Sergeant Keeler and Yon were already scrambling over the stanchions.

He started up the welded steps and paused for a moment before his head topped the edge of the conning tower to get a third grenade, cursing as he changed it from his left hand to his right and pulled out the pin.

There were four men in the tiny bridge section, all holding their heads and stumbling and staggering into the stubby, waist-high periscope pedestals and the azimuth compass, obviously stunned into near stupor. What mattered now were the men still below.

Jumping on to the bridge, Ned reached for the circular hatch in the top of the conning tower, looked down and saw several white faces staring up at him. He dropped the grenade on top of them and swung the heavy hatch shut.

In five seconds' time, he though grimly, that banger should spoil the German second-in-command's concentration enough that he will not realize he could save his boat (perhaps at the cost of the Captain's life) by submerging just a few feet – enough to float off his attackers. But the second-in-command can't tell what's happening and until the third banger explodes at his feet down there – there it goes – he only knows there have been two violent explosions up on the bridge.

Ned cursed that he had no Sten gun and wrenched the commando knife clear of the sheath inside his jacket. He stepped across to the blond seaman, who was still staggering like a hopeless drunk with the Schmeisser in his hands and suspended by the sling round his neck. Suddenly the seaman's eyes focused just long enough for him to raise the barrel and aim it at Ned, now less than a foot away. Ned slapped the muzzle to one side with his left hand and lunged forward with his right, and as the commando knife thudded into the man's stomach the Schmeisser fired a burst.

Ned waited for the pain: obviously, from the whiplashing and ricocheting bullets round the inside of the bridge, he had not pushed the gun far enough away, and he clutched his stomach with his left hand as he pulled the knife from the collapsing body with his right. But no blood, no pain, no holes. His left hand revealed it was just imagination.

And there was Keeler's head coming up over the far side of the conning tower, bellowing (Ned could see the man's mouth opening and closing, but the earplugs kept out the words) and in a second sitting astride, aiming his Sten at another lieutenant and a seaman. Ned suddenly realized that the U-boat Captain, riddled by the Schmeisser, was sprawled on the deck: it was his blood that was running in broad zigzags across the steel plating as the U-boat rolled and pitched.

'Keep them covered but ready with your grenades!' Ned yelled as he tugged the pin from his last black banger, lifted the hatch, dropped it down and shut the hatch again.

As Ned waited for the explosion Jemmy appeared at the after side of the bridge, obviously having scrambled up on to the gun platform, followed by the Croupier and Yon. Marines followed, elbowing them aside to get to Sergeant Keeler, who announced in a sudden silence: 'If these buggers dive, we're going to get wet feet.'

Before Ned could give any orders, Keeler had pressed the Sten into his hands, flung open the hatch, threw in yet another black banger to one side and started off down the ladder, bellowing: 'Last man down is a sissy!'

The grenade exploded below inside the conning tower as Ned reached the ladder and followed Keeler down into the gloom, his nose tingling and his throat protesting from the reek of the exploded grenades. Someone above was in such a hurry that Ned found his right hand nipped by a shoe, and he looked up to see Jemmy.

'Hold it!' he yelled, but Jemmy, oblivious with earplugs in place, took no notice, forcing Ned to step down faster. He glanced down to see that Keeler had jumped down the next hatch into the control room itself and was now crouched, knife in one hand, grenade in the other, threatening the group of Germans standing rigidly at the foot of the ladder and surrounded by a bewildering number of gauges, wheels and valves.

Ned took one look at them and saw they too were all stupefied by the grenades: they were still on their feet but their eyes were vacant, like a knocked-out boxer in the moment before he hits the canvas.

'Hold 'em, Ned,' Jemmy yelled as he jumped down the last few steps. 'Yon and I will secure the engine room mob!'

He turned and ran aft, obviously quite at home in the pipe-lined tube of the U-boat's hull.

'Shall I read 'em the riot act, Ned?'

As Ned pulled out his earplugs he turned to find the Croupier was the last person down the ladder, which was now crowded with commandos and seamen holding Sten guns and obviously feeling cheated.

'What about the two in the conning tower?'

'Jemmy and I knocked 'em cold: they won't be wasting our time. We've got them down here now. Who shot the Captain? I didn't think you had a Sten, and anyway I heard a Schmeisser.'

'That German sailor waiting to knock off you lot!'

'But he's been knifed!'

'Yes, but get on and tell these Teds they're prisoners – the ones that aren't too deafened!'

Jemmy's bellows from aft brought Corporal Davis and six commandos racing to join him, crouching with Stens and grenades at the ready.

That leaves the forward part of the ship, Ned thought – and the wireless cabin with the Enigma machine. Damnation! The reek of explosives had slowed him down, yet the whole purpose of this operation was to get into the wireless cabin! In the time he had been standing there the wireless officer or operator could have fired a destruction charge and destroyed the Enigma and cipher manuals.

Realizing that he still held the bloodstained commando knife in one hand and a Sten in the other, he ran into the cabin, thankful that the hours spent on board the prize U-boat had made him familiar with the layout.

The curtain was drawn and he ripped it aside. The cabin was in darkness and he felt for the switch and turned it. There it was: a tiny desk to the left had an Enigma machine on it, and to the right was a built-in table with a Morse key in front and a big radio transmitter, its front studded with dials.

He bent over the Enigma. That curious *Ersatz* smell of German synthetics or oil. He lifted up the lid. Yes, it had the four rotors fitted in place: it was a new Mark III German Navy Enigma. All he needed now was the manual giving the daily settings.

He jerked at the drawers in the metal desk but all were locked, and the shelves above the Enigma contained what were obviously only routine reference books.

Steady now, he told himself: we've got the Enigma. The manual giving the setting will be locked up, and the Second Lieutenant will have the key. So – a Marine in here guarding the equipment and another on the doorway.

By now seamen and Marines of the boarding party were rounding up Germans in the forward part of the ship and, following orders, keeping them in groups where they had been found.

There were a dozen Germans in the control room, all sitting on the deck with their hands on their heads and facing the Croupier, who was seated comfortably in a chair facing them, holding a Sten gun. Round them all were control wheels ranging in diameter from bicycle wheels to saucers; gauges as big as grandfather clocks and as small as travelling alarm clocks. At least one – Ned recognized it as the very precise depth gauge – was a vertical glass tube marked with graduations, like an enormous clinical thermometer. The Papenberg meter, or some such name. Every wheel had its label; many of the dials had red sectors. Several valves went directly to pipes – obviously the ones that were closed off rapidly as depth-charges caused damage.

'All the key men here,' the Croupier reported. 'Jemmy just brought in the Ted Engineer and tossed him into the pool. He's gone back to make sure Yon and his ERAs and electrician's mate know which wicks to trim.'

'You've got the Second Officer?'

'The wireless wallah? Yes, he's that wanked-out specimen there, fourth from the left. Except for the Engineer, they're still too deafened and stunned to hear anything or talk sense. What happened, did you drop a banger down here?'

'Yes, it landed in the middle of them.'

'The poor sods will never hear Wagner again! When do we start this cruise?'

'As soon as Jemmy and Yon are ready.'

'Jemmy said all the batteries are topped up, the boat's fairly low on fuel, and everything is working. Want me to question the Engineer?' the Croupier asked.

'Yes, but first I'm going to look around on deck. I keep seeing a Tribal steaming straight for us at full speed.'

'Mind the corpses. Pity it was the Captain.'

'He'd just ordered the seaman with the Schmeisser to kill all of you in the boat,' Ned said quietly.

'Then belay that last pipe and don't invite me to the funeral.'

Funeral...committing bodies to the deep...a prayer or two and a volley in salute. No, Ned decided; no prayers and no salutes: that Captain had just ordered the cold-blooded murder of more than twenty men in an open boat, and Ned could still see the seaman's evil, expectant grin as he cocked the Schmeisser. Two murderers. No, there was going to be no funeral for them; no volley fired in salute.

He climbed the ladder into the conning tower and then up to the bridge. The dead men seemed smaller; death had shrivelled them. He picked up the Schmeisser and examined it, setting the safety as he did so. It was a well-balanced gun.

And the lifeboat was still nearly alongside: Leading Seaman Jarvis had remembered his orders to secure the lifeboat's painter.

With the U-boat still lying beam-on to the seas, the lifeboat had drifted to the full extent of the painter, thirty feet to leeward.

The sky was still a patchwork of clouds and weak blue sky; the wind waves were not above three feet on top of the longer swell waves, which were the ones making the U-boat roll.

It was then he noticed the stench coming up from below: an unpleasant mixture of diesel fumes, boiled cabbage, *Ersatz* materials, the sickly warm smell of hot engines and oil, damp clothing, and the reek of too many men crowded together for too long in too small a space.

He looked aft over the gun platform with its guard rails angled outward like the beginnings of a magpie's crude nest of sticks and mud. Nearest were the twin 20 mm cannons. They had a good field of fire, providing the U-boat was steering away from attacking aircraft. The bigger gun with its square armoured shield was also well placed, although the gunners would be deafened by muzzle blast if the 20 mm cannons fired over their heads.

He took several deep breaths, holding each lung full for as long as he could. Up here it was fresh – he found it easy to ignore the two bodies which were symbols of the depraved side of U-boat warfare. Defenders tried to sink attackers, and vice versa, but until recent times it was accepted that once a ship was sunk the survivors were left alone to save themselves if they could. Hitler's Navy had now changed the rules – just as the Kaiser's Army had been the first to use poison gas – and that crumpled body there still wearing a cap with a white cap cover represented a U-boat Captain who was quite willing to take an enemy ship's captain prisoner and kill other survivors, and the seaman was just a pervert, sexually aroused by killing. Ned realized that this was the example of the way the new Germany went to war. Chivalry to these Swastika-studded thugs was just a joke. He counted the Swastika badges and emblems he could see on the dead Captain's uniform. Five. And another on his cap.

Yes, the first time he had seen the new warfare had been at Kingsnorth in Kent, during the Battle of Britain. Two hundred or more German fighters and bombers coming in high over Romney Marsh had been attacked by three RAF squadrons. For a few minutes there had been the spasmodic howling of planes diving and climbing and the brief stutter of machine guns and cannons; then had come the faint screams, rapidly getting louder and shriller, of crippled planes diving into the ground, the pilots either killed or trapped.

But some of the crippled planes came down in shallow dives, so that the pilots could bale out, and five parachutes floated, as innocent-looking as dandelion balls. Three of the parachutes had come from German planes, two from RAF, and some time after the German air armada had disappeared to the north-westward, towards London, a German Me 109 with a red-painted propeller boss flew in and methodically fired long bursts into the two RAF parachutes. One of them began to burn, the silk crinkling until instead of being hemispherical it was a bundle of cloth falling at an ever-increasing speed, landing close by on a road, where the impact left the shape of a body on the tarmac. The other parachute seemed undamaged, but through binoculars Ned could see the pilot's body hanging inert, slowly spinning, like a lynch victim hanging by the neck from a tree branch. These two examples of the new warfare he had seen himself; the third he had heard on the German radio propaganda broadcasts – Hitler's 'Commando Order'. This really was a direct order by Hitler: the German broadcasters were proud of that. It seemed that Hitler (alarmed or angered by the Allied commando raids on the Channel coast) had ordered that in future any captured commandos would be executed at once. He claimed their activities came outside the scope of the Geneva Convention.

Ned exhaled in what was almost a sigh. Down below Yon would be ready to handle the diesels and Jemmy would have allocated his own chosen submariners to the various valves and levers. The Croupier and the commandos would have the prisoners under guard.

Fifty Germans (less two, of course), but only twenty-three in the British boarding party. The ten seamen and four officers in his party would be doing watch and watch about, handling the submarine, and that left only nine Marines to keep a guard over the Germans. But…but…there was nowhere in the submarine that fifty prisoners could be kept together. Now beginning to feel a chill he knew was not entirely caused by his duffel coat being left in the lifeboat, he had at last fully realized that a couple of determined Germans could lead the rest into retaking the submarine. They might lose a couple of men, but a few fanatics could be persuasive. Indeed, he thought soberly, reverse the roles – a German boarding party of twenty-three trying to hold fifty British submariners…

He turned and went down the ladder, arriving in the control room just as Jemmy came forward from the engine room.

'Ah, Ned! We've trimmed the wicks, checked the gauges and muttered the magic spell known only to us denizens of the deep. In other words, sir, the engine room reports it is ready for you to get under way, on or below the briny waves.'

'Very well. But we have too many passengers.'

The Croupier sniffed and commented: 'I was going to mention that.'

'Very well,' Ned said crisply, seeing quite clearly what he had to do. 'Fetch Yon, and I want you and him to select which German engine room staff you might need.' He thought quickly and decided that for Enigma he needed only the Second Lieutenant, who was responsible for the wireless and Enigma machine, and the wireless operator, who actually transmitted the signals, tapping away at the Morse key.

'I know who we want,' Jemmy said. 'I'll go aft and sort 'em out; then we can dump the rest.'

Ned turned to the Croupier. 'You can be the compère. Start by introducing the officers to me – just point 'em out.'

'Well, that red-headed bugger at the end – '

'Wait,' Ned interrupted, 'we might as well start the dumping. Sergeant Keeler, take Corporal Davis and four men to the forward torpedo room, and made sure that all of them have Stens. We'll use that compartment as the main cell. Don't let them crowd you. And Keeler, although there's no need to be trigger-happy, make sure Davis takes no risks. And have a man get the Schmeisser – I left it on the bridge.'

Ned turned back to the Croupier, who went on: 'As I was saying, that red-headed bugger at the end is the First Lieutenant and a troublemaker. He's already threatening me with what will happen to me personally when *Der Führer* invades England.'

'He's a candidate for the torpedo room?'

'Carried unanimously,' the Croupier said. 'He probably has dhobi rash and crabs as well as fetid breath, and he'd be the kind of golfer who'd move the lay of his ball when you weren't looking.'

'A real bounder, eh?' Ned said in a pukka-sahib voice as a Marine came down the ladder carrying the Schmeisser.

'An absolute cad,' the Croupier echoed.

'Very well, who's next?'

'The fourth man from the left, he's the Second Officer. Seems a quiet type.'

'Just check he's also responsible for the wireless. Make it casual.'

The Croupier made a comment to the First Lieutenant, and then said something in a similar tone of voice to the Second Lieutenant.

'Yes, I checked with Barbarossa as well. Usual division of duties – First Lieutenant responsible for torpedoes and gunnery; the Second is wireless – which covers the box of tricks, I assume. The Sub-lieutenant is navigator.'

The red-headed First Lieutenant barked a question, but the Croupier appeared to ignore him, telling Ned in a conversational tone: 'He's asking where his Captain is.'

'Tell him, at a suitable time, that he was accidentally shot dead by the blond German with the Schmeisser.'

'Nothing will give me greater pleasure. Who's next?'

'The Engineer.'

'Ah, a very intense little chap with a thick Hamburg accent. He's aft with Yon, and ERA Brown's keeping an eye on him. Then there's the Sub-lieutenant – the red-faced kid next to red whiskers.'

'Who comes next – a warrant officer?'

'Yes, the *Obersteuermann*. The portly character, seventh from the left, who looks like a cartoon of a chief petty officer. Quite a lad, I suspect; one of the seamen boasted that beer-belly served with Schepke but was down with VD so he missed the last trip from which Schepke didn't return.'

Again the red-headed First Lieutenant barked his question and the Croupier answered him casually, as though dealing with a persistent small boy.

The effect was extraordinary: with an enraged bellow the First Lieutenant dragged an automatic from his pocket, pulled back the slide to cock it and aimed at Ned, who was between him and the ladder, towards which he prepared to make an awkward leap.

The metallic squawk of the Croupier's Sten was deafening in the confined space and the red-headed man's body crashed against the foot of the ladder as Ned moved to one side. Ned picked up the pistol, slid over the safety catch, and said calmly to the Croupier: 'Thanks, I didn't expect anyone to have pistols: we'd better search the rest, but I was getting tired of his interruptions. Now, we need the wireless operator.'

'Wait a moment,' the Croupier said, eyeing the body of the First Lieutenant. 'He's dead all right, isn't he?'

'Very,' Ned said. 'Don't go for a head shot next time, though: too risky. At that range, hits in the chest or stomach solve any problems.'

'I was just showing off,' the Croupier admitted. 'I noticed he was tensing up for a leap, and the ladder seemed the obvious destination. Sorry about his automatic.'

'Sitting birds,' Ned chided.

'Yes,' the Croupier admitted, 'but I don't think we'll have any more – hello, the Second…'

He broke off as the white-faced and swaying Second Lieutenant fainted, bouncing off the *Obersteuermann*'s stomach as he fell.

Ned said: 'Ignore him. Let them think we'll kill 'em all without compunction.'

'This mother's boy will, too,' Jemmy commented, having just arrived from the engine room. 'I wondered what was going on. Ned, let me have that pistol. I can keep a watch for the odd joker while you and the Croupier have your gossip. What did red whiskers do, use bad language?'

Ned handed over the pistol and reminded the Croupier: 'The wireless operator.'

The Croupier spoke rapidly in German and a small, round-faced youth with protruding teeth stepped nervously forward.

'Well, there he is, the Third Reich's answer to Marconi and Samuel Morse. Looks about eighteen years old.' He asked a question in German and then said to Ned: 'Sorry, nineteen. Bavarian, from his accent.'

'Right, I want the Second Lieutenant (when he recovers), wireless operator, cook – or chief steward, or whatever they call him – and *Obersteuermann* to stand fast; the rest can go forward to the torpedo room.'

'Not all at once,' Jemmy said. 'Send half, and the rest once we've dived. We'll never trim a strange boat if we start with all that weight forward. Might even store some of 'em in the after torpedo room.'

'You'd better see how many torpedoes are left,' Ned said. 'We might as well fire 'em off and save the weight.'

'I wish you'd asked the First Lieutenant before the Croupier potted him,' Jemmy grumbled, and then questioned the pot-bellied warrant officer.

'He says five left out of the fourteen,' Jemmy said. 'Four in the forward tubes, one in the stern tube.'

'Fire 'em when you get bored,' Ned said.

He beckoned to two of the boarding party, Ordinary Seamen Keene and Beer. 'Get the duffels and suitcase wireless transmitter out of the lifeboat and bring them down. Don't bump the wireless too much: it's supposed to be shockproof and waterproof, but... And then pull the bung out of the boat and cast off the painter.'

Jemmy pointed at the dead First Lieutenant. 'Some of his mates can hoist him up the ladder. Giving 'em a funeral?'

Ned suddenly had second thoughts. 'What do you think?'

'Those two up in the conning tower are thugs and this fellow is the same. Funerals for bastards who can massacre survivors in a lifeboat? Leave 'em on the casing, so when we dive...'

Jemmy had echoed his own ideas. He ordered a couple of Marines to go up the ladder and guard the Germans hauling up the body. 'Perhaps you would be so kind as to order half the Teds forward, and a trio to take their late lamented Lieutenant aloft and place him beside his late Captain?' he asked the Croupier with mock formality.

As half the prisoners in the control room stood up and shambled forward, herded by Marines holding Stens, three German seamen began hoisting the First Lieutenant's body up the ladder, cursing because it was so flaccid, some limb flopping and jamming in the steps the moment it was not held.

Ned said to Jemmy: 'I see the Second Lieutenant has recovered. Is Yon going to give me fuel reports, and so on?'

'If you want, but I got the answers from the German Engineer.'

'Before we do that, shall we dive?'

As Ned said it, he knew his unfamiliarity with submariners made it sound like an invitation to dance.

'Whenever you're ready,' Jemmy said thankfully. 'I feel more naked with this boat surfaced than ever I did in the lifeboat.' He pulled Ned's arm and led him over to the wireless cabin out of earshot of the rest. 'Ned, have you thought of dumping two thirds of these Teds in the lifeboat? Having to guard the sons of bitches twenty-four hours a day is going to be a strain.'

Ned shook his head. 'I had thought of it, but suppose another U-boat finds them, just like this one spotted us? Dönitz would know at once that we've got a Mark III Enigma, the Triton manual – the lot. So he'd change the Triton cipher. It'd only take him a month – until all the boats now on patrol get back and are given new books – and we'd be even worse off.'

'There's another way.'

'Yes, I thought of that too.'

'Why so squeamish?'

'Putting thirty or forty Teds in a lifeboat and then ramming it is just the sort of thing we're supposed to be fighting this war to stop, Jemmy.'

'They were going to mow *us* down with that Schmeisser.'

'The Captain and the blond seaman were, and they're dead.'

Jemmy shrugged his shoulders, his head jerking in twitches which indicated that the depth of his feelings belied his quiet voice. 'You're the boss, Ned, but warn the Marines that they should shoot the moment there's any trouble. A Sten bullet won't go through the hull plating. Just keep clear of the gauges.'

'I was going to tell Keeler that anyway. Stopping that crazy First Lieutenant dead in his tracks was a lesson to the Teds: you saw how the Second Officer passed out at the sight!'

'Yes, but he's a thinking man. Yon Cassius with a lean and hungry look. Remember Caesar's warning – such men are dangerous.'

'The thinkers sometimes outsmart themselves!'

'By the way,' Jemmy said, 'we can put twenty prisoners in the after torpedo room.'

At that moment three thuds and a hail from the Croupier warned that the Marines who had guarded the German seamen as they hoisted the red-headed Lieutenant's body up the ladder were now back below again.

Ned walked over and told the Croupier: 'We're going to dive, and as soon as Jemmy has stuck a trim, or whatever he calls it, we'll shift the rest of these chaps aft – Jemmy's offering the after torpedo room.'

The Croupier looked round at all the dials and gauges. 'What happens if I accidentally put a bullet into one of these dials?'

'Jemmy will be very cross. I've just been talking to him about it. The hull plating is all right, though, but if you shoot as well as you did with our red-headed late friend, the bullets will stay in the target.'

'Can't guarantee it,' the Croupier said cheerfully and then added, an anxious note in his voice: 'Have you ever been down in a sub before, Ned?'

'No, and I'm not looking forward to it. Flying in the face of Nature as far as I'm concerned. Submarines and aeroplanes. Fins and wings, ughh!'

Yon came through the narrow space leading from the engine room, a small corridor lined with bunks on each side, and grinned at Ned. 'All tickety-boo, Ned; both diesels ready to start purring, all the gauges poised to say the right things, ammeters and voltmeters show the batteries are fully charged and topped up. So as far as the engine room is concerned, we're ready. The Blohm and Voss diesels are fantastic.'

Ned listened carefully. Yon's voice was confident – in fact this would be how he reported to the commander when serving in a British submarine. Since he too spoke German, he had no trouble reading gauges and labels on valves.

Ned turned to Jemmy, nodding towards the group of Germans who were now sitting in a corner of the control room and watching the Croupier with all the paralysed fascination of a rabbit trapped by a stoat. 'You don't think these fellows will try to rush you as you take her down?'

'No, but let's see what the Croupier thinks.'

The Croupier was more than confident. 'I've been telling them such horrifying stories that their blood is running cold. So cold it is nearly coagulating. They hardly believed their eyes when I got that red-headed bird on the wing. I gave you credit for doing in the Captain with the Schmeisser, Ned. I've told them we are a special anti-U-boat commando, and this is the first time we've ever taken prisoners...'

'Carry on, Jemmy!' Ned said, grinning at the Croupier's story.

'Diving stations!' Jemmy bellowed, and the seamen among the prize crew went to various levers and gauges at the forward side of the control room.

Yon said: 'I'll go and see how my chaps are getting on, and be ready to turn the wick up when you're ready. By the way,' he told Ned, 'this Jerry Engineer is good, and co-operative. Although one of my chaps keeps close to him, I think he's the sort of dedicated man who doesn't really care who owns the diesels as long as he's allowed to look after them.'

'Mind he isn't scheming to drop a spanner into a set of vital gears,' Ned said.

'He's been warned,' Yon said. 'I told him his only hope of living, let alone ever getting back to Germany after the war, depends on those diesels and batteries. He understands that quite well.'

A klaxon screeched and Yon hurried aft. The group of prisoners looked first at the British seamen at the controls and then at Jemmy who, to their obvious surprise, was commanding the submarine, not Ned.

For a few moments the boat seemed strangely dead; then the conning tower hatch slammed shut, and Ned looked up and watched a seaman securing it. A red light winked out on what seemed to be the control panel, which Jemmy was watching closely, to be replaced by a green beside it.

Jemmy spoke quietly, levers were pulled, valves spun, and a seaman watched what seemed to be an elaborate vertical spirit level, the Papenberg. There was a deep humming noise from aft as the batteries started to turn the electric motors, and Ned heard the screws begin to turn.

Ned said to the Croupier: 'I want to talk to the Second Lieutenant as soon as you can listen and check my understanding of German: it's a bit rusty.'

Ned beckoned to the man, who scrambled to his feet and stood uncertainly, obviously alarmed at having been picked out.

'You speak some English, I believe?'

'Very little, sir: it is several years – '

'Come with me.'

Ned led the way to the wireless cabin on the starboard side just forward of the control room. The Marine guard stood to one side as Ned reached for the curtain.

'You can help guard the prisoners in the control room,' Ned told him, and gestured to the Second Lieutenant to follow him to the cabin, where the other Marine guard stood smartly to attention.

'Take over outside for the time being,' Ned told him, and as soon as the curtain closed sat down on what seemed to be a typist's seat in front of the Enigma machine, and swung round to face the German.

'Sit over there, on the wireless operator's chair.'

The German sat perched nervously on the edge. The colour had come back to his face but his movements were hesitant. Highly strung, or scared stiff, Ned decided. Perhaps both, but much more important, he was not the bluffing arrogant Nazi.

'Tell me your name and describe yourself.'

'Heinz Wellmann. Born in Kiel. I'm twenty-six. I studied physics and was teaching until the July of 1939, when I began naval training.'

The man stopped, as though those few words described his life so far.

'Born in Kiel, eh? So you know the Navy war memorial, and the Tirpitz Pier.'

Wellmann's face became more animated. 'Oh, you know Kiel, then?'

'I've been there. Sailing in regattas in Kiel Bay before the war.'

'It is a fine city,' Wellmann said nostalgically, 'particularly with – how do you call the *Nord-Ostsee-Kanal*?'

'The Kiel Canal.'

'Ah, how flattering for us. Well, with the Kiel Canal running through to Brunsbüttelkoog, there are always many ships passing to the North Sea. Until the war, anyway.'

'Did you volunteer for U-boats?'

'No. Because of my physics and mathematics I was put down for navigation and wireless work. I did three cruises in late 1940 as sub-lieutenant in a U-boat; then in 1941 I was ill and missed a cruise from which the boat did not return.'

'So all your shipmates were lost?'

Wellmann shrugged his shoulders, and Ned was not quite sure whether the gesture meant that he bore the loss stoically for the Fatherland or did not care for his shipmates.

Now the motion of the boat was changing: the slow roll gradually stopped, he felt the bow dropping slightly and the hum of the electric motors took on a deeper note: he thought he could feel rather than hear the beat-beat of the turning propellers.

With a nonchalance he did not feel, he asked Wellmann: 'Who commanded this boat?'

'*Oberleutnant* Schmidt. He was due to be promoted *Kapitänleutnant* when he returned. We'd done three cruises. This is the third.'

'These three cruises – you had successes?'

'Yes,' Wellmann said warily, and seeing that Ned expected details he added: 'In the Atlantic. Three ships on the first cruise, four on the second and three up to now.'

'Those earlier cruises in 1940,' Ned said. 'What happened?'

'The usual successes, and on the fourth cruise, when I was sick, the boat lost contact.'

Ned reflected on the phrase 'losing contact'. It was, of course, quite correct, meaning that the captain no longer signalled his headquarters (presumably still Kiel at that time) listing his successes, and when the wireless operators in Kiel tapped out the call sign of his boat there was no reply. Contact was lost. It was an easy way of saying that the boat had been hunted by the Royal Navy – by the 'Tommies', as the Germans called them – dropping depth-charges, and at a certain point the charges had dropped so close that the hull – Ned involuntarily glanced at it, grey-painted and glistening with condensation – was punctured or crushed, and the U-boat filled and slowly sank a couple of thousand fathoms until it settled on the bottom, an intruder among primeval debris.

'What happened to you then?'

'By now our boats were moving to bases in south-western France – Brest, Lorient, Saint-Nazaire, La Pallice, Bordeaux, La Rochelle. The Lion – this is our nickname for *B der U*, Admiral Dönitz – moved to Kernével, which is near Brest.'

'Tell me,' Ned asked, hoping to answer a question of little consequence, but which had puzzled ASIU, 'how did the Lion and the SO West work together?'

Wellmann shook his head. 'The Senior Officer West, as far as I could see, commanded all the surface ships and looked after the work at the ports, like building the concrete bunkers for the U-boats when the RAF began its bombing. The Lion,' he said proudly, 'was responsible for U-boats and reported directly to the Führer.'

The U-boat had dived and the lack of motion was uncanny: down here – whatever depth they were at – they were below the surge of swell waves, and he found no difficulty in guessing the number of revolutions at which the electric motors were turning the propellers – about sixty a minute.

There was a knock on the door frame – curtains replaced actual doors – and Jemmy came in.

'We're cruising at fifty metres, and she went down very smoothly,' he reported. 'Handles very well.'

'You got over the snags, then?'

Jemmy looked puzzled. 'But we didn't *have* any snags,' he said. 'It all went perfectly.'

Ned laughed at the expression on Jemmy's face, like a child allowed to choose the best chocolate in the box only to have it taken away before he could eat it.

'I'm teasing. How many knots?'

'Four kilometres an hour. Actually, I came to ask permission to get rid of the fish.'

Ned scratched his head and then, to warn Jemmy that the German spoke English, introduced the Second Lieutenant.

'Yes, I've been thinking about them. Must we get rid of them?'

'What good are they to us? We aren't likely to sight the *Bismarck*, or the *Scharnhorst* and *Gneisenau*, and with the weight of the fish and all those prisoners up forward I had a hell of a job getting a trim. We've got all the rest of the prisoners ready to go aft. If we don't get rid of the weight of those torpedoes, if we do a crash dive she'll be so bow heavy that we'll probably go down like a harpoon and stick in the mud at 2,000 fathoms. That's four miles deep or thereabouts. This bucket will start springing leaks below about four hundred feet and probably flattens like a squashed can of peas at eight hundred.'

'We can go down to 100 metres,' Wellmann said.

'Oh – ah, yes, thank you,' said a startled Jemmy. 'Well now, that's nearly 350 feet, although it doesn't affect firing those fish.'

Ned knew he was being absurd: he simply disliked being in an unarmed ship.

'We can keep the one in the stern tube,' Jemmy said, as if reading Ned's thoughts, 'and we've got the guns.'

'Very well, get rid of the four. But wait ten minutes, I'd like to watch.'

'You just say when,' Jemmy said cheerfully, leaving the cabin.

Ned turned back to Wellmann. 'So what happened to you when you recovered from your illness?'

'I was promoted to *Leutnant* and sent to a signals school near Hamburg.'

'Why? Did you expect it?'

'Yes,' Wellmann explained patiently, 'because I guessed I was to serve as Second Lieutenant in a U-boat and would be responsible for signals and ciphers.'

Ned waved to the Enigma. 'And this machine?'

Wellmann's eyes dropped.

'This is your first cruise with the Mark III, I suppose,' Ned said conversationally. 'Have you had any trouble with the extra rotor? An extra rotor and a new cipher – we were surprised Admiral Dönitz took a chance trying out both at once.'

'That's true,' Wellmann agreed, nodding his head. 'But he was right – we've had no trouble with the machine or Triton – ' he broke off, appalled at having used the word.

'Yes, Triton isn't really any more difficult than Hydra,' Ned said easily. 'Really, it was just the extra rotor. Having more to choose from is no problem?'

'No,' Wellmann agreed, apparently reassured. 'And of course it is much more secure, giving us four settings, three of which we change daily, and the fourth changing with every message, and a choice from eight rotors. So we have a theoretical choice of more than 150 trillions. It's completely unbreakable, a cipher and a machine like that.'

Ned said nothing, and Wellmann stared at the steel deck for a full two minutes before looking up again, his face once more pale, and pinheads of perspiration suddenly leaking out on his brow and upper lips. 'But it *is* completely unbreakable,' he repeated. And then, still trying to reassure himself: 'The Lion would not continue using the machine with a new cipher if it wasn't, would he…?'

CHAPTER FOURTEEN

'Give me your keys,' Ned said quietly, and when the bemused man handed them over, added: 'Where is the manual giving the Triton settings?'

'In the Captain's safe. Behind the aftermost panel in the Captain's cabin,' Wellmann said and then, as if excusing himself to an invisible Gestapo witness: 'You'd have found it anyway, now you have the keys.'

'Of course,' Ned agreed. 'Now, you must have the easiest job on board the boat! What do you do with your spare time – read books?'

'Spare time!' Wellmann exclaimed. 'I have to stand a watch, so I have no spare time. Well, not until the transmitter broke down.'

Ned felt his body chill. 'The transmitter does not work?'

'No. About four days ago something burned out. A pair of final valves. We had a spare pair and, because the operator was in the middle of transmitting an important signal, he fitted them and started transmitting without waiting for them to warm up.'

'So that's how the spare pair burned out, too?'

'Yes,' Wellmann admitted shamefacedly. 'I had enciphered the signal on the machine and given it to him, and he was sending it to *B der U*. I suddenly needed – ' he stopped, trying to find the phrase.

'To relieve yourself.'

'Exactly, otherwise I should have insisted that we find out what the fault was. It is routine. The man was excited.'

'Why?'

'We – well, we were reporting.'

'On an attack?'

'Yes. We had sunk two ships,' Wellmann added defiantly, 'which made a total of three for the cruise so far.'

'With five torpedoes still left.'

'Exactly. We could hope for at least one more.'

'But with no transmitter?'

'*B der U* might wonder if we had been lost, but breaking off suddenly like that in the middle of a transmission – the receiving operator at Kernével would probably guess something had gone wrong with the transmitter.'

'The *receiver* still functions?'

'Oh yes. We can receive orders but can't acknowledge them. Or we could until now, rather,' he corrected himself.

'What time does Kernével come on the air each night?'

'I do not feel I should be talking so freely.'

'The Gestapo would make you talk.'

'Yes, but…'

Ned let the pause hang in the air, with its implication that the Royal Navy and the Royal Marine commandos could teach the Gestapo a thing or two.

'Well, I suppose you'd find out from the wireless log since it gives all the times of origin,' Wellmann said. 'We listened at midnight Greenwich to see if we were on the traffic list. If we were, we listened three hours later and took the signal.'

'What if another U-boat sighted a convoy and wanted reinforcements?'

'We'd pick up his report and decipher it with the Enigma, but of course we would not change our position until we had orders from *B der U*.' His smile was superior as he added: 'We have so many boats in the Atlantic now that he has no trouble in assembling a pack.'

Realizing that he needed to keep the initiative, Ned smiled back. 'Yes we know how many boats, and their reported positions.'

Wellmann nodded, accepting the significance of Ned's words. 'For how long have you been able to read Triton?'

Ned raised his eyebrows and shrugged his shoulders. 'When did you start using it? A month ago, five weeks?'

'And before that, Hydra?'

Ned nodded. There was no harm in the fellow knowing the British had read a cipher which had now been replaced.

'What will be happening now because your transmitter is not working?'

'I suppose *B der U* will continue calling us, assuming we will repair our transmitter. He would not consider us lost for another three or four days because he knows we might be shadowing an enemy and keeping radio silence.'

'Thank you,' Ned said, adding: 'No one will ever know what you have told me.'

Wellmann looked first startled and then puzzled. What had he told this hard-eyed man who seemed to be telling *him* things? That the Tommies knew about the Mark III Enigma, and the introduction of Triton, for instance. Then Wellmann began to feel fear; had he betrayed the Führer and the Lion? His comrades? He could not see how, but this Englishman was thanking him for *something*, and that could only be secret information. He vowed to keep his mouth shut when the others questioned him about what the Tommy had asked. At that moment he realized that he was effectively the senior surviving officer. The Engineer was technically second-in-command to the Captain, but he took no interest in anything but diesel engines and dynamometers. So the men must now be looking to him as their leader – the man the Tommy's senior officer had just thanked for being so helpful.

As Ned pulled back the curtain to let Wellmann out, he was startled to see that the once crowded control room was now almost empty. Four of his own seamen were seated at various controls. The Croupier must have taken the rest of the prisoners aft.

Then he called to the rating sitting at the nearest of the two wheels, controlling the forward hydroplanes. The man pointed up the ladder, to where it disappeared up into the conning tower.

Ned hurried up the ladder to the conning tower, hauling himself into the small circular cabin which could only be described as a small apartment one deck above the control room. He looked up and saw that the ladder continued right up to the hatch to the bridge. He was looking up in just the same way as the Germans were when he dropped a black banger on top of them. The shock must have been enormous: it was unlikely that any of them had ever seen or heard of such grenades. Having one dropped down the ladder when as far as they knew the Captain and his men on the bridge had, while taking the Tommy captain out of a lifeboat, accidentally caused an explosion on the bridge and fired a Schmeisser burst, must have been quite a shock.

The inside of the conning tower was circular, the size of the straphanging section of a London Underground train opposite the sliding doors. Jemmy was sitting on what looked like a bicycle saddle, peering into the eyepieces of a periscope, which he seemed to be turning by manipulating two wooden handles which stuck out like bicycle handlebars. As the periscope turned, so did the seat. Then Ned saw that Jemmy was turning it by a foot-pedal fitted to the seat, and the handles were presumably for focusing.

A rating stood nearby and there was another periscope to one side, presumably for spotting aircraft.

Jemmy stopped the periscope turning, slapped up both handles, and said briskly: 'Down periscope!'

The rating did something that Ned could not see and there was a humming noise but Jemmy, startled to find Ned standing behind him as he turned, said with mock sternness: 'Only the captain and watchkeepers allowed up here!'

'A miserable little crow's nest you have,' Ned commented.

'Certainly a different way of doing it,' Jemmy admitted, 'and I still prefer our system, where the skipper is down there in the middle of the control room and everyone else within earshot. But this system isn't so bad. Look.'

He pointed to the thick stubby periscope with its two handles, and beneath it a bicycle seat mounted on a small platform, like a miniature merry-go-round.

'And this – ' he turned and pointed to something that looked like a three-foot-square grey fuse box, with a dozen or so dials on its front, and various large circular switches – 'is the torpedo fire-control gadget: like the Fire Control Table in a surface ship; you feed in ranges, bearing, own and target speed and courses, and it hums and hahs and comes out with angles and settings.

'Next to it are the firing controls. "Fire one, fire two..." and so on. "*Los*" in German. Over there is the aircraft periscope, for searching the sky for magic portents, flying dragons, airborne cherubs, and – if you're a Ted – Sunderlands and Liberators.'

Ned coughed and assumed a mock serious voice. 'I suppose you have this noisy toy pointed in the right direction?' he asked, nodding at the helmsman who was at the wheel on the forward side of the conning tower.

'More or less. If you steer east until you see land, and then turn left, you find England.'

Jemmy's bantering voice belied the care with which he had drawn in the course for the first few hours of the long voyage to the United Kingdom.

Ned gestured to the second seaman to go below and then took the opportunity to tell Jemmy: 'The U-boat's wireless transmitter is busted. We can't warn the Admiralty that we've captured this boat.'

'Je-sus!' Jemmy said, exasperated rather than angry. 'All that careful planning with Captain Watts and the wireless intercept boys. What was it they're listening for – "Spree" repeated three times on the U-boat frequency, wasn't it? Now what? Haven't even got a bloody tom-tom, have we, except the lifeboat wireless.

Wrong frequency anyway, and nowhere near the range. And there's no chance of staying on the surface and calling up a British frigate with an Aldis and saying we're really on their side!'

'Not a hope. Any aircraft or ship sighting us will immediately bomb, depth-charge or fire salvoes at us and to hell with signals. Anyway, we couldn't risk it – losing the boat at this stage…'

'Quite apart from our precious skins,' Jemmy said fervently. 'Unless we can do something with the lifeboat wireless, we're going to be like a magpie perched on a telephone line and the farmer underneath aiming with a 12-bore.'

'Yes. If one of our hunting groups find us, we're going to be able to give them a good report on their techniques.'

'If they fail,' Jemmy pointed out. 'If they succeed, *they* write the report.'

Ned gave a dry laugh. 'I have a picture of us surfacing beside the tug that opens the boom gate on the Clyde, waving a white flag.'

'You can wave me,' Jemmy said, his voice resigned. 'Taking a sub that far in peacetime with all the proper charts is bad enough. If I had to take this dam' thing in, my hair would go so white you wouldn't need a flag.'

'I notice you're getting a bit thin on top,' Ned said as he started down the ladder to the control room.

Back in the wireless room and before he opened the top drawer he told the Marine sentry: 'Pass the word for the German Second Lieutenant, our wireless operator, and the German operator.'

Then he sat down, unlocked the drawer and opened it. He took out three slim volumes which had blue covers and the double-headed eagle with outstretched wings ('the ruptured vulture' someone had called it) which seemed to be stamped, sewn, embossed or painted on anything connected with the German Navy. The Second Officer had the badge on the right side of his jacket.

The books were printed in German script on poor-quality, greyish paper. He opened the second drawer. It contained several printed pads which were obviously signal forms, and another set which were laid out differently. The third drawer was full of paperback books and magazines, all obviously pornographic and – he flipped through one of the magazines – in poor taste: blowsy and fluffy-haired fräuleins wearing little more than a leer.

The Croupier appeared at the doorway, looked round the tiny cabin, and said: 'I've suddenly realized that to like submarines you have to understand the mentality of a sardine when he settles down in the tin. Do you want us all in here?'

'Just you for a moment: the others can stay outside. Look through these, will you?' He passed over the three volumes as the Croupier slumped down on the wireless operator's chair.

He turned the pages quickly. 'Not much interest to us. This one on top is a German reprint of our own Admiralty List of Wireless Signals, Part I; the next is the German equivalent of our Part II, and the bottom one is the Germans' own List.'

Ned nodded and passed over the pads.

'Standard signal pads – ah, this is a form used with the Enigma. Yes, here are the panels where the decoder types in the random setting, rotors setting, plug settings, addressee, time of origin and all that jazz. Anything else?'

'Only some dirty books in the bottom drawer.'

'That's nonsense: there must be the daily manual for the Enigma somewhere.'

'Yes. There's a safe behind a panel in the Captain's cabin. Here's the key. Would you get it – and see if there's anything else to interest us? And call that wireless operator in – the German.'

As the Croupier flicked through the books, the man came into the tiny cabin as warily as a cat entering an alley after being chased by a dog. His beard was sparse, his face even whiter than the rest of the men, and the acne scarring his face emphasized that he was still in his teens. His thick, open-necked jersey was obviously new; Ned had the feeling this was the youth's first or second cruise.

Ned questioned him, finding his German improving fast. Günter Hauser, aged nineteen, from a village in Bavaria. He and the hydrophone operator kept wireless watches when they were running on the surface, and they both took turns at the hydrophone when submerged.

'The transmitter – what exactly is wrong?'

The man explained, with Ned making him repeat and explain again the technical terms.

'There are a pair of final valves,' the youth said. 'They've gone. When using the transmitter it is necessary to switch it on and let it warm up for about three minutes. You cannot just switch on and transmit.'

'Why?' Ned demanded, although he knew the answer.

'You'd burn out valves. That's how – ' he flushed with embarrassment, the first colour Ned had seen in his face, 'that's how it broke down.'

'But you have spares, surely?'

'Yes, sir, one set.'

'So what happened?'

'I was nervous sir: we had just been in action. When the valves burned out I took the spare pair and put them in...'

'And started transmitting again before that pair had warmed up.'

'Yes, sir.'

'And there is no third pair on board?' Ned decided to check up on the Second Officer's story.

'No, sir.'

The Croupier, who had not yet left the cabin, said: 'I think this chap is telling the truth. He made some sort of elementary mistake: he's very ashamed about it.'

'I'm not surprised,' Ned said. 'Ask how he came to do it.'

The Croupier listened carefully as the German became more and more excited, gesticulating at the transmitter, at the doorway and at the seat Ned was occupying.

'Well,' the Croupier said, 'this started some days ago. Apparently they'd sunk a ship or two and then were driven off. I think no one thought the Commander pressed home the attack very strongly. Morale was very low and the signals from *B der U* were a bit curt and reduced to asking for weather reports, fuel consumed and position.

'The Commander was blaming the First Officer who was bullying the Second, and so on. Then three days ago *B der U* sent a signal which, when the Second Officer put it through the code machine – the Enigma – told this boat to stand by for special orders, and to acknowledge receipt.

'This chap reckoned it meant acknowledge the special orders when they were received, but the Commander got very excited and said that this warning must be acknowledged. Anyway, there was a screaming match involving the Commander, the Engineer (who of course was second-in-command), and the First and Second Officers. Finally the Second Officer came in here and sat where you are, typed out an acknowledgment – with the Commander standing there cursing him – and gave the encoded signal to this operator, who tuned in the set and was waiting for it to warm up to tap out the signal when another furious row started between the Commander and the Second Officer, with the First shouting from the control room. This made our fellow very nervous, and he started transmitting, but suddenly his set went dead. The Commander began raving again – obviously anxious to get the special signal – and Hauser here tracked down the fault, found burned-out final valves, replaced them, and at the first tap of the key the new parts burned out. The Captain nearly went berserk but didn't blame Hauser – whose fault it obviously was: he hadn't waited for the new valves to warm up.'

'Yes,' Ned said, 'that's roughly what I understood. Not the rows, just the lack of warming up. Anyway, where's the wireless log? What did that special signal say?'

Hauser's reply was an excited gabble.

'He says that *B der U* never sent the special signal, presumably because the first one wasn't acknowledged, but Kernével has been calling this boat at intervals ever since. We can pick up Kernével, of course, because the receiver is working.'

Ned shook his head wonderingly. Apart from the Commander going berserk, it could have happened in anyone's navy. Well, the German operator was still excited from telling his story and being the focus of attention from two officers. 'Give him the keys,' Ned told the Croupier. 'He knows where to find the wireless log and the Triton manual in the Captain's safe.'

Watched by Ned and the Croupier, the operator walked the few steps to the Captain's box-like cabin, brushed aside the curtain at the doorway, and went in. Since both Ned and the Croupier were used to surface ships with their comparatively large cabins, the U-boat commander's quarters reminded Ned of either the bathroom in a very small house or a single berth sleeper in a railway train, second class and probably Spanish. The cabin was simply an indentation on one side of the corridor leading from one end of the boat to the other.

The wardroom was worse. Anyone wanting to pass from the forward torpedo room, POs' quarters or galley aft to the wireless room, control room and conning tower (which meant watch-keepers in particular), had to pass through the wardroom. However, this was not a case of simply saying 'S'cuse me, sir.' There were four bunks in the wardroom: two were one above the other, welded piping with mattress, blankets and pillows, on the outboard side of the corridor and two more on the centre-line side. To eat meals, the officers obviously had to hinge the upper bunks up out of the way, and use the lower ones as seats, with a table astride the corridor between them.

Ned had noticed that in the Captain's cabin the bunk had a wood lining against the steel hull. Hauser, selecting a key from those given him by the Croupier, went straight to the panel beside the head of the bunk, pulled it out to reveal a grey metal safe door behind it, fitted the key and turned it. The safe contained three shelves crammed with books, most of them of a uniform height.

'So that's where they kept the CBs,' the Croupier commented.

'An obvious place for Confidential Books, when you think about it,' Ned said ruefully. 'Whichever officer was on watch would decipher a signal, which the Captain would want to see at once, so the most convenient place for storing the Confidential Books would be in the Captain's cabin.'

Hauser took out a slim, bound book and a cardboard-covered volume which looked like the radio log, brought them back to the wireless room and handed them to Ned.

'If this lemon only knew what a tense moment this is for us,' the Croupier said as casually as he could, 'he'd stop eyeing that bottom drawer and actually ask if he could have one of those dirty books.'

'Very true, very true,' Ned said heavily. 'But don't overdo it. Just give that bound volume a casual flip.'

'Aye aye, sir,' the Croupier said sarcastically. 'I was obeying your orders that the German prisoners must not know why we captured the boat, even though for security they'll be kept prisoners in a special camp.'

With that he asked Hauser if he was married, at the same time looking at the blue book. Hauser was young enough to blush and say he was engaged, and had hoped to be married at the end of this cruise.

Something in the man's voice made the Croupier look up and ask a question. Hauser's face went redder as he stammered an answer.

'What's all that about?' Ned asked impatiently.

'The girl's knocked up.'

'The wedding ceremony's going to be delayed a year or two,'

Ned said unsympathetically.

'That's just dawning on him. Trouble is that the girl hasn't told

her parents, who are very strict.'

CHAPTER FIFTEEN

The Croupier said with carefully controlled casualness: 'This is the Triton manual all right.' He slurred the word 'Triton'. 'With the daily settings for three months, not just one month as we expected.'

'Toss it to one side carelessly,' Ned said, 'and start reading out the last few signals from the Lion at Kernével.'

The Croupier threw the Triton cipher manual on to the wireless operator's table like a gambler discarding a low card and opened the log. He scanned the half-dozen pages of entries.

'These chaps lead a dull life! I see they decipher all signals they pick up, whether the signal is intended for them or not. That way I suppose they can get some idea of what's going on.

'Well, first signal is from this boat (calls itself ULJ) to *B der U*, reporting its position – having cleared the Bay of Biscay. Various signals intercepted from *B der U* to other boats, and various boats to *B der U*. Some sighting reports, others giving weather. *B der U* tried to get a pack together to attack one of the HX convoys about four days out of Halifax but they were driven off. Ah, by Jingo, the good old *City of Norwich* was sighted and reported, by a boat whose call sign is UL, but too far off and travelling too fast to be attacked.

'That's interesting, Ned. They don't try to catch up on the surface.'

'Not surprising,' Ned said. 'We were usually making sixteen knots, which they could calculate, and these things only make sixteen to eighteen knots on the surface, less even if there is much of a sea running, so at best it would overhaul at two nautical miles in an hour. Say she sighted the *Norwich* three miles ahead, and the U-boat needs to get into an attacking position well ahead, and the *Norwich* is zigzagging...'

'You sound like Jemmy!' the Croupier commented. 'Been going to night classes? Well, there are routine signals, Daddy Doughnuts asking about fuel and fish remaining, positions, weather reports and so on. Ah, the famous "acknowledge receipt" signal that got everyone agitated and led to John Willy here blowing the gaskets on the transmitter. Then – don't forget they've now no transmitter – Daddy Doughnuts calls them every twenty-four hours, when his staff calculate the boat will be running surfaced in the dark, charging batteries, telling them to report their position. Looks to me as though he thinks they were surprised on the surface and sunk while preparing to receive the previous "acknowledge" signal. So, Ned me boy, we have our alibi already – ULJ has been sunk. I wonder when they rub her off the blackboard…'

Ned nodded, and for a couple of minutes he tried to picture Dönitz and his staff working in a big operations room at Kernével. *B der U* was supposed to be in a castle there. Considering how much radio traffic it put out there must be more serials poking up than ever there had been lances belonging to quarrelsome knights. Now, he realized, was a perfect – and perhaps the only – chance they had of finding out everything about the way a U-boat operated. Capturing the boat now called *Graph* gave all last year's technical information – speed, tonnage, fuel consumption, type of electric drive, battery capacity and so on – but how was a boat operated day by (all too often) boring day?

'Let's find out from Hauser what the drill is for receiving and passing signals,' Ned said. 'Start with surfacing at night.'

The Croupier questioned the man in rapid German, giving the impression that he was not particularly interested in the answers. Finally he turned to Ned.

'Fairly straightforward. They surface as soon as it's dark and stoke up the wireless. Hauser listens on the U-boat wavelength, particularly for any signals addressed to ULJ, this boat. But as Kernével never call two boats at the same time, he usually jots down any signals he hears, and passes them on to the officer of the watch.

'They're in cipher, of course, so Hauser never knows what a signal says. The signal, written on one of those pads, is given to the Second Officer if he's not on watch, but whoever gets it comes along and types the enciphered signal as received on to the Enigma, and gets out (on a page from that other pad) the deciphered signal, which he then takes to the Commander, who reads and signs it. The officer then enters the deciphered signal in the log, with date and time.'

'What happens to the original signal in cipher?'

'John Willy doesn't know, but he thinks it's kept for twenty-four hours, in case there are queries, and then destroyed.'

'That's pretty much as we would guess,' Ned said. 'What about making signals?'

The Croupier asked Hauser another series of questions and then told Ned: 'The same thing in reverse. The Commander writes the signal in plain language on a pad. One of the officers then checks the settings of the rotors on the Enigma against what the manual says (even though the machine has already been changed to the day's setting), types out the signal (thus changing it from plain language to the Triton cipher), copying out the ciphered letters as they light up, and then gives the ciphered version to John Willy to transmit. There's the usual warning to the bridge for watchkeepers to stay away from the aerials and insulators to avoid shocks and burns, and away it goes towards Kernével.'

Ned nodded as the Croupier added: 'Oh yes, the officer who enciphered it enters the plain language version in the radio log as soon as it has been sent, so that he can add the time of origin.'

'Any trouble in calling Kernével? Long traffic lists causing delays, that sort of thing?'

'No. I've got Kernével's – or rather *B der U*'s – call sign, and Hauser says they answer at once, static permitting. Good operators who rarely ask for a repetition.'

'Very well. You'd better get our own signalman in and translate any question he has for Hauser. See if there's any chance of getting that transmitter working again. Might only be a solder-and-insulating tape job…'

With that Ned picked up the Triton manual and went over to sit in the Captain's cabin. He shut the safe door, hinged back the panelling (thick plywood faced with *Ersatz* leather, the edges held by round-headed tacks) and sat back on the narrow bunk which acted as chair, settee and bed. The only other furniture was a rectangular hand basin which had a flat lid covered with Bakelite and which, when hinged down, formed a desk – providing one sat on the bunk. At the foot of the bunk was a small hanging locker, in which the Captain could hang up a few clothes. Again Ned was reminded of railway sleeping cars and that no one travelled first class in a submarine. A voice pipe, for the moment plugged with a whistle, probably led to the conning tower, and an adjustable lamp completed the fittings.

He flopped back in the bunk and stared up at the deckhead. The pillow smelled from the last – the late – Commander, who obviously used some pomade on his hair, but of the sort even the gaudiest whore in Brest would sniff warily.

But just lying here for a few minutes was luxurious. Pity there was no door to shut off the cabin from all the noise and movement; just a green curtain, the same type that separated the wardroom and the wireless room. Yon was aft in the engine room which, with the two diesels shut down, was comparatively quiet: only the electric motors were humming. An electric motor – previously Ned always thought of one as being the size of a bucket, but ULJ had two which each developed five hundred horsepower, drawing their strength from great banks of batteries set low in the boat. Each motor was connected directly to its propeller shaft: there was no gearing apparently because the electric motor's speed was varied by juggling with rheostats and the like, always keeping a sharp eye on the voltmeters and ammeters which showed how much charge was left in the batteries. And of course, when the boat was surfaced with the diesels running, these same motors acted as generators, charging the batteries.

What had Jemmy said about this particular boat after questioning her Engineer? The electric motors could push her along and underwater at a maximum of about nine knots, although they only turned the wick up that high in an emergency because it flattened the batteries in an hour. But at a sedate one or two knots, ULJ could stay submerged for up to three days, though by then the air would be foul.

This was bliss: admirals in their flagships must feel like this. Jemmy was up in the conning tower with the helmsman, or down in the control room keeping an eye on things there – on the two men sitting in front of two large wheels which reminded Ned of the type that turned old-fashioned mangles with wooden rollers, but in fact controlled the hydroplanes at bow and stern, and thus the angle of dive. Dozens of dials and gauges to watch – a large one in front of the big wheels, he remembered, showed the shaft speed. Electric wiring in protective trunking passed wherever there was space between the gauges, like dry ivy. Twenty or so small wheels, operating vital controls, grew from the hull by the conning tower ladder like toadstools from a rotting log. Grey boxes of ammunition for the Oerlikon cannons were dotted about, ready to be handed up through the hatch to the gun platform but in the meantime acting as stools. He disliked the claustrophobic effect of the access up to the conning tower. It was a circular skirt of thin plating, like a big oil drum without top or bottom and fitted to the deckhead with a welded-tube ladder through the centre of it. Up half a dozen rungs and your head was emerging from the drum into the conning tower, with the two periscopes, the helmsman and, if submerged, the officer of the watch or the commander.

This class of submarine was designed for a crew of fifty. Now it had twenty-three extra men from the prize crew, minus three men from her original crew. A forty per cent overload. Ned had not gone to look, but the Croupier had reported that the prisoners fitted well into the two torpedo rooms, allowing ten to spill into the petty officers' quarters. He had allowed this, he explained casually, because he could only get twenty men in the after torpedo room – more than that crowded the Marine guards. For the same reason twenty had been the safe maximum in the forward torpedo room, so ten petty officers had been allowed into what had been their own quarters.

No, he had assured Ned, there was no chance the prisoners would try to sabotage any of the machinery. The Croupier had emphasized to the prisoners that any such sabotage would first perhaps result in the boat sinking, so any such attempts would be suicide, and second, those guilty of any minor sabotage would be severely punished.

He told a laughing Ned how he had threatened that such malefactors would be dealt with. The boat would surface and the whole group of ten or twenty would be marched out to stand to attention on the casing. The boat would then dive slowly. Those who wished to prolong their agony could wear their lifejackets. The prisoners, the Croupier assured Ned, believed every word.

But Ned was certain that the prisoners would cause no difficulty: their leaders – the Commander and First Officer – were dead, and thanks to the Croupier's combined role of Satan and Goebbels, they were convinced the Tommy prize crew was really looking for a good excuse to massacre them all, and they were determined not to provide it.

Submarines... He could understand Jemmy's twitch: another week and all the prize crew would have twitches. Anyone who volunteered for submarine service must either have a vocation as strong as the one that led a man to be a priest, or be a bit batty. Not just a bit but wholly and completely batty.

Ned pummelled the pillow to raise his head high enough to look through the doorway into the control room. There were Jemmy's chosen men sitting at the controls for the hydroplanes;

Jemmy and the helmsman would be up there in the conning tower, Marines guarded thirty Teds forward and twenty more aft... and there Yon had just walked in with the German Engineer Officer, who was explaining something, gesturing at one gauge and then stepping sideways to point at another, obviously making a comparison. Yon nodded and the German was pleased. Curious how certain activities, like engineering and medicine, had a freemasonry among their devotees. A stranger looking at Yon (greasy grey flannel bags, nondescript brown woollen jersey) and the German (greasy grey cotton trousers, blue jersey with more holes than material) would not be certain which was the Tommy and which the Ted.

But this U-boat had been at sea for weeks. It stank of – he selected and identified the smells: rotting vegetables, diesel fuel, bilge water, hot lubricating oil, stale sweat (so stale it seemed to be lodged in petrified lumps), mildewed bread (he had seen half a loaf, covered in a pale green patina and spotted with yellow eruptions, sitting on the desktop), sour fruit (that must come from spilled fruit juices), unwashed bodies (hardly surprising since presumably fresh water was not allowed for washing), and...well, others too that he could not name but guessed were from *Ersatz* materials. The blue-grey rubber oilskin coats for instance, which had been dumped in the conning tower, had a sharp, sweet, almost surgical odour.

Oh yes, and hams and German sausage. He had first noticed them while standing in the crowded control room in the minutes before the Croupier shot that red-headed First Lieutenant. Hanging down from the deckhead wherever there was space were German (perhaps salami) sausages, like bunches of mummified limbs, and ten and twenty pound hams, their net bags brushing electric conduits, hydraulic piping, voice-pipe tubing, each ham leaving greasy marks which also showed the maximum pitch and roll since the boat had sailed. And the boxes, cartons and cardboard drums: wherever there was space in the boat, containers of provisions were lodged or lashed down with codline, and his German was adequate to read the stencilled contents: butter, oats, flour… Parts of the U-boat looked more like a half-stocked delicatessen than a fighting ship.

Yet, the German U-boat today was perhaps the most sophisticated and effective fighting ship at sea, even if submariners always referred to them as 'boats', and spent most of their time under the sea. With ULJ, the German designers had taken two big Blohm and Voss diesels, each as tall as a man and longer than a large car, two electric motors, a vast amount of diesel fuel, air compressors, and fourteen or so torpedoes and their fire control gear, and fitted them into a hydrodynamically highly efficient steel cigar which could withstand the pressures of great depths. But the men, from the captain to the cook, and the food they needed, were in effect left to fit in where they could. The Captain's cabin was the size of a second class sleeper on a British train, the galley from a quick glance looked a good deal smaller than would be tolerated on a cruising yacht sleeping four, although it had to provide three meals a day for fifty men…

He realized that he was deliberately avoiding facing the problem. Very well, problem, step forward and be recognized. But first, the preliminary to the problem. The Prime Minister had told him to collect a group of men of diabolical cunning and somehow capture the key (the manual, in other words) to the Triton cipher and a Mark III, 4-rotor Enigma machine. Very well, he had done that and, though he said it himself, it had been done with the sort of qualities that the Premier had in mind.

But what perverted mind could place cipher, Enigma and boarding party a thousand miles from England, home and beauty in a German U-boat with a busted wireless transmitter and no way of passing the message to the Admiralty that would tell them of success – the single word 'Spree' repeated three times, on three successive nights, on the U-boat wavelength? How Captain Watts would have enjoyed seeing that word in an intercept; the name he had given the operation. Nor was there any way of saying 'We're friendly' before a corvette, frigate, destroyer or aircraft rained shells or depth-charges down on them like sleet across Ilkley Moor.

Right, that's dragged the problem out into the open, if this dank steel tube humming along a hundred feet below the surface can be called 'open'. How do we get back safely? Certainly the Teds are winning the Battle of the Atlantic, but they're losing boats all the time – thirty-seven in July, twenty-five in August, nine in September. They are losses that do not matter a damn to Dönitz because, despite all 'Bomber' Harris' claims on behalf of the RAF, who are losing an appalling number of aircraft, many more new boats are being launched than we manage to bomb in the shipyards or sink once at sea.

While the Germans launch more U-boats than the Allies sink, and those U-boats sink more merchantmen than the Allies can build, it needs no great feat of mathematics to see who is winning. And that was while we were still reading Hydra; when we knew every order and report passing between Dönitz and his U-boats in the Atlantic.

Yet the Battle of the Atlantic when viewed from a U-boat itself and ignoring Dönitz, Ned suddenly realized, gave a vastly different perspective. Thirty-seven, twenty-five, nine – as U-boat sinkings on the ASIU chart they might not look very impressive as a percentage of the U-boats known to be operating in the Atlantic, and no doubt to Dönitz they were a mere pinprick, but they still added up to seventy-one, and that averaged six a week. So bearing all that in mind, the chances of getting this literally dumb boat into British waters without being sunk by a wary British corvette captain or the excited pilot of a Liberator or Sunderland were not very great. Six in a week. Maybe Sundays were regarded as close season for U-boats.

It occurred to him that the swilling back and forth was bilge water inside the boat, like an open sewer sluicing forward and aft and athwartships with every pitch and roll. Surely there were bilge pumps? Admitting to himself that as far as the wireless transmitter was concerned he had a problem but no answer, he pulled himself out of the bunk and went through into the control room.

'What about pumping the bilges?' he said to Yon, who was still talking to the German Engineer.

'Certainly sir, I'll just clear it with the skipper because it means leaving some oil floating on the surface.'

He shouted up the ladder to Jemmy, and then came back. 'That's fine, sir.'

Yon asked the German a question and then pressed the buttons he indicated.

Ned thanked him and realized that he had absolutely nothing to do. Jemmy commanded the U-boat, the Croupier...well, come to think of it the Croupier knew as little about submarines as Ned did, and Jemmy did not have enough watchkeeping officers, even if he stood a watch himself.

Now they had the prisoners sorted out and the Croupier had put Sergeant Keeler in charge of arranging guards, there were still some housekeeping jobs to arrange: the German cook must be found, threatened with hellfire and damnation, and put back to work in the galley. He was the only man who knew how it all worked and what provisions were available. Yes, stewards, too. The wardroom steward could look after the British officers, and the POs' steward could look after the seamen and Marines.

He could go through the chest of charts. Thanks to the time spent in ASIU he was more than familiar with the German gridded chart of the Atlantic, each tiny square numbered and lettered. He remembered the signals from Dönitz to particular U-boats, sent in the Hydra cipher and intercepted and deciphered by BP. A typical one would be 'Proceed at once to AS 57', and then giving the course and speed of an Allied convoy expected there. Sometimes *B der U* would be more urgent: 'All boats with torpedoes' would be ordered to a particular grid square when a convoy had been sighted.

Now Ned was actually inside a U-boat, he could better understand why Jemmy in the ASIU office used to dismiss derisively any idea that the Germans after assembling a pack of submarines then put an ace commander in charge. Jemmy had always maintained that the boats arriving at different times and from different directions just waded into the convoy as soon as possible, leaving only when out of torpedoes, running low on fuel or pinned down by an escort for a couple of days so there was no chance of catching up the convoy again.

At that moment he saw the Croupier crowded in the wireless cabin with the German operator and the British. These two had the casing off the transmitter.

Ned caught the Croupier's eye and the lanky lieutenant came out of the cabin.

'Where's your Sten?' Ned asked. 'These dam' prisoners might...'

The Croupier gave a lopsided grin and from each jacket pocket pulled out an automatic. 'Look at 'em, nine millimetre, hold six rounds each. That means twelve individually aimed rounds, which would pay more dividends with all these pipes and gauges around than a squirt with the Sten.'

Ned nodded. 'Perhaps Jemmy, Yon and I ought to have one each.'

The Croupier grinned again. 'I've got all the pistols and the ammunition stowed in that drawer – ' he pointed at the Enigma table, 'and I was going to suggest we issued them.'

'Now, what about the transmitter?'

'Our chap, Hazell, is checking it over now. Says the Teds were crazy to sail with only one spare pair of final valves.'

'When do we know if he can repair it?'

'He doesn't think so, but he'll know for certain in half an hour.'

While sitting in the lifeboat, Ned had found himself dreading the possibility of diving in a U-boat, but now it had happened, now the U-boat was cruising along a hundred feet down, he felt a strange reluctance to go back to the surface, where a sudden attack could come as a passing Sunderland or Catalina or Liberator, or a frigate sighted their grey hull, or the bow wave and spray. Any surface ship had a visual advantage: the higher the eye, the more distant the horizon.

'We must monitor all traffic once we're surfaced,' Ned said. 'We can read all the signals from Kernével now we have the Triton cipher.'

'Won't do us much good except as records,' the Croupier commented gloomily. 'If only we could transmit a few bogus sighting reports so that old Doughnuts concentrates all his boats in an empty part of the ocean!'

'Yes, except the moment Kernével realizes the signals *are* bogus, Dönitz knows we've either captured one of his boats or at least got a Mark III and the Triton manual. Or, life being what it is, we might get all the U-boats concentrated and then one of our convoys really does steam into sight.'

'Yes,' the Croupier said sourly. 'Excuse my mad burst of poor humour: I had thought of all that.'

'Have you checked what frequencies Kernével used to transmit to the boats?'

'No, damn it, I haven't. I thought the receiver would be pre-tuned just for the U-boat frequency.'

'Or there might be a limited number Kernével uses.'

'The fact is,' the Croupier grumbled, 'that none of the rest of us know a damn thing about wirelesses!'

'I prefer gramophones,' Ned said. 'Come on, we'd better spend some time with that Triton manual; then we can set up the Enigma machine so that at least we can decipher anything we hear tonight.'

He thought for a moment and then said: 'Leave Triton for a moment. I'm getting hungry and so is everyone else.' He then explained his intentions about the cook and stewards, and the

Croupier went off to find them.

CHAPTER SIXTEEN

As soon as darkness fell, unseen but waiting above to hide or trap them, Jemmy prepared for surfacing. Those due for the bridge watch sorted through the grey-green German oilskins and found coats and shoulder-high trousers that fitted. Heavy leather boots, which had thick cork soles as insulation against the steel plating of the deck, were more difficult to choose.

Finally, adopting the German method of controlling the boat during surfacing, Jemmy went up into the conning tower to use the periscope, Ned standing by him and acting as the first lieutenant, with Yon down in the control room ready to give the orders which would blow compressed air into the ballast tanks, driving out the water and making the boat buoyant. The German Engineer stood close by, a Marine guarding him, but it was clear by now that his first concern was for the boat; he was determined that mechanically everything should continue to function smoothly and did not seem to realize that he was now collaborating with the enemy; that if ever the Gestapo caught him he would be shot out of hand.

Yon had already checked on one of the U-boat's most valuable commodities, compressed air. Earlier the electrically-driven air compressor had filled all the tanks, those for blowing the ballast tanks and the others which would start the two 9-cylinder diesel engines, letting great blasts of air into the cylinders to get the crankshaft turning until the cylinders had enough compression to ignite the fuel spraying in through the injectors.

When running under water using her electric motors, the submarine was controlled by two sets of hydroplanes, one forward and one aft, like stubby narrow aircraft wings, or fish fins. Each pair turned together so that when those at the bow were angled up they steered the boat towards the surface like an aircraft climbing; angling them down drove her deeper. The pair right aft did the same to the after part of the boat. Two rudders, one abaft each propeller, steered the boat whether on the surface or submerged.

Surfacing was not just a question of blowing water out of the ballast tanks and blundering up like a clumsy whale. That could be done in an emergency, but normally the boat was kept carefully trimmed and brought up to within thirty or forty feet of the surface. The Papenberg showed the final precise distance from the submarine to the surface so that the periscope could be raised only enough for the commander to see over the waves, with him using a control on the periscope itself allowing him to raise or lower it completely or just a few inches.

The electric motors had to be used until the big vents could be opened to allow the diesels to suck in the huge quantities of air they needed. It was important for the men's eardrums that the air pressure inside the boat was equalized with the atmospheric pressure outside, before the hatch between the conning tower and bridge was opened.

Jemmy had decided that he himself would stand the first watch. Normally the commander did not stand a watch but, as he explained to Ned, he wanted to get the complete feel of the boat.

Four seamen now waited in the control room, towels round their necks, bulky in oilskin suits and sou'westers, and each with a pair of binoculars slung round his neck. As lookouts, each would be responsible for a quadrant of the horizon, reporting any object in a particular way. Facing forward, the port side of the ship was divided into 180 degrees from dead ahead round to the left to a point dead astern. The other side of the ship was divided into a similar semicircle comprising 180 degrees and referred to as the starboard side. In peacetime, when ships carried navigation lights, that on the port side was red while the starboard one was green, so the lookouts now used these same colours in their reports. An object on the starboard beam would be 'green nine oh', something half-way between dead ahead and abeam would be 'green four five', an object half-way between abeam and astern would be 'green one three five', while 'red' before the bearing warned it was to port.

The German cook had worked with a will, although the Marine guard reported that he ate ravenously as he cooked. The prisoners were fed first, then the prize crew.

Jemmy looked at his watch. Ned had noticed that, ever since they boarded the U-boat and he had become responsible for her, Jemmy's twitch had vanished. He walked around the boat, in the Croupier's words, like the lord of the manor inspecting how the fruit was ripening and paying special attention to the pheasant chicks.

The German wireless operator was now aft with the other prisoners: he and Hazell had tried repairs, but even Ned, looking at the blackened valves and smelling the hard but sweet smell of burned-out electrical fittings, could see there was no hope.

Just before joining Jemmy in the conning tower Ned had what seemed such an obvious and practical idea that he grabbed the Croupier's shoulder and hissed: 'We'll use the lifeboat suitcase wireless with a big aerial! Five hundred metres, the distress frequency: everyone listens. We'll get hold of that corvette in a few days – she'll be listening for us! Send her a jumbled-up signal to be forwarded to the Admiralty. Watts will catch on!'

The Croupier said nothing; his eyes dropped to the steel plating forming the floor – the control room sole, if one wanted to be accurate, Ned thought, though not one in a hundred seamen (or officers) would know what you were talking about. The Croupier was behaving most oddly. Ned knew that, if he had to describe it in one word, it would be 'shifty'.

Ned felt his sudden elation disappearing, like a barrage balloon punctured by friendly anti-aircraft fire and slowly deflating and falling with all the dignity of an old dowager in the private bar who had drunk too many port and lemons.

'What's happened to it?' Ned asked.

'You remember we told some men to collect the duffels and the suitcase wireless, and then cut the lifeboat adrift.'

'Yes, just before we dived. I saw the duffels being dropped down the hatch.'

The Croupier looked up. 'If any of us had been watching from the bridge, we'd have seen the bloody fools accidentally drop the suitcase wireless into the water…'

Now Ned felt not just despair (and fear, he had to admit to that), but anger. 'Why wasn't I told at once?'

The Croupier shook his head. 'Sorry Ned. Fact is, none of us – you, me, Jemmy, Yon or Hazell – remembered the dam' thing at the time. We'd been so cold and wet so long, I suppose we thought only of the duffels. It wasn't till after we finally gave up on the transmitter that Hazell said we could use the suitcase one, and he'd rig up a better aerial. Then we started wondering where the set was. I started asking questions… I hadn't reported to you yet because I only found out an hour ago, and reckoned you had enough on your plate.'

'Why didn't the men report the accident?'

'Well, they were so excited at capturing this bloody boat, and then seeing the big insulators on the stay-cum-aerial running up the conning tower, they didn't think the lifeboat transmitter was of much importance: as one of them said, they thought we were just going through the drill in bringing it on board because it was government property. And the thing *looks* so like a bloody suitcase…'

Ned grimaced and said ruefully: 'What we need is a tom-tom: I knew there'd be trouble when they gave them up.'

'I'm inclined to agree with you. I know Hazell is so frustrated I'm sure you'll be getting a request from him to transfer to the catering branch.'

'He'll lose his trade pay.'

'I'm sure he's considered that and reckons it's worth it.'

The Croupier pointed to the gridded chart on the chart table and the ordinary navigational chart, folded in half, beside it.

'Seriously, Ned, we've got a dam' long way to go.' He looked round to see if any of the men handling the hydrophone controls, watching gauges or just passing through the control room on their way forward or aft, were within earshot, before he lowered his voice and added: 'I've been thinking about it. Unless we can send a signal to the Admiralty telling 'em that we've captured this bloody boat and telling everyone to hold off sinking us, I don't think we've a snowball in hell's chance off getting back.'

'Don't forget that Germany claims – and Britain believes it – that she's wining the Battle of the Atlantic!'

'Come off it, Ned. No U-boats operate within a couple of hundred miles of the British Isles, and very few inside the range of Coastal Command planes. It's only out here, at the extreme range of our aircraft, that they slaughter the convoys.'

Now, standing in the conning tower talking to Jemmy, no longer surrounded by gently swaying German sausages and hams, lulled by the whine of the electric motors, Ned felt completely defeated. Thanks to a burnt-out wireless part, ULJ and the British and Germans in her were so many Flying Dutchmen. For lack of communication and the speed of a diving plane or an approaching destroyer or frigate, they could call no man friend and expect him to listen: instead there would be a hail of bombs, shells, bullets or depth-charges. The White Ensign or RAF roundels belonged, for all intents and purposes, to the enemy. No white flag would be acknowledged – RN ships and RAF planes would (quite reasonably) assume a trick or a trap and carry on an attack.

Ned was startled suddenly to find himself in the dimly-lit conning tower and with pins and needles in his left leg. He also had an increasingly urgent desire to relieve himself (with thick woollen full-length pants, trousers and oilskin trousers made of *Ersatz* rubber, achieving that relief, he thought, would be like searching for a needle in a haystack), so he tried to focus on Jemmy.

The man, still with no sign of a twitch, was embracing the thick, shiny steel bulk of the periscope as though it was a passionate woman; he was sitting on the seat with his legs wide apart, each foot alternately touching the pedals which revolved the periscope and seat. Jemmy's face was almost completely hidden: the large double eyepiece hid most of the upper part, reminding Ned in a bizarre thought of a masked highwayman bestowing a farewell kiss after relieving a lady of her gems. More than gems, in this pose.

Jemmy suddenly stood up, slapping at the two wood-covered handgrips, and the periscope motor hummed as the tube was lowered.

'Nothing in sight; wind is west about Force 3, sea almost flat, seven-tenths cloud, vis may be a mile. Permission to surface, sir?'

A startled Ned agreed, and then realized that both Jemmy and the Croupier had automatically put him in his place in the hierarchy of the U-boat: he was like an admiral flying his flag in, say, a battleship: he was the ultimate authority for every major move made by the ship (and the fleet), but the battleship's captain and ship's company actually steamed the flagship wherever he directed.

The prospect of being in a similar position to an admiral lasted only a few seconds: Jemmy and the Croupier could not be expected to stand watch and watch about; Ned would have to take his turn. His initial alarm that he knew nothing about submarine procedures was eased by the knowledge that the Croupier did not either. In fact, running the boat depended on Jemmy and Yon.

'Take her up!' Ned said.

Jemmy checked the helmsman's course and then called a stream of orders down the circular hatch to the control room. There was a rumbling below, like a complaining stomach, as compressed air drove out the correct amount of water from the ballast tanks to bring the boat to the surface.

Jemmy stared at the depth gauge, and Ned felt the slight motion of the boat increase as she broke surface and began to roll.

'Must equalize pressure,' Jemmy grunted as he reached up to a valve in the hatch. 'If there's more pressure in here than outside, I'd fly out through the hatch like a champagne cork.'

He unlatched the hatch while shouting 'Lookouts!' and scrambled up the aluminium ladder, followed by Ned and the four lookouts coming up from the control room.

The blast of air down the hatch startled Ned, but as he heard the whining of fans he guessed Yon had switched on powerful ventilation to force fresh air through the boat.

Jemmy had not ordered the diesels to be started, and for the moment the U-boat continued moving slowly under the electric motors. Ned's shins bumped painfully against strange fittings on the bridge: he felt rather than saw Jemmy's bulk and moved to one side as four cursing, night-blinded lookouts fumbled their way out of the hatch, oilskin pockets, binocular straps and shins catching on a bewildering number of projecting lugs and sharp corners all apparently specially designed to injure the unwary.

Ned's eyes grew slowly accustomed to the dark as he gripped the forward side of the tiny bridge – like a midget inside a large dustbin, he thought inconsequentially. Gradually the forward section of the U-boat took shape, a long and narrow wedge of deep black slicing through a grey sea flecked with white.

'Horizon clear,' Jemmy commented to Ned and turned aft to snap at the lookouts: 'Come on, some reports. A quid for the first man to spot Southend pier.'

'Wigan's bearing red nine oh,' muttered one of the men, and Jemmy laughed.

'That's the spirit, but if you don't see a destroyer until it's too late, my ghost will haunt your ghost.'

Jemmy then shouted down the hatch: 'Start both diesels!'

There were muffled thuds as vents opened, deep coughing as though a score of bronchitic bulls were clearing their throats, and then Ned felt the vibration in the thin plating of the conning tower start coming through the clumsy cork-soled high boots as the cylinders began firing. He caught the sudden sooty smell of exhaust fumes from cold engines, swirled forward by a random gust of wind, and heard the roar of air going into the air intakes each side of the cockpit.

'How's your heading?' Jemmy called down the hatch to the helmsman in the conning tower, and as soon as he received the answer, shouted: 'Half ahead both!'

Ned could imagine Yon, happy now his beloved engines were running. By now the noise from those eighteen cylinders would be deafening and Yon and the engine room artificers would be anxiously watching the various dials and gauges which revealed their secrets in the German language and metric measures. The largest dials, as big as frying pans, were the crankshaft tachometers, one high on each side of the corridor running between the two diesels. Then on each side were nine rectangular gauges mounted in a vertical bank, like a stack of large glass-fronted letter boxes, except that the dials behind the glass fronts recorded cylinder temperatures. Nine on one side, nine more on the other, each in effect an eye which revealed what was going on in the cylinders.

Three similar-looking gauges to one side of the vertical bank told the temperature in the exhaust manifolds. Another pair of gauges, as bulky as small searchlights and arranged on each side, were the engine room telegraphs: indicators which made a penetrating noise until an outside pointer was lined up with the inner one, acknowledging the order from the control room.

Ned had marvelled at the clever way the two huge diesels were squeezed in, each separated by the narrow corridor which ran from the control room, through a circular hatch in the bulkhead which could be shut and screwed tight to make it watertight, then into the electric room, with the two big motors which drove the propellers when the boat was submerged. Right now, with the boat surfaced and the diesels running, those motors had been turned into generators and were charging the batteries.

To a layman, the control section for each diesel was a bewildering mass of control wheels, from a few inches to a couple of feet in diameter, with so many different-sized pipes that no plumber's feverish nightmare could equal it. Yet standing in one position an ERA could see the heat of every one of the nine cylinders for which he was responsible, the temperature of the exhaust gases, the crankshaft revolutions, the speed ordered by the captain for his particular engine (and propeller shaft), and a dozen other things ranging from the temperature and flow of the cooling water to the flow of fuel. Just beside him, fans encased in bulky trunking supplied the vast amount of air the diesels needed.

The next section aft was, by comparison, as clean and antiseptic as a medical laboratory: there each of the two big electric motors had its own control panel – ammeters and voltmeters as big as soup plates, telegraphs like those at the diesel positions, tachometers showing the shaft speeds, the rate of discharge of the batteries when the motors were driving the boat, the rate of charge when they were being turned by the diesels and making electricity.

Up on the tiny bridge, Ned felt like a man standing on the chimney of an enormous house: below him, unseen dozens of people slept, ate, talked, as remote inside the hull of the boat as they would be below a tiled roof.

Below and slightly aft on the waterline, the diesels' exhausts alternately thundered and mumbled as waves surged over the vents, reminding Ned of an asthmatic lion lying in the corner of a cage, now roaring, now wheezing. He thought how every turn of the two propeller shafts spun the generators and sent amperes surging back into the batteries: he could picture the needles on the voltmeter dials, as big as dinner plates, gradually moving back up again. Yon will have to check the specific gravity of the electrolyte in the batteries – or, rather, someone will lift up floor plates and climb down on to the little trolley that runs along a beam past the batteries, so he can unscrew the caps and test each cell with a hydrometer, adding distilled water as necessary.

What batteries they must be: two large banks of them, each the size of a large bin, and together providing enough power to drive this boat of 770 tons displacement, seventy-five metres long and six metres in diameter, at nine knots for an hour's spurt, but for three days if she ambled along at one or two knots. And she could do that at a depth of 100 metres...say fifty-four fathoms. And the Croupier had once received what they now knew was a BP intercept of a U-boat's signal to *B der U* reporting that she had survived after being forced down to 245 metres – say 735 feet, over 120 fathoms – to avoid a heavy depth-charge attack. Yes, that was *U-230*, and at that depth, Jemmy had explained, the explosive effect of a depth-charge is reduced to a third, because of the immense pressure of water.

Still, the strain on the submariner's nerves, diving to more than twice the depth for which the boat was designed, must be considerable, knowing that at any moment the hull could be squeezed like a crushed eggshell. Submariner's twitch – doctors at the naval hospital at Haslar ought to publish a paper on it. Except, Ned remembered bitterly, the Navy could not admit it existed, any more than the RAF could admit that air crews were human beings who had a breaking point: instead the Air Ministry invented 'LMF', 'lacking in moral fibre', and that was the label they pinned on imaginative men who finally cracked up after a couple of dozen bombing raids which may well have killed half the men in the mess. The men who ought to receive those labels (the equivalent of the old 'Unclean' from the time of the plague) were those who lacked the moral fibre to face up to the fact that brave men could be driven only so far, and of course the psychiatrists also lacked the moral fibre to stand up to authority...

'Commander Yorke...will commander Yorke please go to the wireless room!'

CHAPTER SEVENTEEN

The sudden call coming up the conning tower hatch startled Ned, who at that moment was comparing going at full speed in a North Atlantic winter while standing on the open bridge of a destroyer with doing the same thing in a U-boat. Though admittedly the U-boat was a vile experience, like being lashed to the high water mark of one of the rocks at the foot of Beachy Head, a submarine at least gave you a chance to cry quits and submerge.

'They haven't got that bloody transmitter to work, I suppose?' Jemmy said as Ned started down the hatch.

'Not a hope. They've probably intercepted an AFO ordering all left-handed armourers to wear clean socks on Wednesday.'

Admiralty Fleet Orders sounded impressive to soldiers and airmen, but to the Navy they rarely rose in interest or importance, as a destroyer captain had once commented to Ned, to the height of Wrens' knickers.

He felt his way carefully down into the vertical cylinder of the conning tower, with its dimmed lights. The helmsman was a shadowy figure, an Essex man called Coles.

'How does she handle?'

'Very odd to start with, sir. She's so long and thin she is hard to turn once she gets off course, but at the same time that helps keep her on the straight and narrow.'

Looking down into the control room through the bottomless dustbin affair of the hatch, Ned decided to practise a rapid drop, of the kind that would be expected of him if he was on the bridge when the time came for an emergency dive.

He held the aluminium sides of the ladder, went down one rung and then kicked back with the other foot. He landed on his knees with a crash and set the floor plates rattling and the

startled men at the hydroplanes swung round in their seats while
Yon hurried over to help him up.

'Sorry, sir: the call from the Croupier wasn't *that* urgent.'

'My fault,' Ned said. 'I was playing silly buggers, just seeing
how fast I could get down the ladder.'

'Without breaking a leg,' Yon added.

'Yes, I shall regard that as par for the course.'

He found the Croupier and Hazell radiating excitement.
Hazell, earphones clamped over his head, was writing rapidly on
a signal form, a number of which the Croupier was already
holding and inspecting like a bridge player who had just been
dealt a perfect no-trump hand.

The Croupier turned to Ned and explained above the dull roar
of the diesels: 'Old Doughnuts is just sending off his night orders
and questions. We've copied signals to five U-boats, and one for
us is just coming over now. I thought you'd like to be here when
I put it through the cash register.'

Ned shook his head with sheer frustration. BP, the Admiralty
and ASIU now had no idea where the U-boats were, thanks to the
switch from Hydra to Triton and the Mark III Enigma, but here
on board the prize U-boat an ASIU group had an actual machine,
the key to the cipher, a pile of signals...and a pair of burnt-out
valves.

Hazell's right hand kept jotting as his ear heard the Morse dots
and dashes and his brain translated them into letters. From time
to time his left hand moved up to the front panel of the receiver
to make a slight adjustment to the tuning.

He tore a page from the pad, handed it to the Croupier and
continued writing on the new sheet.

'That's all for us,' the Croupier said. 'Let's get the book and put
it through the cash register. You have the keys...'

Ned went through to the Captain's cabin opposite, pulled out
the padded panel, unlocked the safe and took out the manual. As
he relocked the door and pocketed the keys, he found he was
holding the Triton manual as though it was an early Shakespeare,

and was startled to find when he returned to the wireless cabin that the Croupier was cocking his Walther automatic.

'Just in case the prisoners have worked out why we're here and try to rush us since we're surfaced,' he explained, reaching for the manual. 'Just think, Ned: this flatulent typewriter – ' he tapped the Enigma machine which was, indeed, like a plump portable – 'and this manual are the key to the Battle of the Atlantic, and the Battle of the Atlantic is the key to the war, and freedom for millions.'

Ned smiled patiently and said: 'Yes, quite. Hurrah and whizzo. I've been wearing my Freedom braces and working on that basis ever since Watts and I went to see the PM.'

'Oh, you're a miserable sod,' the Croupier grumbled. 'Get excited just for once! This is Robin Hood and Christmas and V for Victory and Cowboys and Indians and bugger Cromwell all rolled into one!'

'Yes – but just bear in mind, Red Riding Hood, that you have to keep an eye open for the Big Bad Wolf!'

The Croupier opened the manual. 'Right, I'll translate and read it out, and you juggle with the rotors. Now, let's find the right day.' He flipped through the pages. 'Here we are. Now, these settings for today would have been put on the Enigma at just past midnight.'

Ned opened the lid of the machine, revealing the typewriter keyboard in front, then the three rows of glass-topped letters duplicating the keyboard, and then four rotors already fitted, with four spare rotors in a rack to the right.

'The four-rotor Mark III isn't any bulkier than the models the Wehrmacht and Luftwaffe use,' he commented. 'Perhaps an inch or so wider.'

The Croupier nodded, and with his right index finger marking a place in the manual said: 'Right, from those eight rotors – no, wait a second; take out the four they were using the last time and the four spares. Now, here's the first one we need.' He pointed to the Roman numeral VI. 'Find that.'

Ned sorted through the rotors until he found one with the number engraved on it. 'So I put that one in position, out of the way.' He glanced curiously at the rotor, with its twenty-six letters of the alphabet neatly engraved round it, so that it looked like a huge coin with letters replacing the milled edge.

'Right,' the Croupier said briskly, 'now II…then VII…and finally I.' He had been reading them out so that seven was 'vee one one'.

Ned clicked the rotors in position, put the remaining four spare rotors in the rack to the right, and waited for the next instruction.

'Right, now we have to fix each rotor in relation to its disc, or wheel.' He glanced up at Ned, noted his look of impatience and said: 'Yes. I know, but let's work slowly and avoid mistakes. So here we go. The first disc number is twelve.'

Ned counted on his fingers the letters of the alphabet until he reached twelve. 'L.' The Croupier nodded in agreement and Ned turned the notched disc of the first rotor until a mark on it was against the letter L on the rim.

'Three,' the Croupier said. 'This is like housey-housey. Letter C!' Ned took out the second rotor, rotated the notched wheel, and replaced it.

'Twenty-two…' The Croupier started counting but Ned quickly went back four from Z. 'V – for victory, by jingo!' He adjusted the third disc.

'Now fifteen.'

Ned turned the fourth disc until the mark was against O on the rotor, and after replacing it read out the sequence: 'L,C,V,O.'

'Right,' said the Croupier, 'now we've set each rotor in relation to its own disc. Now we have to set the four rotors in relation to each other.'

As Ned shut the lid of the machine he was conscious that Hazell was still writing on the signal pad, and that he had four or five pages held down under his left elbow.

'Here we go,' the Croupier said. 'Four figures representing letters of the alphabet.'

Ned looked down at the machine. The four small slots in the lid, side by side, revealed a single letter of the alphabet on each of the four rotors, and alongside each window a section of a notched wheel also protruded.

'Ten,' said the Croupier, adding: 'That's the letter J.'

Ned pressed down on the first notched wheel and rotated it until he could read the letter on the rotor in the window.

'Second is nineteen.'

'S!' said Ned, rotating the second wheel.

The third letter proved to be P and the fourth was R.

Ned dropped the hinged front of the box ready for the next and last settings – fitting a series of small plugs into sockets, the whole thing looking like a miniature telephone switchboard.

'The *Stecker*, as the Teds call 'em,' said the Croupier. 'Only four for today – connect the F plug to the S socket, T to M, that's it; then P to K, and S to B. Now we're ready to see what old Doughnuts has for us.'

Ned swung round the back of the chair, sat down in front of the machine and flipped up the on-off switch.

The Croupier put the sheet from the signal pad in front of him and Ned slid a blank pad and pencil close by.

'Right – the preamble, which isn't in cipher,' the Croupier said. 'We might as well write it all down. Ready? "*B der U* to ULJ, time of origin 18.22, 44 letters in text, first part of one part then…" ' The Croupier's brow wrinkled. 'Oh yes, that three-letter bit means it's in the Triton cipher. All the preamble setting is BJEK.'

Ned leaned forward and turned each of the four discs until they showed, from left to right, the four letters BJEK in the windows.

The Croupier picked up the pencil and pad. 'Ready,' he said, 'the magic word is ZCAL.'

Then, with the rotors set at BJEK, Ned slowly typed ZCAL, with the Croupier noting down the corresponding letters as they lit up on the lamp board.

'There we are, WLDP. We're nearly there, Ned!'

Ned turned the discs until the engraved letters on the edges of the four discs showing in the windows were WLDP.

'Let's check,' said Ned. 'First we had the machine on the correct setting for the day.'

'Correct.'

'Then we set the discs to BJEK, which are the random letters chosen at Kernével.'

'Correct.'

'Then we typed the first four letters of the signal, ZCAL, which with the BJEK setting gives us WLDP on the lamps.'

'Correct. Now you set the discs to WLDP...'

'And then we'll get the hot words from Doughnuts,' Ned said cheerfully. 'Right, you read out the letters from the signal, and then as I type you write down whatever letters these lamps show.'

The Croupier read letter by letter and as Ned tapped the corresponding key the Croupier wrote down the letter lit up by the lamp.

Finally, with the last letter typed and its encoded equivalent lighting up, the Croupier groaned.

'Brief and not very exciting. Doughnuts is telling us: "Report position and fuel and torpedo expenditure." '

'Sounds as though we should have made a routine signal last night: and this is the routine reminder.' Ned commented. He swung round on the seat and saw that Hazell was still busy taking down more signals.

'Let's knock out some more of those and see what he's telling other boats.'

The Croupier took the pile of signals forms from under Hazell's elbow and the two went back to work with the Enigma machine. As the Croupier copied down the last letter coming up on the lampboard, he grunted.

'That's more like it. Doughnuts to UL. "Proceed full speed grid square QA 94 convoy reported course 095 speed six knots." '

Ned pictured the gridded chart. 'That's several hundred miles east of us.'

'Right, so let's do the next.'

As the Croupier glanced at it, he commented: 'Ah, this is a boat report to Doughnuts.'

The signal was brief but explicit as the Croupier translated and read it out, explaining that he was inserting punctuation: ' "Sunk two ships ten thousand tons, depth-charged fifteen hours, after hydroplanes damaged. Contact with convoy lost. Returning to base." That's UBT.'

He took another signal 'Another to Doughnuts.'

They began to work at the Enigma again as Hazell pulled up one earphone with a sigh. 'Phew, must have been children's hour for the U-boats! They can keep quiet for ten minutes now, so I can give my hand a rest!'

Again the Croupier grinned. 'Another U-boat reporting to Doughnuts from grid square LA 19 – '

'That's near us,' Ned said.

'…Well, he's damaged. He says: "Attacked convoy grid square LA 19 zigzagging seven knots through mean course 085 heavily depth-charged and lost contact." '

They put five more signals through the machine and found them to be either routine sighting reports, or Kernével requesting meteorological reports and ordering several U-boats to report their positions.

Finally the Croupier looked at his watch. 'Time to give Jemmy a spell.'

'Very well. He'd better have a quick course on this machine before he turns in. We're going to have to put every signal Hazell picks up through the cash register. A week's U-boat signals will be welcome at ASIU and Operations Room.'

'Sobering thought, isn't it?' muttered the Croupier as he switched off the Enigma and gave Ned the manual to return to the safe, 'that these signals – ' he waved the pages ' – are being read by Doughnuts and his U-boats, and by us: the cuckoo in the nest.'

Screaming alarm bells, as though they were trapped inside a bell with madmen hammering the outside, froze all three men for a moment. Hazell automatically shut off the receiver without realizing he did it, and threw open a row of knife switches. Ned grabbed the Triton manual and the Croupier shut down the Enigma lid.

'Alarm,' Hazell said. 'Diving alarm.'

By then Ned was already taking the half a dozen paces into the control room, arriving as the first of the oilskin-clad lookouts landed with a heavy crash at the foot of the ladder, his cork-soled boots acting like mallets on the steel plating, and cursing the second man who landed on top of him before he had time to roll clear. The two men, clumsy as bears in oilskins, looked as though they were wrestling as they tried to get out of the way, knowing two more lookouts and a lieutenant were due any moment. They were too slow to avoid the last two lookouts, although the four writhing and angry men managed to get clear while Jemmy stopped in the conning tower to secure the hatch.

Ned, for once utterly out of his element, realized that he had in a few moments heard a complete sequence of orders, from the bridge and from Yon, who was now standing beside the two men operating the hydroplanes.

First had been the alarm bells clattering through the ship, followed by Jemmy's bellow of 'Clear the bridge for diving!' Then Yon had given orders, repeated on the telegraphs, to stop the diesels and disengage the drives. Then more telegraphs as Yon ordered the electric motors to be engaged with the propeller shafts, at the same time telling other men to close the diesel air intakes and exhaust ports.

Then the engine room had signalled to the control room. 'Ready to dive', the other compartments in the boat had reported they were prepared for diving, and then the four lookouts had done their Marx Brothers act. And, as the hatch closed in the conning tower, Jemmy shouted as he spun the wheel to clamp it down hard on its rubber seal: 'Flood! Take her down fast, Yon!'

Ned stood fascinated but helpless, still holding the Triton manual, as Yon gave a string of orders, his voice loud now the fierce thunder of the diesels had stopped.

Everything seemed to happen at once: there was a great roaring as air was thrust out of the ballast tanks by the sea rushing in; from aft came the ever-increasing whine of the electric motors and the vibration of the propellers turning, and the boat began diving, her bow dipping sharply.

Above and outside the hull there were a couple of crashes as waves hit the conning tower, then the sea was silent as the boat slid downwards below the surface.

That seaman, Ned worked out, is operating the forward hydroplanes and his dials show he has them hard down, forcing the bow to dive. Next to him was Ordinary Seaman Keene, responsible for the after hydroplanes, but a dial seemed to show he had them adjusted for ten degrees, which should mean the stern was lifting slightly and thus helping to force the bow down in a steep dive.

Jemmy, obviously standing at the top of the conning tower hatch, shouted down: 'How's she going, Yon?'

Yon glanced up at the moving needle on a dial.

'Nicely, sir: sixty-five feet and descending.'

'Take her down to a hundred and fifty and put Hazell on the hydrophones. Is the Commander there?'

Ned stepped forward and looked up the hatch. 'What is it, a Number 11 bus?'

'Couldn't be – they go in convoys. No, I think it was a destroyer. If she picked us up on her radar then we can expect a few hours' depth-charging, starting any minute now.'

' "Up Doppler!" eh?'

Jemmy laughed and turned to ask the helmsman a question. Very soon, if the destroyer was turning to attack, they would hear her Asdic pinging. This underwater detection device was based on the same idea as a man in the dark judging the distance of the other side of a valley by shouting and measuring the time the echo took to return. The Asdic transmitted sound waves and, the instant they started bouncing back from an object like a submarine, determined the direction and, very approximately, the distance. It had two drawbacks. The major one was that it did not function if its ship was going at more than about fifteen knots, and the other that it became temperamental and confused when its distinctive ping hit cold layers of water, which acted more like a solid substance. Submarines and sub-hunters were, Ned reflected, probably the only people that knew the ocean was not a lump of water as cold at one hundred feet as it was on the surface. In fact it was like a giant multiple sandwich – between the surface and a hundred and fifty feet, the depth Jemmy had ordered, there might be half a dozen layers of water with differing temperature and salinity. And so on down to the sea bottom (about a mile below at this point).

If the thermometer in the U-boat showed a particularly cold layer, Jemmy would hide beneath it, knowing the Asdic pings would bounce off. From bitter experience of hunting submarines with a destroyer, Ned knew that, just as the destroyer was sure she had the U-boat trapped, it usually found a cold layer and slid beneath. But now he was in a U-boat and about to be hunted, there would not be a cold layer for miles…

Yon called up the hatch: 'Hundred and fifty, sir. I'll start trimming.'

At that moment Hazell called: 'HE bearing red two zero, distant.'

Yon relayed this to Jemmy, who clambered down the ladder into the control room. 'Since we haven't got any torpedoes, I can't think why I stayed up there. Hydrophone effect at red two zero – yes, that's him.' He walked over to the small cabin next to the wireless room, where Hazell was now sitting in the doorway, wearing a headset.

He pulled off one earphone and offered it when he saw Jemmy approaching, and the two men, the submarine commander crouching slightly and the hydrophone operator sitting, listened to the electronic underwater ear trumpet.

Jemmy said to Yon: 'Turn down the wick on those motors and quieten the ship. He may pass close.'

The hum of the electric motors died down and there was something approaching an eerie silence in the boat.

'What's our heading?' Jemmy asked in a loud whisper, and Yon repeated the question up the hatchway to the helmsman.

'Oh nine oh, sir,' he reported, and Jemmy nodded.

It's all a game of blind-man's buff, Ned thought, with the hunter trying to guess which way the hunted is going. Once detected, a submarine can dive deeper but, as the hunter increases speed to get above to drop depth-charges, her Asdic does not register, giving the submarine a chance of swiftly turning one way or the other – or keeping straight on, gambling on what the hunter will do, since the hunter knows the tricks and might herself turn one way or the other.

Ned noted that Jemmy had done what needed the coldest courage – keep straight on until the last minute, and then stop. The destroyer could this very moment be turning to port or starboard, depending on her commander's guess about the U-boat's tactic. But her commander might also reckon he was dealing with an experienced captain, who would try a bluff, or double or treble bluff, whichever it was.

Ned looked at all the dials, gauges, piping and the unworried faces of Jemmy, Yon, the men at the hydroplane controls, and the three other men handling valves and levers in the control room (what had happened to the four Marx Brothers? Their oilskins were hanging up, and so were their binoculars, but the men, not needed, had vanished). No one seemed concerned that at any moment British or American depth-charges might be exploding so close that the cigar case shape of the U-boat would be crushed into tangled metal which would then slowly sink. That was an interesting point – in very deep water did a wreck eventually reach a depth where the water pressure was so great that by some basic law of physics, or hydrodynamics, or some other 'ics', it equalled the weight, so that it just stayed suspended, a metal tomb hovering at some level between the ocean surface and the ocean bottom for the rest of eternity, occasionally nudging other wrecks that had been similarly suspended since the first iron and steel ship sank? (This crushed U-boat would presumably have passed the hovering wooden walls of Nelson's day at lesser depths: a whole Spanish plate fleet, sunk by some storm centuries ago, might be suspended there, like models hung by wires from a museum ceiling.)

'HE green oh five, distant,' Hazell reported.

So the hydrophone effect, the arcane way of describing propeller noises, is passing ahead: the destroyer is passing across what would have been the U-boat's course, and apparently not turning.

'She's not using her Asdic and I don't think she spotted us,' Jemmy said, and Ned realized that he was in fact making an informally formal report.

'Very well: carry on as you think fit.'

'We'll wait half an hour,' Jemmy said.

'HE green two oh, fading,' Hazell said.

'We're losing a good half-hour's wireless signals from Doughnuts,' the Croupier grumbled. 'There might have been exciting orders for us to ignore, like "Sink the *Ark Royal*".'

'According to Lord Haw Haw she's been sunk a dozen times already,' Yon said, not taking his eyes off the dials above the hydroplane controls.

'Perhaps Doughnuts is superstitious and reckons he'll get her on the thirteenth try,' Jemmy said.

'No point,' the Croupier commented gloomily. 'Old Goebbels has sunk her so many times on the German wireless now that if any Ted does manage to sink her, he won't get any credit.'

Ned began laughing to himself. 'Just imagine – say one of Goering's favourite pilots sunk her, but Goebbels refused to broadcast the claim because he'd already reported her sunk so often. Old Fatty Goering would go mad!'

'HE effect ceased altogether,' Hazell reported, sounding rather disappointed, like someone who has run out of counters and has to quit the game.

Jemmy glanced at his wristwatch. 'When is dawn?'

The Croupier flipped through the almanac on the chart table. 'Two hours almost exactly.'

'Damnation take that destroyer,' Jemmy said. 'I want the batteries topped right up so we can get a decent day's run submerged.'

'You don't want to chance running on the surface in daylight?' Ned asked.

Jemmy twitched, the first Ned had noticed for several hours. 'I'd sooner be watching ducks patrolling the Serpentine, but their Lordships gave me this toy to play with. So it's up to you, sir.'

The 'sir' was the unspoken acceptance that Ned was the senior and in command: if Ned wanted full ahead on the surface, Ned would have it: if Ned wanted an underwater run, just pass the word.

Ned went over the arguments again. On the surface they could manage seventeen knots. Yon had worked out that they had enough fuel to reach the UK on the surface. So seventeen knots times twenty-four hours meant four hundred miles a day. With under two thousand miles to go, that meant five days. But it would be madness to spend the last two days on the surface – Coastal Command would be queuing up to attack. Three days and nights on the surface meant 1,200 miles covered, with eight hundred to go. Then running surfaced at night and submerged by day would give two hundred surfaced plus perhaps fifty submerged – just over three days to cover the last eight hundred miles. Three surfaced and three half and half meant six days, probably seven, before they reached the UK. Two days to pass the word, the manual and the cash register to London, two more days for the BP folk to get to grips with it. So it would be eleven days or so before BP was reading Doughnut's signals with the Triton manual, a dozen altogether before the Admiralty had its U-boat plot brought up to date, and fourteen before any convoys would be getting signals diverting them from U-boat concentrations. That was assuming that Hazell continued intercepting signals from U-boats reporting their positions to Doughnuts, so the wireless log would give the Admiralty six days of positions.

Yet a week in the Battle of the Atlantic at this stage was a long time, and furthermore Captain Watts had no idea that in the meantime a Mark III and the Triton manual were heading for him at whatever speed the circumstances would allow. Two weeks' merchant ship losses could amount to...he remembered Watts' grim face when he said the Admiralty reckoned at least a million tons of shipping a month would be torpedoed in the Atlantic when the Germans switched to the Triton code. A million tons... Take five thousand as an average size: that meant two hundred ships, which in a thirty-day month meant an average of six and a half a day. Thirty deck and engineer officers and seamen and twenty DEMS gunners to each ship...roughly 325 men dying each day.

It was an interesting mathematical problem if your blood ran cold and calm enough. A straight surface run except for the last couple of days still meant a six- or seven-day voyage, plus seven days before BP and the Admiralty could light up the Blackout. Fourteen days meant ninety-one ships sunk and 4,550 men killed, wounded or trying to survive. That was the best he could do – assuming that this U-boat reached the UK safely, and that was almost an absurd assumption.

But a complete run surfaced at night and submerged by day would take – Ned quickly worked out a rough total, based on 250 miles in twenty-four hours. That was two thousand miles divided by 250 miles in twenty-four hours...eight days, say nine.

Plus seven more while the Mark III and manual went through the machinery. Sixteen days meant one hundred and four ships sunk, carrying an average of 5,200 men.

So the choice was either a wild dash on the surface taking six or seven days, or a half and half lasting eight or nine. Which meant ninety-one ships lost compared with one hundred and four.

He shook his head impatiently: he was standing too close to the problem. Seventy, eighty, ninety, a hundred ships – to save them by a surface run meant risking (indeed, almost ensuring) that this U-boat would be lost. What were those losses compared with getting the cash register and manual back safely, and saving (at the present rate of sinkings, although they would increase) nearly 2,400 ships a year? There was no choice, really.

'Surface while we're in the Black Pit. Then we'll think again,' Ned said finally to Jemmy, who realized that some struggle was going on in Ned's mind. 'We'll make the last bit submerged in daylight.'

The Black Pit was a broad band of the Atlantic stretching from south of Greenland down to the Azores which was out of range of Coastal Command planes flying from bases in Britain and Northern Ireland, or from Newfoundland. Although every citizen of Eire was fed by British ships travelling in British convoys, she refused to let British warships or planes use any of her ports or airfields, with all the logic of a drowning teetotaller refusing a lifebuoy hurled by a drunk.

Jemmy nodded but the Croupier said questioningly: 'It's not worth taking a chance, Ned?'

Ned shook his head. 'For the sake of a few days? Listen, we've got what we came for and what the PM, Admiralty, BP and the Flat Earth Society are waiting for with bated breath. My sums here – ' he tapped the signal pad on which he had been doing his calculations ' – show we must be losing an average of at least six and a half ships a day. But weigh that against a projected nearly 2,400 ships lost a year: a million tons a month the moment we lost Hydra.'

' 'S'right, guv,' the Croupier drawled.

'I'm in no rush,' Jemmy said. 'I just don't like sleeping alone any more than Joan does. But neither of us wants to see me knocked off in a Ted U-boat marked down as some frigate's "probable".'

Ned nodded sympathetically: Joan was far too full of life to be left to sleep alone, and she was the only person who stood any chance of curing Jemmy's twitch. As Jemmy always maintained, sex outdoes psychiatry every time.

Jemmy looked at his watch and raised his eyebrows. 'The half an hour is up. Permission to surface, sir?'

'Carry on,' Ned said, and turning to the Croupier asked him: 'Would you make a copy of the main part of the Triton manual and keep it in your pocket sealed up tight in a knotted French letter?'

'Yes. Although this volume is only current for three months and I'm not a cipher expert, I think it'll tell the BP boffins enough to let them go on busting it. Shall I make an extra copy for you?'

'As many as you can find carbons and FLs for. Jemmy, me, Yon, Sergeant Keeler, Hazell…if things go wrong surely one of us will survive.'

'It'll give me something to do. This is going to be a long trip and I didn't bring any books.'

Jemmy was standing at the entrance to the hydrophone cabin. 'Any HE, Hazell? Take your time and turn that ear trumpet nice and slowly.'

He looked round the control room and saw that Yon was not there. 'Pass the word for Mr Heath.' The oilskins and binoculars hanging on their hooks jogged his memory. 'And pass the word for duty lookouts to come to the control room.'

Yon came through the circular hatch which could shut off the whole after part of the boat in a watertight section. He had found a clean pair of engineer's overalls and the German eagle, wings outspread, was still sewn on to the right-hand side.

'How about this?' he said. 'You will address me as *Oberleutnant*, otherwise I shall sulk.'

'*Jawohl!*' Jemmy said and turned back to Hazell. 'Well?'

'No HE, sir: all round search. Just the fishes out there, nibbling the weed that's grown on our hull.'

Jemmy rubbed his hands together cheerfully and took down an oilskin coat. 'Must get a supply of towels: these bloody jackets let the drips get down your neck.' As soon as he had wriggled into the coat and speculated about the weather on the surface, he said to Yon: 'Wish I could get used to this German routine. I can't see any advantage in having the skipper up there in the conning tower and the rest of you down here in the control room.'

He stood back as the lookouts trooped in and pulled on oilskin trousers, coats, and boots, carefully winding towels round their necks.

'Hey, where did you find those towels?' Jemmy demanded.

'Whole locker full in the POs' mess, sir.'

'Oh well, too late now. Let's hope there's no spray. Right,' he said to Yon, 'take her up! Proceed to periscope depth, *Oberleutant!*'

With that he climbed the ladder into the conning tower, followed by the lookouts.

Yon gave an order which set the electric motors humming and then, watching the gauges, gave another series of orders to the men at the forward and after hydroplanes.

The Croupier took the Triton manual from Ned and nodded towards the wardroom. 'I'll go through this slowly, just to make sure I haven't missed anything, then I'll begin making the copies.'

Ned waited, fascinated by Yon's confidence at the control panels. His hands moved back and forth with the skill of a juggler; indeed, Ned thought, controlling this damned boat as it moved in three dimensions was about the same as flying an aeroplane.

The needle of the depth gauge was moving round steadily, and Ned noticed Yon keeping a close watch on the vertical Papenberg glass scale. He seemed to be matching the dial against the gauge; then Ned remembered that the art of surfacing a submarine was to stop her just a few feet below the surface, at just the depth for the commander to raise the periscope for a careful look round and, if necessary, search the sky with the other periscope, and the Papenberg had that kind of accuracy.

Yon moved under the hatch and called up: 'Periscope clear, sir.'

Ned heard Jemmy's muffled voice (presumably he was raising the periscope and searching the dark horizon) giving instructions to the lookouts. Finally Jemmy called down: 'Prepare to surface... Surface!'

And this was the moment when they were most vulnerable, Ned remembered: the conning tower was now clear of the water but everyone in the boat was still blind, unable to open the hatch until the valve had been turned to equalize the pressure inside and outside. There were hilarious stories of what happened to men who opened the hatch with the pressure high in the submarine.

Ned felt a slight pain in his ears, then a sudden flurry of orders from Yon seemed to turn the control room into bedlam: an hysterical hissing showed compressed air was rushing into the ballast tanks to drive out the water, the whining of the electric motors stopped, powerful ventilators began sucking a great draught of fresh air into the boat. Yon was giving instructions about opening diesel exhaust and air vents, and with a massive cough first one and then the other diesel started. As far as Ned could make out, Yon was now using the exhaust gases from the diesels to finish blowing all the water from the ballast tanks.

Now the roar of the diesels seemed to take over the whole boat. Ned crossed over to the chart table and glanced along the shelf above, which held almanacs, lists of lights and radio signals, and finally found the rough log. He began filling it in, guessing the meaning of some of the German abbreviated headings to the various columns. He looked at his watch and, timing the entry half an hour earlier, wrote: 'Sighted destroyer on port bow, dived to 120 feet, destroyer passed ahead.' Then, against the present time: 'Surfaced, proceeded on diesels.' Not the skilled prose of a submariner perhaps, but it told the story.

What was that? It was hard to hear but Jemmy seemed to be shouting 'Clear the bridge' – and yes, the first of the lookouts had just crashed down the ladder and was rolling aside so that the next man down did not land on him. And Jemmy was shouting to Yon: 'Take her down fast, Yon! Two hundred feet.' His voice was fainter as he turned to the helmsman and snapped: 'Hard a'starboard, steer…'

The last few words were lost as Yon ordered the diesels to be shut down, air and exhaust vents closed, the diesel drives disengaged from the propeller shafts and the electric motors started up and connected. The boat would dive in a great curve to starboard.

Ned turned to Hazell: 'Start passing hydrophone reports.'

The man picked up the earphones, pulled them over his head, and as he turned a wheel which presumably gave the direction his face went white.

CHAPTER EIGHTEEN

Jemmy scrambled down the ladder after the last of the lookouts and strode straight towards the hydrophone cabin, turning to Ned as he went. 'Bloody destroyer was waiting for us. Must have picked us up on the radar the minute we surfaced, the cunning sod.'

He looked down at Hazell. 'Well?'

'HE approaching fast, green 040, sounds like that destroyer.'

'Yon, use the Tannoy: warn everyone to close down for heavy depth-charging.'

The Croupier ambled out of the wardroom and, rubbing his eyes sleepily, said to Ned: 'Permission to transfer to major vessels, sir. I'm temperamentally unsuited to submarines: they're too noisy.'

'HE approaching fast, bearing the same.'

The sharp tilt as the U-boat's propellers pushed her forward and the hydroplanes drove her down now combined with a list to starboard as the rudders swung her round in an arc directly towards the approaching destroyer.

This time, Ned saw, Jemmy was playing a different game: just as the waiting and watchful destroyer had picked up the conning tower on her radar and immediately got under way to head at full speed for the spot where her captain calculated the U-boat would be when their courses intersected, Jemmy had turned the steeply diving boat *towards* her.

Obviously he was calculating that his sudden jink to starboard at the last moment would not be noticed because as the destroyer increased speed her Asdic would become useless. Which, Ned estimated, gave the U-boat that vital minute or two to dive straight at her so that the destroyer passed overhead sooner than she expected.

So – in theory at least – the destroyer would drop her depth-charges astern of the U-boat, which presumably would continue on the opposite course and gain even more time as the destroyer – after dropping depth-charges – would slow, and then wait for the turmoil of the explosions to die down before resuming her Asdic search.

Ping...ping...ping, and a sound like surf, the distant deep hissing of the destroyer's propellers. The Asdic signals echoing off the hull were as he imagined Tibetan temple bells would sound across a valley. Then they changed – ping, ping, ping, ping, and at the same time the noise seemed to peck at the U-boat's plating.

They had the U-boat! Ned remembered the hours he had spent on a destroyer's bridge, listening to the monotonous ping...ping...ping, and then suddenly everyone's excitement as the echo came back from a U-boat hull – ping...ding...ping...ding. Then up Asdic dome and a high-speed turn on to the bearing, firing depth-charges to port and starboard and rolling a couple over the stern.

But the destroyer's pinging had stopped: by coincidence the destroyer's sudden increase in speed had coincided with the echoes for two or three pings. He could picture the captain's fury, but the man was committed.

Now came the approaching egg-beater swishing of propellers and he suddenly remembered as a boy standing at one end of a long railway tunnel as the train entered the other.

Jemmy was listening on one earphone and Hazell held the other and twiddled the controls. Suddenly Jemmy let go of his earphone and Hazell pulled off the headset, obviously to avoid being deafened.

'They've let go the depth-charges,' Jemmy said calmly, walking to the conning tower ladder. 'We heard the splashes.'

'Starboard thirty...what's your heading?' he called up to the helmsman. Ned did not hear the reply but Jemmy was increasing the turn to starboard so that the U-boat should be sneaking away on the destroyer's port quarter in the underwater noise and turbulence caused by the depth-charges.

Booo...ooo...ooom. Two exploded almost simultaneously, a noise so powerful that it alone seemed capable of crushing the boat. Then two more. Ned was startled to see the control room was exactly the same; the two men working the hydroplanes were still watching their dials, Yon still standing behind them, Jemmy holding on to the aluminium strut of the ladder, the Croupier listening with his head cocked to one side, a quizzical look on his face.

But the steel deckplates had jumped; each explosion was like a giant squeezing the hull; an all enveloping blast of pressure, noise, naked power. How could this narrow cylinder stand the punishment?

'Take her down to three hundred,' Jemmy told Yon.

Yon gave the orders to the men at the hydroplane controls and the boat's bow-down attitude increased with the heel to starboard as water gurgled into the ballast tanks. 'The builder's guarantee expires at three hundred feet,' Yon reminded them quietly. 'No good asking for a replacement if she caves in.'

'I'll remember that,' Jemmy said, but he was listening. The swishing of the propellers had stopped but Ned could hear the whine from the surface which he realized must be the destroyer's generators and pumps.

'She's stopped to listen,' Jemmy said. 'She must have turned to port as well, trying to outguess us.'

Ping...ping...ping...ping...ping...ping... The sound impulses hit the hull as sharp pecks: this is how a termite feels when the woodpecker starts working nearby.

Ned saw Hazell had the earphones on again. 'HE,' he began, and then laughed at the unnecessary expression, 'dead astern, very close. Depth-charges away...one and two, three and four, five and six.' With that he snatched off the headset.

The first two explosions seemed to squeeze Ned and at the same time kick up through the deckplates, which rattled like a building labourer dropping a hod full of bricks on to galvanized sheeting. The second two were closer and the third pair, he guessed, would end it all. Would the great pressure wave as the hull caved in crush you into unconsciousness, or would you drown in the inrush of water at the pressure of three hundred feet?

Three and four seemed to be touching the hull, and all the lights went out amid the crash of falling glass – and yes, spurting water!

'Emergency lights…report damage after the last two!'

Jemmy seemed calm enough in the darkness.

Five and six. Definitely exploding on the other side and higher: the destroyer had passed right overhead.

Lights came on, weak, an emergency circuit, and Ned saw gauges had fractured and thin streams of water came out at high pressure. A seaman, seeming unhurried to the point of being casual, reached across and screwed valves shut. The streams died. These submariners – well, Jemmy had chosen well.

Yon called for reports from the engine room aft and listened to the answers, and by then the forward torpedo room was reporting.

'Nothing significant, sir,' he reported, to Ned's surprise. 'The only leaks forward and aft are valve-seats being lifted, and the packing in the port shaft gland is dripping. We can very easily tighten that.'

Jemmy nodded, his face shadowed by the dim auxiliary lighting. 'Warn the ERAs not to drop spanners – that destroyer has hydrophones, too.'

Yon did not in fact pass the warning because ERAs serving in submarines – as these two had for years – needed no such instructions.

'Shut down,' Jemmy said. 'No pumps, nothing…'

The electric motors whined to a stop. Ned could hear several different drips. Exploring underground caves must be like this: darkness, unreal silence, the steady drip of water, and not knowing where you were going, though the next step might launch you over a steep ledge.

To occupy his mind, Ned leaned over the chart table and twisted the adjustable lamp so that it lit up the German gridded chart of the Atlantic. Hellfire and damnation. They were well over in the western half. A long way from home.

Now Hazell, headset on, was reporting again in a low voice. 'HE red zero four, distant…red zero five, distant…she's stopped.'

'Having a sniff with her Asdic and hydrophones,' Jemmy commented.

'HE effect red four five…Asdic…'

With friends like these who needed…? The hackneyed phrase amused Ned and for a few moments took his mind off the bitter irony of their situation: they had, more effectively than perhaps they deserved, carried out Mr Churchill's orders.

There was, of course, a way of saving their lives at the risk of losing the Mark III, though they could probably save the manual, but there were other considerations. Jemmy, the Croupier, Yon – everyone must be thinking about it, but to their credit none had said anything. The U-boat could surface and surrender, but… Two 'buts', in fact, one lethal and one that ruled it out entirely.

Perhaps he should say it all in as many words to Jemmy and the Croupier and Yon.

'Officers' meeting in the wardroom,' he said suddenly. 'Can you leave those dials and things for five minutes, Heath?'

The engineer nodded, saying something quickly to the men at the hydroplanes and looking at the two men replacing the broken glasses in the gauges.

Four men in the wardroom meant it was crowded and they had to sit two on each lower bunk. Ned pulled the curtains at either end.

'This isn't a council of war,' he said. 'I'm not delegating or spreading responsibility, or asking your opinions, but you must be wondering why I don't surface and surrender to the destroyer and – '

'Never crossed my mind,' Jemmy interrupted. 'I don't want to get myself killed. We couldn't surface and surrender – they'd spray us with cannon and machine-guns to kill everyone who got to the upper deck and than ram us, or do us in with their 4.7s. White flag be buggered. If they saw it in the rush they'd think it was a trap. Let's face it, U-boats *don't* surrender.'

Ned grinned and nodded. 'That covers my first point. We've got to get the Mark III on the London bus, along with the manual. But when this destroyer's finally left us in peace – providing she does – we might later surface and then surrender to the first RN ship we see – '

'Same again,' Jemmy said doggedly. 'Anyone seeing a U-boat on the surface at whatever range is going to get all excited and start shooting, and then depth-charge or ram. Ned, I hate to say it but we have left the Allied fold. We are the clap, Flying Dutchmen, politicians, Typhoid Marys, income tax collectors, enemies of the human race. We can wave white flags like mad, but the first people sighting us are going to start shooting. A U-boat is a U-boat; there's no way we can disguise it to look like Number Ten Downing Street, or a bunch of gladioli.

'A Coastal Command Liberator fitted with radar, a Leigh light and depth-charges will jump us at night as soon as we make a blip on his radar screen. Ned, my old mate, nobody (on our side, I mean) trusts a U-boat. Guns, depth-charges, Leigh light – but sink on sight!'

The Croupier carefully traced his eyebrows with a wetted finger. 'What Jemmy's trying to say tactfully is that collectively we smell.'

'There was a second point I was going to make,' Ned said mildly.

'Are you still alive?' Jemmy asked ironically. 'They sank me with a 4.7 inch shell hit on the conning tower as I waved a pair of Joan's knickers in a friendly sort of way.'

'Always thought you were a bit of a pansy,' the Croupier said unsympathetically.

'I didn't know Joan *had* any knickers,' Ned said, 'but listen. If somehow we managed to get ourselves captured and managed to get the cash register and the Triton manual safely on board the other ship, we've got another security problem. At the moment only twenty-three of us, chosen men and sworn to secrecy, know we've captured a U-boat. Maybe half a dozen of us really know why. None of us will ever talk. The German prisoners will be kept in a special isolated prison camp. So the chances of the Germans discovering that we've captured one of their U-boats and thus Enigma Mark III and Triton are nil.

'But bring a destroyer into it… A hundred men of the ship's company see it happen, some will take photographs, all will be as proud and excited as hell. I don't see anyone swearing every one of them to secrecy. Nor do I see all of 'em surrendering camera film. If even one roll of film stayed in someone's pocket and was developed by a photographer in some market town in the Midlands, people would talk. You can't mistake a U-boat. So the photographer mentions to his wife and his mates in the pub – in complete confidence, of course – and they gossip… Soon the Germans will get the word: one of their boats – one of the thirty or so missing that month – was captured. And overnight – well, as soon as new manuals can be got to the boats – Triton is replaced, and we are back at square one – which is black-out. They can carry on using the came cash register, of course.'

Jemmy gave a startling series of twitches. 'Ned, mate, with our wireless transmitter busted, there's no chance that we can surrender at long range or pass the word to the Admiralty and stop all these people being nasty to us, so it wouldn't matter if you had Mr Churchill, Roosevelt, the C-in-C of the Home Fleet or Veronica Lake on board; there's just no way of surrendering to 'em. You're in a U-boat, mate, and like a wasp at a picnic, if you sit still for a moment you'll never get a second chance: somebody'll swat you!'

Ned laughed, conscious that Hazell was again reporting, and said: ' "Pariahs of the world, unite!" I'd reached all those conclusions in the lifeboat. I really wanted to explain to you why we just can't surface and surrender.'

'Oh, we can surface and surrender,' Yon said. 'It's just that we'd never live to tell the tale, eh Jemmy?'

The four of them suddenly became conscious of Hazell's monotonous reports.

CHAPTER NINETEEN

'HE red two oh, distant but closing...red three oh...still closing...think I can pick up the Asdic...red four oh...five oh... She's passing on a reciprocal course, slow speed, Asdic on...'

Jemmy stood up and walked the half a dozen paces to the hydrophone room and Hazell, seeing him coming, pulled off an earpiece and proffered it.

Just then all of them heard the faint ping...ping... ping...ping... Yon walked over to the men at the hydroplane controls, although every piece of machinery in the boat was shut down. Men no longer used the head because pumping the toilet bowl would make an easily detectable noise.

'Persistent bugger,' the Croupier whispered. 'A headhunter. Wants to add to his score.'

'That's what he's paid to do,' Ned said mildly.

'Fact is,' the Croupier muttered, 'I tend to take against anyone trying to kill me, whether he's a friend or foe.'

'I'm more against him if he's a friend,' Ned said. 'I wish I knew who is commanding this destroyer: it'd be fun meeting him afterwards and telling him the mistakes he made.'

'*If* he makes any mistakes. He seems to have the textbook open at the right page!'

Hazell said: 'He's turning...approaching...'

Ping...ping...ping...and then, as the first of the sound waves hit the hull and bounced off, ping...ping...ping...ping... ping...ping...

'Take her down to four hundred feet as soon as the first charges go off,' Jemmy said.

Yon opened his mouth to say something, thought better of it, and said: 'Aye, aye, sir.'

'I know what he was going to say,' the Croupier whispered.

'So do I,' Ned said. 'That with the charges set to go off at different depths, we're liable to drop into a sandwich.'

'Yes, and Yon said these 'orrible tubs are designed for a maximum of three hundred feet.'

Ned dredged his memory of the last anti-submarine course he had attended at Portland, just before Dunkirk. 'There's some nonsense theory that the deeper you go and the greater the water pressure, the less the effect of the depth-charge. I don't remember the figures, but the strength of the bang is lessened by the square of the distance, or something equally improbable.'

'Yes, I did that course, too. Not very convincing. They'd done trials on an old wreck. I'd have thought the greater pressure of the water increased the pressure wave from the charge...' His voice tailed off. 'No, of course the greater water pressure would *reduce* the charge – '

He broke off as the Asdic pings bounced off the hull as though a boy was throwing pebbles.

'I bet that bastard wears the grommet in his cap,' the Croupier whispered. 'All Leslie Howard and Noël Coward and cucumber sandwiches. If you hear a bump it's because he's dropped a charge on to our bridge.'

'Depth-charges...two...four... Just four, sir,' Hazell said unbelievingly. 'No, there's two more. I bet someone's getting a bottle over that!'

Depth-charge patterns were very carefully worked out. Projectors could hurl them out to port and starboard, well clear of the ship, but the two intended to burst in the ship's wake were usually rolled off the stern on special rails. Hazell's 'bottle' referred to the Navy's slang for a reprimand, which was usually a polite word describing a string of oaths from a petty officer.

The first pair of explosions, separated by two or three seconds and showing that the hydrostatic valves were set to detonate them at different depths, seemed to be above and below the submarine, squeezing it as though it was a horseshoe being shaped on a blacksmith's anvil. The lights went out again, glass clattered on to the steel floor plates, there was the sound of water spurting under pressure.

The roaring finally convinced Ned that the boat was sinking and he thought bitterly that Clare would never know he had succeeded. A moment later he realized that most of the noise was more water sluicing into the ballast and trim tanks, and the electric motors were running to spin the propellers and, with the hydroplanes, drive the boat deeper – just as Jemmy had ordered moments ago.

The next two explosions were the most violent yet: the whole boat creaked under the double blow, there was more water spurting, and Yon called for lights, and for damage reports.

Jemmy's face suddenly appeared on the far side of the control room, a satanic grin on his face, which was lit by the reflection of the torch he was holding up to the depth gauge.

'Going down…fourth floor, ladies' wear; third floor, garden implements; second floor, a bloody big pair of bangs!'

And they came: even nearer than the first two, Ned was certain. The next two would be game and set: a thunderous crash, a roar of water, and it would all be over: the crushed U-boat would be on its way down and no one on board would ever know whether it reached the bottom or stayed suspended…

But the depth-charges continued. Eleven…twelve… Ned found himself counting and at the same time listening to the mad dance of the deck plates, the groaning and crunching of the almost circular ribs which formed the skeleton of the boat over which the hull plating was welded (and riveted, too: God, if any of those rivets started popping).

Yon was shouting orders again, the electric motors stopped whining, the emergency lights came on and Jemmy said in a low voice: 'We're at 425 feet. Just twenty short of the deepest I've ever tried.'

The Croupier, who had also been listening to the creaking hull – to creaks that came from the pressure of the depth, as well as from the pressure waves radiating out from the exploding charges – said languidly: 'Jemmy, old sport, I'm sure you don't want a couple of surface types like Ned and me being able to make the same boast as you, so as far as we are concerned, 425 feet *is quite enough*, old son. Too much, some might say.'

Jemmy was still grinning. Ned was startled at just how satanic he looked, and he glanced up at the depth gauge again, as if hoping it would show another fifty. 'Lads, three of those charges burst *below* us.'

'Let's go up to fifty feet and fool them,' Ned said promptly.

'You won't fool these boys, and they'd have to turn down the volume on their Asdic to stop being deafened by the returns.'

'What are these metallic cracks we keep hearing?' Ned enquired.

'Metallic what?' demanded Jemmy.

'Well, sort of sharp creaks. There! And there!'

'Oh, don't let *that* worry you,' Jemmy said, as though reassuring a nervous aunt having her first ride in an Underground train. 'That's just the water compressing the hull. Actually at this depth our cubic displacement will be less because of it.'

'It'll stunt our growth,' Ned protested, and looked round at Hazell, who had again put on his headset, and was turning the dial of the hydrophone, hunting for sounds and reminding Ned of an old man with an ear trumpet.

'No HE, sir,' he said to Jemmy.

Jemmy glanced at Ned. 'Up to his old tricks, that destroyer: he's sitting up there, a hand cupped behind his ear, just listening.'

'Can he hear all this waterworks?' Ned waved to the dozen or so streams of water criss-crossing the boat from dials and broken gauges.

'No, but we're mending 'em as fast as possible because our bilge pumps are noisy. Hello, Keeler, you look worried!'

The Marine sergeant had just squeezed through the circular hatch and once inside the control room spotted Ned in the dim light and stood to attention. 'Sorry to report a casualty aft, sir. Two, actually, both dead.'

'No damage to the ship?'

'Oh no, sir,' Keeler said in a shocked tone. 'No, a couple of Jerries who'd been a bit upset with that first lot of depth-charging got very agitated when they heard the 'lectric motors start up with the second lot. Then when we started going deeper and things began creaking they started screaming and ran amok. Both were trying to open a valve, with all their mates screaming at them to stop. We didn't know how urgent it was, sir…'

'Knife?'

'Only way, sir with both of 'em. We were getting a whiff of battery gas, so we didn't want any sparks to fly – if you get my meaning, sir.'

'Did it quieten down the rest of them?'

'Oh yes, worked a fair treat, sir. They'd never seen commando knives before.'

'Commando knifework, you mean! Very well, Keeler. Any ideas about the bodies?'

'No hurry about them, sir: they don't upset us, and they remind the rest of the Jerries to behave, or else'. Keeler grinned and continued: 'Wish our chaps up there were not so good!'

Ned pointed at Jemmy. 'We've got a live one here, you know!'

'Yes, I'll remind our lads o' that, sir.' He turned to Jemmy. 'Best o' luck, sir. I'm a betting man meself, 'specially over the sticks.'

Jemmy nodded in agreement. 'This flat racing stuff is very tame. Start a book on how many depth-charges we'll get!'

'Oh, we have, we have, sir,' Keeler assured him earnestly. 'I picked thirty-eight. Reckon I've got a chance?'

Jemmy nodded. 'Twelve down and twenty-six to go, eh? Well, your guess is as good as mine.'

With that a cheerful Keeler squeezed back through the hatch just as Hazell reported: 'No HE except I can hear his pumps and generators. No direction, though: I think he's right above us.'

Jemmy said to Ned: 'I was watching the sea water temperature as we came down that last hundred feet. By luck we've dropped into a cold layer, so his Asdic isn't working so well. If we can stay in or under it, we should be all right. But if it slides around – they do, sometimes, nudged by currents – we may be all naked again, like the fan dancer whose ostrich feather moulted.'

Hazell said: 'HE effect sir, I think I heard splashes. Four – two and then two. Screws – increasing speed…'

'If they sit there they'll be blown up by their own charges,' Yon said, a querulous note in his voice implying that by moving the destroyer's captain was cheating.

'Four,' commented Jemmy. 'They're not sure.'

The first explosion was enormous: Ned felt it slam up through his feet; it seemed to crush his chest while battering on his ear drums, and no sooner had the floor plates dropped back into position and the last piece of glass tinkled out, burst by the sudden and enormous pressure, than the second charge burst: a repetition which seemed certain to crush a boat already bruised and strained from the previous explosions.

But there was Jemmy, inspecting gauges with his torch, and the other moving light was Yon. Both men were stepping round or ducking under spurts of water, and Ned realized that the other blobs of light were the torches of the two men who had been seated at the hydroplanes and were now busy shutting valves.

Ned heard Sergeant Keeler calling from the circular hatch and he walked over to see what he wanted.

'That German Engineer, sir,' Keeler explained. 'I know he was sort of collaborating with Mr Heath when we started. Now he's all excited and keeps pointing along here and jabbering away. I *think*,' Keeler said carefully, 'that he's offering to help. Anyways, I've brought him along so you can talk to him.'

Keeler stood to one side and beckoned the figure behind him. The Croupier had materialized from somewhere and with a brief, 'Leave him to me, Ned,' started questioning the man, who kept on nodding.

'Keeler's right: the chap guessed we must have some leaks and is offering to help sort things out. Says he knows all the valves – yes, and where the spare glasses are for the broken sight valves and gauges.'

'Very well, Keeler,' Ned said. 'You did perfectly right: we'll keep him with us.'

Keeler grinned contentedly as he returned to his prisoners. At that moment the third and fourth depth-charges exploded, but, compared with the first two, much less violently.

'Two deep and two shallow settings,' Jemmy said to Ned. 'Hello, what's old Helmut want?'

The Croupier explained in English, and Jemmy gave a short laugh. 'Can you beat it?' he asked Ned. 'Trying to keep any engineer away from his engines is bad enough, but keeping a German engineer away from his toys at a time like this! Yon! Your mate is back!'

'Thank gawd for that. Tell him to get replacement glasses for these bloody gauges. We're finding the shut-off valves.'

The Croupier translated and the German happily hurried round, opening little lockers no one had noticed, and setting up the glasses like a barman expecting a rush of customers.

Jemmy nodded his head at Ned, indicating the wardroom, and when the two were inside, Jemmy said: 'I don't believe in forecasting the result on the day of the race, Ned, but I think we're nicely parked under a very thick cold layer. We're probably about as deep as Herbert up there has ever chased anyone, and right now I doubt if he has the slightest idea where we are – '

'But the first two of those last four!' protested Ned.

'He was just trying his luck: two set very deep – four hundred feet, I reckon, and that's an absurd depth setting by normal standards – and the last two much shallower. Still deep, probably a hundred and fifty feet. Believe me, when you're using only four charges instead of six, and at such settings, you're groping.'

'Steady on,' Ned said cautiously. 'Talk like that and you'll get the bloody thing bouncing off the periscopes!'

Jemmy shook his head cheerfully. 'No, Herbert thinks he's sunk us and is looking for oil and wreckage, or else he thinks this cold layer stretches for miles and knows he can't cover the whole area to stop us sneaking away. So now we repair the bloody dials and things, tighten up the propshaft packing glands, get the cook to work providing grub – serve our chaps first – and as soon as it's nightfall we'll surface and begin our run for home in earnest. Sorry I let that sod catch me. In the Med the Teds didn't have radar worth a damn. I was crazy to go up like that: the destroyer's radar operator must have nearly died laughing when he saw our blip come up!'

'That slurping of water,' Ned said cautiously.

'Just bilge water. All these gauges and dials peeing away – doesn't amount to much, but you notice it sloshing about in the bilge. We'll pump out in an hour or so, but we'll give Hazell plenty of time with his hydrophone. He's good at it, too.'

'Wish we could get that bloody transmitter working.'

'Don't be crazy, Ned: like this we can choose where we go to. If their Lordships knew we had the boat, the cash register and the cookery book, they'd dream up some nonsense like making a rendezvous with a Sunderland and paddling the goodies over in a canoe, which sinks on the way. Let's keep the ball in our court,' Jemmy said firmly. 'You're the boss, but I'd sooner see you, the Croupier and me turn up at the Citadel in a taxi, the cash register in a suitcase – it's already fitted in its own wooden box – and the cookery book in your hot little hands. No, it's our bird; don't let any of the other bastards claim it!'

Ned carefully pencilled the lines on the German version of the North Atlantic chart, eastern section, used the dividers to measure off the latitude and longitude, and then wrote the figures on the chart.

With nothing else to do, having taken three hurried star sights using the last of the horizon when an unexpected break in the clouds revealed them, he checked over his calculations. No, he had not made any silly error like adding seven and three and writing down nine.

So now they were outside the Black Pit. Beyond it and on the British side of it, in fact. From now on their main enemy was Coastal Command – a Sunderland, a Liberator, a tiny Hudson or even a Catalina diving on them out of a night sky using its radar. The U-boat had neither radar nor radar detector: the German Second Officer had described to Ned U-boat Command's experiments with two different sorts of detector and how both had been given up when sinkings continued. It seemed that the British, realizing the U-boats began diving as soon as the radar detected them, had guessed that the Germans had devised some sort of detecting device, worked out what it was likely to be, and discovered it gave out some sort of oscillation. The cunning Tommies, according to the German Second Officer, then fitted their planes with a special receiver which picked up the oscillations and then flew round listening and with their radar switched off. The U-boats happily cruised along on the surface with their radar detectors switched on and, they thought, acting as some magic talisman. Suddenly they would have about a minute in which to realize that the Tommies had somehow detected them – obviously without using radar – and were dropping enough depth-charges to sink or damage them.

Listening to the Second Officer's story, Ned wanted to say, 'I know the feeling,' but thought better of it. They were in fact gradually approaching home – only it was an enemy coast! No one – ASIU, BP or the Admiralty – had anticipated that a U-boat's wireless transmitter might not work; no one could imagine the lifeboat set being lost. It was inconceivable that Ned would have no way of warning anyone that he was approaching. For the want of a nail, the shoe was lost... And, he realized with a cold bitterness, for the want of a transmitter, Britain could lose the war: this U-boat now thundering along on the surface in the darkness of an ocean night had the key (how literally a key) to the Battle of the Atlantic, but no way of preventing her friends destroying her.

Yet…yet…yet: he saw, like the faint glimmer of a distant fleck of phosphorescence, that there was a slight chance of passing the word without having a whole ship's company watching and later gossiping. A *slight* chance and a *massive* risk. Would it work? He stood up from the chart table, jerked upright by the tension. The Croupier was asleep in his bunk after a tedious watch as they ran submerged, which for both Ned and the Croupier was a far greater strain than running on the surface. On the surface with the U-boat crashing along at near full speed, slamming into waves, slicing great swells in a welter of spray that flew up with the force of flying concrete, they could call on the experience of thousands of hours spent in destroyers and, in Ned's case, MTBs in the Channel during the time immediately after Dunkirk.

Yon probably carried most of the strain: in addition to the responsibility for the entire mechanical workings of this steel box of tricks he, as a result of the German Navy's way of running their U-boats, was second-in-command and responsible for diving and surfacing. In addition, though, he had to make up for the fact that neither Ned nor the Croupier had submarine experience: their wartime lives up to now had been devoted to dodging or sinking them. Yon was at this moment asleep on a mattress spread just beside the chart table, occupying the only six feet in the control room where no one would accidentally tread on him.

Jemmy was on the bridge. Ironically, back at the Citadel in London, when Captain Watts had discussed who Ned should take, Watts had had doubts about Jemmy. Not about his courage or his brains, but because in Jemmy's case both had been stretched to breaking point: no man with any imagination could become the great submarine ace of the Mediterranean without eventually paying an exorbitant price in nervous strain. Finally Ned had insisted on taking Jemmy. All right, he had a terrible twitch, nightmares several times a week, hands that trembled like tuning forks, but Ned knew instinctively that Jemmy had not lost his nerve. He had been under a terrible strain, but the trip in the *City of Norwich*, the week in the lifeboat, and now command of a U-boat had, in a curious and quite inexplicable way, removed the strain. Yes, the twitch which had vanished for a while had now come back, though far less violently, and Jemmy was, instead of being wound up and taut like an overtuned violin, relaxed, jocular and obviously enjoying himself. Both Ned and the Croupier had recognized that Jemmy's apparently casual behaviour during the destroyer attack was the real Jemmy in action, not an act to keep up the morale of the ship's company. Joan, Ned thought to himself as he climbed the ladder into the conning tower, is in for a surprise, and it will also do her complexion the world of good.

He looked up the hatchway. 'Permission to come up on the bridge?'

'Ah, granted sir,' Jemmy called down. 'Turning into a decent sort of night. Wind's chilly. What did the sights produce?'

Ned gave him the latitude and longitude.

'We're well inside the range of the Brylcreem boys,' Jemmy commented. 'A Liberator with radar, a Leigh light and a basketful of depth-charges could do for us!'

'What does a Leigh light look like from down here?'

'Damned if I really know.' He turned to the four lookouts. 'Any of you seen a Leigh light?'

'Caught winkles at Leigh-on-Sea, sir,' one of them muttered.

'Yes, and had to borrow a bent pin to get 'em out: that's the trouble with you Essex people,' Jemmy growled.

'Well, I've seen one fitted on the wing of a Liberator on the ground,' Ned said. 'As far as I know it's a fantastically bright searchlight designed by a chap called Leigh, though whether he's a sailor or an airman, I don't know. Quite a bright idea – excuse the pun. Leigh realized the only time U-boats ran surfaced outside the Black Pit was at night, so even if Coastal Command picked them up on the radar, it was dam' difficult to aim depth-charges from the air and drop them on to a radar blip. So with this powerful spotlight the planes work like a poacher with a torch lashed to his shotgun. Very unsporting – you ever done any of it?'

'No,' Jemmy said. 'Snares and ferrets, but never torches. How does it work?'

'Well, with the torch lashed to the barrel but switched off, you creep along in the darkness to a place where you know there'll be plenty of rabbits – they come out at night to dance and play, you know, and hey-nonny-nonny. As soon as you're sure there are one or two there, you aim and switch on the torch. The light hypnotizes them and they sit up and stare back. You can either aim using your sights – that's difficult because the light dazzles you too. Or, you have to have the torch lined up with the barrel so that if the target is lit you just squeeze the trigger and you're bound to hit.'

'I don't see what's unsporting about *that*,' Jemmy said, snuggling his head down into the collar of his oilskin. 'If you're a poacher, your livelihood depends on knocking off a few bunnies. And with meat rationing the way it is, they fetch a good price, not being rationed.'

'Well, I think it's unsporting,' Ned said. 'Like shooting a sitting bird!'

'That's the only time I can hit the bastards, when they're sitting still!' Jemmy protested. 'But this Leigh light – *that's* bloody unsporting.' All Jemmy's submarine loyalties bubbled up. 'Doesn't give a sub a chance. A bloody great aeroplane screaming down out of the night and switching on a spotlight – why, dammit, the commander might be having a pee over the lee rail just at that moment!'

'You have the vulgar and limited view of a submariner,' Ned said. 'So have I, until we're safely berthed!'

He watched the U-boat's long wedge-shaped bow slicing through the quartering seas and listened to the snoring of the diesel exhaust and sucking of the air vents. Strange to think that at this very moment up there in that blackness a British aircraft might have this boat showing as a blip on the radar, and be arming the depth-charges and getting ready to switch on the Leigh light.

'Yes, well,' he said to Jemmy, making sure none of the lookouts could hear. He then described the idea which had occurred to him at the chart table.

'Bloody risky,' Jemmy commented. 'Might work if we're quick enough. We don't get a second chance, that's for sure. All of us had better do some dummy runs.'

CHAPTER **TWENTY**

As memories of the depth-charging faded, both Ned and the Croupier settled down to submarine existence. For both of them the watch system had been a way of life for as long as they could remember, except for the brief time at ASIU and, for Ned, the long time in hospital as doctors fought to save his arm.

Now well inside the area covered by Coastal Command's searching planes, the boat was being driven hard on the surface at night but moving submerged by day, surfacing a couple of times so that Ned could get some sun sights because, for several evenings, clouds had built up with the last of the light to hide the stars, even though the horizon was clear.

Ned was keeping his balance against the pitching by holding the forward side of the bridge with the lookouts to one side and behind him, each responsible for a ninety-degree sector of the sea and sky, and going through the routine of lifting binoculars, searching the horizon, dropping the binoculars on their strap, rubbing their eyes and looking again.

The wind was from the west, gusting occasionally to fifteen knots, so that the U-boat thundered along eastward in a cloud of her own diesel exhaust, giving the men on the bridge a headache and a metallic taste in their mouths. The long, narrow boat, most of it like the proverbial iceberg, with only its conning tower and upperworks above water, pitched heavily as long swell waves swept under, lifting first the stern, seesawing the hull as the crest passed beneath, and then lifting the bow and burying the stern just in time for the next wave to repeat the sequence.

With the after side of the conning tower open and leading on to a flat gun platform on which the two 20 mm cannon were mounted, with another climb down to the heavier gun, a large following sea was the most dangerous. A rogue sea rushing up astern before the boat had time to start lifting could swamp the bridge and, although in bad weather everyone wore a safety harness securely clipped to rings in the conning tower, Ned had long since noted that the harness only stopped you being washed away; there was nothing to stop a heavy sea smashing you against the steel plating, staving in ribs, breaking arms and legs, or cracking skulls. In a heavy following sea, Ned reckoned, the boat would momentarily submerge, a proposal which shocked Jemmy, who suddenly found himself in a minority.

Ned found that, providing he forgot about the cash register and the cookery book, he enjoyed his watches. The low conning tower, the feeling of being perched astride an enormous log being driven along by some unseen force, was exhilarating. For the first ten minutes of the watch, anyway... Then, if it was not raining, a rogue wave would slap the side of the conning tower, dodge up and over the spray deflectors, and deposit a few gallons of water on the heads of the five men. Never an honest bucketful hurled at a man's back or sides, where it would just run down the oilskin coat and trousers and boots tucked inside the trouser legs. No, it always hit the face, at the side or front, so that it squirted down to soak the towel carefully wound round the neck to seal the openings that no oilskin designer had yet managed to close successfully, and after a couple of minutes of has-it-or-hasn't-it, the first of the drips would start their chilly decent along the spine, inside woollen underclothes and jerseys.

It was, Ned thought wryly, like sailing before the war: though thrashing to windward in a yacht was more uncomfortable than pounding into a head sea in a submarine because the submariner, at the end of his watch, could go below, hang up his wet clothes to dry, rub down with a towel and turn into a dry bunk, and the cook would provide hot food and drink. That never seemed to happen in any yacht he sailed in.

Clare – it was now about two o'clock in the morning in London. Was she on night duty? Was she asleep in the nurses' quarters? Was she having a couple of days' leave and staying in

Palace Street? One thing was certain – she would not be writing to him. Although she had no idea exactly what he was doing, she knew there was no way of him getting mail.

He turned and called to the lookouts over his left shoulder.

'You fellows asleep? Haven't heard any reports!'

'Not exactly a busy shipping lane, sir,' one of them said.

The two to starboard merely cursed the spray settling on the lenses of their binoculars. It took a lot of rubbing and polishing to get rid of the smears.

Down below, lights dimmed, Jemmy, the Croupier and Yon would be sleeping, the green curtains drawn across the front of their bunks. Hazell, who never seemed to sleep, would be in the wireless cabin, listening on the U-boat wavelength, faithfully copying down anything he heard and calling the Croupier if he picked up a signal from *B der U* for this boat. The big Blohm and Voss diesels at this distance were a comforting burble of exhaust. An ERA at the forward end of the engine room could watch the dials and gauges of both engines. Exhaust manifold temperature, cylinder head temperature (eighteen of them)... The electric motors would be spinning, making electricity instead of using it, and feeding it into the great banks of batteries. The air compressors would have refilled all the big tanks with compressed air, used for starting the diesels and blowing the water out of the ballast tanks when surfacing.

He turned up the faint light on the dim bridge gyrocompass: the quartermaster was steering well. He hauled back the sleeve of his oilskin enough to look at his wristwatch. An hour and a quarter left of the watch.

He should marry Clare when they got back. It would change nothing, except it would all be legal. She would have a husband and a mother-in-law. And get a widow's pension if he was knocked off. Curiously enough they had never really talked of marriage in terms of a date and a ceremony. He almost laughed aloud at the thought that lovers in bed together rarely discussed wedding rings.

Suddenly the bridge, the whole boat and the sea turned a brilliant white: a Leigh light! This was it! Would it work? He crouched over the hatch and yelled: 'Hard a'port, quartermaster...slow ahead port, full ahead starboard...' To the nearest lookout he snapped: 'Grab that signal lamp, call up the bloody thing!'

The great white eye was diving steeply: any moment the bombs or depth-charges would be bursting round them. He slammed down the hatch and clamped it shut: a near-miss could send tons of water below. The sharp turn and change in speed will have told Jemmy all he needed to know.

Come on! He looked aft and the enormous light was diving steeply but not quite directly at them: the U-boat was just beginning to turn under rudders and engines.

Would it work? When Ted dive-bombers kept up their attacks on the destroyer *Aztec*, when he found himself senior surviving officer, he had tried to guess whether each attacking pilot was left- or right-handed, assuming a right-handed man turned more easily to the right. And that was the reason why he and Jemmy had planned this sharp turn to port the moment they were caught in a Leigh light: they hoped that by the time the boat was turning the bomber would be too low and too committed to swing round to conform.

Christ! A stick of bombs erupted along the starboard side like half a dozen fire crackers: fifty yards away and at least three of them sending up water spouts in what would have been the U-boat's length had she not turned. They sound like sharp cracks up here; down below they must seem almost like direct hits.

He flung open the hatch and Jemmy came up like a jack-in-the-box.

'She's all yours, Jemmy,' Ned said quickly. 'Give me the Aldis,' he snapped at the lookout, who had been so impressed by the bomb bursts he had stopped signalling.

That was her still turning, Leigh light blazing away: Ned guessed that as the plane climbed away the pilot had seen the U-boat on the surface and had reckoned the bombs had so damaged her that she could not dive. Or could not dive because of some other attack...

Dot-dash...dot-dash...dot-dash...

The Morse letter A, and used for calling up. Ned kept fingering the second smaller trigger and felt rather than heard the mirror clicking as it aimed the narrow beam. Dot-dash...dot-dash...dot-dash...

The plane was not answering – a signal lamp was unlikely to be as close at hand as a packet of sandwiches – but she now shut off her Leigh light: instead she was starting a slow circle round the U-boat, like an enormous owl inspecting its prey.

There – a long dash: acknowledging the signal: but the pilot was staying well out of range.

Ned aimed the Aldis carefully: dash-dot-dot-dot...dot-dash-dot...dot-dot...dash... Quickly he spelled out 'British', by which time the plane was well astern, in a perfect position to make another bombing run.

But Jemmy must have the boat back on a straight course again, both engines full ahead.

Ah, there was a dash in reply.

Damnation! The suddenness of the Leigh light going out had left him almost blinded. Where the hell was the plane now? Oh yes, she had put on navigation lights. Wary...they knew all about those twin 20 mm cannons and, although curious about the signalling, were not going to get themselves shot down.

Ned aimed again: dot-dash-dash-dot...dot-dash-dot... Slowly he spelled out 'prize', received an answering 'T' and, with the plane turning ahead, saw her signal lamp flickering urgently. He read the letters aloud. 'Stop…no…more…men…on…deck.'

'Fair enough,' Jemmy said. 'Now tell 'em all about it, Ned!'

Ned's index finger was already aching, but, pausing after each word for the acknowledging 'T', and having to dodge round the periscopes as the plane circled, with one of the lookouts keeping the flex clear, he continued the message.

'Signal… Admiralty…attention… ASIU… York…' He had to repeat his name twice before getting a 'T.' …Spree…successful… need…air…cover…stop… Yorke…to…pilot…highly…secret… do…not…radio…and…use…scrambler…phone…stop… Report…our…transmitter…busted…report…our…position.'

After the series of 'T's a brief signal winked back.

'What…about… Whitstable…'

Ned laughed: the pilot had a sense of humour in the way he was checking up whether they were really British.

'Don't…eat…natives…when… R…in…month.'

The plane, on the port beam, suddenly switched on its Leigh light and came low so that it had the U-boat in profile.

'Wave, you buggers,' Jemmy snarled at the lookouts. 'Smile…look happy, just in case he hasn't believed a word of it and is going to straddle us with another stick.'

But the plane roared over, shut off the Leigh light, and continued circling with its navigation lights on. Its signal lamp winked again.

'Remain…surfaced…give…course…speed.'

Ned replied: 'Wilco…zero…eight…zero…sixteen knots.'

Jemmy laughed. ' "Wilco" – masterly. That'll get 'em. No Ted would know that.'

'Wilco' had become RAF wireless slang for 'will comply', but as with all slang it sounded wrong the moment it was used even slightly out of context.

Again the plane's signal lamp winked. 'Is…that… ASIU…?' Ned spelled out: 'Anti… Submarine… Investigation… Unit… that's…our…mob…tell… Captain… Watts.'

The plane then asked: 'What…phone…number?'

'Jesus,' Jemmy said, 'They're *really* checking up on us.'

Ned answered: 'Whitehall…9000…tell… Joan… Jemmy… sends…love.'

The plane sent one last signal before flying off: 'Have…good …trip…please…report…my…eggs…landed…closer.'

The navigation lights went out and Ned handed the signal lamp to the lookout.

'Put it back in its box, very carefully. It's worth a hundred times its weight in gold!'

The Croupier's plaintive voice came up the hatch. 'Permission to come on the bridge and share the fun?'

'Granted. The show is over,' Jemmy said. 'Ned won the box of chocolates.'

'From what I heard from the conning tower, we ain't home yet,' the Croupier said. 'Those Brylcreem boys will balls up the message and kidnap Joan, too.'

'A great big white flag,' Ned said. 'Lash it to the periscope. Get some chaps to work on it,' he told the Croupier. 'Four sheets sewn together, if there's nothing else.'

He turned to Jemmy. 'Joan's going to have to take her chance, and I've got to go down and play with the charts to see what time that plane will get back to England, and the soonest another one will come out. What brand was it?'

'A Liberator, as far as I could see. Certainly not a Sunderland or Catalina: neither can make sharp turns like that thing did.'

Ned went below and sat at the chart table, measuring distances with dividers. The Liberator probably had hundreds of miles to fly back to its base in the UK. Certainly with that news it would fly direct. At say two hundred knots. Four or five hours. A couple of hours to get the word to Admiralty, an hour for ASIU to react and get approval for whatever it proposed, and another five hours for a plane to get back here and find them. The position the Liberator reported would not be very precise. Thirteen hours before anything could happen that would affect them. He glanced at his watch. That would mean noon

tomorrow.

CHAPTER **TWENTY-ONE**

The day began as though winter had stepped aside to let autumn return for a day or two. The air was cold but the wind had dropped to ten knots from the north-west, pulling broken cumulus clouds with it so that from time to time a weak sun played on the sea like a cinema usherette using a torch with weak batteries.

Jemmy was on watch but Ned stood on the tiny bridge beside him, and both men were wearing thick jackets, the German equivalent of short bridge coats, instead of the usual oilskins. The lookouts were cheerful, the heavy binoculars coming up to sweep the four quadrants with something approaching eagerness.

'You know what could mess everything up, don't you?' Jemmy said lugubriously.

'Many things,' Ned said. 'The most likely being us sighting another blasted frigate and having to dive just before our plane comes back.'

'That's what I was thinking. We'd need to get down fast before the frigate got a sight of our laundry.'

The 'laundry' was the huge white flag sewn out of four sheets, and now streaming out from the periscope standard and slatting from time to time.

'Aircraft red four five!' a lookout called. 'Sunderland.'

Ned and Jemmy lifted their binoculars, and simultaneously saw the flying boat just beneath the cloud layer. 'Flying boat,' commented Jemmy. 'Appropriate name. Just a boat hull with wings.'

Ned's finger hovered over the alarm button warning of air attack, but the warning was to prepare to dive.

'Plug in the signal lamp and test it,' Jemmy ordered. 'And make sure there are no kinks in the flex.'

He lifted his binoculars and looked at the flying boat again.

'She's seen us all right. Ah! She's calling us up!' he exclaimed as a white eye started winking.

'I'll take the call,' Ned said, mimicking the pompous tones of a self-important businessman addressing his secretary.

One of the lookouts passed him the signal lamp. He lined up the aircraft in the cross-wire sight, and squeezed the large trigger which switched on the light and then the smaller trigger in front of it which aimed the mirror. Dash: the Morse for 'T', the answering or acknowledging signal.

'Who...is...Clare?' the plane flashed, and Jemmy began chuckling.

'That's Captain Watts being cautious!'

'What the hell do I answer?'

'She's your bird,' Jemmy said unsympathetically.

Ned aimed the lamp. 'Future... Mrs...Yorke.'

'She...sends...love,' the plane signalled as it began a long, slow turn astern over the U-boat's wake. Then, having made what was in effect a challenge, and been satisfied with the reply, began signalling again: 'Will...drop...parachute...and...canister...one ...mile...ahead...of...you...for...marker...dye.'

'Box of chocolates from Captain Watts,' Jemmy said, and then yelled down the hatch for the Croupier to come up and watch the fun.

The Croupier arrived sleepy and surly, thinking he was being called on watch, and sprang completely awake when the Sunderland was pointed out.

The plane's signal lamp began again. 'What...is...sea...state ...wind...direction...and...strength?'

'Wind...northwest...under...ten...knots...sea...strength... two,' Ned signalled back.

'Hard to distinguish sea conditions from a plane,' Jemmy said. 'Always looks smoother. Right, you men,' he said to the lookouts, 'you'll find boathooks stowed under those gratings. Off oilskins and stand by on the foredeck.'

He shouted down the hatch: 'Steady as you go, quartermaster... Half ahead both... I want four seamen on deck sharpish, no oilskins!'

The U-boat's bow wave subsided and the growl of the diesel exhausts was muted. The Sunderland was now on the starboard beam, and Ned realized that she was cannily doing a complete circle round the boat to make sure there were no other vessels around.

Then from dead ahead she dropped low, flew down towards the U-boat, passing very low, and then turned slowly over the wake.

Now, unexpectedly, her signal lamp blinked again.

'Reckon...I...can...land.'

Was it a statement or a question? Ned raised his eyebrows at Jemmy and the Croupier.

Jemmy nodded. 'I've seen 'em landing at Calshot in far worse than this.'

Ned signalled back a bald: 'Yes.'

The plane's lamp flickered again. 'Will...pick...up... Yorke ...plus...rotors...and...manual.'

Ned acknowledged the signal, and then added: 'What...about ...prize?'

'Have...orders...to...stop...to...give...our...inflatable...boat ...a...lee.'

Ned acknowledged, gave the signal lamp to Jemmy, and – as four seamen came up the ladder and then scrambled past to go down the ladder beside the gun platform – said to the Croupier: 'Let go below and sort that lot out.'

The two of them stood in the wireless cabin, looking down at the Enigma machine in its case.

'Take the whole bloody thing,' the Croupier said. 'By the time we've packed up eight rotors and padded 'em, you'd have a parcel that size.'

Ned nodded, his mind made up. He pulled off the heavy leather boots with their cork soles. Hazel had guessed what was going on and disconnected the lead from the Enigma to the electric socket that kept its battery topped up, closed down the lid, locked it with the key that had been kept in the top drawer, and put his wireless log on top.

'There's some useful decodes in there, sir,' he said.

By that time the Croupier had come back into the cabin with the Triton cipher manual. 'Anything else?'

Ned shook his head. 'Lots of seabags. Put the cash register, log and manual in one and secure the opening. The put that bag upside down in another; and those two – '

'I understand,' the Croupier said impatiently and then, like a nanny addressing a small child, said with a grin: 'Clean underclothes? You're sure you don't want to pay a visit? And comb your hair, you never know *who* will see you.'

'Buoyancy,' Ned said. 'I want the seabags tied to something buoyant, so they won't sink if the dinghy capsizes.'

The Croupier bellowed into the control room.

Hazell suggested: 'One of those big Bakelite drums they store the salt herring in, sir? Lid screws down!'

'Get one quickly,' Ned said. 'Don't worry if you have to pour the fish in the bilge!'

'It's all right for you,' the Croupier grumbled. 'You're flying away from all our cares and stinks.'

Suddenly half a dozen empty seabags came flying though the doorway. 'How many do you want?' Yon called.

'That's enough,' Ned yelled, noticing that the German seabags were made of rubberized material, not the thick canvas of the British type.

The Croupier undid the four wingnuts which secured the Enigma box to the table and Ned held open the top of a seabag. The Croupier carefully slid the box into the bag, pushing down the wireless log on one side and the Triton manual on the other.

'Ship's log,' Ned reminded him. 'Our latest position is on the chart and the calculations for the star sight are on the pad.'

As soon as the Enigma was padded they tightened the drawstrings, and while the Croupier held open another bag, Ned upended the sealed bag into it. They repeated this until the Enigma was inside four bags. By that time Hazell and Keeler had arrived in the wireless cabin, Hazell with the Bakelite herring tub and Keeler with an armful of different pieces of rope and light line.

'Here, Ned: we can put this into the tub and screw down the lid: then it'll be waterproof and float and we don't need lashings! Look,' the Croupier said. 'Why don't you go and say goodbye to our chaps forward and aft while we secure this?'

'Lifebelt, too, sir,' Keeler said, 'if what Hazell says is true. I've seen these bloody silly blow-up dinghies those airmen use. And I'll put a line round this container so if the worst come to the worst – ' his voice dropped, as though it most certainly would, 'you can grab hold.'

Ned crouched as he climbed through the hatch in the forward bulkhead, and found the seamen and Marines guarding the prisoners completely unaware of what was going on. Conscious that by now the Sunderland was probably about ready to land, he explained that the Admiralty wanted to get him back to England quickly and had sent a Sunderland. A quick handshake all round, the Germans watching almost open-mouthed, wondering why the British leader was saying goodbye in mid-ocean, and he was scrambling aft, past the roaring diesels. As he hurried aft past the engine room telegraphs, he saw that Jemmy had gone on to slow ahead; then there was the confusion of explaining and saying goodbye to the men in the after torpedo room.

He returned to the control room to find that Keeler and Hazell had already hoisted the herring tub into the conning tower and were shouting up to the bridge.

Ned turned to Yon and was surprised to find he had the German Engineer Helmut with him.

'Ned,' Yon said carefully, 'I'm not very struck on shaking hands with Germans, but – '

'But Helmut has been a great help,' Ned said.

'Yes. So much so he might be victimized if he was put in the same camp as the rest of the crew.'

'Leave it with me.' Ned said. 'He'll be taken off the moment you dock, wherever that'll be.'

He shook hands with Helmut, and then with Yon. 'I hope to see you in a few days!'

He turned to the Croupier. 'Seems a long way from the Citadel, doesn't it? Still, we did it, even if it all drops overboard and sinks, or the bloody Sunderland gets shot down by a herring gull.' He took the horseshoe-shaped lifejacket. 'Come up and wave,' he said as he climbed the ladder.

He looked across at the quartermaster, Taylor. The sailor shook his head sadly. 'Fer me, sir, I like staying on the surface, but in an emergency I don't mind divin'. But I can see no occasion for ever going up in the air.'

Ned grinned and slapped him on the back. 'Just think, Taylor, in a few hours' time I'll be knocking back Naafi tea!'

Jemmy was shouting down the hatch. 'Come on Ned – all your luggage is ready on deck, the chambermaid's been tipped, we've made a lovely smooth, and young Brylcreem is just landing on it with your taxi!'

On deck, blinking in the bright sunshine, Ned saw that Jemmy had brought the U-boat round in a great curve, and her wake had made a smooth semi-lune of water. The Sunderland touched down well beyond it – clearly the pilot wanted the smooth area for boat work.

One flurry of spray...another...another, as the underside caught the wavetops, and then the great plane was the plough, making a white furrow in the sea which was broadening out as she slowed down.

'Not quite the way he said,' Jemmy explained. 'I called him up with the lamp and told him I could make it smoother. I hope their rubber dinghy hasn't got a hole in it.'

Ned looked down at the herring tub with its precious contents.

'Is that making all the stink?'

'Yes,' Ned said. 'Hazell wiped the inside, but the silly bugger forgot the outside.'

Jemmy shouted orders down the hatch and slowly the U-boat came to a stop. 'You'd better get down before we lose all our way, because she's going to roll. And here – ' he held up the lifejacket, pulled it over Ned's neck and tied the tapes.

'Give my love to Joan,' he said.

The roar of the Sunderland's engines was sharp, almost staccato, to ears accustomed for days to diesels. The rubber raft, rowed by four muscular airmen, was larger than Ned expected, and the seamen soon threw them a line. Looking down into the raft Ned was surprised to see a grey metal canister, which the airmen carefully handed up.

'Commander Yorke, sir?'

'Yes.'

'All Admiralty orders, charts and so on are in here, and I am to hand them over to whoever takes command of the boat.'

Ned grinned because he could imagine Captain Watts' voice in London thundering over a scrambler telephone, and he said: 'Jemmy – charts, orders and a stick of rock in here!'

Seamen hauled the canister on board.

'You next,' one of the airmen said.

'No, this smelly container next.'

As the seamen handed it down to the airmen, Ned called to them: 'That cask is what it's all about. Whatever happens, that's got to get to the Admiralty, even if we swim with it.'

Once on board the Sunderland, the Australian pilot gave a brief explanation as he prepared for take-off. If the sea was rough, he was to parachute the metal canister down to them – it contained charts and orders; if it was smooth enough – and no

one had expected that it would be – he was to land and take off

Commander Yorke and hand over the canister to whoever was

left in command.

CHAPTER **TWENTY-TWO**

The Sunderland pilot pointed through the port side of the windscreen. 'I imagine you recognize that lot, sir.'

'Just about. Isle of Wight, the Needles, Lymington River, Yarmouth, Cowes and the Medina River…where are we going, Calshot?'

The pilot nodded. 'You've caused a fair commotion, sir. I'm to transfer you to a high-speed launch before I pick up a buoy!'

'Suits me,' Ned said. He tugged his beard. 'The sooner I get scissors and razor to this lot, the better.'

The pilot looked startled. 'Why, it's a splendid beard, sir: I thought all submariners had 'em.'

'They do,' Ned said, 'but thank God I'm not a submariner.'

The great flying boat made a leisurely turn. 'Our runway,' the pilot said, pointing to a double row of small round buoys on the surface of the sea. 'And there's your boat tearing up and down. Perhaps you'd go back and wedge yourself in for landing…'

There was a full commander in the tiny cabin of the launch which, from the roar of its engine, was clearly powerful. Ned shook his hand but speech was impossible. By now the Sunderland's crew had become very protective of the Bakelite herring container, and one of them, a sergeant, jumped down into the launch and gave brisk and positive orders.

The commander left the cabin, the sergeant climbed back into the Sunderland, and the launch roared away. The commander came back into the cabin just as an alarmed Ned leapt up to make sure the container was safe.

'Jesus,' the commander shouted. 'I've got three men here with Stens guarding what smells like a box of herrings. Been fishing?'

'Yes, and hold on to the cask, sir. Where are we going?'

'The Hamble River: car and motorcyclists are waiting at Warsash for you. The C-in-C's Humber, actually. I say,' he said as a thought struck him, 'you won't put your – er, luggage – in the boot, will you?'

'Not likely,' Ned said. 'That stays on the seat right next to me until I get to the Citadel! Why?'

'Well, it has a certain pong about it. I was thinking that when the lady admiral – the C-in-C's wife – next goes for a ride, she's going to look at her husband in a strange way!'

The drive to London began with two naval motorcyclists ahead making a way through traffic with their thumbs on their horns, and two motorcyclists behind returning all the rude gestures.

But the Humber was warm and comfortable, the driver a three-badge AB, who drove with his mouth shut and his eyes wide open. The Marine sitting next to him, Sten across his knees, looked back from time to time, as if to see if Ned was still there. But Ned, his feet resting on the cask, was soon sprawled back, fast asleep.

The depth-charges had finally smashed open the hull, rivets were popping, and he struggled to the surface to find he was half asleep with the car stopped by the Captain Cook entrance to the Citadel, and Captain Watts tapping impatiently on the window with his signet ring while the Marine guard was holding his Sten with complete nonchalance, waiting for orders from Ned.

Ned unlocked the door from the inside and Watts pulled it open, eagerly reaching forward. Suddenly he stopped, and his face dropped.

'Christ, I can just about recognize you behind that beard – but where's the stink coming from?'

Ned got out of the car and found the ground swaying beneath him. It would be a couple of days before he got his land legs back.

He bent over into the car and handed out the cask to Watts. 'Present, sir, from your loving nephews, Ned, Jemmy and the Croupier, and Yon Heath, too.'

Captain Watts stepped back cautiously. 'What is it?'

'The bucket thing once contained German salt herrings. The seabags inside – there are several, one tucked in another, like a Chinese puzzle – contain – ' suddenly he remembered they were still standing by the Captain Cook memorial, 'your Christmas presents.'

Watts embraced the bulky container and without another word lurched with it into the old entrance of the Citadel.

An ancient guard on the door saluted him but held up a hand to bar Ned. 'Pass, sir?' From the tone of his voice and the way he eyed what was obviously a drunken fisherman, he knew no pass would be forthcoming.

Watts, realizing that Ned was not behind him, turned and shouted: 'It's Commander Yorke, if you look closely.'

Just as Ned felt the cold mosaic floor reminding him that he had left his boots in the control room of the U-boat, the attendant peered closely. 'So it is. Grown a full set, eh sir?'

'Yes,' Ned said. 'So embarrassing growing it while one's in London.'

Ned followed Captain Watts down to the ASIU, the container sounding like a damp tom-tom as it bumped at corners, and soon they were marching into Captain Watts' office, where an excited Joan hugged and kissed him and then reeled back.

'Darling Ned – Commander Yorke, if you wish – have your best friends never told you?'

'No fresh water in a submarine. Jemmy sends his love.'

'Ned – you did it? She whispered, moving over to lock the door.

'Yes. Sorry about the smell – German herring juice.'

'Bugger it, Joan, give me a knife,' growled Watts, crouched over the cask. 'These fools have tied Boy Scouts' knots!'

'Only scissors.'

'In the Admiralty and only a pair of scissors!' Watts wailed. 'When I was a youngster every matelot wore a knife.'

'They were just whittling the first wheel about that time, weren't they, sir?' she asked sweetly.

Captain Watts took a deep breath. 'Tell me, Ned, what's in here?'

Ned grinned cheerfully. 'One Mark III Enigma, which was in full working order when bagged but may have been damaged in transit; one U-boat log covering the whole of her last voyage; one U-boat's wireless log, with all the entries up to yesterday...'

Watts' face fell. 'So you didn't get – '

'...and one Triton manual,' Ned added.

Watts roared like a Viking, shook Ned's hand fiercely, gave Joan a noisy slap on the bottom, and then collapsed in his chair. 'Damnation – here I have all the riches of the world, but I can't get at 'em because Joan's too lazy to find scissors, or a knife, or – hell, even a sharp stone.'

Ned was so weary he said: 'While you're going through all this, perhaps I could have a zizz, sir?'

Watts slapped his own head with annoyance. 'Of course, of course. And the bloody C-in-C Portsmouth's car and outriders are still waiting outside. Tell 'em to drive you to Palace Street. Then send 'em home to Portsmouth. Let's empty this container, then you can take it with you. Makes a fearful pong.'

'Well,' Ned said lamely, 'I think the boys would like to keep it as a souvenir.'

Watts raised his eyes to the ceiling. Ned suddenly said: 'I haven't got the key to the Palace Street house.'

'Oh, there's bound to be someone there,' Watts said airily. 'Or just kick in a panel of the door and we'll send round a chippy to mend it in the morning.'

The Humber pulled up in Palace Street, and while the four motorcyclists revved their engines to stop the plugs oiling, Ned thanked the driver and Marine guard, waved to the motorcyclists, went to the door and rang the bell.

The door opened almost at once and an angry Clare, looking past him into the street, said: 'What's all this noise?'

'Sorry,' he said and she stared up at him wide-eyed, and managed to murmur, 'That beard!' before she fell into his arms.

A week later, clean-shaven and in uniform, Ned sat at his desk in the Citadel. The room was strangely empty without Jemmy and the Croupier. Where was ULJ?

His uniform was newly pressed, his collar overstarched, his tie carefully tied because, with Captain Watts and the First Sea Lord, they were lunching at Number Ten Downing Street, and he was expected to tell the Premier (who had been abroad for several days, a fact which was still secret) the story of the cash register and cookery book.

And he was exhausted. Not tired, just physically exhausted. He had clung to Clare as though life was trying to tear them apart, although that was what death was trying to do. Yet exploding bombs added a hungry intensity to their love-making.

He took the latest U-boat sinking reports from his In-tray and put them squarely on the blotter. That had been a fascinating second visit to Bletchley Park yesterday: it was thoughtful of them to invite him down to watch them using the Enigma Mark III. It was a bizarre experience seeing the Enigma machine that Hazell and Keeler had put in kitbags and stuffed in a salted herring cask now plugged in at a Victorian mansion and clicking away, surrounded by half a dozen boffins who were as excited as punters reading the names of horses coming off a teleprinter and finding they'd all backed winners.

They had only one question to ask him (apart from demanding the complete story of how the U-boat was captured), and that was why the Enigma and the manual had smelled so strongly of herrings.

Ned felt completely flat. Part was a sexual surfeit and relaxing; but the other part was a combination of the sudden let-down of tension when the Sunderland had taken off with him on board, and the worry of what had happened afterwards. At that moment his telephone rang and a crisp voice he did not know asked: 'Is that Commander Yorke?'

'Yes, Yorke here.'

DUDLEY POPE

GOVERNOR RAMAGE RN

Lieutenant Lord Ramage, expert seafarer and adventurer, undertakes to escort a convoy across the Caribbean. This seemingly routine task leads him into a series of dramatic and terrifying encounters. Lord Ramage is quick to learn that the enemy attacks from all angles and he must keep his wits about him in order to survive. Fast and thrilling, this is another highly-charged adventure from the masterly Dudley Pope.

'All the verve and expertise of Forester'
– *Observer*

RAMAGE'S CHALLENGE

The Napoleonic Wars are raging and a group of eminent British citizens have been taken captive in the Mediterranean by French troops. The Admiralty traces their location and sends the valiant Lord Ramage to effect their release. As Ramage and his crew negotiate the hazardous waters off the Tuscan coast, they soon begin to doubt the accuracy of their instructions. Ramage comes to realise that in order for his mission to succeed he must embark upon a fearful and highly dangerous escapade where the stakes have never been higher.

Ramage's Challenge is another action-packed naval adventure from the masterful Dudley Pope.

Dudley Pope

Ramage and the Guillotine

As France recovers from her bloody Revolution, Napoleon is amassing his armies for the Great Invasion. News in England is sketchy and the Navy must prepare to defend the land from foreign attack.

Lieutenant Ramage is chosen to travel to France and embark upon the perilous quest of spying on the great Napoleon. His mission is to determine the strength of the French troops – but his discovery will mean the guillotine!

'The first and still favourite rival to Hornblower'
– *Daily Mirror*

Ramage's Prize

Lord Ramage returns for another highly-charged and thrilling adventure at sea. Instructed with the task of discovering why His Majesty's dispatches keep unaccountably disappearing, Ramage finds himself involved in a situation far beyond his expectations. Based on true events, *Ramage's Prize* is another gripping story from Dudley Pope.

'An author who really knows Nelson's Navy'
– *Observer*

Dudley Pope

The Ramage Touch

The Ramage Touch finds the ever-popular Lord Ramage in the Mediterranean with another daring mission to undertake. He soon makes a shocking discovery which dramatically transforms the nature of the task at hand. With the nearest English vessel a thousand miles away, Ramage must embark upon a truly perilous and life-threatening course of action. With everything stacked against him, he has only one chance to succeed…

Ramage at Trafalgar

Lord Ramage returns to fight in the most famous of Britain's sea battles. Summoned by Admiral Nelson himself, Ramage is sent to join the British fleet off Cadiz where the largest battle in naval history is about to take place. Finding himself in the front line of battle, Lord Ramage must fight to save his own life as well as for his country. The result is a thrilling, hair-raising adventure from one of our best-loved naval writers.

'Expert knowledge of naval history'
– *Guardian*